LOSING OUR MARBLES?

A Dot to Dot Story

Angel Capelli

angelcapelli.com

ISBN-13: 9781739400002

Cover design by: Angel Capelli

With thanks for the encouragement of my wonderful other half and family and of those friends who kindly read the early drafts, even those who after the first few pages begged me to use a pseudonym to preserve their anonymity.

CONTENTS

PROLOGUE – JOINING THE DOTS

"This is not the end. It is not even the beginning of the end. But it is perhaps the end of the beginning".[1]

Everything was blank as if peering through thick fog in dark glasses. Where to start? The white page had nothing at all to say for itself. It just stared back at me like a freshly ironed bed sheet. There were no wrinkles, rumples or crumbs to give any clue to its dreams, appetites or passions.

The silence that comes with a heavy snowfall filled the room. Even the tinnitus of conspiratorial whispers that often plagued me seemed to have taken a trappist vow. I put the pen down again and tried to remember what my therapist had said. 'Pick a dot. Then imagine you are floating in a bath. It's so deep you can barely keep your head above water. Okay? Now just pull up the plug and let it all flow out.'

When I say therapist, that's how I thought of him although he called himself a doctor. A friend had suggested the guy might be able to help me. He did warn me that the Doctor's approach could be a little unorthodox, eccentric even, but this didn't adequately prepare me for my appointment. I arrived at 8.37am on the dot[2] as requested by the small card I had received a few days earlier through the post. For some reason I couldn't understand the word "dot" was missing, but the meaning was clear from the enlarged black spot after the words "on the". I suppose it could have been a perfectly positioned circular ink blot covering up for a sudden mental block, but that seemed unlikely as the word "dot" is a pretty simple one.

Out of ingrained routine, I took a circuitous route to the address on the card. It was in a quiet suburban area of Kensington, not far from London's green lung, Hyde Park. Several times on the way I instinctively ducked behind a hedge for a minute or two or waited stock-still behind a tree to check that no one was following me. The small plaque by the door read "Mindbender" which seemed odd until I realised that my brain was up to its tricks and was carrying out some subconscious editing. It actually said "Mindmender" and underneath that "Doctor K.P.Bacon - Consultant in Psychiatric Engineering". Names always intrigued me. I wondered what the initials stood for and whether many of his patients were vegan.

The room I found myself in was completely covered in bright tiles decorated with a menagerie of exotic animals. Although windowless it was cavernous, allaying any concern that it might trigger my claustrophobia. Beckoning me in with an impatient wave of his hand and no other introduction, Doctor Bacon explained brusquely that it used to be a Turkish sauna. Perhaps as a memento of this, I noticed a hookah next to the lava lamp on the corner of his desk. It looked as if it had been in recent use as the mouthpiece was still smoking, but there wasn't time to take much more in as it seemed that within seconds I was lying on a large red divan with ice cubes on my eyelids.

In a hypnotic bass voice that hummed down my spine as if through an organ pipe, the Doctor invited me to explain my troubles. He told me to take it at my own pace, so I did. I was still in the witness protection programme and needed to exercise great care although I had been assured that the Doctor was the epitome of professional discretion. It was a risk I had no choice but to take and I was careful to omit names and anonymise events wherever possible .

When I eventually finished, I realised it must be getting late as the ice cubes had melted and my voice had that squeaky edge it gets when I talk too much. It makes me sound like a cartoon character or someone who has blown up too many helium balloons for a children's party.

As my eyeballs thawed out, I was able to see that the Doctor was leaning forward, elbows on knees and fingertips pressed together in a pagoda shape. His chin rested on the pinnacle in an inverted triangle that sharpened into a ginger goatee beard. In the freckled shadows cast by the glass droplets falling like rain from the large chandelier the Doctor's eyebrows sprouted in dense thickets of carroty undergrowth, shifting from a glowing orange to angry red as the waves of light from the lava lamp swept over him. His sunken eyes reminded me of pictures I had seen in coffee table books of cobalt lakes in the craters of extinct Indonesian volcanos. Although I must have been droning on for hours the disconcerting intensity of the Doctor's gaze convinced me that he had retained a tightrope concentration the whole time.

'Yours is an unusual case, Angel.'

I was blessed at least in that my height, facial features and the pitch of my voice when not overstrained all lent themselves readily to disguise, even of gender. I had dressed androgynously in jeans and a knitted jumper. One day I could be Angelo and another Angela. Today I decided on Angel. After all gender gives roughly half the game away and, as I mentioned before, concealing my identity had become a habit I couldn't easily shake off even when seeking therapy.

The Doctor continued, 'It seems from what you say that your whole framework for making sense of your life and of the past has unravelled. You've given me a hotchpotch of random events but it's hard to trace any guiding story or shape.'

This seemed a fair summary. Constantly changing secret locations while on the run had taken its toll. I never knew when another assassination attempt would be made. Fear lurked around every corner and the effects of a caged existence weighed heavily on me. I felt like a castaway who could only cork up thoughts in bottles and throw them into the sea knowing that they might never be washed ashore or found. Studying history through the many hours of enforced isolation had been a way to fight back by reasserting my sense of chronology and of cause and effect. This helped, but my mind was still as delicate as a dandelion blanched of colour and vigour in its transformation to a gossamer ball. I could feel a breeze blowing through it, softly teasing the fragile halo apart.

'You say that while in hiding you have had to adopt many different disguises and identities, and of course this will have deeply confused your sense of self. There are a number of techniques that may alleviate the symptoms. We could for example try the tarantula position. But in your case I suggest joining the dots.'

I had no idea what he was talking about. On the shelves that lined one side of the room I caught a glimpse of various intriguing items. They included some tarot cards, an astrolabe and what appeared to be a set of electrodes, although it wasn't obvious what part of the anatomy they were designed to be attached to. There was also an enormous glass snow globe, or perhaps it was a crystal ball, and a large collection of books on astrology, philosophy, alchemy, phrenology and teleportation. In the short pause while the Doctor took a sip from a cut glass tumbler on the desk, I seized the chance to unleash my curiosity.

'What is the tarantula position?'

'Oh, it's a complex tantric yoga move where you spend several hours crouched in a corner while focusing all your mental energies on visualising yourself as a spider that has been poked with a sharp stick.'

'I'd rather not try that. I suffer from arachnophobia, and it sounds painful.'

'It is. The pain is what brings patients back to reality. Most of them are euphoric about their lives once they realise they are not spiders after all.'

'So, what do you mean by joining the dots?'

'This is a much more philosophical method based on the concept of dot-to-dot.'

'Like in a child's drawing book?' I must have

looked doubtful because I was, but I told myself that I needed to keep an open mind. A fleeting memory came back to me of the trouble I had got into at primary school for joining up the freckles on another child's face with an indelible marker pen.

'Exactly, but an adult version.' With the smooth assurance of a well-oiled piston the Doctor slid into an explanation he had obviously delivered many times before.

'Dots, as I term them, are nodes of consciousness and anchor points through which we organise what we think of as reality. They often crystallise around facts but include every aspect of our intellectual, sensory and spiritual perception. Think of them as the pegs on which we hang and shape our narratives of ourselves, the turning points in our past and indeed history generally. Once you understand this, you will begin to see how learning to re-join dots can help you.'

'So will this treatment restore my sense of reality?'

'We can come onto that later, but it depends on what you mean by reality. As the great philosopher Douglas Adam's said, "We are constantly reminded of how startlingly different a place the world is when viewed from a point only three feet to the left." The reason I am suggesting that the dot-to-dot technique will help you is that it offers a more systematic approach to one you have been subconsciously following already in your history studies and seem to have found helpful to some extent. You obviously believe that there is such a thing as history?'

'Yes ... or at least I used to believe in it until a few days ago when everything began to melt into chaos and coincidence,' I replied. 'Now the past seems more like a smashed windscreen after a car crash. All crazy opaque pieces barely held together by the laminate.'

'Presumably, when you study history you use various props like dates and lists of kings and queens as starting blocks, then moved on to concepts such as trends and periods to organise your thoughts. Joining the dots of experiences, feelings and thoughts that seem most striking to you will help you to start to see where you are and where you are going again.'

The Doctor turned and pressed a small red button on the desk beside him. Immediately a large screen unrolled soundlessly from the ceiling. On it I could see a few bright dots against a black background.

'Join these up in any shape you like.'

'Where shall I begin?'

'Ah yes, beginning is often the hardest bit, but you'll soon get the hang of it. Anywhere can be a beginning or an end, or both for that matter. Just head in any direction joining one dot to another. Let your imagination run free and you can't help creating a picture. We are all natural artists if we just allow ourselves to be, even if we get no further than doodling.'

Taking the thick crayon he was holding out, I quickly drew some glowing silver lines between the bright spots on the screen. Standing back, we both could see that although the shapes were crude, they were the rough image of two kites, one larger and the other smaller one flying above it in the opposite direction.

'That's very interesting. You have just updated the constellations of Ursa Major and Minor. Those points you have joined up are its brightest stars. Ancient peoples saw these patterns as two bears, the little one upside down above the larger.'

'But bears have stubby tails. These shapes have long tails, as in my kites.'

'True, but the Greek myth has an answer for that. Zeus flung the bears into space by their tails and that stretched them.'

'But even then it's very hard to picture them as bears. And anyway, I still don't see how stars can put my mind back together.'

The Doctor leaned back in his chair. He clearly wasn't going to be hurried. Fortunately, while on the run it had become a matter of self-preservation to be a good listener. One missed footstep in the dark behind me could have meant I was a goner.

'I think a bit more context will assist. People have always used the stars to help them navigate when travelling over long distances, particularly the Pole Star at the end of the tail of the smaller kite you have drawn because that's so closely aligned to the Earth's axis that it seems to be the only fixed star in the northern sky, a celestial flagpole for North. They also invented stories that connected the stars to remember the patterns that would literally guide them in this way but also to give a metaphysical direction, shape and meaning to their lives. That needed not only stars, or dots, but imagination.'

The Doctor had his eyes turned upwards as he leaned back on his leather chair in mid monologue. He didn't notice the three cats who had materialised as if from nowhere, their tails twitching like wands in a witches' spell contest. Two were rubbing themselves against my legs as I perched on the edge of the divan and the third was swiping at the gold tassels that dangled enticingly just above the floor.

'The first stellar pictures and stories were often of Gods, monsters, heroes and animals, like these bears. Many of them are half forgotten now, except through the zodiac and horoscopes, or are seen differently. We usually call the brightest part of the constellations of Ursa Major and Minor, the Plough. If you look again at your large kite I'm sure you will now recognise it. Americans prefer to call them the Big and Little Dipper. Among other peoples in the past they have been called the ladle, the drinking gourd, the great and little wagon or the salmon net.'

While the Doctor purred on I took a quick look at the tags on the cats' collars, Melchior, Caspar and Balthazar. In a sudden epiphany I realised it couldn't be a coincidence that these were the names of three wise astronomers who followed a star to became a bit part in an all time bestselling story. As if echoing my thoughts the Doctor continued ...

'All of these pictures weave stories around the stars. In one, for example, the Big Dipper is a bow from which no arrow is ever fired in case it hits the Pole Star because that is the rivet that holds the universe together. In Arabic tradition, the bowl of the Big Dipper is a coffin and the stars behind it are mourners. All these stories are different ways of making sense of oneself through patterns and involve selecting some stars while leaving out others.'

The Doctor paused and, suddenly noticing the cats, took a silver tin out of the pocket of the jacket draped over the back of his chair. Absent-mindedly he peeled back the lid and dangled a sardine for each of his feline companions in turn. These offerings were swallowed with fastidious ferocity and not the slightest indication of gratitude. My own pursuers were just as ruthless but wouldn't have worried about leaving a mess.

Turning, Doctor Bacon now pressed a small yellow button. So many stars filled the screen that in many areas the tentacles of light fused, blotting out the blackness of space. They were blinking like thousands of lighthouses suffering from mass hysteria so that even the original stars of the Big Dipper became almost impossible to pick out.

'The problem is that our ability to draw pictures like this is now collapsing. When we were unaware of all but the three or four thousand stars we could see with the naked eye from Earth we felt more secure, more certain of where we were. Now the harder we look the more stars we discover...a never-ending number. At the same time, we have come to understand that the relationships we thought existed between the stars are illusory. They are all at very different distances away from us, linked only by the level of brightness we perceive. Everything, and not just the universe, is expanding and becoming more complex, and what makes things worse is that the rate of expansion is accelerating.'

Melchior, the white Persian that looked like an inflated feather duster, had clearly heard enough. He mercilessly shredded several of the gold tassels, transforming them into tinsel. I was becoming concerned he would lacerate my ankles next, but the Doctor did not break stride.

'The point is that everything we have discussed

can be applied to all dots. Stars are just one example. Take history. We just have too much data now to make any sense of it. That's causing mental overload. As we draw our pictures, and through them our stories, more and more dots are appearing, creating chaos and coincidences too numerous to absorb. Selecting dots to tell our stories becomes increasingly difficult and we are overwhelmed by the knowledge that the patterns we design leave an infinite number of dots unaccounted for. Eventually our minds grind to a complete halt, sometimes called a breakdown.'

'So you are saying I am suffering from an overload of dots?'

'Yes. The technical terminology is that you're going dotty. But that at least is better than having the perception that all the dots are disappearing, which specialists in the field call losing your marbles. There were some worrying peripheral symptoms of the marble syndrome in what you told me, but I'm satisfied that the primary diagnosis is going dotty. The good news is that you are definitely not round the twist, which is when all the dots are sucked into a never-ending loop-the-loop. That's very hard to unwind.'

'So, how does all this help me?'

'Your condition can be completely cured with time and practice by going back to the basic principles of dot-to-dot. Just focus on the dots that most attract you, the brightest stars if you like, and rigorously exclude the noise from all the others. It seems from what you told me earlier that you have been involved in some startling events, even if at present you describe them all as if they were isolated fragments. Just take it a dot at a time and begin linking them together to recreate your own story.'

'Easier said than done. What you call imagination for me too often becomes hallucination ... terrifying shadows following me.'

'That's because you have lost sight of the dots altogether and you are just making up random stories based only on your paranoia. But you've already shown you can re-boot and get back to using your imagination positively to join the dots. That's what you did when you drew the kites. Because you didn't initially know those dots were stars or recognise the Dippers you started again from scratch. Why kites? I suspect it's because you have been in hiding for so long. They probably represent the freedom you're seeking. Given more time we could have uncovered the story in your subconscious that made sense of those dots by drawing that picture.'

'You said you would come back to how joining dots would restore me to reality.'

'Well, not quite. I said it would give you back a sense of reality and that would be a healing process in itself, a form of therapy if you like. Take another look at your picture. It's probably a lot closer to the actual star pattern than the two bears. Just a different point of view. I accept that underneath all of our different perspectives there is only one reality, but the kites may be as near as you can get, at least without a singularity where all the dots fuse and merge so that there is no longer any relationship between them and no room for their configurations to shift or change.'

Seeing that I still looked confused and doubtful, he continued. 'With all the distractions we create by inventing our own stories or becoming lost in those of others, finding reality is like blundering around in a blizzard looking for a little white flag marking the North Pole. You just have to hope you don't freeze to death in a tent wondering if you ever got there and doomed anyway not to return, like Captain Scott. The best you can do is set off, pick a dot, join it to another and start writing the story you imagine yourself to be caught up in. Don't worry that a lot of dots are left out altogether. They may come in useful sometime.'

I was getting up to leave but could see that the Doctor had one final parting shot to make.

'If you are concerned your story is too outlandish to be believed, remember that fact really is stranger than fiction. For example it probably never occured to you, but my first name really is Kris.'

This certainly hadn't crossed my mind, but remembering the nameplate by the door I struggled to keep a poker face. The Doctor finally seemed to be showing a scintilla of humour.

'Ok, I'll give your recommended treatment a go. One last thing. Where do the ice cubes come into all of this?'

'Oh, I just had a few too many in my whisky and had nowhere else to put them.'

Once back in the flat I was renting, I sat looking out. The window frame sealed the chaos that I knew was prowling outside within reassuring squares, but the skeletal limbs of the beech trees were shivering as they twisted upwards bereft of their green summer sleeves.

Doctor Bacon's advice seemed less and less convincing, but he was right that my mind was under strain and overloaded so I felt I should at least give his remedy a try. I had also been struck by his comment that we are all stories and whatever stories we make up about ourselves, others will tell a different one. I needed to tell my own story while I could before someone abruptly finished it for me with the sort of painful end I would rather not think about. A dead end.

I still wasn't sure if I could link together the whirling fragments that the Doctor had called dots, but he had assured me that even if the result initially appears disjointed, the mind can do the rest. So picking up the pen again, I closed my eyes, imagined I was in the bath and pulled the plug out. As the whirlpool twisted down the plughole my story started to rush out of me almost more quickly than I could write it down.

When I say, "my story" I was really only one dot, one star, on the edge of a distant constellation that may simply be a pattern that exists only in my mind. Many of the other dots come from what I was told by the Italian police Inspector who interviewed me when I had already been in witness protection for some time and from sources that I cannot disclose. The result may be disjointed but, as the Doctor suggested, I have just used my imagination to create connections that seem to me to make sense of it all and paper over the many cracks.

CHAPTER 1 – A NIGHT AT THE MUSEUM

If a man insisted always on being serious, and never allowed himself a bit of fun and relaxation, he would go mad or become unstable without knowing it.[3] – Herodotus

The Ashmolean Museum in Oxford wasn't accustomed to being a scene of chaos. The stone spindles of the balustrade guarded the perimeter, marching to attention in serried ranks above the pavement. Turning sharply inwards on their heels they came to an abrupt halt at the massive blocks that framed the black cast iron gates. There, the classical columns, accepted the salute in solemn silence. As doorkeepers, they demanded respect from anyone approaching the museum's hallowed halls. This was, after all, a shrine to some of the greatest treasures of antiquity and only the reverent were welcome. Ascending the pyramid of steps, visitors sensed the gravity of the great stone architrave above their heads. The two top edges of its shallow triangle rose upwards towards the apex like giant eyebrows, surprised that anyone would have the nerve to come so close. Newcomers instinctively feared that if the eyebrows dropped down into a frown of displeasure they would be crushed, even before the mighty doors gaped wide to swallow them in shadow.

Just inside the cavernous hallway, a paunchy ticket collector was sitting slumped forward on a slatted wooden chair that seemed barely able to support him. Although lost somewhere in his early thirties, Joe's stooping frame and sparse sandy hair suggested that he had emerged from some more distant era, possibly primeval, an impression that his outlook tended to confirm. The uniform would have been smart had he not managed to wear it like a bin bag. It had been a long day ... mainly just sitting, but every half hour or so he had wandered round the vast ground floor. A complete circuit seemed to take an age and he was desperate now for closing time. Desperate for a fag.

Joe gazed down at the tiled floor and noticed that his shirt had ruckled up again. One of the middle buttons had popped off so that the blue cloth bulged open, revealing his navel. The rim of this miniature crater was stretched into an oval as it surfed the crest of a wave on a beer belly that rose majestically between deep troughs of flesh. He had always been quite proud of it.

Most of the navels he had ever seen reminded him of the abandoned burrows of some small animal, probably a caterpillar that was now extinct. His own had started as an "innie" but had now become an "outie" – more of a knob than a button. Perhaps, like the valve on a pressure cooker, it was giving warning of the build-up of unseen forces beneath. It perched amid the curling hair like a crenelated castle keep or perhaps a tiny pork pie. The pinched edges of the knot reminded him of pastry crust. His mother told him that the midwife had made a bit of a bodge of the knot, but Joe couldn't see anything wrong with it. It was a bit itchy and he scratched it gently, then quickly covered it up. Health and Safety had caught him doing this once before and had given him a verbal warning for, 'Indecent exposure in contravention of professional conduct.' A bit over the top for an innocent belly button, he thought. Anyone would think he had been mooning at the visitors. Still, better not take any further risk.

Joe sighed then grunted. With the slow deliberation of a water buffalo reluctantly leaving its favourite pool, he shifted his bulk forward so he could get to his feet[4]. Time for the last inspection of the afternoon. As usual, there were bound to be a few stragglers in the galleries, often American tourists or academics lost in some obscure corner of ancient history. They would need to be jolted back to the present and swept out of the door.

Joe didn't want to be late for his tea. His beloved West Ham were playing Chelsea tonight. He had a nagging feeling that the game wouldn't be an uplifting experience, but until the final whistle there was always hope. As Joe rose, he was oblivious to the events that were shortly going to make this an inspection he would never forget.

On a bench by a bus stop half a mile away, a young woman took out a small silver make-up mirror. Pouting to kiss the air, she re-applied a vibrant cherry red to her lips with a few adept strokes and then carefully added a little more mascara to eyelashes that curved to infinity.

Many women had told Cassandra that men were totally unreliable. Her own experience was that they could nearly always be counted on for three things: stupidity, predictability and attention. She was hoping that they wouldn't break the habit and let her down this evening. As she swiftly ran a small brush through her golden curtain of hair, the craning neck of a striking young man on the opposite pavement turning in her direction reassured her on the last two points. A double-decker bus drawing up at the kerb in front of the bench suddenly sliced off the young man's view before she was able to see proof of the first. When it pulled away, she saw from the window that he was still staring as he strode along.

Tom's moment of disappointment that the bus had obscured his vision of the beautiful girl didn't last long, but even from a distance, and apart from the glorious hair, he retained a fleeting impression of vivacity and perfect classical features set within an elfin face of pale olive complexion. It seemed only a few seconds before an entirely different face was swimming into focus. A large, round and dough-white shape wobbled in and out of his consciousness.

As the heavy metal drumming in his head faded, he could see that the kindly features belonged to an elderly woman dressed in a nurse's uniform and realised he was lying on a hospital trolley.

'You're in Accident and Emergency, love. It'll be a couple of days before we can discharge you. You will look like a panda that's been in a punch up for a while but it will wear off.'

It was only sometime later that Tom discovered he had fractured his skull after walking into a lamppost. Apparently, a traffic warden found him face down across a double yellow and obstructing a parking space. Thankfully, the warden called the ambulance, although he told the ambulance driver that, if it hadn't been a Friday, he would have just stuck a parking ticket on Tom's forehead and booked a tow vehicle to take him to the pound.

Cassie did not see her admirer meet with the unfortunate accident that would have confirmed that her first assumption about men was as accurate as the other two. She paused, holding onto the rail as the bus lurched off again. Looking down the length of the aisle, she could see it was fairly empty. There was a surveillance camera in the usual place, but she wasn't worried about that. Could come in useful, in fact. She made sure she was in shot but didn't look towards it.

A couple of elderly ladies sharing a seat about three rows in front of her were locked in conversation, or more accurately in two monologues that criss-crossed without seeming to make contact. Both were talking at the same time, oblivious to what the other was saying, and from a few snatched words it seemed that the topics were entirely different. Only occasionally did the two strands momentarily weave together to make something almost meaningful, but that was probably more confusion than communication.

'... My grumpy neighbour ... named John ...'

'... lost my glasses, Gladys, when I was out gardening ...'

'... Yes, he has been very keen on his garden recently ... we started calling him John Innes ... after the compost ... odd to always be digging so late at night.'

'... Must have lost them near the cherry tree ...'

'... She loves cherries, his wife that is. John Innes even called her Cherry....or was it Cherie? ...a bit strange but I haven't seen her for months ...'

'... Oh, cherry trees don't like being disturbed ...'

'... Dug the patio up during the night and then re-laid it ... Just after I last saw her ... Same paving, so you couldn't see any improvement ... and he broke the bird bath.'

'... Broke my last pair of dentures on a cherry stone ... Dentist said I should be grateful that it's cheaper to replace them than a gold filling.'

'... New Bentley on the drive ... Told me he'd found a pot of gold under the patio so it had been a double win ...'

'... Or a double crown ...'

'... Not sure what he meant by double ... I'm sure he just mentioned gold but maybe they were gold crowns ...'

Cassie wondered if either of them had their hearing aids plugged in. There were also a few students, presumably going to or from lectures. Most of them also had electronic devices in their ears, but these were intended to isolate their users into their own little worlds rather than connect them with each other in this one.

In just a few minutes she would be at the museum. She hoped that the men she was relying on this time had already arrived, although, to be fair, they had no idea she was coming or who she was.

Joe had now almost finished his inspection. As he entered the last gallery, his heart sank. Among the few visitors who hadn't yet left was a distinguished gentleman with a long, wild beard. He had a marked resemblance to an old Russian portrait of Rasputin[5] just before his murder which was currently on loan from the Hermitage Museum in St Petersburg. Joe knew, however, that he was a professor of Eastern Studies who visited the museum nearly every Friday, always in a waistcoat. When unbuttoned it revealed a remarkable purple lining in silk, embroidered with phoenix rising from leaping flames. Joe thought he must be a bit odd, like a lot of these academics. They sometimes chatted and Joe had discovered that he was writing a treatise on the mystic rituals of some old Persian kingdom, but the Professor didn't know much about football, so mercifully that soon left them both with nothing much to say.

One of the museum's greatest treasures was a richly enamelled Persian bowl which depicted the signs of the zodiac and a grotesque figure with three bodies and two heads wrestling with a dragon.[6] The Professor was particularly fascinated by this item. He could often be found studying it, notebook in hand as he scribbled down his most recent theories as to how to interpret the meaning of this curious artistic jumble. Joe thought that it might have some connection with the waistcoat and had heard rumours that the Professor was a member of a secret sect. Joe thought it had some connection with fire worship but he wasn't sure about this. He could have asked the Professor but had no intention of doing so now, with tea and West Ham waiting. That would just guarantee a further delay in closing time. Instead, as soon as he saw the Professor lingering as usual before the cabinet containing the cup, he just switched off the lights. Five minutes later, after the oaths that came out of the darkness as the Professor bumped into various displays died away, he switched them on again to confirm that the room was empty.

There was a rather battered mahogany desk in the small dingy office in the front hallway. Joe used the small key that hung from a chain around his neck and opened the top drawer, extracting a much larger iron monster surely designed for a dungeon and with enough teeth to turn any alligator a brighter shade of envious green.

The real protection of the museum's treasures now relied on its computerised security system, but Joe did not trust it and still preferred to physically lock up as well. Along with his colleagues, he now spent a lot of his day monitoring the screens which continually scanned each room. He had however been firmly told by the IT Department to watch, but never touch, any of the controls. Despite endless training sessions, Joe had long ago proven his determination to live a balanced life by ignoring virtually all developments in technology other than the TV and the phone ... landline only[7]. He knew where all that stuff could lead, people like that Bill Gates guy reprogramming your brain and turning people into androids.

The IT team finally gave up after the third time he had clicked on scam emails that introduced computer viruses to the system, paralysing the museum for days. All Joe now had to do when he left the museum was press the red button that set the alarm system for the night and close the door behind him so the latch clicked.

Then he always took satisfaction in using the great key in the side door exit, unaware that IT had long ago removed the mechanism. Once he had left he would then check furtively that no one was looking before hiding the key in one the large plant pots just outside the building.

This evening he didn't get that far. He was in the act of reaching forward to press the red button when he noticed that the other lights that were usually lit up on the security console were off. As he glanced up, the surveillance screen itself went blank. Before he had time to think or blink, the side exit burst open. Three burly men in camouflage fatigues with balaclavas over their heads piled through it and Joe found himself crushed against the wall. There was no time for him to react or resist, but even if he had, they were all built like bulldozers. The largest of the three forced him to the floor and sat on him, then the other two ran into the museum.

'Cloze da tong and shut up da mowff or ...'

Joe wasn't very good on accents and had never heard one like this before. Maybe Geordie or Brummie? But there was no need to ask where "or" was leading. His captor left nothing to the imagination by drawing a grimy finger across his throat while from deep down inside it came a disgusting sound Joe had last heard from a tanker pumping out a cesspit. If you are as flat as a lilypad struggling to stay afloat under a squatting bullfrog you have no breath for questions. In any case Joe's mind was already elsewhere. There was now very little time left before West Ham kicked off, so he was already feeling a rising anxiety. Joe just hoped that these guys were West Ham supporters. Or even Chelsea supporters, because then they would still want to watch the match ... although then revealing his own colours might be a lot more risky.

Over what seemed like an eternity but was probably no longer or more nail-biting than the average time for a penalty shoot-out, Joe watched a whole load of treasures disappear rapidly out of the door. His head was crushed against the parquet floor so hard he was left in no doubt what a poor job the cleaners were doing, but he could still catch most of the action out of the corner of his eye. With the systems all down, the burglars could pretty much take everything they could carry, and that turned out to be more than most removal men would manage in a week without tea breaks. Joe realised that they must have a van outside and wondered if the robbers had remembered to pay and display. One of them opened his fist triumphantly as he passed to show Joe's captor a couple of the smaller items which Joe immediately recognised as the Alfred Jewel[8] and the Ballyshannon Sun Disk[9]. The museum's Curator would have a heart attack! Then came the surreal sight of one of the burglars wearing an elaborate Samurai helmet[10] while carrying the Guy Fawkes lantern[11]. The Renaissance dish, depicting a head composed of interlaced penises, ignited a laughing exchange between the burglars. Joe couldn't share the joke not only because of the pain from his rib cage but also because they were speaking in some guttural foreign language[12].

At this point the beast sitting on him jumped up with a startling agility that would have caught a sumo wrestler offguard and roughly tied Joe's hands behind his back before joining his partners in crime. It soon became apparent why, as all three of the brutes came staggering past with the sarcophagus of a mummified Egyptian priest who Joe had always nicknamed "DJ". Djed Djehuty Iuef Ankh was a bit of a mouthful and difficult to pronounce.[13] Finally, Joe saw the Persian bowl vanish into the dusk. The Professor would be heartbroken.

With only five minutes to go to kick off for the match, the door banged shut. Joe managed to drag himself to his knees and, with the frenzy of a Viking berserker, head butted the red button on the security console and every other button in sight. As the security alarms, fire alarms and sprinkler system all went off, he staggered to his feet and lurched out of the door. Within a couple of minutes he could hear the melancholy undulation of police sirens in the distance and was satisfied they were on their way. No time to get home but there was always the pub.

It was while the raid was still going on that Cassie's bus pulled up at the top of Beaumont Street only a hundred yards up the road. Bang on time, even though as usual it was in a small swarm of several buses on the same route. She walked calmly down the street and past the parked white van towards the Museum's side exit. Although small and slim she neatly hitched up her skirt and scaled the balustrade in a trice.

As she stood stock still behind one of the columns of the portico, Cassie could see through the door a large man pinned to the floor by a colossus in fatigues. Fortunately, both were facing away from her. Cassie opened her small shoulder bag. It was made of soft Italian leather, unmistakably Gucci. She was sad that she would need to get rid of it afterwards, but needs must. Taking out some light plimsols, she slipped them on in place of the stilettos which she placed in her shoulder bag. Then, as the giant got off his prisoner and disappeared into the museum gallery, she stepped silently round behind Joe's prone body and followed.

Cassie only wanted one thing. Her planning was meticulous, as always, and although she had never visited the Ashmolean, she was as familiar with its layout as she was with every shade of eyeshadow you could buy. Not wasting a second, she glided through the dark, imagining she was a black panther like Bagheera moving with subtle sophistication. Cassie remembered that life was, after all, a jungle and the laws of the jungle should therefore be taken seriously.[14] She was immaculate not only in her preparation but in her clothing, right down to her bare necessities.

Cassie counted carefully in the dark. Forward thirty steps, ten left, twenty-five right, then fifty ahead. Pause. Slip on a pair of thin rubber gloves. Feel for the door frame.

The small room at the end of a long passage was hardly somewhere most visitors would pay much attention to. There were no great treasures in here to pull the crowds. Just a selection of coins and minor artefacts that the museum hadn't found space to display in the main exhibitions. In fact, the descriptions in the cabinets that danced under the pencil beam of her tiny torch all suggested that not much was known about many of these exhibits. What they shared was the fact that all were ancient and showed exquisite workmanship that made them worthy of further research.

Cassie took a selection of miniature tools out of a

pouch so neatly packed it seemed to be able to hold far more than was possible for its size. Then she levered up the glass and removed just one item from the fifty odd small exhibits that glistened on the black velvet cloth underneath them. Quickly taking an exact replica out of her shoulder bag, she placed it where the original had been before gently reinstalling the glass lid. No need to worry about the alarms as the other raiders on the premises had done the work of disabling them for her, as she had known they would.

Time to go. Almost the perfect crime, but then nothing is quite perfect. Just one long curving eyelash now lay inside the cabinet next to the fake treasure she had placed there. The lash was virtually invisible against the black background – but virtually is not quite completely.

Cassie reached the main atrium just in time to see the gang that had preceded her staggering towards the door carrying DJ. It looked to her like three huge undertakers carrying a wooden coffin and it was a few seconds before she realised it must be one of the museum's Egyptian mummies. As one of men lurched and almost dropped his load, Cassie thought they were being a bit ambitious. Surely there were easier pickings to be had? Anyway, that was their self-inflicted problem.

Leaving by the same exit would risk running into the gang, the museum's doorman or the police. Instead, now that Cassie was inside, it was easy enough to find and open a fire exit which she made sure to shut quietly behind her. Forcing herself to stroll rather than quickstep down a back street behind the museum, she heard sirens approaching. Emerging again at the top of Beaumont Street, the red glow of the white van's taillights stained the dark in one direction as three police cars passed it coming the other way and screamed round the corner towards the museum entrance. Cassie turned her face away as she passed an elderly couple shuffling down the pavement towards her, then slipped into the Randolph Hotel[15], leaning hard against the heavy swing doors that parted as reluctantly as a tenant resisting eviction. The uniformed doorman, shoulders festooned with sufficient gold braid to delight an Italian admiral, had his back to her. She guessed he was chatting to one of the waitresses although she couldn't see past him. The door to the Ladies was on the opposite side of the lobby. Ducking inside, Cassie found it empty, save for a haughty woman adjusting her necklace in the enormous mirror. The pearls were a string of demolition balls that must have given their oysters indigestion. Once safely in a cubicle, Cassie slipped into a pale blue silk dress and folded the clothes she had discarded back into her bag.

A glance under the door allowed her to see a pair of powerful stockinged legs stomp away like a triceratops, cracking a couple of tiles but leaving the coast clear. Once swiftly detached, the blonde wig revealed a short crop of black hair that she brushed into place in a trice. As Cassie left, the doorman peered round but, as his epaulettes blocked his vision and he was poised in mid chat-up line, he resumed his conversation without offering her assistance.

Later that night, Joe could have been found perched awkwardly on a small stool with his eyes fixed on the TV screen at the Bird and Baby[16], just around the corner from the museum. The publican hadn't been able to untie him because the burglars had used some very professional-looking cable. Fortunately, Joe knew the guy well and he was a friendly chap. Every now and then, as he served other punters, the publican paused to lift Joe's pint to his lips so Joe could take a swig from it.

The end of the match was marked by a crash as West Ham scored in the final seconds to win. Overcome, Joe had slid off his stool to the floor in blissful oblivion. He had refused to allow the publican to try and find help to untie him until the end of the game, but with Joe now out for the count, it seemed like time to call 999.

The operator must have heard the post match commentary still going on in the background.

'What's the result? I've been on shift all evening?' he asked. The publican told him.

'You're havin' me on mate. That's brilliant ... a lot of the ambulances are at the ground for the pitch invasion and celebratory punch up, but if your bloke is West Ham I'll get one there right away. At least it's a real emergency. Not like a lot of 'em. The previous caller was just asking if the peas you use to take down swelling in a sensitive place should be frozen or mushy.'

When Joe finally came round, he found that he was in a bright white room filled with light. Perhaps the joy of that glorious finale had made his heart pop and he was now in the lobby in front of the pearly gates. If so, he could rely on his faith to get him through. Faith that St Peter must be a West Ham supporter and would let him in along with all the others. The mixed leaf salad topped with a tomato and two small kidney beans on his bedside table made him reconsider. Surely in Heaven there would be something more substantial, like pies or burgers with chips? Maybe he was being sectioned and everything had been a dream, but the hospital staff soon reassured him that West Ham really had won and he had just been brought in for monitoring as a precaution after passing out in the pub.

As instructed, he took plenty of fluids through the tube he found hanging at the side of his bed until a nurse pointed out that he was sucking the end of another patient's catheter. In one of those many small coincidences which make up our lives but which we never even notice until someone else connects them, Joe soon found that the bed was occupied by a young man with a bandaged head called Tom who ruefully admitted he had walked into a lamppost while eyeing up a blond bird. Although a University nerd Tom also loved footie, but as an Italian by birth supported Fiorentina which Joe had always thought was a pizza topping.

Dr Carver was late. Striding down the path towards the operating theatre he was trying to work out how he would fit in the five NHS vasectomies scheduled that evening while allowing time for the private work that paid for those little extras in life – the convertible and holidays to the Bahamas. Perhaps he should just not bother with the bedside manner. That would save precious time. After all, most of the patients would in all honesty prefer him to cut the chat, or anything else, rather than the tubes to their scrotum. As he passed Ward 13 a shimmering jellyfish shot through the open window. It landed at his feet, bursting on impact. Only as he stared at the bedraggled remnants on the gravel and a loud cheer echoed from the ward did he recognise it as a colostomy bag.

Joe tried to explain to the ward sister the following morning that they had been re-enacting West Ham's winning goal, but she just didn't understand. Joe could only assume she was a secret Chelsea supporter, like the patients who had complained of his and Tom's rendition of *I'm Forever Blowing Bubbles*[17] in the early hours. His suspicions were strengthened by the fact that she was wearing a royal blue uniform; Chelsea colours with no hint of West Ham's claret and sky blue.

At least the midnight Zimmer frame race down one of the interminable hospital corridors had proved a resounding success. The hospital chaplain confirmed that it had raised morale and given several patients to whom he had already administered the last rites a whole new lease of life.

As soon as he and Tom were discharged, Joe was interviewed by the police. As he was about to leave the police station one of the ladies from the HR department at the museum turned up to check on his welfare and offer him counselling after the night's trauma. Joe was bemused. Why would he need counselling for one of the best nights of his life?

CHAPTER 2 – GRIM UP NORTH

[18]

Space isn't remote at all. It's only an hour's drive away if your car could go straight upwards.[19] – Fred Hoyle

Two months later, and only half a mile from the Ashmolean, the morning flooded the main quadrangle of St Barbara's College with mellow sunshine. It was surprisingly warm for an Oxford November and Archibald Templeton, the Dean, could see small motes of dust drifting as if they had lost their way in the shafts of light that pierced the windows of his study. He was a strangely emaciated man with a head that poked out of his jacket a bit like a skull on a stick. At present, he looked serene. Indeed, the college matron might have been tempted to take his pulse to check he was still alive were it not for the flinty eyes that gleamed below a wide expanse of forehead and a few wisps of thining grey hair. Had she done so it would have been a grave mistake. The Dean was known to have a terrible temper. The head of HR had only recently shown courage that, in other circumstances, might have earned her a VC by suggesting he would benefit from a course in anger management. The Dean listened to her advice in silence and reflected on it for at least thirty seconds before blowing his top. He then called the porter to clear her desk into a dustbin liner and had her marched off the premises.[20]

His mood had indeed only just recovered from the previous morning when he looked out at around the same hour to see that the words, "Screw Archie," neatly cut into the lawn. An immediate interrogation of a ferocity that would have made any Jesuit squirm resulted in the sobbing confession of three Classics students. Their transparent attempts to suggest their crime was intended as a celebration of the invention of the screw by Archimedes, the Greek philosopher[21] but that they had simply got the words back to front sealed their fate. On reflection, the Dean was delighted to have the chance to expel three troublemakers before they got up to something worse.

At his orders, the entire college gardening team descended on the lawn with every mower available. Within minutes the grass had been shaved to a short bristle that erased all evidence of the infamous offence.

So now the Dean stretched out his long, spindly legs under the massive desk from which he surveyed his domain while sipping his capuccino. The coffee provided a perfect foil to the exquisite mixture of chocolate dusted foam and he sighed with contentment as he reached for the newspaper. He fully expected that the front page would still be entirely taken up with the gradually-emerging details of the Ashmolean raid. This had created a massive shock throughout the University and there was little talk or thought of anything else.

Already, reams of print had been devoted to the priceless nature of the stolen treasures. The Egyptologists were normally a reclusive bunch with their heads lost in hieroglyphics. But they were distraught that the thieves had somehow managed to get away with Djed Djehuty Iuef Ankh. Repeated reference in print to the priest's lengthy name was already having a small, but nonetheless detectable, impact on tree-felling in the Amazon, among other unexpected side effects. Several interviews with journalists were cut short with the words, 'I'm afraid that's all we have got time for,' before Dr Babel[22], the head of the Egyptology Department, could get beyond the name itself.

Matters were made worse by his meticulous corrections of the journalists' stuttering attempts to pronounce the name correctly, or at least as intensive, but inconclusive, research suggested it might have sounded phonetically nearly three thousand years ago.[23] Dr Babel therefore never managed to fully explain the really interesting bit, the story of the mummy's curse that anyone who stole his body would themselves be entombed [24] alive in a pit filled with cobras. Equally the journalists had no time to satisfy a curiosity irrelevant to the supposed subject of the interview by asking him privately why he had no eyebrows[25].

Instead, the headline that confronted the Dean was "Words Phallus" and the huge image below left him choking with rage. There, staring back like a selfie you would desperately delete, was a distorted image. But, even through the thick veil of milky froth that he had split across the page, it was close enough to reality that no-one in university circles at least would have any doubt who it portrayed.

All morning, the rain had been falling in a shroud that smudged the charcoal line of distant North Pennine hills. Tom could feel the bleak moorland soaking into him. Pools gathered in the tarpaulins that sagged across the hidden delving of the dig. The deep mud and trenches were a scene reminiscent of the Somme. At least he didn't have to go "over the top" like those poor sods in the First World War. Adding insult to injury, it seemed from the forecast that the South was basking in a late autumn heatwave.

The excavations had been hurried. Working all hours when the weather allowed, the team were torn between their passion to preserve the imprint of the past and the relentless advance of the earthworks that nipped at their heels. From that point of view, the icy monsoons of the last few days were welcome. A pause for rest before the angry herd of earthmovers and trucks started bellowing behind them again.

The construction company was more concerned about penalties for delay than the risk of erasing history. The planning permission for this new spur of the A1 required them to excavate ahead of their road building. If anything of sufficient archaeological interest was identified in their path, they would need to literally stop in their tracks to allow time for detailed excavation. Naturally, they would prefer to swiftly bury any discovery again so deep that it would never remerge into the light of day. The construction foreman called the archaeologists, "the moles," at least when he was being relatively polite. Having to pay for the moles as part of the project infuriated him. And the moles knew that the builders were itching to whack them with their spades given half a chance.

Tensions reached breaking point a couple of days earlier when some bones and shards of rusted steel were unearthed directly in the line of the roadworks. The bones hadn't yet been analysed in any detail and might not even be human but there was a heavily oxidised sword hilt among the steel fragments. The embossing suggested it could be Roman. Now, digging would need to slow to a pace that would seem to the foreman like a snail going into reverse gear.

Tom's thoughts blew around in the blustering wind. The Romans would have had plenty of time to dream of the sun, vineyards and olives of home while they marched north. They would probably have preferred to risk wading through hot lava in Pompeii rather than ending up in Britain. The poet Ovid, banished to a similar forgotten outpost of the empire on the Black Sea, had composed self-pitying verse hoping to earn a reprieve from exile[26]. Tom's own misfortunes gave him a miserable sense of empathy, but he doubted that any poem could touch the hard hearts that would determine his own fate.

At least now a sickly sun was finally filtering through the cloud. It reminded him of the curtains twitching at a care home, giving a momentary glimpse of a pallid face blinking in the thin light. But even this colourless greeting seemed like a hopeful sign after the deluge. Perhaps his luck was starting to turn.

The wide brim of a battered hat obscured his view of the sky. Spirits lifting, he took it off and looked up. Yes, even the fine spray that had followed the earlier waterfall from the heavens was thinning to nothing. The air was noticeably brightening and, as the light increased, it was split into its primary colours by the arc of a rainbow.

He was jerked out of his reverie by a wallop on his forehead. The blurred grey fuselage of a gull swept in a broad curve past the crook of his eye, it's legs flattened against the sky but still slightly apart. The sleek head craned back over its shoulder at the impossible angle only birds can achieve, but from the ground Tom couldn't wring it's neck anyway. He was no ornithologist, but there was little doubt that the gull was grinning as if it had just taken part in the Dam Busters' raid. It was already circling back to admire its kill. Wiping away the lime only made matters worse, smearing Tom's hair with dirty white streaks. He gave up and abruptly launched himself into a stooping sprint before ducking into a tent at the edge of the excavations to escape another attack.

'Hey! Watch the pole or you'll bring the whole lot down!' The disembodied exclamation came from somewhere inside the tent.

Tom's eyes gradually adjusted to the gloom inside. He was still doubled up in the entrance when a cup of steaming tea was thrust towards his face almost searing his skin, as if it was being wiped by a scalding flannel. The tea was dark, as murky brown as the waters of the Limpopo when stirred up by mating hippos. This wasn't just an image Tom had plucked from his fevered imagination. As a boy, while on an expedition with his father, they had crept silently at dawn through the scrub to a riverbank to watch these impressive aquatic antics.

Tom took a slurp of the rusty liquid. He was secretly concerned that so much tannin might be corrosive. He preferred coffee, ideally espresso. Still people seemed to survive the tea here in Yorkshire. His father would just have added a generous glug of whisky from the hip flask that accompanied him everywhere. 'Medicinal,' he always said. 'To kill the bacteria.'

Tom knew he had been an unspoken disappointment to his father. But then it wasn't easy to follow in the wake of an explorer who had partied in full regalia with Zulu warriors and shown that it was possible to herd llamas from the top to the bottom of South America.

He remembered, as a child, plotting the progress of the llama expedition across the magical colours and folds of the map bought for him in a second-hand bookshop. His father had marked his route plan on it with indigo ink. It stretched from the curious quiff of land that reached into the azure Caribbean at the northernmost tip of Columbia, then descended to follow the broad spine of the Andes. At each stage the coils of the path wound down the map like a shimmering thread through bright pictures of local wildlife. There were toucans with beaks so large in proportion to their bodies that it seemed they must overbalance and topple out of the trees in which they perched. Apart from llamas on pinnacles of rock, there were other similar four-legged creatures which he learned were alpacas and guanacos. In places, the heads or tails of pumas could be spotted, stealthily peeking out of verdant jungle. None of the images were to scale and so the guinea pigs were enormous compared with the pumas or even the whales that spurted fans of water into the air just off the coast of Argentina. His father told him that these furry creatures were really only the size of a rat and were great local delicacies, eaten on sticks like large flat lollipops.

Tom was however much more interested to hear that chocolate had first come from South America[27]. His mother, who loved the laidback lifestyle of the Mediterranean, always said that it was true to character that the Spanish discovered tomatoes bursting with taste and colour as well as a flood of gold, enough to drench their churches and fill the coffers of an empire. By contrast, the famous English buccaneers who went all the way to the Americas brought back potatoes, dull tubers of English starch.

As well as animals, there were historical scenes such as the temples of the Aztecs [28]and moustached Spaniards hauling away chests of jewels. Finally, the route ended at the tip of Patagonia where the whole great South American landmass cooled its curling dragon's tail in the icy seas. Here, his father had drawn a small tent with a flag sheltering under a much larger slice of his favourite Victoria sponge cake to mark the end of the expedition.

'Your lucky day?' The voice was measured and dry now, but had a hidden edge to it.

'What? Oh yes. I looked up at the wrong moment. Sorry to crash in, but the wretched bird was coming back for a second strike.'

'Cracking shot. It's luckier if the bird shit lands on your head, you know. Something to do with the rarity of a direct hit between the eyes. You should see it as a sort of blessing[29].'

'I don't think it can be complete chance. I'm sure

it was deliberate. That gull had me in its crosshairs. Just waiting for me to catch sight of the rainbow. I could see it in those mean gritty little eyes and the way it opened its beak afterwards like a smiling assassin. Hope that doesn't dilute the luck though. I could do with some.'

As the steam cleared Tom could see that Professor Gillibrand was crouched on her haunches. Grey eyes and an angular but haunting face that in the right circumstances might have conveyed a wild beauty. But these were not the right circumstances. Her tawny mane came down to her waist and would have been magnificent if it had not been matted and unwashed. She must be edging towards fifty, but with her tough and wiry build it was hard to tell in her current unkempt state. Fiercely dedicated to her work as lead archaeologist, she was usually referred to by the team, with an affection mingled with fear, as Boudicca[30] and he understood that Gillibrand meant flaming sword.

Like the Iceni queen, she was more than a match for the foreman of the construction company in their regular clashes. From bedtime to boarding school, piano lessons to make up, punk rock to student politics, every stage of Boudicca's life had sparked opportunities to make revolt her status quo, all of which she had seized upon. She chose archaeology as a career when her parents suggested that she should go into nursing, and because the dead could be relied upon not to impose pressure on her to do anything that she would instinctively be compelled to resist.

She and Tom, as he said he preferred to be called, hadn't had much time to get to know each other since his sudden and unexplained arrival a couple of days earlier. He looked as if he had the athleticism and broad shoulders for digging and the blue eyes were alert and enquiring, but would he have the determination to slog it out day after day on site in these conditions? Whether he could or not, she found herself suppressing a fleeting thought that he might be good material for an earthy encounter in a trench if he stayed long enough. Digging up the past was fascinating but being surrounded by ancient bones made you aware that death lasts a very long time. Plenty of time to regret what you didn't do when alive, especially when only the dead were watching as they were very good at keeping things to themselves.

Boudicca had simply received a request from the Dean at St Barbara's asking if a junior lecturer on the college staff, Tommaso rather than Tom according to the formal letter, could join her excavation. Short of help and under pressure from the roadworks she agreed without asking for an explanation. But Tom had known he would need to give one sometime and, lubricated with hot tea, he was as ready as he would ever be. As he was to come to realise, Boudicca never started with the obvious.

'St Barbara's? Never heard of it before.'

'Not that surprising. It's the most obscure college at Oxford. Founded in the fourteenth century but very small and not many people have come across it. The University doesn't like to draw attention to it as it's really a sort of landfill for academics and students who don't fit in anywhere else but might conceivably have some potential that no one can quite put their finger on. It also helps the University's statistics as nearly everyone comes from state schools, so that comes in useful.'

'I was quite struck by the coat of arms on the Dean's splendid letterhead. What's the significance of the lightning bolt across the middle?'

'Barbara was the daughter of a wealthy heathen. He was pretty upset when she converted to Christianity. In fact, he went completely bonkers and planned to torture and behead her. But on his way home he was struck by a divine bolt of lightning. So, after she was sanctified, people used to pray to her in thunderstorms.'

'You could have told me before. A few prayers to her over the last couple of days might have come in handy. Unless of course you tried, and we have you and her to thank that it's clearing up?'

'I didn't think of it. But, if the builders start dynamiting again for the next section of road after we've given them the all-clear from the excavation, I'm prepared to give it a go as that would certainly play to Barbara's specialities which include mining. Apparently, when guns and fireworks came along, sudden death by explosion became much more common so prayers to Barbara were increasingly popular as an insurance policy. That's how the college was established. The widow of a knight who was blown to bits by a malfunctioning canon at the battle of Crecy[31] gave an endowment in memory of St Barbara. She hoped this would save other poor souls from exploding, whether by accident or spontaneous combustion[32]. The failure of the Gunpowder Plot gave Barbara's appeal a massive boost and the college received a lot of other rich legacies as people gave her the credit for the exposure of the plot in the nick of time. Bonfire Night at college is quite a celebration.'

'The Dean mentioned you've been doing some

research, but he was very vague, and I haven't seen anything published. I'm not clear why you were you posted up here ... in a bit of a rush, it seems. I called him and asked when he would need you back at college. He asked if it could be treated as a long-term posting. To be truthful the word was "lifetime" rather than long-term. When I mentioned that you might find it mucky work, he suggested that it would suit you down to the ground ... and hopefully at least six feet under it. A warped sense of humour, I suppose?'

Tom felt like a seal sliding off an ice floe. There really was no way back now except to swim or sink. Awkwardly, he began to explain.

'All a bit unfortunate really. The Dean has never much warmed to me. I was doing my best to keep a low profile but thought at least I could earn a few brownie points by taking a field trip of students to study Iron Age sites in Dorset – Maiden Castle and all that stuff. Anyway, we had an overnight stay in the pub at Cerne Abbas. Of course, we went to see the famous giant and I gave the group a talk on it. We discussed whether it really was Iron Age or a seventeenth century fake as some think.[33] I suppose that must have put the idea in their heads.'

Tom remembered the evening very clearly ... or at least the beginning of it. It was the last day of the field trip. The eight students were in high spirits, and they would be heading back to Oxford the following day in the St Barbara's minibus. Everyone had far too much to drink of course. The local ale was nectar and Tom soon lost count of his pints. The students were usually too skint to be generous, but they had all stood him rounds with a relentless encouragement that, with hindsight, should have aroused his suspicions. As he couldn't recall going to bed it seemed likely they had carried him up when he finally passed out. In the morning – well, almost lunchtime – he came round fully-clothed with a head like a volcano in mid eruption. After a while, he managed to crawl on all fours to the bathroom. Then, with great care, he drew back the curtains to let in some light.

The room provided a magnificent view down the valley. On one side, the slope rose to meet it and the giant stood out clearly where it had been etched in the chalk. Over one hundred and eighty feet high, it dominated the scene, waving its huge club above Britain's most famous phallus. The students inevitably insisted on measuring this impressive appendage, allegedly as part of their research. They noted that it was over forty feet high in its full state of excitement, although various studies suggested that it had undergone significant enlargements as it had been reinvigorated by new carving over time. Against his better judgment Tom was prevailed upon to take a group photo with four of the students sitting on each testicle. This immediately went viral around college, but Tom felt confident that none of the students would share it with the other staff and at least, as the photographer, he wasn't in it.

Nothing about the giant was therefore a surprise to Tom that morning. He had seen it all before. But what no one had previously seen was the even larger replica giant that now confronted the original from the opposite side of the valley. In most respects it was a strikingly good likeness of the original. They could almost have been twins, except for one thing. Tom's horror rooted him to the floor. He stood open-mouthed, then rushed for the bathroom as his stomach seized on this moment of weakness to rebel and lurch up inside him. The bubblelike head of the original below the waving club looked very like an alien, but its new rival was unmistakeably the Dean.

'So, as you can imagine, when the Dean saw it splashed all over the press, my days were numbered. He couldn't easily dismiss me as it would look too obviously like payback time and the students confirmed that I didn't have anything to do with it. Also, it would just look even worse in the press if he couldn't laugh it off as a student prank. So that's why I'm here ... as far away from college as he could send me.'

He looked like a small boy lost in a supermarket, but Boudicca was laughing out loud now. Head thrown back and oblivious to the fact that her tea was spilling everywhere. When she finally stopped, the rain had as well and the digging could resume. As the day wore on, the team discovered more and more bones. But it was Tom who made the find that really did show that the bird poop had worked its magic.

He was in a shallow trench that cut across the site when his trowel revealed what looked like a mangled piece of bronze. Gradually he worked around it with painstaking care. This took some hours as it was quite large and another time he might have given up, bored, but this looked like something worth finding. Only when he had finally freed it all from the clinging soil could he begin to see what it was. A statue or figure of a bird with out-stretched wings. Similar in size to the large gull that had attacked him, but it wasn't a seagull. Boudicca knelt beside him and whistled as they both gazed at his find.

'You know what that looks like, don't you? And if it is, then there's only one of those we can't account for.'

The same thought had been slowly dawning on Tom, and what it might mean, but he was almost overcome. Boudicca had to steady him as they gently carried the metal lump into a tent for washing before others could realise what it might be and get over-excited. There was a lot of research to be done before anything could be confirmed and it was important that there was no leak to the press. The site itself would also need protecting as the scale of the discoveries generally was becoming clearer.

Tom heard later about Boudicca's showdown with the foreman of the construction company when she told him that his workers would have to take a three-month break. The Romans came in for a stream of expletives but it was a fight Boudicca was always going to win.[34]

CHAPTER 3 – STRANGE ENCOUNTERS

[35]*A collision at sea can ruin your entire day* – Thucydides Book 9[36]

A gondola slipped quietly through the water and bumped gently against the quay in front of the Doge's Palace, the heartbeat of Venice with its long arcade topped by the pink and white bricks of the upper stories. The tall, dark-haired gondoliere took the priest's hand to help him onto the wharf, then removed his straw hat with the striped bow round the brim before bowing his head in respect. Father Matteo knew that a few prayers would suffice in place of a fare. It wasn't as though he would be denying the boatman a living. There were plenty of rich pickings to be had from tourists with more money than sense[37] and these elegant ferry services were a bargain compared to coffee or a meal in the restaurants on St Mark's Square.

The priest exuded a calm authority that would not be rushed. That was a good thing, as his aging and portly body showed the signs of many happy decades of the finest red wine. Any abrupt movement would have caused him to trip over the tassels of the long emerald and crimson robes that gave him the appearance of an overdecorated Christmas tree. He had recently returned to Venice after conducting a survey for the Vatican of the major relics held in Churches across Italy[38]. This confirmed that most were maintained in good condition and were generating a substantial financial return from donations. His conclusion however recommended that there was scope to extract more and he had been charged with overseeing the plan to achieve this.

As he alighted, Father Matteo caught only a glimpse of the Bridge of Sighs[39] in the small canal behind the palace. His path took him instead along its front façade. The towering red brick finger of the campanile[40]reached upwards. It seemed to him that the sharp tip scraping the fading night sky might explain the stars that still gleamed like pinholes through to another world of light. The huge square opened out into a vast apron to his left. Only a few days ago the *alta acqua* – the high water that regularly submerged the city - still rippled across its surface and church services had been suspended. But now the floods were receding, and the cathedral always reopened its doors as soon as it could.

The basilica of San Marco stood before him like the dream of a confectioner who had escaped from an asylum; it was an enormous pavlova with the meringue and cream of the marble crowned by domes, dusted with frescos and jewelled with the glitter of gold mosaics. Father Matteo's footsteps reverberated around the nave until he reached the high altar of the saint and knelt there[41]. Deep in prayer, he nonetheless thought for a moment that he could hear a rough scratching that seemed to be coming from behind the altar. It was as if large stones were grating against each other, followed by a rustle and then faint scraping that called to mind the painstaking glass engraving of Murano. It must be either mice or his imagination as it was still thirty minutes until the Matins service was due to begin and the church was empty, save for an old gentleman folded up asleep on one of the pews like a discarded newspaper.

The priest went to the side aisle where the confession box stood and sat down inside, pulling the red velvet curtain shut behind him. He slipped his rosary out of the pouch in his robe and quietly intoned Hail Mary's, sliding the smooth worn beads through his plump fingers. After a while, boredom overwhelmed him. He had hoped to have a little snooze, but there was the risk that his snoring habit would give him away and be put down to a lack of devotion. Instead, he changed tack on his incantations to stay awake.

At the end of the nave, the elderly gentleman slid off his pew and onto the floor. Shaking his head and picking up a battered blue rucksack, he limped slowly and soundlessly down the aisle to the confession box and slid inside. He put his ear against the curtain, listening intently. Yes, a priest was there but the old man wondered if his unreliable hearing was playing tricks on him.

'Eeney, meeney, miney, mo ... tinker, tailor, soldier, sailor ... rich man.' There seemed to be a lengthy pause at 'rich man,' as if for contemplation, then the voice continued. 'This little piggy went to market, this little piggy stayed at home …'

The old man coughed and the rhymes stopped abruptly.

Father Matteo was taken aback. He quickly pulled his sock on again, then pushed his toes back into his shoes. A low male voice came from behind the red velvet curtain that covered the grill.

'Bless me, Father, for I have sinned. It has been fifty-nine years and three days since my last confession.'

'That is a long time, my son. What are your sins?'

'Shall I tell you in chronological order, Father.'

'Maybe that would be best.'

'I have kept a diary, Father. But I keep remembering others from my earlier years before I began recording everything. I can clearly recall I stole a football from one of the other boys in my class; I wrote a very rude word on the blackboard in the classroom during morning break and left a dead frog on my teacher's chair; I played truant from school in the afternoon, upsetting my mother, and I fed rat poison to my sister's gerbil.'

'How old were you then?'

'I was five years old, Father.'

'And how far does that take us in your diary?'

'That was the first day.'

'And how long is your diary, my son?'

'I have the first three volumes here with me in my rucksack and the other volumes are still at home.'

'Perhaps we should just deal with your top three biggest sins today, my son, and you can come back for the others, although we might need to find a junior priest so you can block book a suitably lengthy appointment.'

'It's hard to say what the top three are, Father. But, just as an example, I suppose I could mention pushing my father-in-law down a well so I could claim his estate.'

'That is truly shocking, my son. But why would his money come to you? Surely his direct family members would have had a prior claim?'

'Well, you asked for three, so I was just going to come on to that, Father. The money would have gone to his wife, my mother-in-law, but I nudged her off the edge of the campanile here in Venice when we were admiring the view. Then, after my wife inherited, she was blown up in an unfortunate incident involving a gas barbeque ... so then I was next in line.'

Father Matteo's head was swimming now and he felt a panic attack coming on. He said faintly. 'I don't feel well, my son. Have you committed many other similar sins.'

'Oh yes, Father, lots, and I'm not sure that these are the worst. That's why it's taken me several weeks just to write a summary. Fifty-nine years is, as you said, a long time.'

'Come back tomorrow, my son, while I think what to do. Yours is a tricky case.'

Father Matteo reached into his robe and took out a packet of Valium. He popped a couple in his mouth and, picking up a hassock from the floor, propped it behind his head.

It was only a couple of minutes later that he heard a rustling. He would have liked to pretend he wasn't in the confessional box but that wasn't a realistic option, so he bent forward towards the confessional grill.

'I'm ready to hear you, my son or daughter.'

He had barely finished speaking when a hand wrapped in white cloth punched through the grill and grabbed him by the throat. It was some time later before his dead body was found slumped back on his seat, eyes fixed wide with fear.

Back in Oxford, Tom had spent the last few weeks putting the final touches to the article that, after considerable scrutiny, had just been published in *Veni Vidi Vici*[42]. This was the most pompous academic periodical journal for the Roman period as well as the most prestigious although commonly referred to by the students as *Three V's*. Only the high regard in which Boudicca was held had convinced the stuck-up editor to reluctantly accept Tom's paper; that, and recognition that it could be a major scoop. The site of their excavations on the A1 lay not far north of York, where the lost Ninth Legion had been based. The total disappearance of this huge fighting force had never been properly explained and remained one of the great mysteries of British history. It appeared that the legion had just vanished into thin air. But the dig had started to uncover what could only be the edge of a huge battlefield and a mix of Roman and Pictish weaponry had already been recovered. The bronze legionary eagle Tom found put matters beyond reasonable doubt. It was the Eagle of the Ninth Legion, which, it now appeared clear, had been wiped out by a surprise ambush close to its headquarters while marching northwards to crush a Pictish raid.

The news of the find and Tom's article had already sent seismic shock waves through the scholarly world and attracted colossal attention[43]. Collecting his paper at the corner shop the previous day he was astonished to see it had even made the headlines *The Eagle has Landed* and *Pict Apart – The Nemesis of the Ninth.* On his way back to St Babs, a professor who had never previously given him the time of day, came striding up, beaming and waving to ask if Tom would give a quote for his new book *Sewers and Drainage Systems of the Ancient World.* When Tom pointed out that he hadn't read it, his new friend replied. 'Oh, don't worry about that. I can just draft something if that would be easier. "An extraordinary work of scholarship that should take pride of place on every bookshelf," or something like that. You don't even need to see it. That's the way it all works. Once you're in "the club," everyone helps each other out. Where do you think all those superlative reviews come from and how do you think we all get our books published and sold? Welcome aboard the gravy train. You scratch mine and I'll scratch yours.'

Tom recoiled at the idea of having anything of his scratched, but he skimmed through the lengthy tome for a couple of hours. It largely contained endless descriptions of the author's exploration of the sights and smells of sewage systems in the dark with a head torch, made far worse because many of them were still in use. The highlight was a fold out diagram of the underbelly of ancient Rome tracing its main sewer, the *Cloaca Maxima*, from the Forum to the Tiber and then through the Pontine Marshes to the sea.

At this point, Tom gave up and wrote, "A plumber's guide to every chamber and passage in the bowels of the ancient world. This work is an unrivalled dungheap of information. Plunging into this stream of effluent, even the most avid enthusiast will encounter the full pungency of the sights and stench of ancient

Rome in a level of detail that will bring them up gasping for air. An opportunity literally not to be "wasted", to jump down the plug hole of the distant past and dive into depths that redefine the meaning of disgust."

The author was initially incandescent with rage when he read it in pride of place on the back cover until he was told by his publisher that the graphic review had massively boosted sales of the book. Instead of the tiny number of academic institutions who might have felt compelled to add it to their collections, a whole range of unexpected readers were now clamouring for a further print run, particularly gardeners who thought they might pick up some new composting tips and lovers of horror fiction. The Rome tourist board also bought a large number of copies to meet increased demand from the rising flood of visitors to the *Cloaca Maxima* and were forced to review safety procedures on the narrow walkways including issuing lifebelts .

Tom tried to keep a very low profile following his return to college, only slipping out when he knew the Dean would not be around. He knew, however, that the call would come and hoped that the reflected glory from his article, in which the whole of St Barbara's was already basking, would at least go some way towards diluting the acid of the Dean's rage. During recent days Tom had left the phone ringing on a number of occasions when he knew the call came from the college office but now there was a knock on the door, and it would be high risk to pretend he wasn't in. The porter was standing there with the expression of a vicar administering the last rites. Tom followed him, as requested.

Tom had been in the Dean's office a few times

before but preferred to forget them. It had always been in connection with some misdemeanour[44]. He wasn't therefore surprised by the large stag's head on the wall, although this seemed rather outdated in a more environmentally-conscious age. There was also, of course, the First World War German Pickelhaube or spiked helmet. The Dean used the spike for all his correspondence. Apparently, it had been kept as a trophy by the Dean's father after he stormed a machine gun emplacement single-handed during a night attack in only his underwear having leapt from his sponge bath as the call to arms unexpectedly sounded. The Dean himself walked with a slight limp that he claimed came from a stray bullet fired by another member of his party while stag hunting, but unkind rumour had it that it that he had dropped a ball on his foot while ten-pin bowling. The desk in the centre of the room was an enormous mahogany affair designed to intimidate. Across this expanse Tom forced himself to meet the hooded stare, knowing that the Dean was itching to announce that a certain junior lecturer was leaving the College as he had joined it - fired with enthusiasm. There seemed no likelihood of forgiveness, but Tom tried to glean a crumb of hope as he saw that the Dean fighting to pull his mouth into a thin-lipped semblance of welcome.

The Dean was indeed finding it difficult to restrain himself at the sight of Tom and his fists were clenched under the desk. After his outburst over the giant, he had been forced to take medical advice for high blood pressure. He had at least been able to prepare for this meeting by doing his morning yoga. Now he also forced himself to do the deep breathing exercises he had been given. For a few uncomfortable seconds his self-control teetered as close to popping as the bung in an overfermented barrel of cider . Then he abruptly introduced another man that Tom hadn't noticed and who was sitting in an armchair in the corner by the sash window.

'This is Mr Cavatappi. He has outlined a very interesting proposition for St Barbara's in which you might play a useful part.'

The gentleman in the chair seemed relaxed, almost languid, although his eyes danced in his aquiline face with a mercurial mix of amusement and hidden edge. Tom felt he was being fastidiously dissected, as if a diner was checking for fine bones in a Dover sole at a restaurant. Yet, at the same time, the charm flowed as easily as olive oil and Tom had no doubt it was *extra virgine.*

'Tommaso or Tom, if I may call you that. It is a pleasure. I would like to congratulate for on your recent article. Quite a coup.'

His slicked-back dark hair with threads of silver enhanced the impression of sophistication. The dark blue suit was immaculately cut. It hung perfectly on the stranger's slim frame, complemented by a crisp, white linen shirt. A green silk handkerchief in the top pocket matched his tie. Black leather shoes refracted light from the chandelier.

'Tom is fine. Only my mother calls me Tommaso…or my relatives on the rare occasions I get to Rome these days.'

'Ah, yes? Well, as you will have guessed from my own name, I am also of Italian heritage but, like many of my grandparents' generation, they were forced to leave Sicily for what seemed the brighter prospects of America.'

The New York accent was unmistakable, but Tom could also trace the Italian in the rolling r's, like the engine of a Ferrrrrrrarrrrri revving at full throttle on the front line of the grid at Monza. Tom waited. He wondered if the Dean had selected him to give this guy a guided tour of the college library and began to think up excuses. But Mr Cavatappi hadn't finished.

'Maybe if you are ever over in Manhattan, I can take you to the pizza restaurant my grandfather set up and my father still runs, *Margherita Amore Mia*, or just go yourself, ask for the chef, Alfredo Vermicelli, and mention my name. But finding time for such diversions is never easy, so let me cut to the chase. I represent a hedge fund owned by a group of very wealthy investors with considerable interest in history. They have far more money than they know what to do with and enjoy investing in other projects. Finance can often be very boring, but they understand history is not all just 1066 and Tudors and Stuarts which I believe is all British children learn about at school? Perhaps you understand this and that's why you chose a career in history? My colleagues have no intention of making a similar financial sacrifice to the one I imagine you have made in becoming an academic, but one of the main benefits of being so successful is that they can use part of their gains on matters that bring them more enjoyment and have an element of excitement. An art collection is all very well, but not so intriguing. They have therefore established a specialist subsidiary fund called the Promotion of Educational Studies Trust through which they would like to support the setting up of a small team to investigate some of the great mysteries of history and I have been discussing with the Dean the prospect of locating it here at St Barbara's.'

'And where do I come into this?'

'Well, we would like you to lead the team. That's why we are thinking of St Barbara's.'

'Are you sure I'm best qualified?'

'No need to be modest. As I have been emphasising to the Dean here, you have captured the attention of the world by uncovering the fate of the Ninth Legion and it exactly fits our project. A major historical mystery that has eluded researchers for years now solved and it's the real mysteries, the famous ones, that we are interested in exploring. What's more I understand you are doing some work on the lost kingdom of Atlantis ... That would of course also fit the bill perfectly.'

How did Cavatappi know this? It wasn't exactly a secret but there were literally only a couple of people he could think of to whom he had lightly mentioned the Atlantis research that had taken up a lot of his time over the last year or so. In fact, it was for this reason that he had neglected other aspects of his work and the Dean had hauled him into this office more than once before. Tom's instinctive wariness urged caution, but he could not stop his heartbeat rising at the mention of his pet project.

'What size of team would you be prepared to fund?'

'That would partly depend on your considered assessment of what would be needed. For example, you might wish to investigate more than one mystery at a time. We would expect you to provide a detailed business plan but envisage you might easily need a team of five or six full-time researchers plus some support staff. A new faculty office area could be built here at St Barbara's for your work as this is a long-term project – our investors know that answers can't be found to such tricky matters in an instant. Then, from time to time you might need local support, for example, archaeologists in certain other countries.'

'So … these mysteries we investigate could be foreign ones?'

'Oh yes, of course. Like Atlantis. Britain, after all, only has so many significant historical mysteries and many of the most exciting ones will be elsewhere.'

'No limitation on time period or other parameters?'

'No, none. You have a free hand, although we would prefer matters that date back more than a century or so. Otherwise they haven't had time to mature into proper historical mysteries. That requires a certain mythology to grow up around them as, of course, you appreciate. The sense of mystery is half the attraction.'

After discussing a few other details, the Italian stood up to go. The handshake was somehow superficially relaxed yet unforgiving. Cavatappi's movement in reaching out his hand exposed a livid scar running upwards from his wrist and disappearing under the cuff of his shirt sleeve. The suave financier also had some strange marks across the knuckles, as if he had been wearing wedding rings on every finger. But Tom didn't take much notice because he was in a daze, already thinking about the business plan Cavatappi wanted him to produce by the end of the week.

Apart from the project itself, Cavatappi had explained that the finances and purely administrative issues were matters for the Dean. When he mentioned a start-up fund of perhaps two million pounds and monthly amounts of three hundred thousand as possible starting points, subject to the business plan requirements, Tom thought for a moment that he must be hallucinating. But the Dean's office always had the kind of chilly micro-climate maintained in the polar enclosure at the zoo. This icy atmosphere only allowed for reality and Tom didn't take drugs[45]. At least he now understood the pressure on the Dean to persuade him to accept the proposal. Without him, St Barbara's wouldn't get the massive injection of cash on offer or a project that would hugely increase the reputation of the college, and therefore its Dean.

Nonetheless, when Tom's own proposed salary was mentioned at a figure he knew from the college's published accounts was more than the Dean's, he thought for a moment that the Dean would be sick. Tom could see there were now going to be huge opportunities for him to get his own way on virtually anything. He intended to make every use of it, particularly where freedom from the Dean's tyranny was concerned.

Over the following weeks several things happened, some possibly connected and others probably not at all. If you have ever tried to fit together thousands of pottery shards from an archaeological dig, you will know how frustrating, or even impossible, it often is. Many parts are likely to be missing, ground into dust over the ages, and many vessels are very similar so it's very easy to get pieces confused. Museums the world round are filled with ancient jars made from reassembled fragments that don't actually belong together[46]. Often you can see the sections that have been filled in and painted over to fit the imagination of the archaeologist rather than the original design. But, of course, that is how the dots are joined to make history.

Tom's mother called him from Rome by video on her mobile. There was raucous laughter and music in the background and Tom could see that she was, as usual, at a party and that the Prosecco was running freely. She was thrilled to see the news about his article on Rai One, the Italian state TV station. All her family and friends were astounded, and she was hugely enjoying the kudos it had given her. Silvio Berlusconi had even invited her to have tea with him. She asked Tom if he thought it safe to accept, given *Il Cavaliere's* reputation[47].

This was a question to which there was no safe answer. Tom tried as diplomatically as he could to suggest that, as she was no longer in high school, she should feel as secure as she would if at mass with St Francis of Assisi. At this reference to her age however, his mother, always highly emotional, emitted a piercing scream that brought several other guests running to her aid and that Tom feared may well have burst his own eardrum. After several observations that any Italian would have understood as rude in the extreme, she cut him off. Tom thought the comment about his parentage was a little rich coming from his own mother, but he knew that the steam from her rages evaporated as quickly as it boiled up. Only a few minutes later he received a text from her saying how much she adored her son, even though he could be a complete *cazzo* - a dick - at times.

Near Kandahar in Afghanistan a goatherd woke up just as the first hint of dawn crept above the dry red bones of the encircling mountains and lapped across the dust of the plain. He had been sleeping in the mouth of a small cave just outside the city. An instinctive unease stirred within him as he raised his head from the bundle of rags and blankets he had wrapped around himself to keep out the intense cold. The goats weren't far away. Some were resting, but others were already on their feet and trying to find the few sprigs of grass still clutching onto life amid the ancient ruins that encircled the cave. Abdul counted and none of his precious flock appeared to be missing. He was about to unroll his small prayer mat when a strange white figure suddenly emerged from behind one of the stunted columns. He shrank back. Could this be a ghost? Or perhaps the *Mahdi*, whose coming was said to signify the end of time?

An article appeared on the front page of the Italian newspapers. It reported the sensational news that the body of the apostle, St Mark, which was the chief treasure of San Marco in Venice, had been stolen. Thieves had not only broken into the chamber within the high altar where the embalmed body had been preserved but it seemed had also murdered the only priest in the Church at the time in his own confession box.

This scandalous and sacrilegious act had aroused a huge wave of popular anger across the country. The Italian police and Interpol were involved in the investigation as it was thought the criminals might be part of some international gang. However, no one could understand the motive. Even a private collector would have to be mad to steal a relic so distinctive that it could never be sold. It was, after all, a very old corpse, not a work of art that could be visually appreciated. Body snatchers like Burke and Hare may have stolen bodies in the past, and even murdered for purposes of medical dissection, but after two thousand years it seemed unlikely that St Mark's remains would have much value from this perspective. This ruled out the trade in organ transplants as an explanation, and, in any case, the priest's own body had been left untouched. There followed a lengthy and heartfelt obituary to Father Matteo which, rather unusually, was written by the owner of his favourite restaurant in St Mark's Square as apparently this was where he had spent most of his time when in Venice. It ended with a lengthy list of the priest's favourite puddings.

CHAPTER 4 – A SUDDEN BRAINWAVE

Just realised ... if tomatoes are fruit, that makes ketchup a smoothie – Anon.

Finbarr was staring through the glass on the seventy-third floor[48] of the Blot in London. It had been designed as a landmark that, according to the architects, would be the signature on the City's skyline. They had originally called the glistening tower Nirvana but it had been popularly rechristened after Prince Charles described it in a speech to the construction industry as a blot on the landscape. His proposal that it should be immediately demolished, even prior to opening, and replaced with a low rise neo – Georgian mansion, had however fallen on deaf ears.

The bank Finn worked for had recently taken space there, although they were quickly beginning to think that had been a mistake. A number of clients had made claims for compensation after complaining that the glare had damaged their eyesight as they entered the vast ground floor atrium and all guests were now warned to come in very dark glasses. Members of the public were advised only to look at the building through a pin hole as for a solar eclipse. Of more concern to the bank, all the offices enjoyed such mesmerising panoramic views across the Thames and London that productivity had dropped by forty five percent. Urgent meetings were convened by the Chief Executive. It was rumoured that his plan was to black out the windows of all offices except his own and those of the senior management. The hope was that keeping everyone warm but in the dark would revive performance, stimulate spectacular growth and keep the spirits of the workforce sky-high, much as it does for cannabis plants.

Finbarr idly drummed his fingers on his desk. He was trying to count the number of taxis he could see crawling like ants across London Bridge and further afield, fetching and carrying their sustenance particularly along the familiar pathways to and from the mainline stations. This was a game he regularly played with a select group of trusted colleagues and there was a weekly league table. On Fridays, the losers bought the champion as many rounds as he or she could handle before sliding under the bar at the *Up in Arms*, a nearby pub. The secret of Finn's recent run of success was a cause of much speculation, but the answer was simple. He had bought himself an extremely powerful set of binoculars with a magnification even sufficient for stargazing.

The league scoring was carefully encrypted on the office system so that only those in the know could access it. Finbarr and his friends had technology skills far ahead of those in the IT or Risk Management departments, so there wasn't much to worry about there. The problem was that none of this really solved the boredom.

Finn had always been a mathematical genius, even at school where he and Tom first met and became best mates. Getting a job in the Financial Sector proved easy and Finn was now paid far more than he had ever imagined he would earn. But he felt deeply dissatisfied. He reflected that, since the wild escapades he and Tom had shared, life had been all downhill. It was not what he had expected at only thirty. He smiled slightly to himself, remembering how he and Tom were expelled together after two earlier suspensions. Three strikes and all that. As the headmaster told their parents with increasing exasperation on each occasion, "Fair is fair, but rules are rules."

They had been holding a Viking burial on the lake in the school grounds for the headmaster's dog which had been killed that afternoon by a cricket ball. The opposing team were making mincemeat of the first eleven and their star batsman slogged an amazing six well over the boundary. Poor Cerberus never saw it coming. He was wagging his tail and waddling round outside the boundary when the ball hit him smack between the eyes. A very gentle black Labrador who brought far more humanity to school than his owner, he was deeply mourned by all the pupils.

As usual it was Finn's idea, but his trusty follower Tom was enthusiastic, and, after recently reading Beowulf in English classes, it had seemed a fitting farewell. Certainly, the groundsman's rowing boat made a magnificent blaze out on the water after Cerberus had been carefully laid on a pile of old branches doused in petrol that had been siphoned out of the school lawnmower. Whether by coincidence or serendipity, it was just as Finn was recalling Tom's funeral speech in Cerberus's honour that his phone began ringing and Tom's name flashed up on the screen.

'Still obsessing over those spreadsheets, Finn? I hear you "excel" at them.'

'Ha Ha and how are you getting on with finding the Ark of the Covenant, now you're so famous, Indiana?'

'Seriously Finn, I'm hoping I can tempt you with another job studying the development of something with even more cells in it than a spreadsheet. It's called a human. I know you have always been intrigued by the riddles of the past, particularly so-called mythology that turns out to be true.'

'What like the Minotaur turning up in Birmingham Bull Ring?'

'Don't mock, we're talking about a much more enjoyable form of problem solving than you will ever find in your algorithms. I think I might actually be getting somewhere with my Atlantis research and I've now got the offer of some serious funding. Only pocket money as far as you're concerned, but a bank, Finn? Come on, there's more to life! If you are so indispensable to global finances that the stockmarket crashes you can always change your mind and go back again later to save the world or catch the plummeting pound. The only real risk is death and that's not a risk either, it's a certainty except for the timing. Do you think those dinosaurs were all craning their necks looking out for an asteroid?'

'Tom, finding the Eagle of the Ninth is incredible, but the odds of solving another mystery like that are vanishingly small.'

'Improbabilities happen Finn. No one believed there was another untouched pharoah's tomb in the Valley of the Kings in 1922, so if you had been Howard Carter back then Tutankhamen would never have been found. If you want to block out everything that isn't probable then you might find it challenging to meet Tsutomo Yamaguuchi who was in Hiroshima for the first atom bomb then travelled to Nagasaki just in time for the second but still survived, or Roy Sullivan who was struck on seven separate occasions by lightening.'

'Really, is that guy still alive?'

'You mean Roy? Sadly no. He committed suicide over an unrequited love whereas the actuarial charts predict with a 94% degree of confidence that you will finally become defunct in your slippers watching repeats of *The Simpsons* at the average age for a UK male of 81 years and 53 days. That's provided you don't take up smoking and keep your alcohol units below 21, so… let me just work it out…that gives you until August 24th 2061 and the most common time of death is around 11 am, soon after breakfast so make that one a full English with extra black pudding and all the works. You'll need it for the next life. In fact we may as well get your tombstone engraved now. Except of course I'm sure that's not what will really happen except in your virtual world of probabilities. My guess is that you're more likely to be electrocuted by a malfunctioning sunbed or something weird like that. In any case it's much more fun looking for improbabilities.'

After a few more light-hearted exchanges Tom

said, 'Just meditate on this Finn. You're only young once ... and that's already becoming ancient history.' Finn only promised to think about it but he didn't need long. Tom had for once risen to the challenge of taking the lead and his words instinctively played on Finn's nagging boredom and impatience, strumming a lingering chord that gathered a clarifying strength inside him like the note from a tuning fork. The opportunity was too good to turn down. He dashed off a one-line email to his boss saying he was resigning due to, "The suffocating burden of probability". Chucking his security pass onto his chair, he grabbed his coat and headed for the lift to the ground floor.

Abdul's story was dismissed by the Afghan elders of his village. Some said it was a trick of the light. Others that Abdul was still dreaming or half asleep and had mistaken one of his goats for a person. However, over the following days there were similar sightings at several other places in Afghanistan. A patrol of US soldiers near Bagram airbase opened fire on a strange white figure but this seemed to have no effect on the apparition. Two members of the patrol were flown home afterwards as they had clearly been unhinged by the experience and kept babbling about it. Bad for morale, the Bagram commandant had concluded.

In his room at St Barbara's Tom received an email from a strange address but passing on a brief message. It was from his father who was in Papua and New Guinea and must have asked someone else to send it from a remote outpost with internet in which he had briefly surfaced. Reading the message, it was quickly clear that news about Tom's own discovery hadn't yet reached that part of the world, but his father believed there were good prospects of finding a new tribe. He was therefore as excited as Tom's mother had been on her last call, but for entirely different reasons. He reminded Tom that it was the anniversary of Uncle Albert's death and asked Tom to go and pay respects on behalf of the family as a whole. Tom sighed but sent a message back promising that he would, although he doubted his father would ever receive it.

Cassie sat waiting on a bench in Hyde Park. The autumn leaves floated down to drift across the grass in a mix of fragile gold, pale yellows and dappled browns – as if a dragon had scraped off its old, dry scales. A few people came past, hurrying to secret destinations to fulfil unknown missions, most of them probably humdrum, but who knows?

Finn was one of them, walking with a sprightly step and a sense of freedom as he headed past the embassies at the western edge of the park and out towards his flat in Notting Hill. But, of course, Finn and Cassie knew nothing of each other. She glanced blankly at the young man of medium height with startlingly green eyes and tousled ginger hair only because he was wearing a grey city suit in a slovenly fashion with a garish tartan tie at half mast, but anything she registered had been erased within seconds. For his part, Finn clocked a petite but striking-looking young woman with the bone structure of a bird within a triangular face; short, spiky black hair; very dark eyes and roller-skates.

The Ashmolean escapade had been exciting and that's exactly what Cassie was constantly seeking from life. It was the intoxicating freedom of riding the invisible tides of the sky that she craved, not the slow, underground existence of a turnip. She wanted to feel the surging force of a waterfall running through her. So many people seemed to be ground down, on anti-depressants or in another world altogether. Even some of her friends often behaved as if they were wandering alone in endless sand dunes, shading their eyes in search of a wavering mirage.

Cassie's father tended the lemon and olive groves on Lesbos as his family had for generations. These plant and ancestral roots were one and the same, sustained by the same soil and water, feeling the encouragement and the harshness of the same sun. Around this and the *cafeneon* – coffee shop- the rhythm of all life turned and nothing could make it either hurry or pause. The sounds were all of sheep bells and floating snatches of gossip, rudely fractured by the loudspeaker from the truck that passed though with the day's gleaming silver catch of fish.

In what little spare time the groves allowed, her father was the island's only magician, astonishing children at village parties with his ingenious tricks, producing cards or even pigeons from behind his ears with ease. When she was still little, Cassie had helped. She remembered the painful clench in her stomach the first time she had been sawn in half. It was as if she had swallowed a whole *galaktoboureko*, a Greek custard pie enriched with pastry, syrup and nuts. Her father promised her that he would zip her up again. Sure enough, when she finally dared to peek, there was no mark at all on her tummy, except for the small button that had always been there but that she was too scared to press in case something happened. She revelled in it all, particularly the theatrical dressing up and the vanishing tricks, the feather boas, mirrors, collapsing boxes and smoke.

Sometimes, things hadn't gone quite as intended. The knife juggling often popped a few balloons and, on one sad occasion, impaled a dove that had escaped and then tried to fly overhead during the performance. Her father told the children that the poor bird was just resting but wept afterwards and blamed himself for not securing the door of the birdcage. After they had been away for a few days visiting relatives, he put on a show without first checking all the equipment and surprised himself as well as his child audience by pulling not only one rabbit from his top hat but also eight babies. When he vaporised one small boy and then couldn't make him reappear, his parents screamed blue murder and called the police. Fortunately, the victim was found hiding backstage before matters got completely out of hand.

Cassie's Greek mother smelt of lavender and made the stickiest *baclava* and *halva* from the beehives she tended in their garden. Both she and Cassie's father brought Cassie up to breathe the ancient Greek myths as if they were a part of her, particularly Homer. Somehow all these childhood ingredients, entwined with Cassie's own passion for adventure and history and the excellent English hard taught by her uncle, had taken her to London where she was currently studying at Kings College for a PHD on whether or not the Trojan war really happened. She found it fascinating to draw back the curtain of the past and look for its myths, mystery and magic in the present.

But research didn't quench her need for the active excitement that could only be found in the remote outer fringes of each moment. That came from pushing her own sense of being to its limits, standing on the very edge of a cliff in a storm or cutting tracks through an untouched duvet of snow on an unknown mountainside. Moments when you had to pinch yourself to make sure you were really in them.

After a few minutes, another slightly older woman approached from the direction of the embassies and Cassie rose to greet her. They kissed each other on the cheek, and both sat down again on the bench. Cleo was a cultural attaché at the Greek Embassy. As compatriots of a kind, she and Cassie had met at a lecture at London University that the embassy sponsored the previous year on the ancient Greek legacy.

'I saw the newspaper reports. Seems like the gang weren't quite as stupid as we thought. They apparently got away with a major haul and there are no signs that the police are making much progress. But how did you get on?'

'No bother,' said Cassie airily. 'They did all the hard work for me and took down the CCTV before I went in. It doesn't seem as if anyone has noticed my visit. Interesting that those hulks even managed to get away with a sarcophagus. That was a complete surprise and could be a real bonus for us.'

Cassie's yearning for mystery and adventure had led her down some untravelled paths. Looking for thrills of an unconventional kind, she had taken up cat burgling while still studying for her first degree. This had started when she shimmied up the tower of Westminster Abbey to let off a firework for a friend's birthday. Exhilarated by the climb, after that she secretly began to make regular night-time excursions, often into museums or the houses of famous people when they were out.

Sometimes she "borrowed" items she found for a day or two but always pushed them back through the letterbox or returned them by post before any major hue and cry could arise. It was only in the last few months that she had begun to realise the wider potential for her skills as a sort of modern-day Robin Hood, working for a more equal society to temper the injustices of capitalism. This had led her to redistribute any stray cash she happened to come across in her nocturnal adventures, liberating those who in her view had more money than they could possibly know what to do with. The beneficiaries included an eclectic range of charities mainly for the homeless and asylum seekers. These talents were now also being used for the first time to assist her other great passion.

'Brilliant work. And did you get it?' asked Cleo with just a tinge of impatience.

Glancing up to check that no-one was close enough to see or hear, Cassie took a small black box out of her pocket and opened it. Inside nestled a gold signet ring with what looked like a seal bearing the profile of a young man's head. Closer inspection revealed rams' horns curling around his ears. There was some lettering underneath, but it was too small and irregular to be immediately legible. Although it was only early evening the sun was already retreating, the light cold and fading.

Cleo nodded. 'That's it. Better get this to somewhere safe rather than hang around. Any other news?' She took the ring from Cassie, putting it in inside the pocket of her own coat.

'Only that I'm thinking of applying for a job in Oxford. Nothing that will interfere with what we're doing. I can tell you about it another time. But also, I've had some further thoughts about our plans. Let's go ahead with the first stage as we agreed but I think we then need to follow it up. We should be more ambitious.'

'First things first, then. We can meet with the others next week and talk about it. But in the meantime, let's get on with stage one, as you say. That should create a real storm on its own.'

The two women pecked each other again swiftly and parted in opposite directions, Cleo striding out briskly and Cassie threading her way in and out of the lampposts on her skates.

Tom had spent the previous few days in his room in Oxford feverishly putting together his project plan for Cavatappi. He was hopeless with financials, which was what had first prompted him to think of calling Finn. He knew Finn cared little about dosh, although he was swimming in it, but had been half joking when suggesting maybe Finn might want to come and work for him. He was amazed when Finn called back only minutes later to bite his hand off. Now Tom just hoped this new venture wouldn't prove to be too good to be true, but then he had always been an optimist.

Once the plan was at least in reasonable shape, Tom called the number on the business card that Cavatappi had given him. A woman with a rich lilting voice and strong Italian accent answered, introducing herself as Norma. When Tom mentioned that Mr Cavatappi had suggested he speak to his secretary but thought she had a different name, Norma laughed. 'I'm on the day shift, but Papa may have mentioned the nightshift. Puttanesca does that, was that the name he gave you?'

Tom thought it was, but asked, 'Papa? Do you mean Mr Cavatappi?'

'Oh yes, he may have called himself that, but we all call him Papa. He's the big guy, the boss!'

Something bothered Tom about this conversation. He felt as if the answers to a difficult crossword were lurking in the recesses of his mind, but his brain couldn't quite spit them out. Every time he tried to stretch out to them, they drew back into the shadows just beyond his reach. Tom knew that the best way to deal with this was to think about something else completely and suddenly the solutions would come as if from nowhere. Often this happened when he went out jogging. The rhythm seemed to help his mind float free and release the ideas he most needed, although as far as he was aware he wasn't even thinking about them at the time.

Cavatappi – it seemed absurd and impertinent to risk calling him Papa – had told Norma that Tom should meet him at the Palline Congelate[49] Gelateria in the centre of town. As Tom's Italian was reasonably fluent, he appreciated the joke but was sure very few of the good citizens of Oxford picked it up. A gelateria seemed a slightly odd place for a business meeting but Norma said the boss loved ice-cream. Sure enough, when he arrived Cavatappi was already sitting at a table near the window with an espresso and the lengthy menu of gelati flavours in front of him. He was smoking despite the polite request on the card in front of him and the law, but he was obviously too good a customer for the staff to intervene unless someone complained.

Tom chose *zuppa inglese* out of curiosity. The menu said it was based on the British trifle and was apparently very popular in Italy. Cavatappi ordered *puffo*, a bright blue aniseed concoction embroidered with smarties, which he explained was named after the Smurfs because of its colour. Cavatappi clearly wanted to get to know Tom a little better and the conversation was charming and relaxed. Tom explained his unusual upbringing – half English boarding school and half Amazon rainforest or other remote locations. No, his parents weren't separated. It was just that they spent quite long periods apart as it was difficult to reconcile the lives of an Italian socialite with that of an eccentric English explorer.

Cavatappi revealed that his wife Penny was looking after their home, Casa Nostra as he called it, in New York and their two young sons, Orzo and Ziti, who Cavatappi missed a great deal. Tom could see his eyes were moist as he spoke of them and began to warm to the man, a sentiment that was reinforced when his host ordered another round of coffees and ice-cream.

This time Cavatappi chose *baccio* in honour of his wife, or so he said with a wink. Tom selected *riso*, or rice pudding flavour. He had been forced to eat a version of rice pudding every day at school that was so disgusting it was rumoured that it was made from powder supplied by the plasterers who had renovated the school hall. As he expected, the Italian version was a wholly different and delicious experience.

When they began to discuss Tom's plan however, Cavatappi's eyes seemed to harden swiftly, losing their colour and sensitivity like pebbles drying on the beach as the tide recedes. The questions now stabbed out at Tom so thick and fast and from so many angles that he felt he was fencing for his life, parrying one after another as best he could.

Eventually, the pace eased. Cavatappi seemed satisfied with most of the answers Tom gave and, equally, Tom had enough grace to realise a lot of weaknesses had been exposed that he still needed to think through in more detail. Cavatappi was particularly impressed by the financial projections, thanks to Finn's input. But, to Tom's surprise, his main concern seemed to be to increase the budget, not constrain it.

The charisma returned instantaneously with the flick of an invisible switch as Cavatappi settled the bill with a large tip for the delighted waitress.

'The first instalment of your funding will be in the St Barbara's account by tomorrow morning, so you need to press on and recruit your team.'

'Do I need to confirm them with you or the Dean?'

'I don't know what skills you need and the Dean has been told to keep out of all operational matters or otherwise the project will be immediately suspended. You have complete discretion ... and, of course you carry the can, Tom.'

If this was intended to make Tom feel like he was surfing the crest of a wave, it worked like magic. Before this meeting, part of him had been nervously holding back, unsure if this breaker was the right one or whether he should wait for the next. Now he was up on the board, arms outstretched and somehow standing. He would never have a chance to ride a bigger wave than this. It was exhilarating and he was determined not to fall off. Any menace in Cavatappi's silky closing words washed over him like foam.

As they put on their coats, Cavatappi said, 'What I like about you, Tom, is that although you are very intelligent, you are like car headlights. You only see what's in your beam and are blind to the dark corners. That's good. Keep it that way. Our investors think confidentiality is a matter of honour and that honour is something worth living and dying for. As you speak Italian you may be familiar with the term, *omertà*?'

The words were spoken lightly but somehow conveyed a potential tension, a slack loop of rope that with one jerk would become a noose. Caught on cloud nine, Tom was hardly listening. The words seemed to float to the back of his mind, and he only understood them much later when he thought back about the conversation.

Cavatappi could see Tom was not concentrating, so to underline his point he smiled again and casually turned over the menu. Although this was primarily a gelateria it also offered a very limited selection of pasta dishes. These were listed on the opposite side to the gelati and drinks. Pointing to one of them, Cavatappi caught Tom's eye and said, 'See, I can't escape my wife anywhere ... think about it, Tom.'

Tom looked and tried to think, but his mind was still buzzing with historical mysteries and the skills he would need in the team to explore them. He shook his head and Cavatappi laughed. 'When you work it out, remember what I said. Knowing when to be silent can be as important as not putting ketchup or pineapple on pizza to Italians ... matters of life and death.'

The truck driver was exhausted. He had set off from Jalalabad to Pakistan three days earlier. His ancient lorry had struggled to inch its way up the endless climb over the Khyber Pass and then on down to Peshawar before heading towards the border between Pakistan and India. Fortunately, the engine still had heart and, apart from one breakdown that Rajah had managed to fix himself at the roadside, that heart was still beating. Every panel of the battered vehicle was festooned with brightly coloured images. Like many Indian truck drivers, Rajah also doubled as an artist, turning his truck into a psychedelic otherworld that both gave him a creative outlet after hours behind the front wheel and acted as a warning to oncoming drivers who were as bone-tired as he was. Among the bright pictures of gods, goddesses, princes, princesses, movie stars, temples and geometric patterns were sage fragments of advice, such as, "Horn, Please!" and, "After Whisky, Driving Risky!!"

They had arrived at Rajah's usual overnight stop in a dirt area just before the bridge crossing over the Indus. Rajah crouched down on his haunches and was warming his hands at the small stove he had lit to boil rice for his evening meal. The tarpaulin at the back of his truck must have come loose as he could see a corner lifting in the wind. But then, a thin white shape emerged from under the covering. It paused for a moment and turned its head as if assessing its surroundings, then jumped down and vanished. Rajah sprinted to the nearby stall where several other drivers were huddled round the fire drinking chai. No one mocked him as they had done Abdul. Word had been spreading of similar sightings and superstition as to what it might mean was rife. No one was prepared to go out and try and find answers in the gathering dark. They promised each other they would all help search every truck thoroughly in the morning, before setting off.

The request from Tom's father was still weighing on his conscience, but in any event, he now had another reason to visit the Pitt Rivers Museum. This huge gothic monstrosity stood on Parks Road and housed Oxford University's extensive anthropology collections. As expected, he spotted Ming bent over at a desk in the Balfour Library in a tightly-sprung question mark and wearing a Hawaiian shirt of orange clouds over an erupting volcano that gave some advance warning of his quirky side. When Tom tapped him on the shoulder, Ming jerked back as if returning from another world, which he probably was. However, he quickly refocused and nodded when Tom suggested they have a coffee in the museum café.

Tom was genuinely interested in his friend's research but also knew that starting there was the best way to get him on side. 'What's the core of your PhD thesis Ming? I know it's about the Rapa Nui peoples of Easter Island, but nothing else.'

Ming swept back his fringe of thick black hair so he could see and Tom asked himself as always why he didn't just get it cut. 'I'm developing a new theory about how they moved those huge statues. As the island's a volcano, a bit like this on my shirt, and the stone heads were all quarried and carved near the summit, it was always downhill to the sites where they are now located. I think a team of men with ropes could have managed to drag them down more readily than many people suggest in those soft volcanic soils. The practical hurdle is I need the funding to get out there and give it a go. If I can raise the money, why not come along if the trip appeals to you? You will need to build up those biceps but the weather is supposed to be great and the scenery spectacular.'

'I've just let my gym membership lapse, Ming. In fact I was hoping to rope you into my new team rather than vice versa! I'm pretty confident you would find it much less onerous and in fact it may even be possible to make your research into one of our projects which would solve your funding problem. What I need are your meticulous research skills and creative thinking.'

Tom told Ming as much as he needed to know, assuming of course that Cavatappi's funding arrived as promised. At first, Ming was incredulous, then when he saw Tom was serious, fascinated and excited. He wasn't ready to abandon his PhD thesis, but of course he was up for being the anthropology and ethnography advisor within Tom's team, particularly as he had told his parents back in Shanghai that he was doing an MBA so could hardly ask them for financial help.

Happy with this outcome, Tom knocked on a door marked, "Private – Staff Only." An efficient-looking lady with her hair in a bun as tight as a clenched fist opened it after a pause so long that Tom had already turned on his heel, assuming the office was closed. The hard slashed line of her mouth pursed into a sow's arse as she glared at Tom and the disapproval only deepened when he explained the reason for his visit. She asked for ID and then briskly led him down an endless corridor to a large airy room and left him to his own devices.

The ceiling was immensely high as it went

up to the gables of the museum roof. Every wall was lined with shelves filled with objects in the museum's collections not currently on display. There were a couple of extendable ladders and, checking the catalogue reference the woman had given him, Tom moved the longest one to the far wall and began to climb the rungs with care. On his ascent, he passed carved eggs, strange daggers and huge fishhooks. Eventually he came to section A, shelf K, row 47 and there, sure enough, Uncle Albert was staring straight back at him.

Albert had been an ethnographer who conducted many field trips with Tom's father when they were both still in their early twenties. Unfortunately, he had somehow become caught up in some tribal strife deep in the Amazon and now found himself included in the shrunken head collection. Tom's father had always been adamant that, given the brothers' shared admiration for tribal culture, which Albert considered far more civilised that that of the modern West, he would have preferred to be an adopted part of it. Since the alternative was to have what was left of him buried in a dank hole and forgotten in some English churchyard, there seemed to be a certain logic to this.

Albert's head was now only about the size of a tennis ball and his cheeks had certainly hollowed out, but he appeared to be grinning and Tom hoped he appreciated the visit. As instructed Tom left the card his father had posted for this purpose on the shelf where Albert could see it and descended the ladder, although he sometimes wondered about their relationship. The card read "Sorry I'm not in contact much, but then neither are you. Hope you aren't having a hell of a time."

The following evening, after a long run through Christchurch meadows, Tom took a hot bath. As the steam rose around him and his brain unwound as if stretching itself out on a deckchair in Ibiza, there was a mental click and somewhere inside his head a rusty lock opened. Tom leapt out of the bath and ran naked to the laptop on his desk without even pausing for a towel.

Not Penny, of course, but *Penne*. That must be the connection Cavatappi was making between the menu and his wife's name. And *Puttanesca*? Yes, now he thought about it he recalled this was a rich pasta sauce, supposedly with its origins in the bordellos of Naples and hence its "spicy" name. That was why Norma had laughed when she said Puttanesca was doing the night shift. *Norma*? He wondered, but surely not. A quick search on google read: 'A traditional sauce from Catania. The main ingredients are aubergines and tomatoes. This sauce was supposedly first named by a Sicilian comedy writer who, tasting it after listening to Bellini's opera of the same title, exclaimed, "*Chista e na vera Norma*" or, "This is a real Norma" – in other words, a masterpiece.'

And *Cavatappi*? Yes, a hollow tube of macaroni twisted like a corkscrew. This increasingly seemed an appropriate characterisation of his mysterious benefactor. So, following the thread he was mentally unravelling, Papa, as he had assumed it must be spelt, was in fact *Pappa* for *Pappardelle*. The Big Pasta! That's what all his associates called their boss and Papa was what Italians called the Pope, but this Pappa had a double "p" showing who was really in charge. So, *Pappa* to his colleagues but *Cavatappi* to everyone else, reflecting his schizophrenic nature. And hot on the heels of this revelation, two other pieces of the jigsaw dropped neatly into place. *Orzo* and *Ziti*, Cavatappi's baby sons, were two different types of very diminutive pasta.

Cavatappi had deliberately given Tom the key when he showed him the menu. Now the penny ... or *penne* ... had, at last, dropped. The mentions of *omertà* and *casa nostra*, hinting at *cosa nostra*, now assumed a new significance. Somewhere in the background to all this, he was being told there was a mafia connection. Staking so much money on finding treasures that in many cases might mainly be of archeological value seemed a longshot to a hard-nosed investor. A vanity project didn't seem likely either. Without seeing the financial details that the Dean was keeping very close, it was hard to say what was going on and maybe it was safer not to know. What was clear was that he was being told to keep his mouth firmly shut and that no questions should be asked about the identities of the investors, all of whom were to be referred to only by codenames based on pastas and pasta sauces[50].

With his head in his hands, Tom considered his options. He told himself he was already in too far. The first tranche of money had arrived bang on time and the Dean had already announced the setting up of the new department – with Tom as its head – to a blaze of international publicity. His best mate, Finn, had given up his job on the strength of Tom's offer and Tom could hardly let him down by admitting what a fool he'd been. But, above all, Tom was still riding through the foaming exhilaration of that wave and he wanted to stay with it, wherever it might take him.

He made up his mind. He was pressing on. If there

was any payback he would just try and dodge it in the hope it would fall to the Dean. That's where it properly belonged as the Dean had introduced him to the whole business and was supposed to be taking care of all the due diligence and finances.

As he steadied himself, Tom's heartrate began to drop back from a sprint to a brisk trot. This was a time to prove what he could achieve, to reveal himself to the world! He closed his laptop and got to his feet. As he did so, he happened to glance out of his window. The music had been blaring out from the party in the flat across the road all evening, but he noticed that everyone had stopped dancing and were gathering by the windows. He could see now that they were all in fancy dress and thought he could recognise some of the characters. The one in the toga was obviously Julius Caesar. John Lennon with the round glasses and guitar. Mahatma Gandhi with the shaven head and long white robes was standing next to someone with an ice-pick that he assumed might be Trotsky. A Russian princess who had been dancing with an Indian chief was now with a clean-cut American in a suit. Anastasia, Sitting Bull, JFK? He wondered what the fancy dress theme was[51].

As if they were telepathic and were trying to assist him in working it out, the partygoers all began turning towards him, staring open-mouthed as he stood in front of the open curtains of his sitting room, so he went right up to the glass to get a better view. The full beam of their attention had turned his way as if they were transfixed. It could only be because he had become a celebrity himself already, but he hadn't yet got used to it.

Of course, it would take some time to adjust.

Shyly at first he smiled and waved. They pointed. He waved again. As a modest person Tom was unaccustomed to such recognition but he could already sense that being the centre of attention, perhaps even adoration, was something he could easily get used to. Still rather clumsily not knowing how to respond, he did a little pirouette and even blew them a kiss. Then he looked down and yet another penny dropped – he was still stark naked.

CHAPTER 5 – DEATH, LIFE AND HOW TO MAKE MORE OF BOTH

I'm not afraid to die. I just don't want to be there when it happens – Woody Allen

Inspector Marcelo Panettone was within a stone's throw of his destination, or at least the edge of it; St Peter's Square in the heart of Rome's Vatican City. He wasn't in a hurry. Usually he stood at the bar for his morning espresso, but today he was at a table on the corner of the pavement overlooking the busy crossroads. He wondered what would kill him first, the exhaust fumes or the nicotine.

The Inspector always liked to be well-prepared, but how could you prepare for a private audience with the Pope? He needed a little pause for contemplation, but there was another more fundamental reason for taking his time. He was trying to coax out every faint trace of pleasure from his cigarette. The tip briefly glowed as he inhaled pure contentment and the lazy curl of the fumes perfectly complemented the sense of profound relaxation it gave him. This was polluted only by the knowledge that it was his very last cigarette. Not because he was expecting a firing squad but because he had decided to give up.

True he had made the same commitment ninety-nine times before, but this was the hundredth and it would be different. He had proven his iron willpower in countless other situations and had now steeled himself, forging the iron into something even stronger.

An abrupt telephone message a couple of hours earlier from some Vatican functionary had disrupted the Inspector's normal calm. By coincidence, he had at that very moment been smoking his penultimate cigarette while visiting his mother. Well, he called her his mother but, in fact, she was his grandmother. She had brought him up after his parents left him an orphan when electrocuted by lightening while taking a romantic dip in a hotel swimming pool during a storm. Now, the only mother he could remember had summoned him to her death bed. This would have been even more upsetting if it hadn't happened every few weeks for the last thirty years or so.

Imagining her own passing was what kept her going. She wrote a new epitaph for her tombstone each week and was constantly amending her funeral manual[52] and the list of those to be invited to the event itself. The manual was a large loose-leaf diary that set out her wishes for every miniscule detail of the ceremony, from the mix of flowers in the bouquets to the particular fragrance of incense to be used. In the last version Panettone had seen some months earlier, he noticed that his mother had ordained that her beloved cat Felix, should be dug up and placed in her coffin with her and that if his successor, Felicette, should pass away after her, she should also be buried with them. He was relieved that his grandfather, who had died of exhaustion many years ago trying to keep up with his wife, was to be left undisturbed in peace.

As usual the old lady had been lying like a tiny antique doll in her vast four poster bed. The sea of pristine white sheets and pillows billowed around her almost exactly matching her parchment complexion, so it was at first difficult to see she was there at all. The bedroom ceilings were so high that it was almost impossible to change the lightbulbs. Most of them had burnt out long ago. Had it not been for the immensely tall windows containing more panes of glass than the greenhouses at the Botanical Gardens, it would have been necessary to keep the gigantic silver candelabra that stood on each side of the bed continually lit.

It was because his mother loved lighting candles, despite the risk of sparking a conflagration, that Panettone had been able to persuade the local fire brigade to come with a cherry-picker from time to time to change the lightbulbs. Opening the windows sufficiently to allow the cherry picker to be extended through them and reach the ceiling inside was a complex operation. The chandelier weighed at least a ton and contained over two thousand glittering jewels of cut glass. One false move and it would have crushed not only the old lady but her many visitors. Panettone knew his mother was very well connected, but even so he put the number of visitors down largely to her generosity with the champagne. A jeroboam of Moet or Bollinger was constantly open in a gilt wine cooler which was kept continually topped up with a mountain of ice. This presented its own problems. Often, when a new bottle was opened, passers-by would call the police to report a gunshot from inside his mother's palazzo.

Panettone had banned his mother from trying to open bottles herself since a cork had struck the previous butler between the eyes and killed him instantaneously. It was only after a large amount of compensation had been paid over to buy off his relatives that they had conceded he would always have wanted to go out with a bang. Now the task was strictly reserved for the new butler, who always took the added precaution of putting on the crash helmet he wore when arriving on his Vespa each day.

On this particular morning, Panettone had approached the bedside in trepidation, manoeuvering his tall gangly frame into position with the ungainly precision of a crane at a building site. His anxiety had been increased by the prospect that the beastly Felicette might be waiting as usual to spring on him, but fortunately today there was no ambush. He asked his mother how she was feeling as she lay there as usual with her eyes closed, waving him a graceful farewell with her lace-gloved hand. She responded to his concern by feebly making the sign of the cross, sighing dramatically and going limp. Her glazed eyes were apparently fixed on one of the many pockmarks left in the ceiling where a champagne cork had made a hole in the plaster. As always, the Inspector could not control his sudden anxiety. She was a hundred and three, so, however often this happened, he knew that sometime it would be for real. When he approached the bedside, he really wasn't able to tell. He stooped to gently close her eyelids. She loved him doing that, even if it was all a performance. This time, however, she seemed genuinely cool to his touch and remained so still he held his own breath. Deep within him he felt his heart pause and contract. Calling for a priest now seemed pointless. But suddenly, she bounced up in the bed like a puppet on strings, laughing.

'Mother, what is it with all this fake dying?' he complained.

'It's not fake! We are all dying all the time. It's just a question of how long it takes, but eventually I do look forward to catching up with old friends and listening to my own eulogy.'

Panettone loved his mother, and he would be grief stricken when she finally snuffed it. But a small part of him wondered if she ever would. Perhaps she was immortal and would outlive him. Whatever happened, it would have a big influence on his future. She was constantly changing her will and, depending on her whim at the time, he might either be able to retire immediately as an immensely wealthy man or otherwise be forced to work until he was a pale shadow and then live a modest existence on a police pension[53]. The fact that he was her only child should have given him some assurance, but his mother's greatest fear was that she would become predictable and her caprice as a result knew no bounds.

This was made worse by her tendency to see everything in black and white, often making extreme judgments about people almost instantaneously on the flimsiest of foundations. As a lover of Dante, she was accustomed to using his divisions of heaven, purgatory and hell as convenient pigeonholes into which nearly everyone she met could immediately be categorised. These judgements were, however, equally capable of sudden and dramatic revisions without any regard for balance or consistency. So, for example, if the post came late, the postman might metaphorically be cast abruptly into the ninth circle of the Inferno where he was fated to be chewed alongside Judas and Brutus in the mouth of the boggle-eyed Beast so graphically described in Revelation. The following day, if he made an extra visit to drop off one of the many parcels the old lady was always ordering, he could hope to be promoted to join Dante's heart-throb Beatrice and share the delights of Paradise. Although she was always quick to say that she harboured no grudges towards anyone, the obvious joy Pannetone's mother took in reading certain obituaries suggested that for some any opportunity for redemption in her good books had perhaps come just a little late .

These mercurial tendencies were exaggerated still further by the attentions of other members of the family who were constantly seeking to ingratiate themselves in the hope of receiving a slice of her fortune. Sometimes she saw through them but at other times she either played along with their flattery or perhaps believed it really expressed some heartfelt affection, Panettone was never sure which.

It was while he was reflecting despondently on these matters, at the same time as toasting his mother's latest resurrection at her insistence with a glass of champagne, that he had received the Vatican call.

Reluctantly recognising that there was now nothing

left of his cigarette but the filter, Panettone glanced at his watch. It had stopped but he had no need of it. He had long been running on his own time scheme measured by the rhythm of his yearning for a smoke rather than by hours. This was remarkably accurate and even as he regretfully dropped his very last stub to the ground he knew it was once again, as always, cigarette o'clock. Now that he had finally given up smoking, perhaps his ability to tell the time in this way would gradually fade with his longing. Only time would tell but in this present moment it was definitely time to go.

The lights at the crossroad had been taking turns to slice the continuous strings of traffic, first this way then that, into standard lengths like spaghetti. Every time they changed a band of small boys swapped from one axis of the intersection to the other, taking advantage of the moments when the drivers were stationary hostages to weave through the cars begging. Most of the drivers avoided eye contact and swiftly closed their windows to seal out the small irritants as if they were vermin. Just a few tossed out the odd coin and a couple even a note.

As Panettone disentangled his long legs from the table, the lights directly in front of him went green again. Accelerating away abruptly one car caught the shoulder of a street urchin as it sped off, hurling the boy into the gutter by the kerb. Twenty minutes later a harassed member of Rome's Social Services took a call.

'I'm a police Inspector. There's a boy at the bar of the Café Vaticano on the Via Rusticucci who needs looking after. Probably only seven years old. He's being exploited by a gang and no sign of any parent. Just been hit by a car, although only badly bruised this time. Can you come and pick him up?'

'Romanian? These gangs are everywhere. We are overwhelmed. Inspector who?'

'Panettone.'

'Inspector Panettone! Are you having me on? The Panettone? I didn't think street kids were your level. Have you been demoted or something?'

'Perhaps this may turn out to be the one thing you and I were put on earth to do. Call me to let me know when you've collected him.' The Inspector's voice was mild, even kindly, with no hint of rebuke, but it allowed no room for argument and at the other end of the line it stung like lemon juice on a paper cut.

Panettone left the small boy sitting on a bar stool with an enormous ice cream watched over by the café manager who was clearly wavering between his instructions to keep his charge safe and his desire to get rid of him by facilitating an escape. Now the Inspector was late and crossing St Peter's Square took a while, although less time than he normally had to wait in the call queue for customer services when trying to get the Council to empty his bin.

Finally ascending the steps, Panettone arrived at doors flanked by the Vatican's Swiss Guards with their poleaxes barring his way. He could see his own reflection in the broad shining blades. Clean-cut, classic suit in light grey matching a perfectly trimmed moustache beneath his imperious beak of a nose and sardonic grey eyes. The misty depths hinted at a sentimentality that might seem inconvenient in his profession. As for the guards, they were all half his height and showing their age much more as their elaborate uniforms hadn't changed since the

Renaissance[54]. Tradition had it that Michelangelo designed them. The bright colours made them stand out like peacocks in a herd of zebras. Certainly they weren't equipped for undercover investigations. And that, of course, was why Panettone had been called upon.

As he straightened his tie he suddenly sensed that his jacket pocket was empty. The discreet bulge on one side was his Beretta, but sure enough on the other side his wallet had gone. As Panettone had only just been to the bank there had been enough cash in it to stock a whole ice cream shop. Still, he could hardly turn back now or explain to the Pope that he had been robbed, even less so as it had been by a seven year old, not the mafia at gunpoint.

Cardinal Cantucci was seated at a desk in white robes. A small red skull cap embroidered with a cross perched on the high pale dome of a forehead that might have been modelled on the basilica itself . He was engrossed in looking at some graphs relating to his role in leading the Vatican's Multiply Mission. The blue line showed the sharp decrease in the Italian birth-rate over the last ten years, now the lowest in Europe. The green one showed an equally abrupt increase in the number of household pets. The apparent correlation between the two was astonishing[55]. This seemed to confirm the concerns he had recently expressed to the Pope that people were transferring their parental affections to their pets, which of course were far less expensive and generally much cuddlier and easier to train than children. Perhaps this was the real secret of declining birth-rates around the developed world, a trend contrary to all the Church's encouragement that its flock should go out and make babies without constraint.

Perhaps some saw that as an odd message coming from a bunch of elderly men living a life very detached from the world and sworn to celibacy, but it was, after all, the traditional teaching of the Church. The Cardinal could appreciate that, very occasionally, the faithful might temporarily lose their way and resort to contraception, but surely the rumours that such disobedience was widespread must simply be a conspiracy theory. From the Vatican it seemed as far-fetched as the suggestion that Italians may have been brainwashed into adopting the Chinese one child policy or that they had become so shy of dating that they found it easier to relate to emojis like some Japanese.

Based on the graphs in front of the Cardinal it seemed much more plausible that, in fact, many of the faithful had committed themselves to abstinence while buying puppies as surrogates for children. Who would have thought it? The world's most amorous nation, the land of Romeo and Juliet, Sophia Loren, Casanova and Bunga Bunga, had forgotten how to make love. It seemed incredible. Mamma Mia! But if things went on this way Italians wouldn't be able to say that anymore.

What else could the Catholic Church do? In the past the rhythm method had been promoted as a clever tactic to encourage more love-making in the knowledge that it was so erratic it could be relied upon to increase the population. As one young father had once said rather too frankly to the Cardinal, it was a bit like trying to persuade someone with a loaded gun to reduce the risk of shooting themselves by playing Russian Roulette because there was a five in six chance of a blank. Wouldn't it be far better to tell them to just put the gun down reducing the risk of a bullet, or by analogy a diary error, to nil ?

It seemed clear that a new approach was needed to boost procreation. The Cardinal had recently been inspired by reading about how rabbits were introduced to Australia[56]. Soon there were over twenty billion of them, as numerous as the grains of sand on the seashore, just like Abraham's descendants in the Bible. Surely there was some way to encourage the flock to copy their example, creating a tidal wave of procreation. All this needed discussion at the next cardinals' convention.

As Panettone entered the Cardinal rose and came forward to greet him and explain why the Inspector had been summoned. In a voice as dry as the parchment of the Dead Sea Scrolls[57] or a biscotti not yet dunked in espresso, he left his visitor in no doubt as to the utmost importance of recovering the corpse of St Mark. Panettone spread open his large hands in a gesture that sought explanation rather than absolution.

'How will I be able to identify the saint, Cardinal? In my line of work I spend a lot of time looking for skeletons, not all of them in cupboards or closets, and it's critical to find out where all the bodies are buried.' Panettone had a great weakness for idioms but often adapted or used them inappropriately. It was a sort of mental tic that he couldn't even account for himself. The Cardinal looked confused.

'What have cupboards got to do with it? The saint's body is wrapped in layers of linen. I can't describe it in detail as it was last moved from the crypt to the altar of San Marco two hundred years ago and no one has inspected it since then. I can tell you it was embalmed and when moved at that time was reported to be in reasonable condition, except of course there is the argument over the head. There may have been a skull interred with the Saint's body once but if so it doesn't belong to him. It seems the real head was left behind when the body was brought to Venice in 828 AD. The Coptic Orthodox Church claim they have the original in their cathedral in Cairo.'

'So to summarise, the saints head is not screwed on and it's in the wrong place. As you know its best to keep your head, Cardinal, even when all around you are losing theirs. Is there anything else you can think of that might assist the investigation?'

'You might keep your eye out for an arm.'

Panettone sighed, 'So the saint has lost an arm as well? These tiny details can be important you know, Cardinal. Is it his right arm and are we certain it's not an arm and a leg?'

'No, you misunderstand me, Inspector. When the San Marco relics went missing on a previous occasion in 1094 AD, the saint himself revealed his own whereabouts by an arm that, according to contemporary accounts, extended itself from a pillar in San Marco and pointed out where his relics were.'

The Inspector observed that this would certainly be very convenient. If any of the priests at San Marco saw anything similar happen again it would be very helpful to be informed as it could save a lot of police time in investigating the crime. Perhaps detecting an undertone of scepticism, the Cardinal asked Panettone if he believed in such miracles to which the Inspector responded, 'I believe in Maradona'.

'I think I misheard you. Did you say "the

Madonna?"'

'No, no Cardinal. Maradona. Did you never go to see him play at Napoli? I'm sure the Vatican could have arranged some free box seats. No? Well but you must have watched him for Argentina in the 1986 World Cup. It may not have been an arm but he was helped by the Hand of God. He said so himself.'

With the interview over, the Cardinal motioned the Inspector through another door at the back of the room which opened to reveal a small chapel. Panettone immediately recognised the figure in blinding white kneeling before the altar rail as the Supreme Pontiff. He and the Caridinal waited quietly until the Pope had completed his prayers and then, getting to his feet, turned to face them. Panetonne bowed his head for the blessing. Then all the Pope said was simply, 'Inspector, we and all the faithful are relying on you to restore St Mark to his ordained place of rest.'

No pressure then, thought Panetonne, as he and the Cardinal exited together. The Swiss Guards were exactly where they had been, as motionless as mannequins. In Panettone's view, the uniforms were far too dressy for the role, making them look like jesters or clowns. Michelangelo would have done better sticking to painting ceilings and, even when it came to interior decoration, the Inspector was a man of very plain tastes. Had he been Pope, his first act would have been to whitewash the Sistine Chapel[58].

At the base of the steps out into the square, a small white vehicle was waiting for them. The Cardinal waved the Inspector in. Panettone realised it was the Popemobile that the Pope used on trips abroad when navigating the crowds. It had a glass top like an ice-cream van. He half expected some cheerful tunes to start playing. It was slightly disconcerting to see a nun at the wheel dressed in white robes from head to toe but with a black and white head scarf. A huge Vatican coat of arms was embroidered on her chest which luckily offered ample room to display the regalia in its full glory. The Cardinal introduced them to each other and whispered that Sister Felicity used to be a formula three driver before she took holy orders, so the Inspector could rest assured he was in safe hands. As the vehicle carried them out of the square a crowd began to gather, expectant that they might see the Pope. Cardinal Cantucci jabbed the Inspector in the ribs with his elbow.

'Give them a wave, Inspector. Our flock is often confused but as shepherds we must keep them content when we can.'

With considerable embarrassment, the Inspector did as he was told. An uncertain cheer rose, attracting yet more people, some of them running. At that point, Sister Felicity sped up slightly, leaving them trailing in her wake and turned out of the square. As the van moved onto the road, a red Ferrari came screaming past. Like a flash, Sister Felicity was in hot pursuit, closing the gap with alarming speed before drawing up at the red lights.

'She just can't help herself, although she knows there will be a penance to do afterwards,' said the Cardinal.

Panettone noticed he was swiftly buckling himself into a three-point safety harness. The Ferrari was right alongside them at the lights with the engine revving, but even this was barely audible above the noise blaring from the speakers. The Inspector had broad tastes in music, even extending to experimental jazz, but this sounded like a nest full of starving parakeets against a backing track of colliding refuse trucks being used as dodgems. In the driver's seat was a mean-looking guy in dark glasses with slicked back black hair and sideburns. The unbuttoned shirt revealed a gold chain thick enough to anchor the Titanic. His sleeves were rolled back to flash a gold Rolex with a face the size of Big Ben. In the passenger seat was a youngish lady with a platinum blond beehive, a deep fake tan and enough make-up to drive a mime artist into a rage of envy.

The driver gave a sneering grin and, as the lights changed, hit the peddle. But he was ahead for only a few metres. Sister Felicity had pulled round the lights onto the pavement and roared past on the inside, making a gesture that left Panettone open-mouthed as she did so. An elderly lady jumped back into a shop doorway, virtually strangling her small Pekinese. It flew past into the alcove having been jerked off its feet by its lead. A minute later Panettone saw why the Cardinal had been using his phone. A police car pulled out from a side street forcing the Ferrari to a screeching halt as the Popemobile rocketed on at a pace that blistered the tarmac. In the wing mirror the Inspector saw a Vatican policeman getting out with some handcuffs at the ready.

A couple of miles down the road, Sister Felicity made a hand break turn into a gateway, just missing the columns on each side. Finally slowing to a funeral crawl, she brought the Popemobile to a halt in front of an enclosed grass area.

Panettone stepped down and virtually fell over,

still in as much of a spin as a child getting off a roundabout. Out of shock and habit, before he knew it, he had taken out and lit a cigarette to calm himself down. Well, too late now. He couldn't waste it. Especially as it had now become the very last.

As he shakily pulled himself together, the Cardinal said, 'Confidential, of course, but this little vehicle's got the engine of a Boeing 747 concealed in the boot there, in case we need to get the Pope out of sticky situations in a hurry. Sister Felicity feels she needs to blow out the cobwebs once in a while.'

The Inspector was too dazed to answer. He had been about to ask whether the Cardinal had seen the nun give the finger to the Ferrari driver as she overtook him, but on reflection held his tongue. Drawing attention to this might simply mean that Sister Felicity's penance would be doubled.

On the grass, Panettone saw that the papal helicopter was waiting to whisk him straight to Venice to inspect the crime scene. If the Cardinal had been seeking to emphasise that there was no time to waste, he couldn't have done so more graphically. It was a good job that some sixth sense had prompted the Inspector to put his toothbrush in his pocket before leaving home. Although he had won several medals for courage in the face of extreme danger, he was terrified of his dentist and dreading the outcome of a recent scan. The whine of the drill would cause him to break into a sweat, so he was obsessional in cleaning his teeth in order to stave off any treatment.

The helicopter lifted off moments later with the solid *thuck, thuck, thuck* of a lumberjack cutting down trees and the regularity of a metronome. Still feeling distinctly queasy and with his knees knocking against his chin due to lack of leg room, Panettone rested his forehead on the window and watched Rome unfold below him. The Colosseum, where over half a million gladiators were estimated to have died, the great dome of St Peter's, the Forum where Caesar was assassinated, the Castel Sant'Angelo, the Pantheon, over two thousand fountains, seven hundred churches and more than three hundred thousand cats with special rights of protection. This was the place burned while Nero fiddled, the ancient Rome where the unibrow was once the height of female fashion and where urine was used to wash clothes and brush teeth. A city of holiness but also of papal scandals.

The Inspector must have drifted off to sleep because it seemed only a few minutes before the helicopter touched the ground again. A Mercedes arrived before he had even opened the door to run stooping through the wind whipped up by the whirling blades. He remembered the four bronze horses flanking the bronze doors of San Marco as he went through the small gate to the side of them and his steps rang out on the flag stones of the towering nave. An officer from the Venice police force showed him the taped-off areas around the high altar and the confessional box. At the back of the altar, the stones had spilled out onto the floor. It would have taken considerable force to do this. The Inspector used a flashlight to illuminate the dark hole this violence had left and the rough chamber within. There was nothing much to see. Forensics reported that they hadn't found anything except for a few fibres that had been taken off for analysis.

There was nothing obvious to find in the

confession box either, now Father Matteo's body had gone. Again a few fibres had been found on the fractured struts of the grate. It seemed that this must have been broken by some very blunt instrument from the hole punched clean through it without any signs that the mesh had been cut.

An elderly man with a blue rucksack seen exiting the Church on the morning of the theft and murder had been identified. Police records showed that he had been repeatedly investigated for suspected involvement in a whole host of crimes including murder of most of his family and arson but had never been successfully charged due to lack of sufficient evidence. The Inspector knew he must not rule anything out at this stage. The theft of St Mark and the murder of Father Matteo might not be linked at all. But if not, it was quite a coincidence.

The two crimes had also taken place on the morning of All Hallows, or the Day of the Dead, when many Italians believed that the spirits of the deceased came back to Earth and it was possible to commune with them. Some half-eaten dog biscuits had been discovered on the high altar, but on closer inspection Panettone realised that they were Ossa dei Morti, cookies shaped like the bones of the dead which it was customary to offer to the spirits of the departed for sustenance on their journey. Was this another clue, a red-herring or a literal dead end?

For the time being, the most likely hypothesis was that a group of thieves had stolen the Saint's embalmed corpse, as the damage to the altar could hardly have been inflicted by one man acting alone, and that for some reason they had murdered Father Matteo on their way out. But why, if he was in the confession box already and hadn't seen them? Unless, of course, the robbers thought he had seen them and was hiding there. The Inspector instinctively felt that the key to unravelling these crimes must lie in the motive for stealing St Mark in the first place but that wasn't clear to him at all. What would a few old bones be worth unless to some mentally unhinged private collector? They would have no value without clear evidence of their provenance and, even with it, there was no prospect of ever selling them on the open market.

The Inspector retired to his hotel to play online chess. He often found this helped to rattle his brain around until possible solutions fell out of it without warning.

CHAPTER 6 – A GAME OF MARBLES

[59]

The work of art is already within the block of marble. I just chop off whatever isn't needed.[60] – Auguste Rodin

If you told any child with a yo-yo that the highest point, when the yo-yo is back in your hand, is Heaven and the lowest point, when the whole string has unwound, is Hell, they would have been able to describe Tom's current position[61]. He was in Hell, having only just hit Heaven and swiftly rebounded, spinning down to the very end of the string. But even worse than that, he wasn't going to rebound straight back up again because he was "walking the dog." This is where the yo-yo just keeps on spinning at the bottom of the string for a long time – in other words, in Hell.

When he had been asked to accompany DC Peel down to Oxford police station, Tom imagined it would be an easy matter to explain the misunderstanding. He had tried to be nonchalant, but perhaps the build-up of nervous energy over the last few days meant that he hadn't handled things quite as well as he could have done. A natural rebellious streak in the face of authority, which also lay at the root of his repeated clashes with the Dean, certainly didn't help. It was a trait that had got him into trouble in the past. When the Council had put yellow lines outside his flat, making parking more difficult, Tom had painted them out overnight and matters had escalated to a point where there had been talk of a prosecution for criminal damage[62].

Tom had tried to take the initiative in the interview by asking how the police were getting on with the Ashmolean case. He had never had much respect for the intellectual abilities of the police. However, his feigned sympathy in suggesting that their task in trying to track down a gang of guys built like weightlifters in the centre of Oxford carrying a large sarcophagus must be like looking for a needle in a haystack, was with hindsight a little provocative. He knew this would strike a particularly sore nerve as, only that morning, the Oxford Oracle had published the abysmal record of the local police in successfully resolving reported crimes, but he just hadn't been able to help himself.

DC Peel was tall and fresh faced. Even the fading acne suggested he was not long past puberty although Tom assumed there must still be some minimum age for joining the police. However Peel showed remarkable restraint and maturity in the circumstances by responding that he could not of course comment on live investigations, adding a little citric twist by suggesting that perhaps Tom's case would help improve the statistics for successful prosecutions.

Now Tom found himself sitting at a table in an

otherwise unfurnished interview room. DC Peel offered him a cup of tea after taking down his details, then went through to update his superior. Tom distinctly heard the word, 'Smart-arse,' through the open office door. The tea took him by surprise and seemed magnanimous in the circumstances, but what he'd heard quickly aroused his suspicion that he was being softened up. He had watched enough crime drama on TV to see the old good cop, bad cop routine coming. Sure enough, when DCI Boyle introduced himself he gave every impression of being someone not to be messed with. Ponderous in speech and gait, he had the broken nose and cauliflower ears of an ex rugby player, probably a prop or hooker, and pulled out a chair like a butcher grasping a meat cleaver. But, having dug himself into a hole, Tom seemed unable to put his spade down and continued across the Rubicon[63].

'So, what's the plan, first I'm to be peeled, then boiled?'

The two policemen glanced at one another. Someone who knew Boyle well, and there weren't many of them, would have noticed a barely perceptible downward movement of his brow and heeded the warning.

'Okay Sir, we were ready to just make it a parboiling, but when the tatties just won't soften up we find mashing usually squashes out the lumps. Given your razor sharp intellect you will no doubt be easily able to fend off a few simple questions from blunt instruments like us.'

After ten minutes Boyle put down his pen and looked at his notebook, then in the low-level monotone he had used throughout, said, 'So, let me summarise.

You admit that when you saw people from the party expressing their shock and pointing to your state of undress, you took no action to cover yourself. You also accept that you responded by coming right up to the window, laughing, waving and blowing a kiss. You say you did this not to mock them but because you thought you had suddenly become a celebrity and they were all therefore desperate to take a closer look at you.'

Tom tried to fight back, but whatever he said DCI Boyle seemed to twist his words into a hideous trap.

He continued. 'Do you think then that its usual for celebrities to expose themselves? Lady Godiva and a few unfortunate celebrity garment failures on stage are hardly convincing examples, are they? Are you saying that you had a wardrobe malfunction that somehow extended to all your clothing in your own home? Okay, so you were distracted because you were googling something on your laptop. Presumably something so urgent that you had completely forgotten you were stark naked. What exactly?'

When Tom told him, he said, 'I see. Pasta shapes and sauces ...'

'I thought I had overlooked something important.'

'Perhaps the recipe for disaster? Or did you have ambitions to become another naked chef?[64]'

At this point, the DCI lent back in his chair without waiting for an answer and said, 'I think we have all we need. Is there anything you would like to add?'

Even now, it might not have been too late had Tom not muttered under his breath something about *Animal Farm*.

Boyle scratched his head as if bemused. 'Sorry, sir. Like most policemen, I'm illiterate. Is that the book in which the pigs take over? Orwell's warning against authoritarian oppression? Sadly I seem to recall that Winston didn't fare too well in his struggle against the overbearing state in 1984.'

Tom realised things had gone not just badly but catastrophically wrong. DC Peel was getting up to escort him, at least so he assumed, to the cells down the corridor as a gaunt man strangely reminiscent of a stick insect suddenly entered.

When the Dean first heard of Tom's arrest he was euphoric, but after only a moment's reflection he was then torn by a terrible dilemma. Just over a week ago, he would have taken great satisfaction in pouncing on this perfect excuse to have Tom dismissed from the St Barbara's staff and cast him into outer darkness forever. Now, much as he was tempted, he could not risk sacrificing the huge injection of cash promised by Mr Cavatappi. This prestige project that he fully expected would put himself and St Barbara's at the pinnacle of the academic world would also give him enough money to indulge his favourite hobby. The cast-off skins of rare snakes were extremely expensive, and the Dean had found himself outbid by several other collectors with deeper pockets in several recent auctions. A huge Bolivian anaconda took pride of place like an enormous green banner over his fireplace, but he had yet to acquire the skins of a Dog-toothed Cat Snake, Speckle-bellied Keelback or Tibetan Bamboo Pit Viper.

Tom was never sure what exactly the Dean said to the two policemen, but overheard a few snatched words.

These seemed to suggest the Dean told them some sob story about Tom having a breakdown after learning that his father had been roasted by pygmies in Papua New Guinea. As far as Tom knew, his father was in fact alive and well. But he supposed that this might be a plausible story, if anyone bothered to check, given his father's colourful life and the fact that no one, other than Tom through his recent exchange of messages, would have spoken to his father for at least a couple of months. Peel and Boyle were clearly doubtful at first, but it seemed the Dean was gradually winning them round. Finally, Tom was grudgingly released with a stern warning and found himself again outside the police station, drinking in the heady air of freedom. Without waiting for the Dean, he almost sprinted back to college, determined not to waste the chance to get on with the project.

The Dean's mountain of grievances against Tom was already so high that adding this ingratitude to it was much like throwing another milk bottle top onto a landfill site. In order to persuade the police, the Dean confirmed that all the complaints made by those at the neighbouring party had been withdrawn. This had only been achieved with great difficulty. The Dean promised that Tom would be evicted from his current flat and rehoused elsewhere so that there could be no risk of a "new moon," as the Dean diplomatically put it, ignoring the technicality that Tom had been facing the window rather than away from it.

It was pouring with rain as Colonel Budimir Krushtin crossed Red Square and approached a side door in the wall below the onion domes of the Kremlin. He had dreamed of being a stand-up comedian as a young boy, but fate had dealt him a different hand. It still left a bitter taste. Not many called him Bud.

The guards on either side of the doorway had been standing as still as stone monoliths, seemingly impervious to the curtain of water that fell from the peeks of their military caps. Now they snapped into salutes with the speed and precision of overwound clocks. Turning sharply on his heel as he entered, the Colonel took the lift. It eventually grounded with a clang in the bunker ten floors below ground. There he was greeted by the harsh strip lights and concrete walls of his hidden domain – innocuously named the Department for International Monitoring.

The Colonel shook out the rain from his umbrella. The small skull and crossbones on the umbrella handle was a reminder that it was standard issue, tipped with polonium, so to be handled with care. He propped it against the wall below the map of the places he and his young wife had visited on their honeymoon, given to them as a wedding present by his departmental colleagues. He had at the time just been appointed to his current role as Head of DIM and Tatiana had been keen to support him in his new responsibilities. If she had been surprised to be taken on a tour of the gulags of Sakhalin Island he hadn't noticed it. It was true that the accommodation they had shared with the commandant of each camp had been a little cramped and sparse but everything is relative and when they compared it to the quarters of the inmates they realised it was the height luxury.

He was pleased to see that his new bride was speechless, even stunned, with the clothes he had given her. As a former ballerina in the Bolshoi she had been used to setting heads spinning in frivolous dresses but there were hardly any other women in this region and he knew she was shy. The most wonderful aspect of their relationship was that they were always on the same telepathic wavelength. The Colonel didn't need to waste time asking to feel certain Tatiana wouldn't want to stand out too much. As most women liked everything to match, the dungarees were the same shade of grey as the concrete, barbed wire and leaden skies.

The newlyweds travelled enormous distances and, although at first rather silent, after a while Tatiana seemed to begin to take delight in the tiny differences between the height of one pine tree and another or the barely detectable rise and fall in the endless tundra. That was a good thing as the Colonel was a man of detail and there wasn't much else to talk about. He was delighted to see how his wife took comfort from the reassurance the frozen wasteland could provide. She once even went so far as to say that she could see it was a preparation for the life that stretched in front of them.

The only disruption in their journey came when they spotted a couple of penguins. That was when he heard her cry out with pleasure for the first time. In fact also, now he thought about it, the last as well. The penguins were trying to escape from a polar bear, but that didn't last long. Anyway, this was all a long time ago and since then his plans on the matrimonial front had all been accomplished – twelve sons all now enrolled in the Russian army. Job done.

Next to the map, above the Colonel's vast mahogany desk were three imposing portraits. On one side Ivan the Terrible[65], on the other Vlad the Impaler and in pride of place Josef Stalin with a crowbar across the middle of his face on which the Colonel had modelled his own moustache. Spread out on the desk itself were a number of files. One was titled Kitty Chaos, the name of the anarchist all female band whose work the Colonel had recently been ordered to suppress, but the red file that lay open was marked Operation Porridge. It was the latest in a sequence of projects involving the clandestine activities of the secret services in Britain, all with distinctively English names. This had started with Project Umbrella and then of course there had been Project Tea[66]. Now Porridge seemed particularly appropriate since the unit that would be carrying it out were *The Bolshie Bears*[67], a branding that had already proved very useful in shadowy missions by giving them a cuddly image that deceived foreign security organisations into underestimating them.

This latest operation was intended to highlight British security failings in subtle ways that would attract enormous publicity and generally shake the foundations of public trust in the competence of the government and public services both at home and abroad. The President had been delighted by the Bears' recent successful raid on the Ashmolean Museum which cleverly tapped into international debate about the ownership of ancient artefacts obtained during Britain's colonial past. It conveniently highlighted not only the ineptitude of security arrangements at leading British institutions but also of the police in finding any trace of the perpetrators. The extent of the resulting furore was even more gratifying than the irritation caused to the French by passing a law that all sparkling wine produced in Russia would be called Champagne[68], while anything imported from France must be labelled Sparkling Wine. Operation Porridge[69] was going down a treat and just thinking about it gave the Colonel a warm feeling inside. He couldn't recall who had said it but there was no doubt this porridge was "just right".

Cassie was sitting in front of her laptop in her London apartment, sipping a cup of strong black coffee. She shared the flat with a couple of other students and her own room was deceptively spacious. In other words it looked bigger than it really was, although by a remarkable deception of their own estate agents have convinced us and themselves it means the opposite. Among her other pastimes, Cassie had always been interested in technology and a few years ago taught herself programming and hacking skills. For a while she took part in an informal group called *Funnelweb* that set itself various hacking challenges just for the thrill of it. This took her to some interesting places, including revealing some of the inner workings of the Pentagon. It felt to her like a sort of autopsy in which she was lifting up the skin of everyday life to uncover its hidden nerves, tendons and bones, except that the patient was still very much alive. Some members of the group however then became obsessed with cryptocurrencies which Cassie found boring, so she dropped out, losing touch with most of the others but retaining a couple of useful contacts.

It was while idly following a few threads of her own that she had stumbled across the Bolshie Bears and their plans to raid the Ashmolean as part of a wider campaign of social disruption. That had given her the idea of piggybacking on their nefarious activities to assist her latest passion – AA, as she called it. Not Alcoholics Anonymous but Artefact Activists, whose core purpose was to achieve the restoration of historical treasures dispersed all over the world to their original cultures by whatever means available. Top of the agenda for the clandestine subgroup that she and Cleo had now formed was the *cause célèbre* of all activists – the return of the Elgin Marbles to the Parthenon in Athens. As Cassie took another sip of her coffee, she saw that Cleo had just texted her with the code words, 'The shooter is in the ring.[70]'

Scrolling through the home pages of the papers she could see the news was just breaking. As usual, the British press were taking a balanced and objective approach to the story, particularly the tabloids.

Hands off our Marbles

You would think everyone would be grateful that Lord Elgin rescued the Marbles from the Parthenon from decay and destruction. Not a bit of it. The grumbling Greeks are making yet another grab for them. The Greek Cultural Attaché, Cleo Popillopolis, has today renewed the demand from the Greek government for the Marbles to be returned to their homeland. They say that the Marbles, now in the British Museum, were stolen in an act of imperial piracy. The recent Ashmolean theft is being used as new ammunition in this long-running dispute.

Ms Popillopolis cited it as clear evidence that our museums cannot be trusted to look after anything including even a sarcophagus. She alleges that the Greek Embassy has received an anonymous tip-off that not all the items stolen have yet been identified, leading to additional questions about competence and whether the British even know what treasures they have. This has caused an increasing crescendo of international pressure. Other countries, such as Egypt, have joined in.

Minister of Culture, Sir Benedict Cloudesley-Shovell, has been forced to issue a hasty statement today saying that there is no safer place for ancient artefacts than Britain, that the Marbles are as safe as the Crown Jewels[71] *and the perpetrators will very soon be brought to book. He has provided a complete list of the stolen items saying that any suggestion of confusion over this is, "preposterous piffle."*

Scotland Yard certainly needs to get a grip and track down the Ashmolean raiders if the situation is not to get completely out of hand. But perhaps the Greeks should remember that they have not been averse to a bit of pillaging themselves – after all who was it that sacked Troy? And it's a bit rich for them to lecture us about security. If they had taken better care of Helen, the Trojan War needn't have happened at all, and had it not been for Greek neglect it wouldn't have been necessary for the Marbles to be removed in order to preserve them for posterity. Three cheers for Elgin. After all, these treasures are known worldwide as the Elgin Marbles for a reason and, as the old saying goes, finders keepers!

Cassie's mind was racing, but for the next few hours she forced herself to concentrate on her research. Her mind could often seem like an unbroken stallion in a rodeo, but eventually she calmed and corralled it to a point where she could make progress. She needed to have something to say to her PHD supervisor next week.

After a few hours she closed her laptop at last

and, glancing at her watch, grabbed her coat, scarf and, as always, her skates. The street outside was lined with the terraces that formed the Victorian arteries of so much of London, many almost indistinguishable from each other and clogged by the smoke and traffic of over a century. At least hers had lime trees at intervals, although their roots were so hemmed in by kerbs and flagstones that they had to fight for their attic window to the sky. Reaching the crossroads at the end of the road, she skimmed past the welcoming wink of orange from a cab. At the next corner, she dodged swiftly around a couple of pedestrians and zipped past the Buddha fitness salon whose neon slogan urged passers-by to 'Stay in shape.' Twenty minutes later she was outside *O Live!* – a small Greek restaurant in Bayswater just round the corner from the Greek Orthodox cathedral of Santa Sophia. A small sign by the restaurant door read, 'Get stuffed' and underneath, in small print, 'Vine leaves are a house speciality.'

There were only a few tables taken inside, but in any event, Cassie headed through another door at the rear into another smaller room with a low-beamed ceiling and one central mahogany dining table. On the walls were a few pictures of Mount Olympus and other Greek mountains, islands and temples. Around the tables, a small gathering of six or seven were tucking into plates of moussaka, accompanied by what looked like a feta salad.

Cleo was already there and as soon as Cassie had taken a seat, Cleo initiated the meeting as chairperson. The group called itself ROT, Return Our Treasures. Cassie had only met the others a few times before. Two were also Greek, a young man she hadn't met before and Helena, a rather bitter elderly widow with what could only be described as the face that sank a thousand ships. There was also an Egyptian man, a Polish woman and a lady from Nigeria who wore enormous, hooped gold earrings and was robed from head to foot in the dazzling pink of a watermelon. The recent proposals for the peaceful return to Nigeria of the Benin bronzes[72] by some museums had given the group considerable encouragement, but everyone recognised that the Elgin Marbles would be a completely different ball game. Running through the agenda, Cleo finally came to "next steps".

'The recent press coverage has gone very neatly to plan. The Government are now on the record in the press with a statement that nothing else is missing from the Ashmolean, so at the right moment we can reveal the theft of the ring. That will shove it up Cloudsley-Shovell. Cassie mentioned that she had some additional ideas as to what else we can then do to ramp things up further.'

All heads turned expectantly in Cassie's direction.

'Well,' she said. 'After all the Russians managed to take the sarcophagus. In fact the mummy was enclosed in three sarcophagi inside one another so perhaps the raiders thought they were like those Russian dolls. Anyway three would have been much heavier than one and they still got away with it. I did wonder if it might be possible to make contact with them. They might be willing to try a raid on the British Museum. If they could take just one of the smaller segments of the Marbles hostage, you could certainly call it a bargaining chip.'

Helena interjected. 'That would be ridiculously risky and would need a crane or a fork lift at least.

Who knows what else the Russians would want in return, even if it would also fulfil their aim to cause more embarrassment to the Brits. Also, the British Museum security may not be impregnable, but getting something so large and heavy out of there is likely to be much harder than at the Ashmolean.'

'Agreed. So I've thought of a couple of other possibilities ...' Cassie outlined her suggestions, which caused initial alarm. However, the Polish lady was supportive. She was from the city of Wroclaw and gave everyone an entertaining insight into the bizarre and imaginative ways in which many in her city had protested against Soviet control when Poland was still part of the Soviet bloc. This included filling the streets and monuments overnight with hundreds of gnomes which would then disappear again by the following day. Protestors would also gather in the main square, lie down and beat themselves saying this would save the Russian soldiers doing it for them.

Encouraged by these examples, and after discussion, Cassie's alternative suggestions were approved unanimously. All the risks seemed to be ones Cassie personally would be taking, not the rest of them, and they were desperate to tuck into the *galaktoboureko*. This glorious Greek pile of custard and filo pastry had been tempting them for far too long and they could no longer think about anything else. After that of course they would need to drink a lot of *ouzo*, dance wildly to the banshee wail of a *bouzouki*[73] and smash a lot of plates. Otherwise, diners next door might become suspicious as to whether their meeting was really a proper Greek party as Demetrios the restaurant owner had told them.

CHAPTER 7 – WHERE THERE'S A WILL

... you will miraculously discover many long lost relatives from previously unknown branches of your family tree who will flock to pay their last respects – Angel Capelli.

In Rome Panettone was one move away from defeat. There were still about half of the pieces left on the board and the points were even. It was a long time since he had lost a game but his online opponent on this occasion, ChesstWig, was unrelenting. The Inspector wondered for a minute whether to resign, but that would be a first and a precedent he didn't want to set. Giving up could become a habit. Better to go down fighting like Thermopylae, Rorke's Drift or the Alamo[74]. Hunched forward, with his fingers spread wide and pressing against his temples Panettone tried to stretch his brain beyond its natural horizons, wide as these were. The black and white squares swam before his eyes. Two pedestrian crossings printed over one another in opposite directions, but which would save him from being run over? Knight to Queen five seemed to offer some short-term prospect of salvation.

His phone interrupted him. He must change the ringtone. *Bella Ciao* didn't chime well with his mood when he was in the middle of a homicide investigation. It must be the dreaded call from his dentist, or as he secretly nicknamed him, The Marquis de Sade. He steeled himself, but a quick glance showed him it was his mother's number. What a relief. She must be dying again.

He took a moment, made his move with the Knight even though the permutations were now so complex he wasn't at all sure quite where it would take him, then answered. The familiar quavering voice said theatrically, 'Father Giovanni is here. Please come so I can see you one last time ...'

Father Giovanni was such a regular visitor, he was pretty much part of the family. He now came to his mother's mansion to give her the last rites more frequently than he presided over mass at the parish church she attended. Still, it might all be worth the priest's while. A relatively small part of her estate would keep the bells of Santa Gummarus ringing for many years yet[75]. The Inspector sighed but, compared to the dentist, visiting his mother's death bed would be like celebrating *Mardi Gras*.

Tom viewed the strange package in front of him with suspicion. Was it one of his students' pranks? He was now sitting at a new desk in the large office he had been given in Clancarty Quad. Along with Boaks Quad, these were the most recent additions to the buildings at St Barbara's, both named after famous old Barbarians. The college careers guidance team loved to use them as examples, pointing the way to the plethora of opportunities that might lie ahead for St Babs graduates in the great wide world.

Lord Clancarty's title tripped off the tongue rather more easily than his real name, Brinsley Le Poer Trench. He was a ufologist and founder of the world's leading UFO publication, *Flying Saucer Review*. Rather confusingly his book, *The Sky People*, suggested that aliens in fact lived below the earth's crust and emerged from tunnels at the North and South Pole. The highlight of his career came when he was invited by a saucer cult in Japan known as The Cosmic Brotherhood to officiate at a ceremony on a top of a place that the cult had identified as a sun pyramid. Here, aliens had descended centuries earlier to teach humans to grow vegetables. If proof of this is needed one has only to see how many vegetables are now successfully cultivated on earth.

Boaks had been a Lieutenant Commander in the Royal Navy during the war but after 1945 dedicated his obsessive energies to repelling a new invader, the motor car. His plan was to cause such traffic chaos that people either took to the bus or helicopters, for which a national network of public landing pads was to be constructed. He waged his campaign by repeatedly blocking pedestrian crossings by wheeling prams full of bricks across them and by sitting on a deckchair in the middle of the A40 while reading the newspaper[76]. A small plaque on the wall of the college chapel commemorated his sad passing. This was all the more poignant because it occurred in a traffic accident for which the motor car was not responsible. He fell off one of his own buses and banged his head.

In any event Tom was delighted with his new

facilities, which included a suite of rooms for the team he was in the process of recruiting. The tall windows allowed great slabs of sunshine to fall into the room. The view across the college lawns to the Bodleian Library encouraged tranquillity for the research that would be needed if historical mysteries were to be unravelled. In front of him was the object that had arrived that morning by courier. It was one of the natural segments of what must have been a bamboo of massive girth. This formed a sort of organic compartment into which a lid had been cunningly cut. When Tom untied the loop of creeper that held the lid shut, he found inside a number of sheets of silver bark on which he now recognised his father's writing in some form of ochre-coloured ink. It was very rare for his father to write but, when he got round to it, his letters were often both long and strangely moving. This one was no exception.

It started with an account of the West Papua expedition to track down a tribe with no previous contact with the outside world. There were thought to still be around forty such tribes in the region but they were increasingly under threat, in danger from the brutality of the Indonesian Army or people seeking to exploit their ancestral lands. Contact risked disturbing their fragile way of life[77] and in particular the possibility of transmitting diseases that these tribes had never encountered before, leading his father to the eventual conclusion that the expedition should be abandoned. Instead he had decided to seek to explore the Songlines of aboriginal tribes in Australia.

Tommy, I'm writing to you in the light of a campfire in the bush near Uluru. I wish you could see the sky here.

The glowing sparks floating up from the flames seem to cool and merge into the scattered silver of the stars that, like all natural things, are part of the Songlines[78]. These are the pathways established at creation that connect the sacred sites of ancestors. The words of the songs preserve, from one generation to another, the sequence of landmarks that enable people to navigate huge distances across the territories of different tribes with different languages. They are connections not only with the land but all physical phenomena, with each person's past, with ceremonies and with the myths of the Dreaming when the world was made. It's hard to explain but there is no separation of time here. Past, present and future are all one seamless whole. Anything that affects one aspect of time affects everything …

There was a quiet knock on the door. He had lost count of time himself. It must be nine o'clock. His first interview of the day. Tom had already recruited Ming as the team's anthropologist and his old mate Finbarr, whose mathematical brilliance was sure to come in useful somehow. Boudicca had agreed to join part-time as an archaeologist. She was still literally up to her armpits in mud in the major dig which had now halted the progress of the A1 extension for the foreseeable future. The construction company was seething, but there was nothing they could do until at least the portion of the battlefield where the Ninth Legion was massacred had been fully explored by the moles. Now that the extent of the site was mapped out and Boudicca's team had been reinforced, she could leave matters in the hands of others when Tom needed her. A couple more people with different skills would give the team the capacity for the work ahead. Tom wasn't quite sure what these skills should be, but the CVs he had received were interesting.

Opening the door, Tom felt the immediate interrogation of azure blue eyes belonging to a very tall woman about his own age with long straight hair as black as a coal cellar. He looked down at the CV in his hand.

'Hi, you must be ...' He hesitated and she filled in the pause for him.

'Puk. It's an old Danish name. It comes from the same Nordic root as Puck the sprite as I was born on midsummer night.'

Then as if Tom's thoughts were printed on a billboard she added, 'Yes, everyone tells me I've outgrown the part but I was a very small baby and my parents made an understandable mistake. In their own defence they always argue, as Shakespeare said of my namesake, that I could "beguile a fat and bean-fed horse".'

'Well, you won't have much problem with me then. Do come in please, Puk.'

Her voice was soft but clear and clipped. 'It's such a lovely day, couldn't we go outside? I saw you have a terrace on the tower above the stairs. Maybe up there?'

Tom wondered for a second if he should be calling the shots, but a free spirit was one of his criteria for the candidate so he could hardly object. He followed her out, carefully balancing the two cups of coffee he had made. There were fortunately two chairs on the roof of the tower which looked over the rooftops of the neighbouring buildings. Puk laughed when she saw the HR sign on the parapet: "Jump at your own risk. If you land feet first in the flower bed you may just survive with serious injury. Otherwise its curtains. You have been warned and the college accepts no liability."

'I'm afraid our HR team aren't exactly brimming with sensitivity,' Tom said apologetically. 'It's not as bad as the sign on the lawn last year which said, "Keep off the grass – unexploded mines." Sadly, one of the students thought it was a joke. The Dean is pretty hard core when it comes to enforcing his rules about the lawns.'

For the next ten minutes the interview roles seemed to be reversed as he parried a maelstrom of questions about the project and his own background and interests, but he didn't really object as they all seemed to come from a genuine interest in everything, rather than any desire to intrude. Eventually, when he managed to ask Puk why she was applying and what it was she thought astronomy could bring to the team, her eyes seemed to grow as wide as the arc of a cloudless sky when you lie on your back in the grass on a summer day.

'Well, how could astronomy not be essential? Studying the cosmos is at the heart of our human experience from the depths of history.' She developed the theme with an infectious enthusiasm, talking with increasing speed about Stonehenge, the Pyramids, the Nazca Lines in Peru and attempts to map and understand the heavens. Tom swiftly learnt that Julius Caesar's most lasting legacy was the calendar that had made the measurement of the year so much more accurate by adding another ten days to it and including a month posthumously named after him; about disputes over the correct date for Easter at the Synod of Whitby; about the effect of the moon on tides and the rotation of the earth on seasons. Surely nearly every historical mystery was likely to have some dimension that involved time and the cosmos?

Tom couldn't fault her fervour but tried to push back. 'Well, I can see some might. I'm not completely convinced, but I'm sure my father would agree with you from the letter I've just been reading.'

Before he knew it, Tom was then head-first into the labyrinth of his own strange family, a mystery no one could understand least of all him. His father was at Ayres Rock spending an unknown period living in the outback with native peoples and learning about the Songlines. Had Puk heard of them? Of course, she knew all about these ancient pathways. No, his mother wasn't with his father. His mother would rather die than go camping or anywhere that might have *serpenti* as she called snakes and other reptiles. She was living the high life in Italy. No, they weren't separated, just both eccentric souls who were still deeply in love but preferred to express it in short bursts a couple of times a year or even less, often meeting at some exotic place and with as little advance planning as possible. Yes, perhaps it was surprising that they had ever had Tom at all, and not at all surprising that he had no siblings. Tom wondered how anyone could draw out information from him faster than Finn could down a pint or his mother a bottle of wine.

Finally, Puk momentarily paused and held her breath when she noticed a student accidentally stepping on the edge of the lawn. Fortunately their shoes only just clipped the verge and was no explosion but Tom dived into the sliver of silence to start swinging the questions around. 'I see your surname is Brahe – haven't I heard that name somewhere?'

'Probably. The most famous member of my family was Tycho Brahe. That's how I picked up my love of astronomy. It sort of runs in the blood.'

It was coming back to Tom now. Tycho was a hugely wealthy Danish nobleman in the sixteenth century who initiated a lot of work for which Kepler, who he sponsored, subsequently claimed the credit.

'Yes, he was an incredible man. It's a bit hazy but I seem to remember that he was the first person after Copernicus to realise that the moon orbits the earth and the planets go round the sun, although he was wrong about the sun going round the earth. Still two out of three isn't bad! And didn't he discover that there were new stars, christening them "supernovas" and that comets are real, not just atmospheric distortions? But, what sticks most in my mind is something to do with his nose and an elk, although I can't recall the details.'

Puk laughed. 'Yes, Tycho was a pretty colourful character. His nose was cut off in a duel as a student, so he used to wear a golden prosthetic one. There were so many arguments about what it was really made of that his body was recently exhumed and it was proven his everyday nose was brass, but he used gold and silver ones for special occasions. And the elk, yes, it's true he had a pet one. Sadly he took it on a visit to a friend's castle and, after the poor animal drank too much beer over dinner, it fell down the stairs and broke it's neck.[79]'

Still a little sceptical about how the astronomy would assist, Tom just had to offer Puk the job for the elk story and her enthusiasm alone.

The next two interviews of the morning were less productive. One was a member of the magic circle who had misunderstood the reference to "mysteries" in the job advertisement and thought he was applying to be a mystery shopper. The other was a professor eccentrically dressed in a waistcoat lined with vivid images of some form of bird that seemed to have caught fire. He appeared to be more interested in persuading Tom to join a clandestine group called the Sect of the Phoenix than in the aims of the project. He kept burbling on about the need for the sect to pass on it's secret ritual and how the phoenix would soon rise again from the ashes, but if the waistcoat was anything to go by it looked to Tom as if the poor creature would instead be reduced to cinders and a few charred wishbones[80].

The monotone of chanting and a faint smell of incense was coming from the door of his mother's bedroom when Panettone arrived. Father Bellagamba was already there, standing over his mother who was propped up on an enormous pile of pillows gazing up at the ceiling. She looked like a pale minnow washed up on a sandbank, struggling for breath. This time the champagne was unopened and clearly very much on ice. On the other side of the bed, the Inspector saw a few close family members gathered round and also recognised the family lawyer, Signor Pelaratti and his mother's doctor, Signor Mezzasalma[81]. You could have heard a pin drop in the sepulchral silence until Uncle Ugo broke it by belching loudly.

With solemnity swiftly restored, the priest beckoned each relative in turn to the bedside. Aunt Chiara almost elbowed the priest out of her path to make sure she was first. Panettone knew she was desperate for a large inheritance to pay off the vast gambling debts she had accumulated over successive years at the Casino in Monte Carlo. Falling to her knees, she broke into loud sobs. After ten minutes of this, the priest gently but very firmly gripped her arm in a half nelson that forced her to rise. It wasn't obvious that his mother was conscious at all, but if she was Panettone knew his aunt's antics were unlikely to make any impression on her. She was very shrewd and had long ago worked out that the regular disappearance of small valuables and antiques coincided with his aunt's visits. Aunt Chiara might not know it, but she had already been cast into the ninth circle of the Inferno.

After a couple of other relatives had paid their respects, Uncle Ugo grasped the arms of his chair to stand up. As he did so however Felicette sprang her ambush, plummeting onto his lap from the chandelier. No one saw her lurking in the gloom above their heads. The impact from height and shock might have given Uncle Ugo a cardiac arrest had it not been for the outstretched claws that sank into the old man's thigh. The acute pain caused him to let out a howl that must have worked even better than a defibrillator by jolting his heart back into overdrive. It was so loud it would have woken the dead if death had already occurred. As it was the eyes of the old lady fluttered briefly before closing again.

Jerking to his feet in agony, Uncle Ugo tried to shake off his tormentor, but this only encouraged Felicette to sink her talons in deeper until, satisfied by a further shriek from her victim, she leapt like a coiled spring onto the bed. She sat there disdainfully licking her paws next to her owner where no one, of course, could touch her. Fortunately, the swinging chandelier just about remained attached to the ceiling although all its bulbs exploded[82]. Since the heavy curtains were drawn as a gesture of respect, this left everyone in darkness save for the banks of candles on each side of the room.

The doctor made Uncle Ugo lie down on a couch until his heart rate had dropped to that of an energetic jogger. He made him take off his trousers behind the Chinese silk screen in the corner of the room, washed and bandaged the perforations in his leg and said he would take Ugo to Accident and Emergency for tetanus and rabies injections. The patient insisted however that he was going nowhere until matters were properly concluded. Uncle Ugo knew that, once the old lady finally passed away, the lawyer would read out her will and he didn't intend to miss that for anything.

While all this was going on, Panettone's mother remained motionless. Any colour she had left ebbed out of her, so her face was now as white and delicate as a starched lace tablecloth. Her tiny hands lay palm down on the coverlet and the Inspector could see the blue river estuaries of her veins standing out as they flowed down to her skinny fingers. Re-emerging from behind the screen, the doctor assisted Uncle Ugo back to his chair and then went to the bedside. He took the old lady's pulse and gravely nodded, indicating that her body was now a husk that her spirit had left. Then he softly drew down her eyelids like blinds with his fingers. Left to last in the commotion, Panettone had missed his opportunity to say a final goodbye. Kneeling uncomfortably now beside the old lady he felt a sudden flood of loss for all she had given him, the kindness wrapped up in all that eccentricity and thirst for life. As he kissed her gently on the cheek and then the forehead, swollen tears welled up and ran down his nose, dropping onto her face. One eye popped open and he was sure she winked at him, but when Panettone jumped up and made way for the doctor to examine her again, he confirmed his former diagnosis and, to reinforce the point, signed off the death certificate. From the way he looked at Panettone the physician obviously thought he had become overwrought by the occasion, but the Inspector had seen a great many corpses in his time, most of them full of bullet holes. Nonetheless the emotional surge deep down within him was hard to control.

Although there was no great affection between them, he and Uncle Ugo hugged each other in recognition of mutual loss. As they unclasped, Panettone found there was now a cigarette between his fingers. He had no idea where it had come from until he saw that there was an open packet in Uncle Ugo's top pocket. It seemed that he had become a subconscious kleptomaniac. Somewhere inside him he must still retain the shoplifting skills that had come in so useful as a young boy when visiting sweet shops before he joined the police and became a pillar of rectitude. He was so overcome now with remorse as well as grief that he couldn't face acknowledging his guilt to Uncle Ugo. An inspector stealing a cigarette! It was impossible to contemplate. The only way to cover up was to pretend it was his and ask Uncle Ugo for a light to face it out. As it was his last cigarette, it would at least he could be confident that it would never happen again.

After a suitable pause the lawyer beckoned the way through to the dining room. The polished mahogany of the dining table, still dressed with place settings, silver and crystal stretched away into the distance leaving the small family group occupying only a few seats at one end. Signor Pelaratti opened a battered leather suitcase and coughed a couple of times, not so much to clear his throat as to make the most of being the centre of attention. The will he placed on the table was as thicker than a full set of Dostoevsky's complete works. Panettone thought that knowing his mother it would probably contain plenty of punishment and knowing his relatives might well provoke a fair bit of crime, but in any event he hadn't got time for this. It looked as if it might take several days to read it all out aloud as the lawyer clearly intended, sustained by the knowledge that he would be paid by the hour.

'I'm sorry, Signor Pelaratti, but as you know I am in the middle of an urgent investigation which the Pope has asked me to pursue as swiftly as possible. Can you give me the briefest of summaries and then you must excuse me.'

'Most irregular,' spluttered the lawyer. 'You must appreciate that I disclaim all responsibility for any summarising that does not reflect the full wording of the will. But in the circumstances, the key points concerning those present are as follows: The deceased bequeaths to her sister the two objects which she describes as having brought her the closest comfort and which have played the most important part in enabling her to enjoy life to the full.'

Aunt Chiara first looked a little confused but then as if she was about to burst with hopeful joy.

'Those are her dentures and her bedpan. To her brother Ugo, the deceased gives a legacy of a thousand euros a month for as long as he cares for Felicette.[83]'

Aunt Chiara was open-mouthed but mercifully as stunned into silence as if struck on the head by a baseball bat. Uncle Ugo was equally dumbstruck, although it seemed he might be about to have another seizure. Perhaps put on alert by the lawyer following the earlier unfortunate incident, the doctor came running in to tend to him before Panettone even had time to call out for his assistance.

'To her niece, Antonella, who she always promised to mention in her will ...' Signor Pelaratti paused to cough, giving Panettone time to register his surprise that Antonella was to get anything at all since he knew his mother disliked her intensely. Pelaratti recovered himself and continued, 'She writes, "Ciao Antonella."

'To her grandson, Marcelo, who she has always regarded as a son, the deceased lovingly bequeaths her entire remaining estate, provided he restores St Mark to San Marco. Otherwise, half will go to the Church and the other half to Felicette.'

Panettone could not help laughing drily. His mother had retained her sense of humour to the last. She would never have wanted her will to be boring and would have relished the thought of the pandemonium she would continue to create from beyond the grave. The aspects involving Uncle Ugo, who she knew had hated the cat for years, were particularly ingenious. Felicette would undoubtedly have come to a sticky end if left in Ugo's hands but now he had two incentives to care for the cat. After its latest attack on him, the mean monthly allowance might not have been enough to keep the cat safe for long, but the prospect that the animal might inherit half the estate would make Ugo rich beyond his wildest dreams. The cat's survival was therefore guaranteed while the Inspector's investigation was on going. If it reached a successful outcome, restoring St Marks to San Marco, swift action would be needed if the cat was to be rescued. If not, then like all police files, it would simply be left open so the cat would continue to be quite safe. Panettone was at least grateful that Felicette hadn't been left in his care.

CHAPTER 8 – LOVE AT FIRST SIGHT

Love at first sight is easy to understand; it's when two people have been looking at each other for a lifetime that it becomes a miracle.[84]- Tom Leveson

Tom was now feeling a bit peckish. Time for lunch. He was expecting one more applicant that morning, but she hadn't showed up. His team was almost complete, and perhaps it would be better to get to see how those already appointed worked together before appointing anyone else. But just as he reached the door and stretched out his hand to the handle it lurched open. The edge caught him between the eyes and knocked him backwards. He lay there for a moment sprawled on the parquet, then sensed someone was kneeling beside him.

'Bit early for a nap, isn't it?'

Cursing under his breath and rubbing his forehead, Tom opened his eyes. Dark brown eyes like pools of molten chocolate, a chic brunette bob of hair beautifully cut and a face as fine as bone china. Her mouth had a soft sensitivity with a hint of mischief, but mercifully no sign of the Botox that so commonly pumped lips up into inflatable tubes – "lilos," as Tom called them.

She was struggling to mask silent laughter with a look of concern. Her profile and the delicate line of her neck as she turned her head seemed somehow familiar ... but like a loose wire in a plug, he just couldn't make the connection.

Perhaps it was the knock on the head, and it would come back to him. Although his feeling of *déjà vu* was tangible, he could see she didn't share it so, rather than make the moment even more awkward, he tried to put it to one side, at least for now, in the hope of working it out later. In any event, a second sensation was already making him tongue-tied.

A couple of lines from sonnets floated into his mind. Tom had always been an incurable romantic, something that he probably inherited through his mother's Italian blood. She was certainly a bundle of passion and emotion, all openly on display in gesture as much as language.

Tom had tried to learn the gestures to accompany his own rather rudimentary Italian but had found it could be very risky. A slight nuance could completely change the meaning. Last time he had visited Rome and tried to thank the taxi driver who had taken him to his hotel, the guy had thrown his suitcase under a bus. As it burst open the Inspector could only watch and try to pretend that the ties, boxers and socks that festooned the oncoming cars were nothing to do with him.

Tom's friends always assured him that there was no such thing as love at first sight. All sorts of research had been quoted at him, demonstrating that feelings of this kind could only be a chemical reaction – a purely physical attraction based on endorphins that gave you much the same buzz as exercise or ginseng. But Tom didn't believe a word of it.

A glance was enough for Romeo and Juliet, although admittedly this did have dire consequences with hardly anyone alive by the end. Or what about Marius and Cosette in *Les Misérables*? At least in that case the lovers survived, although everyone else still died. And these sparks can ignite anywhere. Anna Karenina and Vronsky first meet not at some dreamy Russian ball but when a rail worker falls in front of a train, yet that doesn't cool their ardour. Pip's *Great Expectations* for Estrella are instant even though she then beats him at cards and calls him, "A stupid, lumbering, labouring boy." For a foolish half second, Tom almost spoke the words from Doctor Zhivago that had suddenly come into his mind: "You and I, it's as though we have been taught to kiss in Heaven and sent down to Earth together to see if we know what we were taught."[85]

Fortunately, as his mouth began to open, the tiny remaining particle of common sense still lurking in his skull made a super human effort and he yelped as he bit his own tongue.

'You're going to look like a panda once those bruises turn into black eyes,' she said.

'Well, I'm used to that.' Tom replied. 'I walked into a lamppost only a few weeks ago and spent a few days in hospital. Must take more care to look where I'm going.' He obviously didn't mention that then he also thought he had fallen in love at first sight, but that was with a blond-haired woman who he had only glimpsed for a few seconds on the opposite side of the road. Anyone would think it was a habit, although it was confusing that it was happening again in such quick succession.

'Perhaps you would like to postpone this? I could come back this afternoon. I would suggest another day, but I've travelled up from London so it would be a bit difficult to rearrange completely if you still want to interview me.'

'Definitely ... definitely ...' The words tumbled out, head over heels, getting in each other's way in Tom's haste. It dawned on him that, far from being definite, he had made everything confusingly indefinite. She now wasn't clear if he definitely wanted to re-arrange or to interview her.

He knew he was in grave danger of talking absolute drivel but seized the chance to compose himself so he could prolong this heavenly encounter for as long as possible. 'Let's talk over lunch. Sorry if I've seemed a little distracted but I get a bit faint without regular refuelling.'

The table in the window of the small café overlooked the towpath and the canal. Cassie wished she had brought her skates. It would have been a good place to take a spin after lunch. Tom was regaining his composure, but still looked as if he was suffering from hot flushes from time to time. If he had been a woman of a certain age, Cassie would have known what to put it down to. But perhaps he had a fever.

Tom knew exactly what kind of sickness was affecting him and that it wasn't something any antibiotic would help with. If he could attach any rhyme or reason to it, then the dimple must be to blame. The way it magically appeared and vanished in the smooth olive skin of her cheek was just an enchantment. Lovesickness always gave him a high temperature. Lightheaded and slightly euphoric, he felt at the same time both pleasantly fuzzy yet anxious that he would say something that would jar the conversation.

'Cassie is presumably short for Cassandra?'

'Yes, I'm Greek and my parents liked the sound of it. I'm not sure they realised that Cassandra was the prophetess in Homer who was fated always to tell the truth but never be believed ... and to be honest I sometimes think it is a curse I really have inherited if a name can do that to you.'

'Where in Greece?'

'I'm from Lesbos. It's Greek but very close to mainland Turkey and, for that matter, not so far from the site of Troy. The home of Sappho, if you have heard of her?'

Tom, as it happened had read all the surviving fragments of deeply erotic verse attributed to the legendary poetess. He just hoped Cassie hadn't read his thoughts and was giving him some hint that her preferences lay elsewhere. But, rewinding the conversation, it was obvious that his overwrought imagination was creating hot air out of a vacuum.

The conversation moved on and Cassie explained a bit about her research and soon realised Tom knew quite a lot about Homer and Troy. She also noticed that his behaviour seemed a little erratic. Sometimes he stared at her like a traffic light stuck on red as she waited for him to blink; she wasn't aware that Tom had always been a bit colourblind when it came to self-awareness and thought he was on bright green. At other times, he looked away as if shy and gave her only the clandestine glances of someone pretending to read a newspaper while continually peeking over the top. His laughter was as out of key as an violin stung with fishing line.

Cassie felt a stirring seed of something inside her. She wasn't sure if it might be a tentative attraction, or an almost unconscious sensing of tremors caused by the construction work across the street, or a tiny pocket of trapped wind. If attraction, she was happy to relax. If wind then better to hold back.

'I suppose we might still not have found the site of Troy had it not been for Heinrich Schliemann,' she said. 'He was a wild and controversial character, but he did convince people that the myth might be history after all.'

She crossed her ankles[86]. A moment later, Tom unconsciously did the same as he latched onto the vibe that Cassie quite liked Schliemann.

'I've always had a soft spot for him,' he said. 'Even though he was a rogue. I read somewhere that he was a grocer and then was ship-wrecked as a cabin boy before becoming a millionaire banker trading gold dust in America. Isn't that what gave him the funds to pursue his dreams?'

'Yes, it's true he was a rogue. I hadn't heard how he made his money but I do know that many modern archaeologists curse him now. He may have found Troy, but he excavated it with dynamite, blasting through nine different layers of habitation until he found treasure. Then he dressed his wife up in all the gold necklaces and headdresses, claiming it was the jewellery of Helen, although, ironically, it turned out that it was even older. Level seven is the remains of the city that best fits with Homer, and Heinrich had already dug straight through that without a pause for breath.'

It seemed that Schliemann had now been transformed from Dr Jekyll to the evil Mr Hyde. Tom was momentarily becalmed by this change of tack. He wanted to alter course himself to follow in Cassie's wake, but she had stolen all the wind from his sails. Anything too abrupt would be as clunky as getting out the oars and paddling for all he was worth, and that would appear ridiculous. Just before the silence dropped anchor, he found a fresh puff of breeze.

'Some say Schliemann sacked Troy more thoroughly than the Greeks ever managed to do!'

A close shave but he thought that had brought the gib around quite neatly. She was leaning forward slightly with her palms holding her knee, Tom caught himself just in time as he moved towards the same posture, instead jerking back suddenly to put his hands ostentatiously behind the back of his head.

'Neck pain?' Cassie asked solicitously.

'Yes, must have been a bit of whiplash from that door,' Tom responded, desperate to earn a little sympathy and rubbing his neck on cue.

Cassie seemed oblivious, her thoughts returning to Troy. She sighed. 'I would like to see what Schliemann called Priam's treasure, but the Russians took it during World War Two and carried it off to Moscow.' Another artefact that should be returned to its rightful home, she thought. But if it was returned, Greece and Turkey would fight over it instead. The site of Troy was in Turkey and that's where the treasure was found, but the Greeks viewed Homer's epics as part of their own most sacred and distant past.

'Thanks for lunch. So, what about the job?'

Tom had completely forgotten that this was supposed to be an interview. In a virtual daydream, and, seeing a few students poling their punts down the canal, he had been about to ask Cassie if he could take her out on the water, but her question re-immersed him in the icy tides of reality.

'Oh sure. The job's yours,' he said in a strange, strangulated squawk that recalled the high pitch of a steam engine's whistle when approaching a tunnel.

'Could you tell me something about it first? I'm not sure what's involved.' Cassie asked.

As with Puk but for different reasons the interview went into abrupt reverse as it dawned on Tom that Cassie might not accept. For the next half hour, he used every sales technique in the book, and many more he had just invented, to ensure she would. Cassie was not only smart but, given the proximity of Lesbos to Turkey, was very familiar with haggling in bazaars. Quickly sensing she was not so much pushing at an open gate as being pulled through the doors of an elevator in which the other occupant had already pressed the up button, she took full advantage and then some. She finally walked away with a promise of a salary twice that of the other members of team, leaving Tom with the headache of how he would square this with the Dean and with his sponsors, who though extremely generous, clearly took a very close interest indeed in anything to do with money.

As Cassie walked back to the station, she reflected again that Tom would be quite magnetic if he hadn't appeared quite so keen. That didn't chime well with her own self-image as the huntress not the hunted and perhaps betrayed a hint of weakness on his part. Good looking, but jury out and in any case it wasn't a good idea to mix work and pleasure.

Cavatappi thought the international sociologist, Anita Weiss, was a very perceptive person. He reminded himself of her wise advice whenever he came back to Manhattan: 'I moved to New York for my health. I'm paranoid and it's the only place where my fears were justified.' Oxford had been a peaceful interlude where a bang at night almost certainly was a car back firing rather than someone getting shot. In New York there were lots of old festering scores to settle and he was the target for many of them. Getting from JFK to the restaurant close to Central Park was always a game of pinball and Cavatappi intended to remain in play until he hit the jackpot, not disappear down a pocket.

There was the usual delay at immigration control and, as always, when Cavatappi finally reached the front of the queue and was waved past the yellow line on the floor in front of the glass kiosk, the official was in no hurry. For a good ten minutes he studiously ignored Cavatappi while he took his time checking the latest baseball scores and exchanging wise cracks with his colleague at the next checkpoint. Finally, he banged his palm on the desk as if Cavatappi had been keeping him waiting for a lifetime and took the Green Card.

'So, no terrorist or criminal felonies and no drugs or un-American vegetables?'

Cavatappi was tempted to ask what vegetables were un-American but was fairly sure anything other than a Halloween pumpkin would probably qualify, possibly even a potato, or a *potatoe* as one American Vice-President had once called it[87]. Instead he just nodded, wondering as usual whether anyone had ever been stupid enough to tick these boxes.

'Speak up. Lost yer voice or summat?'

'Just confirming. None of those.'

'Mets or Yankees?'

'Yankees.'

Cavatappi had not the slightest interest in baseball, except when it came to gambling rackets, but his sharp eyes picked up details like an eagle with the all-round vision of a chameleon, so he didn't even need to move his head. He had immediately noticed what team scores the immigration agent was following. Small things could be important, even matters of life and death. This time being alert had at least assisted his quickest border crossing in years.

'Okay, you can go.'

Outside JFK he scrutinised the line of cabs. You always had to be careful of just taking the first. It wasn't difficult for someone to get access to the airline passenger manifest and arrival times so you never knew who might be waiting. A long hard stare at the driver, hanging out of the window of his door to light up a cigarette, didn't give any obvious cause for concern. Nonetheless, caution was in Cavatappi's blood stream as much as nicotine was in the cabbie's. You couldn't just hail a cab from further down the rank without causing a fight, so he let a few other people who were waiting in the queue go ahead of him before proceeding.

'So, you takin' a bite out of the Big Apple?" The cabby tried to make small talk, but Cavatappi ignored him. He knew that this was the city that didn't sleep, and he intended to stay very wide awake until he was home and safe. After a couple of junctions and lane changes, he was pretty sure a black sedan with a group of guys in it was tailing them. The old saying was that, if you saw four dudes in a New York automobile not speaking, they were either making a get away from a bank heist or on their way to commit murder. It had enough truth in it to be worth thinking about.

They would very shortly be crossing the Queensboro Bridge over East River to Manhattan. Cavatappi waited until the car that was following them was obscured by a truck in the lane between them and until the traffic lights had brought them all to a halt. Then he swiftly threw another hundred bucks to the surprised and delighted driver, slipped out onto the pavement and ran to the street corner. Turning he watched as the cab and its pursuers slowed for the toll. A few seconds later the staccato of machine gun fire shredded the air. The cab was riddled with as many holes as a cheese grater.

Cavatappi didn't spare a thought for his unfortunate driver. When it came to prayer, he shared the views of Al Pacino: 'I asked for a bike, but I know God doesn't work that way. So I stole a bike and asked God for forgiveness.' The only thing he was thankful for as he headed for the subway was that the rival New York gangs still seemed to be playing by the same old scripts and didn't have any new ideas of their own[88]. All hoodlums now saw themselves as film stars and were as much acting out Hollywood as they were inspirations for it. He had to admit that since first seeing The Godfather he had always kept a gun in the toilet cistern. Sometimes he even had nightmares that he might wake up to find himself in bed with a horse, although when he mentioned this to his wife she slapped him.

The dimly lit platform was quite crowded, but Cavatappi positioned himself carefully so he could see the bottom of the stairs in the reflections from the perspex covering on the billboard that faced him across the tracks. People trickled down alone or in small clusters, some students, a few businessmen, a large guy wearing what looked like a purple silk scarf with birds on. Then a burly guy in a dark overcoat slowed as he reached the bottom step and looked around. Seeing Cavatappi he turned abruptly on his heel so that he was standing only a few feet behind him but made no immediate move to pull out a shooter. Too many people. He must be assessing his options.

The approach of the next train lit up on the board overhead. It was an express so wasn't stopping. The vibration ran ahead of it along the rails as the rattle of a shaken cutlery draw grew louder. The silver nose of the train emerged from the tunnel as if an eel was darting out of a burrow. Cavatappi sensed the guy behind him launch off his starting blocks to barge him onto the track. He waited, then at the last moment dropped to one knee as if tying his shoelace. The hoodlum flipped over Cavatappi's back in a somersault that would have brought applause from a trapeze artist. Then he was whisked away to Union Square and South Ferry as the train bored into the darkness of the next tunnel section. The passing roar of the carriages guillotined the thud and first syllable of a yell. For some reason the London tube announcement floated through Cavatappi's head. 'Mind the Gap.'[89]

Everything had happened so fast, it seemed it

hadn't happened at all. It was as if that single frame in the spooling sequence of a movie had been snipped out and had been lost on the cutting room floor. Most of those on the platform hadn't moved, still staring blankly in front of them, absorbed in their papers or their headphones. A thin young man standing right beside Cavatappi seemed to be the only one tuned into real time. The colour and shape of his face were changing like a marshmallow on the end of a stick held too close to a campfire.

Cavatappi shrugged. 'A guy in a hurry. I suppose he did kind of catch that train, but most people prefer being inside the carriage. Maybe late for a funeral?'

But the young man had already passed out and was melting into the platform. The gathering knot of do-gooders who were now rushing to his aid gave Cavatappi the perfect chance to slip over to the opposite line. This would still take him into Manhattan, even if by a slightly longer route. The adrenalin was still pumping as he knew trouble always comes in pairs. Sure enough, almost as soon as he sat down on the bench another bloke sat down beside him. He was in a similar overcoat to the first guy. So was half of New York, but there was a bulge in both his front pockets and Cavatappi wasn't taking any chances.

He put his arm round the guy and tapped his furthest shoulder. Then, as his bench companion looked around the wrong way, Cavatappi's stiletto put a deep stitch through the inside of his own coat and his neighbour's. Cavatappi had to catch the backward roll of the guy's head as his eyes turned upwards without a sound. Steadying the body against the bench, Cavatappi swiftly checked the pockets. It seemed the lumps in the front of his coat were just the guy's moobs. Nothing else except a ticket to see Dolly Parton, and Cavatappi had no idea if there was any connection. It did seem that this fella might just have to be put down to unfortunate collateral damage. Still, it was better to jump to the wrong conclusions than be jumped yourself.

When Cavatappi finally emerged from the station at Grand Central, he was only a couple of blocks away from *Margherita Amore Mia*. But the end of a journey is often the toughest and he felt the muzzle of a pistol in his back as two inscrutable men suddenly materialised beside him. They had obviously learnt from Al Capone that, 'You can get much further with a kind word and a gun than you can with just a kind word.' They steered him a short way down the street then through a shop doorway above which, in blazing lights, was a sign saying, *Lucky's Pizzeria*.

Funny; he knew this part of town like the back of his own hand ... surely this used to be a laundrette? The shutters were drawn and all the tables in front of the counter were empty apart from one. He immediately recognised the broad-shouldered hulk who occupied it as Lucky Luciano "Calzone," son of the original[90]. Lucky was hard not to recognise. Pale and puffed up, his bulging body explained the resemblance to an overblown pastry that gave him his nickname. The queasy impression given by his eyes, one blue and one green, mirrored his schizophrenic nature. He could switch in a trice and without warning from calculating and ruthless to irrational, deeply superstitious yet strangely emotional.

'So, Pappa, have a seat.'

Cavatappi's arms became windmill sails whirled

high in a tornado. He thought they might come off altogether as they were twisted behind his back by the two hoods who thrust him into the chair facing Luciano.

'How do you like my new outlet? I thought it was time you gave me a slice of the pizza round Central Park. It's high time for our two families to remember our shared Sicilian ancestry and come together as one big happy clan with me as *Padrone* and you as *Capo*.'

Cavatappi felt the hand he had been dealt was a blind dog in knock-out whist. But even worse, he already sensed that his blind card was the two of clubs and, if he overplayed it, he would soon be in a concrete overcoat. He could only tag along and try and work on Luciano's loose screw.

'How about the split?'

Luciano clicked his fingers loudly. One of the henchmen pressed his shooter just behind Cavatappi's ear while the other disappeared behind the counter and into the kitchen. When he reappeared, he was carrying a large pizza on a board. He lent forward and placed it respectfully on the table then handed his boss an enormous knife. Luciano proceeded to cut the pizza into eight slices. He put one slice on a small plate and pushed it across the table in front of Cavatappi, keeping the enormous platter with the rest.

'One?'

Luciano reached forward with the knife and cut Cavatappi's slice in half, putting the other in his own mouth. His words blurred and thickened through the pizza dough. 'You're rhighth, Pappa. You don't detherve one. I was thrying to be generouth, buth a half will do. Thath's one shixtheenth or shix and a quarther perthent. I'll leth you shoose which.'

Cavatappi gave him a long hard stare. 'If that's all then the quality has to be the best.' He picked up the thin half segment and took a bite. 'Pepperoni ... barely enough to taste but flavour's not bad at all. Although ... not as hot as ours.'

Luciano let out a roar that dramatically cleared his throat of the last pizza remnants and lurched to his feet sending his chair crashing backwards. The knife was slicing the air into thin pastrami strips as he flailed his arms. Then he abruptly stabbed the blade into the tabletop in front of Cavatappi so deeply that the point went straight through, leaving the handle and steel above the surface quivering like a jelly with epilepsy.

'This is a matter of honour. Everyone knows our pepperoni is the best. Order one from *Margherita Amore Mia* and we will force you to eat your words, Pappa.'

As they both knew, the code required all parties to give their honest opinion on issues of honour to other mafiosi[91]. Luciano's henchmen listened carefully to Cavatappi's call to make sure there was no funny business. While they were waiting, Luciano leaned back in his chair and gave Cavatappi a grin that brought to mind a crocodile eyeing up a beefburger.

'So, Pappa. I'm afraid that if you do not choke on your own pizza, my boys will shortly be taking you up to the tenth floor. The Stairway to Heaven, we call it. There they will help you to fly. Perhaps you have some final words for your family?'

Ten minutes later there was a knock at the door. A delivery boy was cautiously admitted carrying a flat square box marked *Amore Mia*. Luciano impatiently seized it from him and tore it open. As Cavatappi and the delivery boy threw themselves under the table a massive blast ripped through the restaurant and the ceiling fell in.

When Cavatappi finally arrived back at *Amore Mia*, he was still brushing the plaster from his hair and suit. Getting home was never straightforward. The exploding pizza was an option he had been forced to use several times before. If he ever placed an order for a pepperoni take away delivery, that's what he got. And the code of honour had been scrupulously observed. He didn't say his pizza was the best, just the hottest and no one who had seen the aftermath of the explosion could argue with that.

If Luciano had been paying more attention that morning then, like Julius Caesar on his way to the Forum, he might have picked up on the subtle signs that his luck had run out. He had got out of bed on the wrong side and put his lucky underpants on inside out. Then he slipped while shaving and not only cut himself but head butted the mirror shattering it into a thousand pieces. His umbrella popped open of its own volition before he could get out of the front door. As he furiously slammed it behind him the horseshoe fell off causing the single magpie pecking at the gold tops on the milk bottles to flap away. Tripping over the neighbour's black cat in the street caused him to step on the lines at the edge of the paving slabs and stumble under the window cleaner's ladder. The large buzzard he had trained so painstakingly failed to do a lucky poop on him as normal. It wasn't the Ides of March, but it was Friday 13th. Luciano hadn't even remembered to look at his horoscope as he usually did over breakfast. If he had he would have read: "In the great pizza wheel of life, the influence of Quattro Stagioni is waning and you will feel a sudden sense of inner warmth as Pepperoni comes into the ascendant propelling you in a new direction towards an orbit around the fiery planet Mars."[92]

CHAPTER 9 – DOWN IN THE MOUTH

All any dentist asks of you is that you put your money where your mouth is - Anon.

Whisky. He had heard that pregnant women often had sudden cravings for fast food and ice-cream but what he suddenly needed was Scotch. Like many of his generation, he was still imbued with a love for single malts. Beer might be called the amber nectar, but the bronze depths of whisky had a far subtler depth of colour and taste, particularly his favourite dram, *Glen Sporran*. Panettone was, in most things at least, a man of extraordinary self-discipline, so a bottle usually lasted him almost a year, eked out from one glass per fortnight to the next. But occasionally, as with smoking, his resistance gave way, corroded by the rusty liquor.

The solid glass base of the chunky tumbler gave an additional sense of heft to its contents. He held it up to the light and swirled the dram slowly, watching for the strength of what aficionados called its "legs" –

the viscosity of the autumnal tones running round the inside of the glass that showed the level of alcohol. The tasting notes that accompanied the bottle verged on the poetic. He thought he could just about smell and taste the peat fire on a Hebridean beach, the undertones of apricot and possibly even the mackerel with a hint of calamari. "Shooting stars dipped in molten liquorice and rainbows dissolved in marzipan," seemed pretentious and a bit far-fetched. It was a positive relief that he couldn't detect the whiff of rubber from the inside of a punctured bicycle tyre or waft from the uncleaned floor of an abandoned hen coop. The taster had either been taking weed at the same time or his flights of fancy had got the better of him. Anyway, *Glen Sporran* was a fine dram. After a double, anyone would feel they could toss the caber at the Highland Games. He wrestled manfully against the thought that the only thing that could bring Heaven closer was a cigarette, but after a lengthy struggle he was eventually thrown and overcome.

Panettone was, to be fair, trying to relax. The call from his dentist had finally arrived, giving him a severe migraine. He needed to anaesthetise himself as swiftly as possible before the appointment and whisky had seemed to provide the second-best option which he had now supplemented with the first. There was afterall something beyond the last cigarette. He christened it the omega cigarette. These indulgences also gave him a brief opportunity to celebrate. The desperate move he had made in his chess game before going to his mother's deathbed had unexpectedly won him the game. Despite his game name, his opponent had not seen the ingenious check mate coming, but neither had the Inspector. Still, it was the result that mattered, and he was pleased to receive a message from ChesstWig.

'That last move was a roaster, ChessNut.'

He resolved to rely on gut instinct a bit more in the future. And, in fact, it was instinct that was telling him that there might be a link between the events at San Marco that he was investigating and another major crime that had recently hit the newspaper headlines – the Ashmolean raid. Both had clearly involved highly sophisticated gangs and the theft of world-famous historical objects that were unique, priceless and would be extremely difficult to dispose of on the open market. Mummified bodies in particular were very rarely stolen not only for this reason but also because most thieves were far more superstitious than they might like to admit[93].

Although the Ashmolean raid hadn't involved any murder, there had been violence against the museum official who had been tied up. Perhaps Father Matteo had also got in the way of these ruthless gangsters and had seen something that might identify them so they could not risk leaving him alive. In any event, there were no other convincing leads. Although the nutter with the blue rucksack had been arrested and questioned, there was no DNA or other evidence to implicate him. The pressure within the police department to just charge him and give the press what they wanted was building, but Panettone knew that the evidence they had was nowhere near enough for a conviction. Besides the guy's account, even if crazy, somehow had a ring of truth, and he was obviously a loner which pretty much ruled him out as far as the Inspector was concerned. It would have taken more than one man to break open the high altar chamber to steal St Mark's body. But that left Panettone in the hot seat with no answers and the Pope was growing impatient with the lack of progress. He resolved that after his dental appointment he would need to fly to England. At the very least, this would eliminate a possible lead and stop the incessant demands for updates from the Vatican.

The clinic was in the basement of a renaissance palazzo quite close to the Pantheon. Panettone thought that Dr Trapano had probably selected premises below ground to suppress the screams of his patients. The Inspector's last treatment in hospital followed an incident in which he had been shot in the arm and then run over by the gangsters' getaway car, but he had taken it all in his stride. Yet, as he was shown into the dentist's surgery, he was so pale you could almost see though him. His heartbeat was shaking him like a tambourine. Trapano's glacial smile did nothing to set him at ease[94]. The rack of equipment on the wall ranged from a tiny screwdriver at one end to what looked remarkably similar to a full-scale pneumatic road drill complete with earphones. It seemed that the cure for toothache was to drown it out with something far worse. The dentist was gesturing to a full-length leather couch surrounded by more spotlights than most football stadiums. As he did so, he gave the drill in his hand a quick burst to check it was ready for action. Although not the largest in his collection, it still looked big enough to make very short shrift of the average breeze block and emitted the high-pitched whine of a thousand angry wasps. Trapano stroked the drill lovingly. To him, no doubt, the sound was of the soprano solo in a cathedral choir.

'This one should do the job but, of course, if we find you haven't flossed, we may have to help you remember for next time by moving to something a bit more powerful.[95]You may feel just a few twinges so perhaps best if I strap you down, Inspector.' When the dentist looked up the patient had vanished leaving the door swinging shut behind him.

Panettone was accustomed to absorbing every forensic detail from crime locations at a glance. The fingernail marks on the arms of the dentist's chair, the earplugs lying on the counter, the bottle of laudanum to quieten struggling patients and the discarded rubber gloves spotted with blood in the waste bin were all reminiscent of some of the most gruesome murder scenes he had attended. As the Inspector sprinted past the desk of the flustered receptionist, she heard him shout something about an urgent investigation and that he had realised he was late for his flight. He also shouted that he would make a new appointment posthumously as then it would be painless. Even the sudden recollection that he had left his cigarettes behind wasn't enough to bring him back.

The great Qattara Depression in the Western Sahara contains the Great Sand Sea where one dune rolls after the other in never-ending waves of gold to the horizon. In the heat of the day nothing living dares emerge for fear of being fried alive quicker than an egg in a pan over a leaping flame. The Siwa Oasis lies in the lowest part of the depression, well below sea level and is one of the most isolated areas of Egypt, inhabited mainly by Berbers who somehow survive in this arid landscape. It does at least contain a real lake, not simply a mirage. At the centre of the oasis, a small mountain rises up and seems to float like a white island above the green palms.

Near the small temple of Amon Ra on the summit of the hill is the pool where Cleopatra was said to have bathed, presumably not in her favourite asses milk as this would have curdled into *gorgonzola* very swiftly in the heat. The camels gathered round the pool stank so badly that it wasn't surprising they were grumpy, although their long lashes gave the misleading impression that they were flirting with the boy who was looking after them. He stridently insisted that he had seen a white figure standing on the altar of the ancient temple. An old Berber who had been drawing water from the temple well saved him from a beating by confirming that he was telling the truth. As word spread, there were further sightings a few days later at the Shallalat Gardens in the ancient royal quarter of Alexandria. Then, after a lapse of a couple of weeks, new reports began emerging from various sites along the southern coast of Turkey.

Outside St Barbara's, Orion was showing off the glittery studs on his belt as Canis Major and Minor bounded along behind him. Inside, Tom was working deep into the night. He had a lot of his own research to catch up on and tomorrow he needed to be ready to discuss potential projects with his new team. But he was exhausted, both physically and mentally. His heart had recently taken to beating three times faster than normal every time he saw, or thought of, Cassie, which was most of the time. He wasn't sure how much more he could take. The desk lamp repeatedly went into eclipse because his eyelids were banging shut as often as the door to the gents at half time in a football match, and no one was holding it open for him.

Everything around him seemed to be swirling amid clouds of dry ice and he found himself on a platform blinded by lights with a microphone in his hand. Opposite was a huge swivel chair. The black leather had more padding than a sumo wrestler. Tom found himself speaking to the dark cavern around the stage where he sensed, rather than saw, a large audience. He was not just speaking, but presenting, far more confidently than in his wildest dreams. Those were often pretty wild and about to get even wilder.

'Welcome to the final of *Mastermind*. We have an exceptionally strong group of contestants, all of whom have fought their way through the preliminary rounds. First in the chair is ... Plato, one of the world's most famous philosophers. He, or at least the shadow cast by the true form of himself, has joined us from his cave[96]. His special subject tonight is Atlantis, a mysterious city which he was the first person in history to mention.'

A grizzled old man with steel wool hair and leaning on a staff came and sat in the black chair.

'Plato, you have two minutes starting from now. Did you invent the ancient civilisation of Atlantis?'

'No. It is history not myth. I relied for my account on Socrates, Solon and Egyptian priests who were all convinced of its existence based not only on legends handed down orally through generations but also ancient Egyptian hieroglyphics. To put it beyond doubt, Captain Nemo visited the city in his Nautilus as faithfully recorded by Jules Verne in Twenty Thousand Leagues Under the Sea[97].'

'Where was Atlantis located?'

'Somewhere in the great Ocean beyond the Pillars

of Hercules which was later called the Atlantic for that reason.'

'I'm sorry I can't accept that answer as sufficiently precise.'

'Pass, then.'

'Explain what happened to Atlantis.'

'Its destruction was caused by earthquakes and floods thousands of years ago. As a result of these upheavals the route to the city was blocked with mud just below the surface of the sea after the island on which Atlantis stood was submerged.'

The buzzer sounded for the end of the round but, breaking the protocol and seizing his opportunity, Plato swiftly turned the tables. He shifted the spotlight and the questions onto Tom, who was so disconcerted that he found himself responding. Having established that Tom was an archaeologist, Plato asked why he hadn't yet found Atlantis himself, what current theories there were about it and whether Tom believed his – that is, Plato's – account.

Stammering a little and now on the back foot, Tom said that there were quite a few theories but the most compelling concerned events within the Mediterranean whereas Plato had been quite clear that Atlantis lay beyond the Pillars of Hercules, or what was now known as the Straits of Gibraltar. One suggestion was a confusion with the submerging of a city called Orobiae and another of a very small island remarkably called Atalante near the coast of Locris in Greece mentioned by Thucydides. Yet another alternative was that it was an echo of events resulting from a volcanic eruption on Thera, now Santorini, that allegedly caused the collapse of the Minoan civilisation.

Many of those who accepted Plato's assertion that Atlantis was somewhere in the Atlantic thought it might have some connection with the mysterious island of Thule or with places to which the Phoenicians had voyaged searching for tin including Cornwall and Ireland. Some thought it must have been in America. But Tom was forced to admit that most scholars now thought Plato had made Atlantis up as a model for his discussion of politics. At this, Plato flew into a rage and tried to smash up a number of spotlights with his staff, until Tom was forced to call security to restrain him. When he had finally calmed down, Tom was able to continue.

'At the end of that round Plato you have scored nine points. You passed on four questions, including the exact location of Atlantis, when your answer was too imprecise. You were also deducted six points for occasions when you insisted on asking the questions rather than answering them.'

'But that's the whole purpose of Socratic dialogue. Instead of making it difficult for yourself like so many philosophers do, you ask questions and get the other guy to do the hard work. Rather than, "I think therefore I am," it's, "You think therefore I don't need to."'

These protests and other complaints along the lines that life was nasty, short and brutish[98] made no impression on the two burly bouncers who took Plato firmly by each arm and ushered him to the side-lines.

'Next, we have Cassandra, a student at London University whose special subject is Troy and the Trojan War.'

Cassie seemed to swim into the chair. She looked stunning with her short turquoise hair and a slinky dress of shimmering scales. Tom gulped and his voice now rasped from a mouth as dry as sandpaper. He had never realised until now that she was a mermaid[99]. Feeling himself blush, he quickly looked down for his sheet of carefully-prepared questions, only to find they had disappeared. There was no choice except to go free style.

'So, Cassandra, what caused the Trojan War?'

'A Trojan Prince called Paris took Helen, the most beautiful woman in the world away from her Greek husband, Menelaus.'

'Most beautiful? I don't think so. But let's leave that to one side for the moment. Did Helen fall in love with Paris or was she taken hostage?'

'That's hard to say. Homer doesn't tell us.'

'And what were Menelaus and Paris like? That may give us a clue.'

'Menelaus was a brutish, ginger bruiser and a great fighter, but he had a very tiny brain so that was probably a turn off. Paris, on the other hand, pranced around on the battlefield in a leopard skin onesie looking gorgeous, but then ran away to bed to make love to Helen yet again, leaving his brother, Hector, to defend Troy.'

'And which type of man would you prefer? Sorry, let me rephrase that totally. What did Helen look like?'

'No one knows because, apart from saying she had fair hair and skin, Homer cleverly doesn't describe her. He just leaves each man to picture his own perfect woman so her perfection could never be challenged.'

'My perfect woman has greeny bluey hair and looks like a mermaid ... I mean, did Helen like all these guys fighting and dying over her?'

'Again, it's a bit complicated. On the one hand, she beat herself up with guilt because all these handsome men were sacrificing their lives on her account. But, on the other, there are quite a few hints that she absolutely lapped it up, really.'

'And what other great love stories are there in the Odyssey and Iliad?'

'Odysseus and Penelope, of course. She waited faithfully for his return, even though he spent seven years enjoying himself with a goddess Calypso, some more time with a beautiful enchantress called Circe, and only just held himself back from deserting Penelope altogether for a princess half his age called Nausicaa. He did come home eventually, with a very long string of tall stories about where he had been for the last twenty years, but then the two got back together.'

'I understand she had a hundred and eight ardent suitors and turned them all down. Would you have done the same?'

'I thought my specialist subject was supposed to be mostly about whether or not the Trojan War happened?'

'Sorry, yes, of course. Let's end it there. You get a full twenty points and another ten bonus points for answering questions outside your chosen topic. But I would just like to ask one final thing while you are here. What is it you find most irritating about men?'

'When they don't listen. Agamemnon was warned by my namesake to be careful when having a bath. But as soon as he got home, he asked his wife to run one for him. Instead of bringing his rubber duck and favourite bath cube, she and her lover then butchered him in it and his life went down the plughole.'

Cassie wriggled her silver tail and glided to sit on a small rock next to Plato at the side of the stage.

'Next, we have Tristram Shandy whose chosen subject is his birth as a very long shaggy dog story.'

A gawky gentleman in a long trench coat, jodhpurs and a bright red cravat creased himself into the chair as if he was performing origami.

'Tristram. Give us a concise summary in just a few words of how your birth came about.'

'You mean the moment of my conception? What is so terrifying is that it nearly never happened at all, or not at that time, in which case I wouldn't have been myself but someone else, because at the critical moment my mother interrupted my father by reminding him to wind the clock ...'

After what seemed like many hours, Tom held up his hand abruptly.

'Enough. We have almost reached the last syllable of recorded time[100]. Just out of curiosity, since we were discussing Helen of Troy earlier, in my copy of your book there seems to be a page missing when you were about to describe her. I was interested to know what you thought she looked like.'

'There's no missing page. I just left it blank as her beauty is impossible to describe.[101]'

'Well, I suppose that proves that, when the mood takes you, you can be the most concise writer who has ever existed. But that just makes the longwindedness of the rest of your work even more difficult to excuse.'

'All I wish is that it may be a lesson to the world, to let people tell their stories their own way. Digressions incontestably are the sunshine; they are the life, the soul of reading. For my own part, I am resolved never to read any book but my own, as long as I live,[102]' Tristram replied sharply before unfolding himself from the chair.

'The last contestant tonight is Humbaba, the very first known literary monster. We are delighted he is able to join us from the Epic of Gilgamesh, a poem from ancient Mesopotamia. His topic, as you might expect, is monsters.'

A collective gasp came from the darkness as a large blob of a creature shuffled onto the stage with a vast jelly-like body and ferocious fangs. As the epic said, he had the paws of a lion, the claws of a vulture, on his head were the horns of a wild bull and his tail and phallus each ended in a snake's head[103].

A voice piped up from the front row, 'Makes Jabba the Hutt look like Marilyn Monroe[104].'

Tom was about to ask a fiendish first question about Frankenstein, but it became clear that Humbaba was a monster of action rather than words. He was much more interested in being a monster than talking about them. Tristram Shandy was already disappearing head-first down his gullet. Gulping down someone who was himself so full of wind caused Humbaba to pause momentarily. The belch that then shook the auditorium gave Cassie, Plato and Tom the chance to take to their heels. Unfortunately for Plato, his long robe tripped him up and it didn't seem likely that Humbaba was ready to engage in any form of dialogue, Socratic or otherwise. But just as Plato's philosophical career was about to come to a sticky and premature end, great billows of dry ice obscured everything. Tom felt that, like Plato, he was also lying on his back concussed as he looked up at a circle of blurred faces. All he could hear were snatches of conversation falling into his mind like raindrops, each contained in its own small world, even if all were born in the same cloud.

Finally he heard a clearer voice he recognised and that somehow he now sensed was directed at him.

'Have you been here all night?'

He gradually came round to find his head was resting on his desk, which explained why his ear felt numb. Cassie was looking into his eyes from only a few inches away. He was about to ask why she no longer had a mermaids tail and had changed her hair back from turquoise to brunette, but then noticed that the rest of the team were standing behind her, looking equally concerned.

Panettone had booked his flight, but before that he had an important duty to fulfil in Rome. "Man does not control his own fate. The women in his life do that for him". These words had always stuck in Panettone's mind. He knew they were from Marx, but he couldn't remember which one. By process of deduction as a detective, it must surely be Groucho. Karl would have talked about men being bound up in chains and slaves to capitalism rather than to women. Groucho had it right as the Inspector was reluctantly forced to accept that his mothers' hands were still firmly gripping the driving wheel of his life, and this wasn't just down to rigor mortis.

St Peter's was already packed out for his mother's funeral. Everyone who was anyone was there, as were plenty of nobodies. Many of the nobodies had in the past prayed they would become somebody, but it now dawned upon them that their prayers should perhaps have been more specific. There were also a great many people who thought they were somebodies but were regarded by the other somebodies as nobody and by the nobodies as one of them. Panettone, on the other hand, was a modest man. He regarded himself as a nobody but, as Italy's most famous living detective who had solved many notorious crimes, everyone else certainly thought he was a significant somebody. Then, apart from the somebodies and nobodies, there were the semi-somebodies, who as a matter of cold logic – although, of course, they didn't accept this – were therefore also semi-nobodies. These were people whose names were on the tip of everyone's tongue but got no further than that because no one could quite remember them.

Tom's mother was in attendance among the semi-somebodies. In fairness she probably was a real somebody, but her problem was that her aspirations to this elevated status mainly came from her presence at parties where everyone ended up wildly drunk. Most of the witnesses who might have supported her claim had very hazy memories of seeing her there and none at all of what they had said to each another, assuming at that stage they could still speak at all. Perhaps proving this point, Tom's mother didn't really know the deceased, Panettone or any of his family but had heard on the grapevine that the social gathering afterwards was an event nobody who was somebody could possibly miss. She didn't consider whether somebody who was nobody might feel the same.

The service itself was one of the most spectacular that the great basilica had ever seen. The old lady had wanted an exuberant celebration of her life and she certainly got one. A leading tenor sang *Bella Ciao* in a booming baritone that echoed around the vault of the nave. For an encore he then performed *Nessun Dorma*[105], which seemed a little ironic since the deceased was presumed to be very fast asleep. There was a reading by Alberto Tomba[106], former Italian downhill skiing champion, who read at extraordinary speed, his voice rising and falling as if he was still slaloming over the moguls at Courmayeur. Many were shocked that the basilica allowed Silvio Berlusconi to give the sermon, which was entitled *Heaven on Earth – La Dolce Vita*[107], but then it was difficult to refuse someone who served as Prime Minister of the Republic in four different governments. His main theme seemed to be that life was often hard, but everyone deserved a little *bunga bunga*.

Finally, the coffin was carried out into the square on the shoulders of six *Corazzieri*, the *Cuirassiers* Regiment of Guards, whose usual role was to protect the President but who were happy to do a little moonlighting on occasion. As they goose-stepped down the nave, the Santa Cecilia orchestra played *Another One Bites the Dust* by Queen and then Elvis Presley's *Return to Sender*. The Archbishop vetoed the Meteor's classic, *She's a Zombie Now*, even though the old lady had included it in her requests, suggesting that it would encourage the congregation to reflect on what they thought about the afterlife. The slow progress of the cortege abruptly sped up when half-way to the door as someone behind the scenes became concerned that everything was running late and switched the music to *The Flight of the Bumblebee*.

As the first touch of dusk began to bruise the

sky above the square, fireworks fanned out in peacock feathers, the quill of each rocket emitting its own bright cascade of plumes. Waiters in black and white wove through the crowd like penguins moving through an Antarctic colony[108], although they were distributing free crostini and bruschetta rather than the catch of the day. The cavalcade of black limousines to the cemetery was led by the hearse carrying the coffin. Continuing the theme of celebrating the old lady's life, it was gold, festooned with balloons and on the rear window in shaving foam someone had written "Just Died – Moving to California."

When they arrived, Panettone and a small family group were finally able to pay their last respects. Panettone knelt down by his mother's side and hunched over the open coffin as the tears rolled down his face. He placed his packet of cigarettes beside her to avoid temptation and as a silent promise to keep to the straight and narrow, although she had never done so. Even in his weakest moments he was sure he would not try and exhume her for a smoke. He kissed her cheek lightly. It wasn't as cold as he had expected so he winked at her just in case. For a fraction of a second he thought again that she was winking back but realized this must be a hallucination brought on by grief. No one else seemed to notice anything and there was no knocking once the coffin lid was replaced so he felt reassured that she must be at peace. He reflected that it was just that someone who had always been so super-charged with life probably still retained a tiny residual charge like a spent battery that could send out a sporadic pulse of light but not illuminate a bulb anymore.

Uncle Ugo had unfortunately brought Felicette

who leapt into the grave and furiously clawed those who, either through extreme bravery or stupidity, tried to extract her. One the guardsmen was eventually persuaded, very reluctantly, to lower himself into the hole by the promise of a benediction from the presiding priest to ward off any curse or bad luck. As gently as possible he put his foot on the cat's tail while manoeuvring her into a sack which she swiftly reduced to ribbons. Grasping her instead in his steel gauntlets, the guardsman managed to transfer her to a cage, although she continued spitting and yowling continuously.

Aunt Chiara was nowhere to be seen. She was probably down at the pawnbrokers still desperately hoping to find that the bedpan bequeathed to her was in fact some priceless antique. Possibly a childhood invention of Leonardo da Vinci during a school project before he moved on to designing helicopters, parachutes, the concept of double hulls for ships, the frying pan, tanks, calculators and a means of concentrating solar power[109]. If Damian Hirst could sell a skull as art for millions[110], then perhaps even the dentures Aunt Chiara had inherited might also have a value.

As night snuffed out the last pale spears of light, the mourners and all vestiges of ceremony drifted away, melting like smoke into the darkness. Only a tiny spot of orange remained, floating like a firefly. Sitting on a cold stone step, the Inspector coaxed every last wisp of life from his cigarette. When it finally went out he bowed his head, caught unawares by the drops that fell in a sudden gust of rain.

CHAPTER 10 – LEAVE THE GUN. TAKE THE CANNOLI

[111]

No one will ever kill me. They wouldn't dare – Carmine Galante[112]

Cavatappi was now seated at the head of a long trestle table in *Mia Amore Margherita*. Every chair was occupied, but there was no one else at the other restaurant tables and he could see the open sign through the glass of the door ... which as he was inside meant that it was closed. Most of those present were in dark suits, creased so sharply that if you bumped into them they would have cut you. Nearly all were wearing shirts open at the neck and white as innocence. The missing ties had probably been used to suffocate someone on the way to the dinner. Anyone entering would have first needed to give a password to the two Rambo characters outside. Cavatappii and all his colleagues used the same one. It was tried and tested always ensuring instant and attentive service without fail, particularly in banks where it was guaranteed not only to give immediate access to your own account but to everyone else's as well : di5iSast1kuP.

Inside, they wouldn't have seen any guns but stacked against the back wall were enough violin cases for the string section of several orchestras and a couple of double bass cases. Someone with an overactive imagination from a military background might have thought they were just the right size and shape for bazookas.

When Alfredo stood, the loud cacophony of banter threaded with laughter and the sotto voce shared confidences were immediately strangled so you could have heard the quiet click of a flick-knife opening. Picking up the menu, the chef read each pasta dish out and, one by one, each diner confirmed his presence. Using code names was a critical precaution. The FBI and other gangs regularly planted bugs and other forms of covert surveillance. One slip could mean a lifetime in prison or worse so, despite having the room swept and checked in minute detail beforehand, no one was taking any chances. Only in a couple of cases was there no answer until the absence was explained by another diner, always addressing Cavatappi, the boss, as Pappa.

'Angelo Capelli[113]?'

'He's in hiding, Pappa. He broke the oath of *omertà* and grassed on us. As you know he kept the books for some of our Italian projects. Maybe he is the loose connection that's blown the fuse box.'

Cavatappi nodded slowly. It was possible and in any case loose wires could cause fatal accidents and needed attending to. He reached for a napkin and wrote on it before passing it to Alfredo who read it – "*dai ai Capelli un ultimo taglio di capelli e trasformalo in un vero angelo* – give Capelli a last hair cut and turn him into a real angel." Alfredo nodded in turn, then Cavatappi continued, 'Genovese Linguine?'

'Ambushed, Pappa, by the Ferrero Roche gang. We don't know if he was given a concrete overcoat and hidden somewhere in the foundations of that new flood barrier for Venice or dropped in a vat in the chocolate factory and turned into Nutella.'

'Okay, otherwise all here.'

Pappa sat down and the first course was served. Spaghetti with walnut sauce, the favourite dish of Al Capone. Alfredo then gave a short report on how the business was going. He explained that a lot of new supplies of "pizza" were coming in from Columbia to supplement those from Afghanistan. International sales were increasing although there was a lot of competition. Even the collapse of Luciano's chain here in New York was only likely to provide a temporary respite. The biggest issue was "washing up" the sales proceeds, but Pappa had discovered a promising new "recipe" for this which involved processing the "leftovers" via PEST and through an educational research charity of impeccable credentials in the UK.

It was meatballs for main course. One fella down the table shouted out, 'Hey, Alfredo, these are a bit tough. I always wondered what you had in that freezer.'

To which Alfredo replied, 'Yes, you're right. Iced testicles. Enjoy!'

But it was no time for frivolity. It struck Pappa as a little confusing that he always had to stand up to get down to business. The greatest setback to other lines of operations was the strange demise of Father Matteo. Although not a member of *Cosa Nostra*, he was a close "friend" within the Church. It was no accident that it was he who had been appointed to carry out the survey of relics, of which one of the most famous was St Mark's body. This had enabled him to ensure blind eyes were turned to assist others to cream off some of the rich revenue stream that the relics generated in donations. To be fair, he really didn't have any option. How else would he have been able to indulge his addiction for fine food and wine, frequenting the most sought-after restaurants to his heart's content. It had never even been necessary to book. A call, even on a last-minute whim, and a table in a prime position that others would need to request months in advance would instantly become available.

Admittedly, like the pasta from which he took his own code name, Cavatappi's mind had been warped into a labyrinth of suspicion and paranoia over many years, most of it completely justified. But, even allowing for this, it wasn't surprising that he was convinced that the murder of Father Matteo and the simultaneous disappearance of such a major relic as St Mark must be linked and be part of a wider plot by a rival gang. It was probably just the first step in diverting the revenue from relic donations or the illicit trade in ancient artefacts into their own coffers. The problem was there were no leads at all. Everyone present at the meeting had a pet theory, but no one had a whisper of new information or word from the street.

Cavatappi's network of sources would have embarrassed Interpol, yet apart from the information about Angelo Capelli, only one other useful suggestion emerged. Alfredo passed on a report from an informer in the National Fraud Squad headquarters in Rome who had been given the task of tracking Inspector Panettone's investigation. Panettone had apparently booked a flight ticket to London in a couple of days' time. A call with Scotland Yard, tapped by the same source, suggested he was interested in the Ashmolean raid.

Cavatappi had considerable, if grudging, respect for Panettone. The Inspector had put more of his colleagues behind bars in recent years than any other detective, although it seemed unlikely that he was yet aware of the relic scam which had no apparent connection with the incident in Oxford. Otherwise, he would probably be staying in Italy to concentrate on enquiries into this aspect. The Inspector might therefore be barking up the wrong tree, not realising the cat was in another one.

On the other hand, maybe he knew something else Cavatappi didn't. If Panettone thought there was a relationship between the two crimes, then it was worth looking into. Perhaps the same gang was involved. Perhaps they really were targeting famous and priceless artefacts for private collectors or even planning to make ransom demands and had no interest in the relic revenue.

Whatever the motive, they had done his own outfit serious damage and Cavatappi couldn't assume that this was just accidental collateral. He urgently needed to know who they were and what they were up to. Otherwise there was no knowing where they might strike next. He roughly remembered Sun Tzu's advice in his *Art of War* that, if you wanted to know your enemy you must become your enemy. But he had always found this confusing, and possibly suicidal, because if you became your enemy then you would be your own enemy and presumably would then try to eliminate yourself. More encouragingly, Sun Tzu had also said that if you wait by the river long enough, the body of your enemy will float past you. But even that seemed less comforting if you didn't know who your enemy was as you wouldn't be sure which body was the right one[114].

For dessert, Alfredo had prepared Pappa's favourite, *bombolini*. The gang regularly used "big bombs" when necessary but in this case the *bombolini* in question were Italian donuts filled with *crema pasticceria*, a kind of Limoncello-spiked pastry cream.

As Cavatappi stood up, the table fell as silent as a cemetery again. Every head turned in his direction. He told them of plans to continue expanding the business here in New York by opening a new outlet called *Pappa Deli* in Luciano's former neighbourhood, a few blocks south around Hell's Kitchen. Everyone needed to remain vigilant. Any intelligence at all that might relate to the San Marco or Ashmolean incidents should be passed on to Alfredo instantly. Cavatappi picked up one of the *bombolone.* As soon as he found out who had murdered Father Matteo they would be crushed in his fist without mercy, like this pastry. The gesture would have been dramatic had Cavatappi not underestimated the explosive potential of confectionery. The pastry blasted its creamy centre over everyone at the head of the table and left Pappa himself looking as if he was a Baked Alaska[115] that had been sucked through a vacuum cleaner.

The large white board on the wall of Tom's office and the flip charts around the room were already busier than Spaghetti Junction in the Friday afternoon rush hour. They could hardly contain the ideas that were colliding with each other like dodgems trying to find an inch of space. The diagrams and arrows in all directions would have left any learner driver paralysed with indecision and fear as none of it was in the Highway Code. But the brainstorming exercise had released a great burst of creativity and the team were buzzing with excitement.

When they finally stopped for a break, Tom's was reeling from lovesickness, an overdose of adrenalin and lack of sleep in that order. His head vibrated with the plodding steps of a mammoth on a long march to escape the Ice Age. He had also never led a team before and felt nervous, but was conscious that was something he needed to both overcome and hide with a strong start. It took several cups of strong coffee to lift his spirits and call everyone together.

'We've got so many ideas here; our problem will be living long enough to do something about even a fraction of them. Now, the hard bit is going to be sieving out the most promising ones and deciding on priorities. Let's try discussing a few and see where it takes us. Puk, you kick off. Pick a possible project. Tell us all in just a few sentences what the mystery is and why it should be on our shortlist.'

'What about another search for the Loch Ness monster? There are still many who think the evidence is compelling ... and I would like to do a bit of diving.'

She paused as everyone turned questioningly to Finbarr. His pained expression drew everyone's attention, although this was partly because he only had one eyebrow and when he raised this dramatically, as now, the lop-sided effect was both striking and strangely mesmerising. Only Tom knew that the loss of the other brow was a legacy of the Viking burial of the headmaster's dog. 'I love spending time in Scotland, but diving in Loch Ness sounds murky and so cold you would need a wet suit as thick as whale's blubber. Not much like the Barrier Reef and definitely no coral. But my real question is, shouldn't we stick to proper ancient mysteries?'

'It is ancient,' Puk bridled. 'The first recorded encounter was by St Columba in 565 AD. He saw some local people burying a man they said had been mauled by "a water beast." One of Columba's followers swam out but, when the monster emerged to attack him, Columba drove it back with the sign of the cross. Since then there have been a great many sightings and, more recently, some photographs.'

'Okay,' said Finn grudgingly. 'But I do remember that the most convincing photograph ever taken turned out to be a hoax made out of a toy submarine bought from Woolworths with a neck and head made from wood putty.[116]'

'I agree with Finn,' said Cassie. 'But for a different reason. We need to think about the skills we have in the team. For example, I don't see the Loch Ness monster giving much scope for Boudicca's archaeological expertise, Tom's or my own ancient research or, to be honest, your own astronomy, Puk.'

'Same goes for a few of the others, like the Marie Celeste and the assassination of JFK,' Finn added. 'As for what we mean by ancient mysteries, I think the latest we should go for is medieval. That would still leave who murdered the princes in the tower; whether Marco Polo ever did really reach China; Prester John and the King Arthur stuff in the net. I suppose, with King Arthur, the question would be what mystery of several would you be trying to solve? There's the whereabouts of Camelot, assuming it wasn't just fable, or the truth about the Holy Grail.'

'The Turin shroud might be a much more realistic project than the Holy Grail,' suggested Boudicca. 'At least we know it exists and where to look for it, but the mystery is how it was made and whether it really is the cloth in which Christ was buried or a medieval fake. What no one has explained yet is the photographic negative image of a man which seems to show marks of crucifixion. There's been an attempt to carbon date it already, but I think the problem would be getting the Catholic Church to allow us to subject it to any further examination.'

'You mentioned Prester John," said Tom. 'I vaguely recall the name but who was he?'

'That's an intriguing one,' said Boudicca. 'We know that the Emperor in Constantinople received a letter in 1165 AD from a mysterious Christian king calling himself Prester John. He was allegedly from India and enormously wealthy and powerful. He claimed his riches included an island made of solid gold, a huge crystal mirror in which he could see everything happening in the world and jewels that would restore the sight of the blind. The letter encouraged the crusaders to think that, in alliance with Prester John's forces in the East, they would be able to crack the Saracen nut between two pincers and recapture

Jerusalem. The letter was widely believed at the time. The Pope even sent a response with a doctor who was never heard of again. It doesn't seem to have occurred to many people back then that the letter might be a fake, and if so to investigate who wrote it. A few theories have been put forward recently but none of them are very convincing.'

Ming had until now been quiet, scanning the white board intently. 'If we really are focusing on ancient mysteries that involve as many of our skills as possible, as Cassie suggests, the most obvious candidates seem to be the Hanging Gardens of Babylon, the Rapa Nui statues, the Copper Scroll from the Dead Sea Scrolls, the Ark of the Covenant, Alexander the Great's tomb, Stonehenge, the Nazca lines in Peru and, of course, Atlantis, which Tom has already been researching.' No one dissented from this summary. 'Just as an afterthought, I know you're doing your PHD on the evidence as to whether the Trojan War took place, Cassie, and another mystery related to that is tracing the route of Odysseus's ten-year journey home to Ithaka, so I suppose those could be put in the mix, too. Any others?'

'I can come up with quite a few more Homeric ones if you really want them,' laughed Cassie. 'No, seriously, Ming, I think that list is more than long enough.'

Thinning down the options caused further heated debate. Puk and Finn were particularly vocal and the temperature was rising. Cassie didn't really express a strong preference but took an impish delight in stoking the fire with a log-like objection every now and then or by pouring a bucket of cold water on suggestions that seemed to be gaining traction. Tom increasingly struggled to keep the discussion from bubbling over into a riot despite the odd more mature intervention from Boudicca. It was Ming who emerged as the peacemaker, quietly leading the discussion back to calmer waters and it was he who suggested that Finbarr might put his maths brain to good use to help reach an objective resolution.

Finn, to be fair, rose to the challenge. His mind began to whirr like an equation gobbling numbers and spitting out all those that didn't fit the formula. 'If we're going to approach this systematically, we need to agree a set of criteria and apply it to all of the options. I can design a programme to do that if we can work out what the criteria are and weight them.'

For the next few hours, everyone's attention was fully absorbed. Apart from Tom's, that is. He had just glanced at his desk diary. Looming up in a few days' time was one that always filled him with a wave of anxiety, Valentine's Day. In his already fevered state, he was seized by a sudden ludicrous sense that this must be the moment, possibly the only moment he would ever have to declare his feelings. He felt as if poised in the open hatch of a plane, teetering on the toes of a decision to skydive out into space or retreat into safety. Who knew if he might be run over by a bus or be crushed by a falling tree on the 15th February? Life was fragile and could end abruptly at any time. He had read that an average of almost five hundred people die falling out of bed every year and nearly two hundred are killed when coconuts drop from trees and land on their heads. Tom wasn't clear what a coconut palm looked like and doubted there were many in Oxford, but nonetheless he made a mental note to avoid the city's botanical gardens. Other new risks were also emerging constantly. A surprising number of people now seemed to fall backwards off cliffs while trying to take selfies. This morning's paper had an obituary for the guy with the world's longest beard. He had tripped over it and broken his neck.

Sometimes such tragedies struck much closer to home. Only last year, one of Tom's own friends, Dougal, a keen fisherman, was casting his line into a canal when the hook got caught in a uninsulated powerline running between the pylons behind him. The resulting bang was mistaken by some other fishermen nearby for the sonic boom of a fighter plane breaking the sound barrier. When they came running, they found only a blackened patch of grass on the bank, the melted shaft of a landing net containing a couple of fried perch and a tin of coffee beans that on closer inspection turned out to be roasted maggots he had been using as bait. The funeral was memorable only for a rather unfortunate slip in the vicar's address, referring to the deceased as a "livewire." Then, in embarrassment, he had catastrophically tried to make light of it by ad-libbing, 'Well, that would be true of anyone who had forty thousand volts running through them.' The verger was seen grabbing a cassock and biting on it to choke off an overwhelming spasm of laughter.

Tom's resolve was solidifying. *Carpe Diem.* He must seize the moment and could hear his father's mantra echoing in his ears: 'Jump, jump and the net will appear.' Although Tom had found this paternal advice enormously encouraging as a boy, it had become less convincing as visits to hospital for various broken limbs and fractures multiplied during his adolescent years. Increasingly it had dawned on him that the logic was inside out, hauling itself up by its own bootstraps by assuming that simply imagining an outcome was enough to ensure everything would be fine by whatever route first presented itself to get there. Still, this time he had made up his mind. Better to do something insane and hope it worked out rather than to become insane wondering what would have happened.

He thrust out of his mind all those negative thoughts of possible, even seemingly inevitable, rejection. Tom knew these fed on paranoia, in particular a deep fear of how people perceived his body that had become engrained at school through his nickname, *T-Rex*. It was only many years later that Tom had come to realise that this had been largely born out of admiration for his physical strength on the rugby pitch after an abrupt growth spurt. For a couple of years this had meant he towered over the rest of the scrum until everyone else caught him up. In his eyes, he thought the nickname was intended to suggest that, like his dinosaur namesake, he was seen as having immensely thick legs and an over-sized head but a puny torso and tiny arms. Frequent checks in the mirror clearly showed him that this was all in the mind, but he found the haunting anxiety difficult to shake off. No, it wasn't the paranoia he should be so concerned about, but the impetuosity that had led him into more awkward corners than a myriagon[117]. Maybe hedging his bets a little with some form of parachute might be a good idea for once. If he jumped and his father's promised net didn't appear, the mess wouldn't be pretty.

The Great Court in the heart of the British Museum had

once been open to the air but was now sealed shut by a vast transparent cover like a Tupperware container. As usual it was flowing with the currents and eddies of the crowds. Many of these were formed of children on school outings, pooled together by their teachers then led off in streams to marvel at the museum's various treasures such as the amazing silver hoard from Sutton Hoo, the mighty bearded statues of Ashurbanipal the Assyrian and the mummies from ancient Egypt. Cassie thought it must be a nightmare to keep these small rebels under any sort of control – a bit like herding lemmings away from cliff edges[118]. She wondered how many had gone missing in the toilets, the cafés or the endless corridors which unravelled in all directions around each floor of the building. Cassie threaded her way through this swarming hive with purpose. Even if a trail of her footsteps would have seemed random as she sidestepped the numerous small creatures that came buzzing out of every crevice of the exhibition halls, she had taken this route so many times before that she was less likely to lose her way than a pack of bloodhounds on the scent of a skunk.

Reaching the Ancient Greek section, she passed a young man holding the hand of his small boy. He was showing his son the display of white marble statues. As she paused behind yet another large school group, she couldn't help overhearing a snatch of the conversation, or at least the father's side of it as she couldn't quite catch the boy's voice above the hubbub.

'No, they didn't always go around naked. It's just so the sculptor could show what their bodies looked like. You can see they spent a lot of time in the gym. More abs than a boxing kangaroo. And yes, the Greeks did have noses and thingies as well. It's just that those bits are fragile.'

In reply to his son's comment, he went on, 'There's no need to worry about that. Yours will be just fine cos you're young. They get brittle with age.' He listened again. 'Yes, a lot older than me. No, it's nothing like lizards' tails.' The boy whispered and his father, added, 'No, no one is collecting them, at least I don't think they are.'

Cassie wondered if somewhere there might be some vast private collection of marble noses and other more personal extremities. She had heard of people collecting all sorts of weird stuff from umbrella cover sleeves and backscratchers to belly button fluff, so anything seemed possible. She couldn't help laughing and the boy's father, hearing her, looked up and winked.

'Well, you never know when a spare might come in useful!' he said.

'And there was me thinking vasectomies were a modern invention,' Cassie responded[119]. Then, crouching down beside the boy, she said, 'So are you going to see the Elgin Marbles? They're just through that doorway in the next hall.' The boy looked up at his father and nodded shyly.

'Did you know that they are two and half thousand years old?' she asked him. 'That's ten thousand times older than your dad! They're the most precious treasure that survives from Ancient Greece, and they really belong on a huge temple called the Parthenon in Athens, the capital of Greece, which is where they were made to celebrate some brave soldiers fighting off a huge invasion – a bit like Britain did in the Second World War. Anyway, hope you enjoy looking at them. Maybe when you are older you can come and visit Greece and see them back in their proper home.'

Cassie caught the question in his father's eye. 'I'm Greek, so maybe I'm a little biased, but that's where they belong,' she said with a barely concealed trace of defiance.

'I've never thought about it much,' he admitted. 'But what about all the millions of other things in museums around the world? Hasn't everyone got lots of stuff that once belonged to someone else, particularly the Americans with not much history of their own but the money to buy up everyone else's?'

'There are no easy answers, I accept. But there are at least some treasures that are at the heart of the history, culture and even identity of a people. The Parthenon Marbles that were stolen by Lord Elgin are among them. And there certainly aren't many foreign treasures in Greek museums, that's for sure. As a country, we only recovered our independence a couple of centuries ago. Being part of the Ottoman empire was no Turkish delight, I can tell you. Recovering the marbles is unfinished business in restoring our heritage. Have you ever been to Greece?'

'I've enjoyed lounging on deckchairs in the sun on a lot of different islands I can no longer name, drinking cocktails,' he said, clearly trying to wind her up.

'Sex on the Beach?'

'No, not my style at all. I prefer an Old Fashioned or Whisky Sour. But just in case you're assuming I don't know any history, I'm not completely illiterate and sometimes manage to struggle through a real history book, like the Da Vinci Code, and even understand the odd paragraph. So a dim memory is stirring somewhere that we helped you Greeks get your independence back?'

'*Touché* ... But that still doesn't mean you can help yourselves to our treasures. Thanks very much for keeping them safe for two hundred years but now we're grown up and can look after them ourselves.'

'It's all Greek to me but it sounds as if you have a compelling case. Unfortunately, I'm not the one you need to convince, but I wish you well. And thanks, by the way, for taking five years off my age just now. That's made my afternoon.'

As they had been talking, they had shuffled along behind an increasingly desperate teacher and his unruly charges. After an intensive interrogation, the poor guy had finally found and disarmed the sniper who had hit him straight between the eyes with a peashooter. Looking up, they were surrounded by the frieze of white marble that they had been discussing, over eighty metres long in a great ribbon of lace turned to stone, showing in fine detail the chariots, horses and booty of a victory procession. Cassie's concentration was however now elsewhere. She had her mobile phone out and was carefully taking pictures of every section of wall and then of the ceiling. When she was able to magnify these, the images would reveal all she needed to know about the security and surveillance systems in operation, but it was already obvious to her that the network of cameras would be a formidable barrier to overcome and, as she already knew, moving the stones themselves without a forklift truck would be impossible.

Having clicked into professional mode, Cassie had forgotten all about the man with his son but, turning to leave, she saw they were standing by the doorway waiting.

'Meeting someone?' she asked.

He looked a little embarrassed but responded, 'Just hanging around wondering if I could think of an excuse to ask for your number.'

'Is that to sell me double glazing? Sadly, I'm still a student not a house owner. And if you've got a family business with your little helper and his mother as well then that's not my scene.'

'Or mine. I'm an architect and freelance in every other respect as well.' Then, seeing that she thought he must be divorced, and glancing down meaningfully at the boy, he pointed to the ceiling and turned his eyes heavenwards.

'Oh, I'm sorry.' Thrown a little off balance now, Cassie was swiftly reappraising the situation. 'Tell you what, I'll take your number and think about it,' she said to buy a little time to wriggle out of this unexpected corner. 'I'm Cassandra, by the way.'

'Cassandra? We're doomed then! I'm Agamemnon.'

She realized she had badly underestimated his classical knowledge. 'Better watch out at bath time then[120].'

He grinned. 'Okay, it's Daniel really. Hope that's a slightly better omen if you decide to brave the lions' den and get in touch.'

CHAPTER 11 – CRISIS? WHAT CRISIS?

Suppose you were an idiot. And suppose you were a member of Congress ... But I repeat myself – Mark Twain

Balanced on the tiny barstool, Tom was finding it hard to relax. Not only was the seat ridiculously small, but the legs were too long, and the fact that there were three of them rather than four made the stool inherently unstable.

'My battery's so dead it must be terminal,' he complained to Finn as they stared into the pint jars in front of them.

'Cheer up, Tom. It all went well today, and we got there.'

Finbarr felt chipper. The software programme he had swiftly designed worked well and that always filled him with satisfaction. When Tom was moody it was usually a sign he was lovesick, and Finn always took full advantage by teasing him mercilessly.

'Anyway, I think she fancies you.'

'Who? What are you on about?'

'Boudicca ... I know you've always fantasised about older women. It's natural for a guy of your immaturity, and she's just your type. After all, *The Graduate* was always your favourite film.'

Tom waivered for a moment then took the plunge. 'Okay, its true I could do with some frank advice from my best and oldest mate. Its not Boudicca though. It's Cassie.'

'Cassie? Nothing doing there, mate. I'm pretty sure she and Puk are an item.'

Finn only just caught Tom as he finally lost the balancing battle with the bar stool. 'Steady on there, mate. I thought you knew. You look like you've swallowed a wasp.'

'With Puk? Really? Maybe that's why she was so interested in Sappho in the interview.'

'I don't know about that, mate. I wasn't there but we may as well get it all out the way at once. It's actually a threesome with Puk and Ming.'

Tom could be very gullible but now he caught the drift. Finn roared with laughter so hard he knocked his pint over and flooded the bar.

'You idiot, Tom. Of course I knew it was Cassie. I've seen it all before. The awkwardness, the sighs and body language falling in with the beloved like a puppet on a string. Remember that Rebecca last year? I thought you'd joined her synchronized swimming team. '

Tom furiously cuffed him across the shoulder and the bar man came running over ready to break up a fight just as Tom's mobile started to ring. Tom glanced at the number and decided that settling the score with

Finn would need to wait. It was Cavatappi and it didn't last long.

The small café on Bloomsbury Square was a bit shabby but the coffee was excellent, and it was only a very short walk from the British Museum. Cleo was already at a table by the window when Cassie entered. They deliberately ignored one another until Cassie had taken a good look around. There were only a couple of other customers. One was an elderly gentleman with a white cane and an overfed Labrador lying under the table at his feet. The other would have stood out like a walrus in a swimming pool. No policeman, even if undercover, would have the imagination to sport an enormous unkempt beard and a waistcoat that seemed to be lined in purple with exotic birds. In any case, neither of them was within earshot of Cleo's table and Cleo would have been checking that no one had followed Cassie in. As soon as Cassie sat down a waitress with an elaborate mountain of golden hair piled up like candy floss and dressed like a Barbie doll came for her order. She took great care to write it down in large loopy handwriting on a small pink notepad with roses in each corner. Her huge lashes were so heavily tarred with mascara Cassie thought she must have gone swimming in an oil slick. The colour of her eyes was impossible to determine as the lashes batted like the wings of an agitated moth.

'That took a while,' said Cassie when the waitress finally disappeared behind the counter. 'Trying to see through those wipers with all that muck on the windscreen must be a nightmare. Perhaps the guy over there could lend her his guide dog. If Ken tries to kiss her he's going to find it hard to get close enough. But perhaps that's the idea.'

Cleo cut straight to the chase. 'The press release has gone out, so hopefully it will hit the headlines this evening. How did you get on today?'

'Fine. I even got the offer of a date as well. I'll need to check the photos carefully tonight to see if the plan is still feasible, but I think it is.' Seeing that Cleo's face had adopted the expression her dad used to use before magic shows when warning her not to move while he was sawing her in half, Cassie added quickly, 'Don't worry. I told him I was married with quintuplets and didn't give him my contact details. But there's a different problem. I've now got to fly out to Italy tomorrow, so we'll have to bring the schedule forward. I'll need to get on with the next phase of our plan tonight.'

'So what's happening in Oxford that's so urgent?'

'We've been sorting through the priority of the potential projects, which as you can imagine is incredibly difficult to assess. But Tom's old schoolmate Finn is a software and maths genius. He devised a programme in a few hours flat that crunches all the parameters and data, then spits out the answers at the push of a button.'

Cassie paused, reliving the moment of suspense. For a few seconds the whole team had felt as if they were at the point on a bungee jump when the elastic is poised between snapping and yanking the jumper back to safety. Finally, a semaphore of fireflies began to light up on the screen. The three top projects it selected were: first, Atlantis, then the tomb of Alexander the Great, and finally Stonehenge. An animated discussion followed with laughing accusations that Finn had rigged the results, when Tom called for quiet.

'But that's surely not why you need to go to Italy?'

'No, Tom also told us the project funders were insisting that one other project be added as a priority: recovering the body of St Mark. You've seen the massive press coverage of the theft and murder in Venice and the appeals made by the Pope in person for information. The funders pointed out that there was both an ancient and a modern mystery to be solved here. If the team succeeds, we can generate publicity and recognition that will virtually guarantee the long-term future and reputation of the new faculty. It could be an even bigger scoop than the Ninth Legion and would engage a much wider international audience, particularly as a murder was also involved.'

'So why does it have to be you? Didn't you object?' Cleo was clearly furious.

'Tom's fully immersed in Atlantis. Finn's already buried in the tomb of Alexander. I'm the only one who speaks really fluent Italian. Simple…and also, I want to do it. I'd have to be mad to turn it down and all it means is we accelerate our ROT plans, so lets get on with that.'

Cleo opened her mouth then shut it again like a goldfish with indigestion. By the time they finished their coffee and left the café, they were both clear what needed to be done. Cassie was soon back at her flat changing and only just remembered to turn on the early evening news in time. The reporter interviewing Cleo was fresh faced, bubbling with enthusiasm. Her dandelion puffball of frizzy hair matched the mood. Perhaps it was the girl's first assignment, thought Cassie. The cynicism would set in soon enough. After a few wavy shoulder length years, she would probably settle into the BBC pudding basin perm of monotone maturity. The interview was taking place in front of a cinema that was reshowing a series of old adventure films. Tonight's show was *Raiders of the Lost Ark*. It seemed rather lacking in subtlety but was probably the perfect backdrop to get the point about the Elgin Marbles across.

As Cassie took her black catsuit out of the bottom drawer, Cleo was telling the puffball that the Greek Embassy had received an anonymous package and letter. The message, as in all good thrillers, was made up of individual letters in varying fonts and sizes cut from newspapers and reassembled. It said that the accompanying package contained another item taken from the Ashmolean Museum, a gold ring from the time of Alexander. Despite several weeks of investigation since the raid, the museum and the British police had failed to even notice it was missing. This was further evidence of the incompetence that showed Britain was not a place that could be trusted with the safekeeping of priceless artefacts which were central to the cultures of the countries from which they had originally been looted.

When asked to give her own comment on this strange turn of events, Cleo said that the Greek Embassy, of course, totally disapproved of theft. It simply placed those involved on the same level as Lord Elgin. She would, in due course, hand the ring over to the police if requested, but only as and when the police were able to recover all the treasures stolen from the Ashmolean and to provide a full public explanation of how the Ashmolean security had failed to prevent a raid of major treasures in the middle of Oxford. In the meantime, the ring would be retained in the Embassy where there could be greater confidence that it would be secure.

In the background Sir Benedict was turning an ever-darker shade of purple. The reporter now turned to him abruptly. She pushed what Sir Benedict at first thought was a dead raccoon on a stick towards his mouth. Then he realised it was a long feather duster microphone.

'What do you say to that minister?'

'Outrageous! Preposterous! It's theft and the police will issue a warrant, seize the stolen ring and pursue arrests and prosecutions if necessary.'

'I don't think you will do that, Sir Ben,' said Cleo, deliberately shortening his name to the familiar while smiling as sweetly as an angel confronting a child raiding a biscuit tin. 'It would be a violation of diplomatic immunity and of Greek sovereignty which would be ... well, I'm sorry to say it, an act of war. As I'm sure you know, embassies are treated as the foreign nation's sovereign territory and English law simply doesn't apply there.'

Sir Benedict tried to speak but the reporter saw her opening to deliver a further mortal blow at this moment of vulnerability.

'And perhaps you could also explain to our audience how your own family accumulated the private art collection which I understand adorns your country home. Is it true that most of this was acquired by your ancestors during their own colonial escapades?'

The minister could only splutter.

Cassie switched off the television. Time to concentrate on the task in hand. The catsuit was designed to be tight and her exercise regime kept her lean, but despite this the stretchy Lycra still seemed harder to squirm into today[121]. Perhaps she had been partying too much.

The following morning Sir Benedict was still feeling unwell when he arrived at Number 10 for the weekly cabinet meeting. As he filed through the door with his colleagues, he was dying for the customary cup of tea served on arrival. However, he saw the PM look up for a second at the housemaid then shake his head. She was holding the large Wedgewood teapot first baptised with England's favourite beverage on the news of the Duke of Wellington's victory at Waterloo[122]. She stepped back as he passed. Flustered, he put his empty cup down, trying to pretend he had changed his mind and decided against tea this morning. He then squeezed past the others who had already taken their places, until he found the last vacant chair at the far end of the table. Around him, his colleagues all sipped their tea with evident relish. Sir Benedict was aware that they not only knew he was in the doghouse, but likely to be boarded up in it for some time.

It was true that yesterday's interview had gone badly. Things had deteriorated further when the Curator of the Ashmolean confirmed later that evening that, on further investigation, it seemed that a gold ring had indeed also been stolen in the raid. It was overlooked because it was taken from a backroom display in one of the minor galleries and because, unlike the other stolen artefacts, a convincing replica had been put in its place.

However, it still seemed to Sir Benedict that the PM was slightly exaggerating the significance of the whole affair until the Foreign Minister elbowed him in the ribs and said, with a laugh so hollow it seemed to cave in on itself, 'Bet the news this morning knocked the wind out of your sails, eh, Ben? Don't worry, old chap. If you need a job, we can always find you a liaison officer posting in Transnistria.'

'Where's that?'

'I'm not entirely sure but I think it's a small breakaway part of Moldova that's still under Russian military occupation, so strategically your role will be of vital importance.'

The Foreign Minister furtively took a silver hip flask from his jacket pocket. Balancing his teacup on his knees below the level of the table out of sight he added a generous glug of something that was much darker and clearly much stronger than tea. 'Sorry you don't have a cup, Ben, or this would help console you.'

The PM was clearly in a very bad mood. His brows were dark storm clouds hanging so low that they seemed to be sinking into his darkened eye sockets. The famous tic that sent an involuntary spasm across one side of his face when angry was twitching noticeably as he called for order. The overall impression was of a large winking owl, but no one was laughing.

'We had better leave the review of the minutes of the last meeting until the end and go straight to item one – The Elgin Crisis. I appreciate not many of you will have had a chance to see the BBC news update only half an hour ago so I think we should all watch it before we discuss what's to be done.'

Everyone turned to watch the screen as the update was replayed. The last of the chimes of Big Ben introducing the morning broadcast faded away and the screen immediately cut to the unmistakable façade of the British Museum. Outside the railings a small crowd were brandishing the blue and white flags of Scotland ... no, Greece, not Scotland. Sir Benedict hadn't noticed before how similar they were. He knew the Scottish Saltire was very ancient and wondered whether the Greeks had just seen a Scotsman using a flag as a towel while sunbathing on holiday on some Greek island and added a few extra stripes.

In the newsroom, the reporter glanced down at the autocue and began to speak. Behind her, the headline read, *Marble Mayhem*.

'Extraordinary developments at the British Museum this morning. When the museum opened, the staff discovered that the Elgin Marbles have been defaced overnight. It seems that someone abseiled down through a skylight. The Museum Director claims that the museum's security is state of the art and that the marbles are protected by a grid of laser sensors and security cameras. The footage has yet to be fully reviewed but Scotland Yard are in no doubt that this was the work of a highly skilled team. While it would be premature to make any link with the Ashmolean raid, separating the two would seem to be stretching coincidence.

So far it appears nothing has been taken from the British Museum, but this latest incident comes hot on the heels of the admission – made only yesterday by the Ashmolean – that it had failed to even notice the loss of a gold ring stolen in the raid of its treasures. Listeners will recall that this was only brought to light when the ring was anonymously delivered to the Greek Embassy's cultural attaché, Cleo Popillopolis.

We have already spoken again to her this morning, and she has expressed the outrage of the

Greek government at Britain's latest failure to protect what she describes as her nation's "stolen heritage." You will see that, already, a crowd of Greek demonstrators are gathering here. Their numbers can be expected to increase significantly before their planned march to Number 10 Downing Street where they aim to demand the immediate return of the Elgin Marbles. So far, there is no comment from the Prime Minister, Number 10 or the Minister of Culture.'

The screen now displayed a series of images of the Elgin Marbles. Moustaches, gaping smiles with vampire fangs and huge outsized ears decorated almost every white marble face in a kaleidoscope of primary colours. The chariots had been given exhausts, number plates, wing mirrors and in one case L plates. Urns were turned into replicas of cups for various football and other sporting trophies. A variety of underwear from boxer shorts to briefs and G strings now protected the modesty of the nude effigies. Sir Benedict ruthlessly suppressed a momentary admiration for the skill and imagination of the artist.

'We have been exposed to international mockery by this debacle,' the PM was saying. 'Serious pressure is now mounting to consider returning the marbles. Previously we have been able to rely on the fact that so many other countries have foreign treasures in their museums, especially the Yanks, but the difference is they take good care of them. But, of course, just giving up the marbles would be unthinkable and where would it end? We have thousands of treasures from other countries.'

'Maybe we could deflect the publicity, Prime Minister.

'What do you mean, Ben?'

'I could call in some favours from some of our political contacts abroad. That would help diffuse things.'

'I think it's a bit late for that, Ben. This nightmare has all happened on your watch. I suggest you come and see me after this meeting.'

Everyone knew what that meant. Sir Benedict looked round the table for support. Three quarters of them had been at school with him at Eton and then on to university at Oxford. The rest were only in the cabinet to satisfy the new-fangled diversity policy. Sir Benedict really couldn't understand what that was all about since the cabinet came from all corners of the Home Counties and their parents managed all sorts of different businesses from arms manufacturers to publishers. The Labour lot all lived in Islington and claimed tenuous connections to mining families, although pits were few and far between in North London. Spending the day underground, digging coal in the dark, didn't seem like good training for government anyway.

Hugo Astley, Minister of Defence, was studiously avoiding catching his eye. They had read Caesar's Gallic Wars and recited Latin verbs together in the last year of primary. Not much sign of *amo, amas, amat* now – or indeed any love at all. He had gorged on Eton mess[123] with the Home Secretary, Clive Cholmondeley; charged over fences on horseback alongside the Chancellor of the Exchequer, Jeremy Penhaligon, and played fives with Lancelot Twistlebottom, Leader of the House. After debates at the Oxford Union, they had all adjourned for port and cigars at the Bullingdon

Club in customary blue tie before sticking to tradition by wrecking the town once they were completely plastered[124].

On one memorable night, Sir Benedict recalled a reckless climb onto the dome of the Radcliffe Camera for a dare. He and Jeremy had lashed themselves to the flagpole and raised the skull and crossbones before being rescued by the fire brigade. The very same Jeremy, who as a prefect he had spared from a caning when his shoes hadn't been shined enough to show the reflection of the large wart on his chin in them, who had been best man at his first four weddings and was godfather to fifteen of his legitimate children. Bitterness seeped into Sir Benedict's mind, laced with the distant memory of the lines he had last delivered to great acclaim as Caesar in the school play. *Et tu ... Jeremy.*

The ladies, or the "Tokens" as they were called, were no better. He had dated Isla, the haughty heiress to the wealthy Bute family. She was now Minister for Equality, but he wasn't surprised to see that she was clearly taking some pleasure in his discomfort. Fair enough, as he had dumped her rather publicly at the Christchurch ball in favour of Pixie Batsford, now Minister of Housing. Quite what Pixie knew about housing, Sir Benedict wasn't clear. The stables at Batsford Towers were significantly larger than most housing estates, but presumably she had occasionally visited the tenant crofts on her father's Scottish estates. Their fling had been ardent and, he believed, a fond memory for both of them – particularly, her enthusiastic use of the crop while still in their riding gear in the bandstand at the end of the lake. As he pointed out to her afterwards, had it been the Grand

National she would have been disqualified. But now when he turned to her, she looked embarrassed and gave him an apologetic shrug with an affectionate but pitying half-smile. She had her career to think of, but it did seem now that, not only was this very small world shrinking to nothing, but that suddenly he was as much a stranger to its charmed circle as an alien from the planet Zog.

For one nano-sliver of a second, Sir Benedict felt years of repressed emotion welling up inside him and he thought he was going to allow the very first tear of his life to escape. Taking a sharp intake of breath, he somehow sucked the shameful drop back from the brink. Just in time, he reminded himself that he was made of tougher stuff. He hadn't scored the winning try in the house rugby sevens or won a blue for tiddlywinks for nothing. He might be down, but he wasn't out. Nelson had triumphed at Trafalgar with only one arm, even if he had been killed in the process. Best to forget how, in that extreme moment, his hero had lost it altogether and asked someone called Hardy for a kiss[125]. Sir Benedict smoothed his moustache and was reassured to feel that underneath it his upper lip was as ramrod stiff as a grenadier saluting the Queen. Any glint of moisture had evaporated from his eyes and they were once more as hard as flint. Under his breath, to calm himself, he quietly whispered the citation for the VC his Great Uncle Barnaby had won in the Zulu wars.

A lone voice piped up breaking the uncomfortable silence. "Surely, Prime Minister, it's hardly the fault of the Minister for Culture that someone is waging a campaign to put pressure on us and that the Greeks are taking advantage."

It was Bob Smith, Minister for Work and Pensions, a pariah post as far as the rest of the cabinet were concerned as the whole point of a silver spoon was to keep as far away from work as possible. You really knew that you had been left marooned on a desert island when your only support came from a state schoolboy who did Media Studies at Keele, thought Sir Benedict.

Reports of a ghost or spirit had continued to surface at different places along the south coast of Turkey, then at Troy and Istanbul and finally in Thessaloniki. The figure had found hospitals and ambulance networks the easiest and lowest profile way of moving around. This was difficult when getting to and from Afghanistan, but returning westwards became progressively easier. A travelling theatre company provided an alternative cover for a few hundred miles. One or two passengers were curious when an ambulance arrived at the steps of a plane sitting on the apron at Thessaloniki airport and a wheelchair containing a figure wrapped in shawls came on board. Bandages obscured most of the patient's face. Probably the poor guy had been involved in a fire and had suffered serious burns. The plane was bound for Heathrow.

CHAPTER 12 – THE POWER OF PERSUASION

I am not in love, but I'm open to persuasion – Joan Armatrading

On that very same morning, Cassie was boarding her flight from Heathrow to Venice and Panettone was also boarding his in the opposite direction. The early publicity of her nocturnal antics had been pleasingly dramatic and would certainly send the government into a tailspin. She assumed that they would soon find out that the paint she had used could be wiped away easily without causing any lasting harm, but it was helpful that this hadn't been apparent when the initial coverage was broadcast. She would check again when she reached Venice, but the next step in their plan was down to Cleo. Cassie's trip to Italy meant that it wasn't something she could take part in. Anyway, she thought it was about time Cleo got her own hands dirty as well.

As they taxied down the runway, Cassie took out

the post she had scooped up from the doormat as she left her flat for the airport. There were three envelopes of varying sizes. She ripped open the smallest. The card simply had a tasteful picture of a heart. The quote inside was from the Odyssey and was deeply romantic. It was one she knew well about the lost hero making love to his wife, Penelope, for the first time after returning from his twenty-year absence. It included the lines that most moved her, about the Goddess Athena holding back the horses that would bring the chariot of the sun over the horizon at dawn so that the newly reunited couple could prolong their lovemaking. Of course, dawn was always "rosy-fingered" in Homer and the sea was always "wine-dark," although some scholars had suggested this was because the poet was colour blind or had just drunk too much.

As if slipping on a bar of soap in the shower, the card caught her off-balance, both through the emotion stirred by the quote and the realisation that it was Valentine's Day. Some slips of paper had fallen out of the envelope as she opened it. She saw these were train tickets from London to Newcastle in only ten days' time, and a booking for a Dark Sky Event at the Kielder Observatory in Northumberland. In a bit of a daze, she now understood why the second envelope was pink. Sure enough there was another Valentine inside, this time with a brightly-coloured hummingbird hovering outside a large beehive. In the entrance to the hive was a bee with an ecstatic smile on its face. The message inside read, "Bee my Bird and let's make Honey!" It was so twee she either had to laugh or be sick. There were some tickets in this one as well, a flight to Paris with a note written on it saying, "Meet me under the Eiffel

Tower at sunset (6pm). I will be wearing a red rose." Unlike the first card, there was no indication that the sender knew her area of academic interest, but that didn't take her very much further. The only person she knew who was passionate about astronomy was Puk and Paris would be anyone's idea of a romantic rendezvous.

The largest card was emblazoned with a chubby cupid of padded velvet, precariously balanced on one toe while firing an arrow. When opened, it started to play an old Wings tune *Silly Love Songs* and she closed it swiftly as other passengers began to look around. It was all very bling, but somehow also endearing and contained a short, typed poem and then a message in a swirling parody of medieval script. "You are holding my heart prisoner as Charles, Duke of Orleans, was held prisoner when he wrote this poem. It is the very first Valentine, written from the Tower of London in 1415 after he was captured at the Battle of Agincourt. Like him, I want to be set free to meet with you, my love." The capital letters were all illuminated in medieval fashion with tiny pictures in bright colours against a background of gold. Some of them had chat bubbles. One showed a frog kissing a handsome young prince, turning him into another frog. The card was accompanied by a small box of *Bacci*, the famous chocolate kisses made in Perugia which had a tag cartoon showing a hunk who looked remarkably like George Clooney whispering seductively in a woman's ear "Chocolate really isn't fattening," as a result of which, inside the card, there was another picture showing her kissing him passionately.

There were also tickets for a special tour to swim

with the seals and hug a gorilla at London Zoo. Cassie loved animals and the assurance about chocolate was encouraging, but she was bemused. She had received plenty of Valentines before but had always been able to work out who they were from. She was mystified by all three of these. The handwriting on each card was markedly different – a bold, swirling script, block capitals and an awkward spidery trail she could barely read. None of them prompted any recognition, although she assumed one or more might be disguised. Well, finding answers would have to wait and might reveal themselves if the admirers were really serious. She first had deeper secrets to decipher.

Rome airport security seemed to be more attentive than normal. Perhaps some heightened alert, thought Panettone as he put his hand luggage on the conveyor to be scanned. A couple of minutes later, he was waved to one side by a bald man wearing sunglasses who gave every impression of enjoying being officious.

'What's the container?'

Panettone had forgotten all about it in the rush and it struck him this wasn't going to be easy to explain to someone who gave no sign of sympathy.

'It's an ice-bucket.'

'And the grey powder inside it?'

'It's my mother.'

'Your mother? She doesn't look very well.'

'No, she passed away recently, and her ashes were delivered to me just as I was leaving for my flight.'

The security guard was looking increasingly sceptical and called over his colleague. 'Hey, Andrea, can you just run the Geiger counter over this. I'm concerned it may be radioactive.'

Panettone unwisely let his irritation show as the checks drew a blank. 'She was pretty lively before she passed away, but I don't think activity of any sort, particularly nuclear fusion, is very likely now.'

'And why an ice bucket?'

'She always liked a bit, I mean a lot, of bubbly and so it seemed fitting.'

'Well, I like riding motorbikes, but I don't expect to be cremated in an oil can. Why didn't you leave her behind?'

'I always promised her I would take her travelling with me, but there was never time.'

The security guy noticed that the small plaque on the ice bucket was in another language he didn't recognise as well as Italian. Although Panettone curtly explained that it was Greek because his mother's namesake was an ancient Greek queen this only seemed to darken his suspicions.

'What age did she live to.'

'No one knows but probably about thirty-three.'

'Thirty-three? Well she couldn't have been your mother then, 'cos you're much older than that.' The guard was triumphant. He could hardly stop himself rubbing his hands.

'Oh, you mean my mother, not the queen she was named after? She was a hundred and three ... and before you say that seems too old, she was really my grandmother. If there is a regulation you are relying on to stop either of us catching our plane, I would be grateful if you could show it to me. '

Panettone waited as the guard desperately leafed through his manual.

'I'll let you go but keep the lid on her. If she

escapes, she will be considered as a separate passenger. I assume she no longer has a passport so wouldn't then be able to get through immigration, but if she does have one I would have to advise the airline to issue another boarding pass and charge you for another ticket. And I'm confiscating that lighter. It's classified in Sub paragraph 9, Section 11 of the 2001 Amendment to the Small but Fiery Objects Act as an incendiary device that could be used by an arsonist.'

Panettone was tempted to ask if the same regulation included an old person's reading magnifier or two sticks that could possibly be rubbed together to create a fire, but thought better of it.

'Come in.'

Sir Benedict pushed open the door of the Prime Minister's study. They had never liked each other since Sir Benedict had lost his balance and accidentally clouted the PM with his mallet when playing polo, leaving the PM with a permanent sickle shaped scar on his forehead which made him look as if he had double eyebrows on that side. The study was panelled in darkened oak and a couple of chairs were positioned round the large marble fireplace with the nodding dog on it that was a less than subtle hint to all comers to toe the line. Behind the chairs, under the window, lurked the PM's desk. This was the cockpit from which, apparently in his own eyes, the PM surveyed the skies above the nation and fought valiantly on its behalf against the forces that constantly threatened to overwhelm it, like a spitfire ace in the Battle of Britain. The desk was neatly piled with the day's red boxes – "done" on the right and "to do" on the left. The silver ink pen the PM always used for matters of state had its cover firmly clipped back on and it lay exactly parallel to the large crystal ink well and the ruler the PM used to underline his most important comments and instructions. This always turned out, in fact, to be nearly everything he wrote, apart from his own signature. He underlined this twice to foreign heads of state, three times to ministers and four times to minions, in other words everyone else. As a result, he was left with little to add further emphasis and so made extensive use of bold, asterisks and exclamation marks when something was truly urgent.

The PM was ready for him but didn't look up from his papers for a couple of minutes, leaving Sir Benedict standing. The delay was deliberate, but the PM was just reading over the final paragraph of a note to the Heath Secretary.

"Alarmed to see NHS waiting lists are getting **longer** and numbers are rising like **a hot air balloon!** Need to **get a grip** **and puncture that urgently. Let's look at how we **count** them. The Treasury has **halved inflation** by taking mortgages out of the rate. Unemployment has been cut by putting them all into sickness benefit. It's easily done. The Police have the right idea. They just **don't record** reported crimes and **exclude theft**, violence and everything that's increasing. That's pretty much everything except traffic offences which **bring in cash** while saving costs by cutting police on the beat. Taking all **weekends and bank holidays** out of NHS waiting lists for example would reduce them by **thirty percent** ☺ and we could announce a major success! If we also took out **all the birthdays** of NHS staff, we could claim to have eliminated waiting lists **altogether !!!*****☺"

Apparently satisfied, he signed it, then rose from the desk, sat down in front of the fireplace and snorted. 'Well, where's your letter of resignation, Ben? I have other things to get on with. Don't stand there like a chump, man. Sit down, but only while you hand it over as there's not much else to say.'

'Have you seen the news, Prime Minister?' he asked. It was clear that the PM had, but wasn't admitting it. 'You've seen that my contacts have turned it all around? The whole debate has been shifted away from us. My friend in the Italian Parliament has put forward a motion that Italy asks the French to return the most dismal painting in the world to Florence even though it's responsible for giving many people depression. It may be the greatest work of Leonardo but, to most of us, the *Moaner Lisa* seems to be suffering from indigestion rather than smiling. Quite why the Italians want it back beats me, but there it is. The anonymous leak to the German papers has worked a treat as Russia now thinks the Germans are hiding the seven lost Fabergé eggs made for the Romanovs that went missing in the Russian Revolution[126]. France is up in arms about that one as well since Fabergé was a French jeweller. Best of all are the rival demands made by our friends in both Turkey and Greece for the return of the gold artefacts Schliemann dug up at Troy, the Germans then looted from Athens at the start of the war and the Russians in turn looted from Berlin. Doesn't sit well, of course, with the Greek claim for the Elgin Marbles. The press spotlight has, in any event, got bored of that and moved on to these other new spats.'

'All good work, Ben. But just damage limitation and it comes too late. I need a head on the block to appease the mob and I'm afraid yours is the obvious one to sacrifice. Think of it as a release. You will have more time to hunt and very probably to get through a few more marriages and sire a lot more children. No point in pleading, Ben. I've made up my mind and as you know I never change it.'

Sir Benedict had no intention whatsoever of pleading. He hadn't spent time at the embassy in Moscow in the early stages of his career without learning a bit about *kompromat* and now was the time to use it. As for the PM's pride in never changing his mind, that was certainly a lie. U-turns were the PM's stock in trade, and everyone knew that, at home, the PM's wife gave their pet poodle considerably more respect. That was probably why the PM felt it essential to spend as much time in his study as possible and rebuild his own self esteem through inflexibility whenever he could.

'Er, Prime Minister, aren't we forgetting something?'

'What Ben?' The PM looked up sharply. 'You aren't still trying to blackmail me with that unfortunate moment when you caught me smoking weed behind the school bike sheds are you? The journalists all know that everyone did that now. In fact, if you didn't they'd label you as odd or not in touch with the electorate. Okay, if not that, then you mean when you found me consoling my PA? That was a complete misunderstanding on your part. He was just coming round after fainting in the heat and had taken most of his clothes off to cool down.'

'No, none of those, Prime Minister. I mean last week. The incident with your lunch.'

The prime minister paled. 'No, Ben, you wouldn't.

I would be outed as a national security risk as well as laughed out of office.'

By luck, Sir Benedict had been briefing the Prime Minister when he had received the code red alert call. This was to tell the PM that Russian nukes had been launched and that he needed to open the Nuclear Briefcase and insert the code to authorise a counter strike from Trident. The PM struggled to find the wretched case until he remembered he had left it under his coat by the desk. When he opened it, to his horror, his wife had stuffed it full of cucumber sandwiches wrapped in silver foil for his lunch and rammed a pork pie against the code panel itself. After a struggle, the PM extracted all these obstructions but then couldn't remember the code. As the levels of hysteria increased, Sir Benedict said in desperation and because both their minds had gone blank, 'Surely not 1066?'

But that indeed had been the answer. The date of the Battle of Hastings. The only date in history most people could remember and the most popular code in Britain apart from personal birthdays. The PM had tried to make it easy for himself as it was also the pin code for his bank account and the number for the many thousands of other codes he now seemed to need in life including cabinet papers, adult TV content and the weekly online supermarket delivery. He was soaked in sweat as he punched it into the panel.

They were both about to scramble for the Downing Street bunker when the phone rang. The Director of MI5 was calling to say that it was a dummy run, but the result was very concerning. Putting it as diplomatically as he could, if Britain was in a hundred metre race for survival, the PM would have ensured that it was still in the starting bocks as the whole island was blown to bits. The true depth of the Director's fury became apparent when the conversation ended. He had clearly turned to a subordinate, forgetting he hadn't yet terminated the call ... or perhaps it was deliberate to get the message through ... and they heard him say, 'We're doomed with that half-wit at the helm if anything really happens. He's the greatest security risk since Burgess and Maclean but he hasn't even got the brains to ask the Soviets to pay him for it.'[127]

Sir Benedict could see he now had the PM by the short and curlies. 'Well, of course not, Prime Minister. And I understand you could never change your mind about replacing me as Minister of Culture. But you could appoint me as Minister of Transport instead.'

'That's impossible, Ben. You know you would be a total disaster. You've already held virtually every cabinet post through repeated blackmail and screwed up every one of them. Transport is in a total mess, and you would turn it into Armageddon. Logjam on the Circle Line, billions of public money wasted on pie in the sky engineering projects like bridges across the Irish Sea or empty new motorways going from your holiday home in Norfolk to Cheltenham Racecourse just for the Gold Cup. I can picture the nightmare.'

'I'm keen on Transport because that's one I haven't had a go at yet to compete my collection. But I could postpone it and settle for another go as Minister of Justice first, if you prefer. I feel my departure last time was premature. I was only just getting into my stride with prison reform.'

'Your stride? There were riots in every prison when you reduced their rations by half, removed all the

TV's and suggested a new deal with Australia to send those with the longest sentences to Botany Bay[128] ... all right, Justice then. Ernest Pembury is as pliable as a play dough, or is it "doh"? It won't be so hard to get him to resign on grounds of ill health if I promise him a peerage in the New Year's Honours List. Perhaps better still I could make him Minister of Culture and call it a re-shuffle.'

'Thank you, Prime Minister. Just one small correction. It was Bondi Beach not Botany Bay and they were to be sent to learn surfing as part of a rehabilitation pilot scheme the Probation Service were insisting on trying out. I was forced to go along with it, hoping that the sharks would get a few of them, but I seem to remember you were very keen on it until the cost came out in the press.'

CHAPTER 13 - EVERY DOG HAS HIS DAY

Handle every situation like a dog. If you can't eat it or play with it, just pee on it and walk away. – Anon.

I have now reached the point where the ciabatta became a bagel. Since seeing Doctor Bacon I have been joining dots like mad, but after his warnings, it's worrying that marbles keep rolling around in the story and even I am confused if they were being lost or found. This seems to depend on whether you are British or Greek but perhaps the picture will become clearer in time. I just have to hope that all the looping lines of narrative don't mean I'm still at risk of what Dr Bacon called "going round the twist."

I accept now that I do need further therapy and I have already booked another appointment with Dr Bacon. But first I should join up some more dots so he can see what I am drawing. So I have been building up my courage to tell you about the traumatic moment I am now going to try and describe. It's when

I came closest to death and my hand is quivering like a grasshopper's hind legs as I pick up my pen again. At that stage I had already been enrolled on the Interpol witness protection programme and had been moved from Italy to London for my own safety, but had not yet been interviewed by Inspector Panettone...

My minder at the time was always urging me to stay inside at the safehouse, but sometimes I just had to escape for some fresh air. Otherwise my head would feel like it was a hive of increasingly angry bees on the verge of swarming.

It was a fine morning so I bought the ciabatta from a small Italian delicatessen run by an elderly couple from Puglia and took it to the park. Sitting on a bench I was just raising it to my mouth when it was almost snatched from my grasp. I managed to hold onto it and was about to make the sign of the horns to ward off the invisible powers of darkness at work when I saw the neat hole that had appeared in the middle of my lunch. At least it started in the very centre of the top crust, but I could see it punched right through the ciabatta at an acute diagonal angle emerging cleanly through the filling at the side. I immediately hurled myself to the ground badly bruising my ribs. The sniper must have been on the roof or one of the upper floors of one of the large Victorian terraces across the road, but I couldn't see anything and he was obviously using a silencer as I hadn't heard the crack of the shot[129].

Just as I was wondering what to do and measuring the distance to the entrance of the public toilet block a few yards away some feet flapping like an overwound toy duck on steroids hurtled around the corner of the path cutting across my line of vision. Alongside the gyrating spindles attached to the feet came another ugly pair of legs but these were even thinner and hairier. The shaggy head of a large Irish wolf hound dropped in front of my eyes and accomplished what the bullet had failed to do by ripping the newly formed bagel out of my hand and swallowing it in one gulp. The blast of hot rancid breath was bad enough as I found out how unpleasant mouth to mouth resuscitation can be for the victim. Worse still I was then waterboarded as the hound slobbered my face with its enormous floppy pink tongue almost drowning me in doggy saliva.

Raising my head just enough to look up beyond knee height I saw that it's owner was doubled up, although seeing my look he reached out and yanked on the monster's collar. Then glancing at his watch and shaking his head bitterly in obvious pain he clutched at his groin saying, 'I think I've strained it just as I was smashing my PB.' It wasn't an abbreviation I had heard before. It must mean pelvic bone although the pain seemed to be lower down around the crotch. The only other thing I could think of in that region didn't usually have a bone in it.

Recovering slightly the guy now realised he should possibly be doing something to help me. 'What is it? If it's an epileptic fit where's the EpiPen and I'll inject you, or is it a heart attack?

He stooped with the obvious intention of trying to lift me to my feet. That would have been fatal for me at least. The crosshairs were surely waiting, poised to slice me into quarters. Fortunately, at just the right moment a coincidence came along. The sniper must have seen me lift my head and was impatient to get the job done. The bobble hat that was part of today's attempt to disguise myself, was plucked off my head by another silent bullet. As the bobble, ripped free, arced over us in slow motion, the hound raced after it nearly catapulting the runner into orbit as the lead yanked tight.

By this stage I had reached the end of my tether as well and dived for the toilet door. In the temporary security of this shelter I brushed myself down and slipped quickly inside hoping for a rear window. There was nothing obvious, but the cubicle was occupied. I put my hands on top of the panel and jumped up to check the back wall for some means of exit. This resulted in an abrupt and high pitched squawk of outrage from inside but nothing more. Fortunately I was in my Angela rather than Angelo persona. The quick peek had confirmed the place was a windowless death-trap. I took comfort from the fact that, as it was the Ladies, no bloke would actually come in to finish me off. There were some lines of decency even hoodlums generally don't cross, or so I tried to convince myself.

Staring around wildly I saw that whoever was in the cubicle must have left her hat on a peg by the sink while washing her hands or adjusting her lipstick. It was a wide brimmed floppy affair that, although sadly not bullet proof, would at least hide my face. My satchel was still firmly attached to my back and I slung this into the corner after changing my shoes for some flatter ones to reduce my height. Then I gave thanks that I had thought to wear my reversible coat out of caution.

To wait would just prolong the agony so, trying to be bold as polished brass, I turned down the passage and stepped out of the doorway, then paused deliberately as if I had forgotten something. One second, two seconds, three seconds passed as slowly as the posters on the wall of the Underground if you walk back up the down escalator. I gained some perverse calm from the thought that if the shot came the marksman would have plenty of time to make it a clean one, but the bluff seemed to be working. Nothing happened except that an intense feeling of pressure building up inside me became uncontrollable because I genuinely had forgotten something important. That was to use the toilet while I was in it, and now it was too late.

Turning down the path my steps were as measured as a grenadier guard on crutches and I had nearly reached the line of trees when the scream came. I checked but it wasn't mine. Sadly the lady in the cubicle had come rushing after me clutching my satchel. She must have thought I had left it by mistake. Whether she was kindly trying to return it or use it to make a report to the police about a Peeping Tomasina, I still have no idea.

My heart used to be as warm and soft as a soufflé but over time with all the hardships I've suffered it's become a bit more like a baked Alaska; slightly crusty on the outside, fluffy underneath but *semifreddo* - partly frozen - deep in the centre. But now my self control simply crumbled. Tears were streaming down my cheeks, blinding me with a murky mixture of mascara and foundation powder. After all, I had nearly died back there. Even when small I had always found the thought of my own funeral deeply moving, particularly the part where all my relatives stand around the grave, regretting that they were not nicer to me when they had the chance.

Lying on damp grass in dense undergrowth for hours is something only twitchers and wildlife photographers' relish. Cleo wasn't either of those. She couldn't tell an ostrich and a robin apart. She had a vague recollection that one had a red breast and couldn't fly but could run like hell, but that was about all. Under her breath she murmured some expletives in Greek that would have made her grandmother reach for the smelling salts. She cursed Cassie for taking the easy jobs, even though the thought of climbing up buildings and abseiling terrified her. It had been bad enough shimmying over the wall of Buckingham Palace into the garden, and even so she had laddered her stockings.

Cassie wouldn't have any sympathy of course. She would have told Cleo to wear something sensible, but Cleo was already wearing her oldest Burberry coat over a Prada dress she had bought almost a year ago and had designated for Oxfam or a skip. As for the stockings, her wardrobe didn't contain any trousers apart from her silk pyjamas, and she wasn't going to risk spoiling those. She grudgingly acknowledged that she should be grateful that before Cassie left she had been able to hack into the Palace's security system and identify a small weak point in the perimeter wall which the cameras and alarms didn't cover.

The mission was critical. Despite the intense pressure on the Prime Minister following the Ashmolean and British Museum debacles, the Government had somehow managed to deflect the press. Journalists were only blessed with the concentration span of gnats and had already largely forgotten the Elgin Marbles in favour of the infighting now going on between a whole series of other countries about their own treasures. The press's excuse was always that they were only reflecting the mercurial interests of the public, but Cleo was never sure who in this endless whirligig was really following who.

What was clear to her was that ROT needed to seize back control of the narrative urgently and bring matters finally to a head.

Still no sound. What had happened? The daily constitutional must have been delayed.

But, just as Cleo was about to give up, a dog came trotting down the gravel path. It was clearly quite elderly, but its pace picked up when it sniffed the air and detected the steak Cleo had hidden under an adjacent bush. In no time, she could see it had clearly found this delicious repast and was wolfing it down. Cleo was relieved. She was no dog lover and had no idea what bait to put out so had just followed her own preferences. Chateaubriand steak of the finest grade. She had even prepared a Bearnaise peppercorn sauce and placed it in a small dish on the side. She had been concerned that a royal dog might be so spoilt that it would turn up its nose at anything less.

The sedative was fast working as promised and she watched as the beast staggered, keeled over and then lay motionless with its legs in the air. Swiftly she ran over and rolled the dog into the sack she had brought along, retrieving the dish so there was nothing for forensics. She was disgusted to see that, while it had gobbled down the steak, the sauce had been rejected.

Corgis are not that big, but they are very muscular and heavy as Cleo now discovered. It was a real struggle to get the unresisting lump to the base of the wall even though this was only a few yards away.

Fortunately, Demetrios, who had been keeping watch on the other side, now leapt down beside her and together they were able to heave the bag over the wall. In the distance, but getting nearer, Cleo could hear a very aristocratic female voice 'Bisto ... Aaaah! Bisto ... and Oxo[130], come here my dear little ...'

The voice trailed away so Cleo didn't hear the last word very clearly, but it sounded remarkably like, 'cube.' Perhaps she had misheard, but then people said all sorts of daft things to their dogs. Presumably, the Queen was calling for Oxo at that moment and would refer to her little 'granule' when calling Bisto. That would certainly be more convenient than the dogs kennel name, which Cleo assumed could only be Bisto in full, "Browns, Seasons and Thickens in One[131]."

The clear patrician tones came again. 'Where are you, my little darling? Come to Mummy and put the seasoning back into my day.'

Well, that could be either of them. Cleo felt almost embarrassed on Her Majesty's behalf, as if she was infringing her privacy – as indeed she was. But somehow, listening in on these endearments seemed worse to her than trespassing on the Queen's property and kidnapping her dog. She was relieved when a car pulled up by the kerb right on time and Helena jumped out. She still didn't look as if many men would be fighting over her, but she showed extraordinary agility for someone of her age. Together, the three of them bundled the sack into the boot and were off in a trice.

On his flight to Heathrow, Panettone had some rare time to think. Although he knew nothing about Cassie, the Inspector had given authorisation for her to have access to the scene of the crime. He had received a formal request from the Head of the new faculty at Oxford that had recently uncovered the truth about the Ninth Legion. There seemed to be no harm in giving its team a chance to bring an archaeological eye to bear on the investigation, particularly as currently there were no real leads. He believed in keeping an open mind and trusting the instinct that had already led him to think there might be a link to the Ashmolean raid, another crime with an archaeological aspect and conveniently in Oxford where the new faculty was based.

Venice was the best skate park Cassie had ever been to. There were steps, bridges and water hazards everywhere to test her skills as she wove in and out of the shifting crowds along the side of the canals. When she found a bit of space in a small piazza, she managed a quick back flip and triple twist. A few passers-by applauded, and a couple gave her some coins thinking she was a street artist.

Arriving at San Marco she was brought to an abrupt halt by a procession of priests in full vestments. In their midst was a large platform covered in embossed silver on which a statue of a young man shot full of gold arrows swayed from one side to the other. He looked sad but remarkably calm. In his chest was a glass door with what looked like a purplish shrivelled plum inside. Cassie had never encountered anything like this. She was surrounded by a crowd of American tourists all jostling for a view and trying to hear their tour guide. One was wearing a T-shirt with the slogan, "When you're born, you get a ticket to a freak show. When you're born in America, you get a front row seat." None of his party seemed to mind, but the cacophony of voices all around Cassie were enjoying the parade.

'Wow, who is that guy? He musta fallen out real bad with some gang.'

'Robin Hood and his Merry Men[132]?'

'They were from France, not Italy.'

'You're thinking of Asterix the Gaul. The little dude. He didn't use arrows. He had a kinda magic potion.'

'You're both wrong and Asterix wasn't real.'

'Sure? I read lots of books with pictures of him when I was small.'

Standing next to her was a guy wearing a baseball cap turned backwards and a camera clicking faster than a tap dancer. The zoom lens was so long it really didn't need to be adjusted because the front element would already be touching whatever could be seen in the viewfinder. Fortunately, his girlfriend was standing a couple of metres in front of him to hold it steady and ensure the guy didn't just overbalance. Despite being American, he had read his guidebook and was able to tell Cassie that the statue was St Sebastian[133], and the prune was his heart.

As the procession progressed through the great doors of the Cathedral, Cassie heard a rhythmic pitter-patter. Underneath the sheet that covered the platform were the numerous caterpillar feet of hidden bearers, bent double under their load, like in those cartoons where the car has no floor and the occupants just run around holding up the chassis.

Cassie joined the end of the procession and followed it into the soaring cavern of the church until a policeman angrily told her to cover her shoulders and take her skates off. When she showed him the pass issued to her with its impressive stamp and Panettone's flamboyant signature he was taken aback. After careful scrutiny, he doubtfully waved her through and pointed out the altar which had formerly been St Mark's resting place. Cassie examined the broken stonework that revealed the empty chamber inside, as Panettone had done. Although not herself an archaeologist she had worked with many experts in the field and helped with excavations. She was puzzled that there were no obvious marks on the stone from the crowbar or pick that the thieves must have used. It was almost as if the chamber wall had been pushed outwards from inside, although that was clearly impossible. She also noticed that among the rubble was the broken corner of an Egyptian sarcophagus. She took a few photos, then asked to speak to the officer in charge.

He could not help much but mentioned that the forensic report had revealed one strange result. The carbon dating of the whitish fibres found both in the Saint's chamber and the confessional box suggested that these were woven around 300 BC. The analysis wasn't wholly reliable, but the usual bracket was within a century either way, and that would still give a date well over three hundred and fifty years before St Mark's death in around 70 AD. Whether these fibres were a thread marking the path out of the labyrinth, or a false trail leading to further confusion, was unclear.

CHAPTER 14 - A WALK IN THE PARK

Outside of a dog, a book is a man's best friend. Inside of a dog, it's too dark to read – Groucho Marx

A gleaming new Rolls Royce drew into the car park at St Barbara's and came to an abrupt halt. The chauffeur, immaculately dressed, spoke to his passenger who was lounging in the back seat reading a copy of The Times.

'Sir, there seems to be someone in your space.'

There was a pause, as these words sank in. Then, in the mirror, the driver saw the paper drop like a guillotine revealing the Dean in the early stages of parking place rage. The Dean had often stolen the spaces of old ladies at supermarkets by simply accelerating aggressively into the slot when they were still timidly lining up to reverse in. But the idea that someone would put their vehicle in his own reserved spot was a declaration of war that could only be countered by immediate escalation.

Ten minutes later a bulldozer arrived, lifted up the battered Mini that was the cause of the offence and disappeared with it[134].

At his desk, the Dean turned to the file of papers on the new History Mystery Faculty. He was delighted that the enthusiasm around the world had already attracted a significant flow of funding from some major educational charities, government bodies, other academic institutions and a few rich philanthropists, all keen to be associated with such an exciting and innovative venture. The accounts showed however that the largest income stream was flowing in ever increasing amounts from accounts in Panama and Columbia which were shown under the entry "PEST". This was matched by almost equally hefty transfers going out to unknown destinations of which the Dean had no knowledge. He simply followed the instructions he was given, happy that the balance was now seven million pounds to the good, despite the extensive sums being spent on the faculty, its staff and his own substantial salary and expenses, which Cavatappi never questioned. The Dean felt that he really had discovered the crock of gold at the end of a rainbow and Cavatappi was its guardian leprechaun. The Dean's only regret was that his own good fortune was so tied to that of Tom and his team. English Heritage had tried to fill in the chalk lines cut in the hillside opposite the Cerne Giant, but it was taking time for the new turf to take root. His features were still recognizable, even if in a different shade of green rather than white.

It was almost certainly paranoia, but it seemed that tourists visiting the college were often lying in wait for him, sniggering. Students, as well as many University colleagues, found it hard to look him straight in the eye. The publication of his recent autobiography, in which he had perhaps gilded the lily just a little in places, met with a savagely critical review in the University magazine which suggested that the Dean's delusions of grandeur were a "phallacy."

The relationship between Cleo and her captive got off to a rocky start. She knew that there would be extensive press coverage of the abduction with lots of photos of the victim, so disguise was essential. The dog was a jumble of colours. Mainly caramel brown but with some white and darker brown splodges, particularly around its head. Well prepared, Cleo had bought some black hair dye and, with some trouble, heaved the dog into her bath. Its legs were so short that she found it quite hard to get her arms around it and pick up the stubby, tree trunk body.

When, finally, she succeeded, the dog sat dolefully but patiently while she ran some lukewarm water and applied the dye. The result was not entirely satisfactory as the animal's coat was so dense it was difficult to get the dye to soak thoroughly to the roots. Still, Cleo donned rubber gloves and used her fingers to work the dye in as best she could before rinsing it away. Then, hauling the creature out again, she subjected it to the hairdryer on max. As the dog closed its eyes in the blasting heat of this hurricane, dye ran down its little legs into pools on the white bathmat. This task finally complete, Cleo turned impatiently back to her desk and emails, leaving her guest to fend for itself.

After standing stock still for a few minutes recovering from the shock of the bath, the dog looked up at Cleo, tilted its head and whined politely but emphatically. He wanted a walk and was used to getting his way. The service at this new establishment seemed to be woefully short of his expectations. Usually he was walked twice a day by the Queen herself along with his friends, who together formed what Princess Diana memorably described as a moving carpet of fur following behind Her Majesty. In between these stately, but not excessively strenuous outings, his every wish was lovingly cared for by two footmen, known in the Palace as Doggie One and Doggie Two.

Perhaps a hard and expectant stare would give this new foot-person the hint. One should at least give the staff a chance to come good before dismissing them if they failed to shape up.

The whining however made no impression on Cleo. She just put in her earplugs and ignored him. To be fair, she had never had a pet. Well, only as a child when she had an overweight goldfish that she had indulged with pellets until it turned belly up and exploded. She hadn't thought about the exercise her hostage might need or why it might be best to give it a regular opportunity to get outdoors. This hound was clearly totally spoilt, and she had no intention of pandering to the sense of entitlement or the airs and graces it had picked up. She settled back at her computer.

The dog could see that his polite request needed sterner reinforcement. When a higher pitched whine failed to produce results, he waddled up to her, lifted his leg and used her as a lamppost. Cleo sprang to her feet with an alacrity that showed she could respond with the attentiveness a royal dog expected if she really wanted to. Perhaps now a short sharp lesson had been administered she would realise that high standards needed to be vigilantly maintained.

Had the hostage not been critical to the ROT plan, Cleo, who possessed a temper that could flare up like a Bunsen burner in a school chemistry lab, might well have shut her canine tormentor in the oven or shoved it out of the window. But this was out of the question. Controlling herself with a herculean effort, she reminded herself that they were both in it for the long haul. The only way forward was to try and make friends.

She lent down, hesitantly stroked her enemy's head and turned up the tag on his collar. Yes, it really was called Bisto. Seemed weird. Why name a dog after gravy, unless you were Korean and planning to eat it? Two dogs in fact including Oxo, presumably to keep the competing manufacturers happy by showing that the crown was impartial. Or, perhaps Her Majesty could not decide which of them she preferred for taste, or whether she liked cubes or granules best. Still Cleo supposed there were worse names, such as Candy, Vulcan or Disco. The fur, still slightly damp from the bath, gave off a very strong and unpleasant odour. Not so much body odour as Bisto odour but BO all the same. She bent down and, with considerable reluctance, quickly stroked her palm over the flat of Bisto's skull while thinking what a tiny brain it probably contained.

No Einstein maybe, but the dog had acute instincts and like most of its kind could tell immediately if a welcome was genuine or feigned. Despite the murmur of his name, Bisto was in no doubt that the caress in truth conveyed an intense dislike tantamount to a declaration of war.

Ten minutes later, having gingerly attached the dog to a long retractable lead, Cleo and her detested companion were walking around the Serpentine in Hyde Park[135]. There were a lot of police in the distance near the public toilets at the edge of the park and a large area taped off. A passer by said that a poor lady had been shot that morning.

Bisto's walk seemed to Cleo interminably slow. She felt like they were trying to push a rotating door round in the wrong direction. If they went any slower they would start going backwards. Some minutes later, however, he suddenly accelerated.

A small Cairn Terrier was coming towards them. Bisto's sudden interest should have warned Cleo, not only that it was female but also that it was in an interesting condition. As the two owners passed one another and Cleo carried on oblivious, Bisto made full use of the extendable lead and, turning with surprising agility, leapt upon the object of his desire.

She was fortunately more than willing, perhaps realising that this might be the chance of a lifetime for a royal fling and even to conceive a royal bastard. As for Bisto, he was simply following in a rich tradition. From Henry VIII to Charles II, Edward VIII and even Prince Philip, the royal family had certainly been very generous in sewing their royal oats. Cleo heard the angry shouts of the terrier's owner behind her just as the lead finally reached its limit and jerked her to an abrupt halt.

She turned to see an unholy scuffle going on as an immaculately dressed lady struggled in vain to wrench Bisto away from her beloved pet while the two dogs clung together passionately, desperate not to be separated. Cleo ran back to help, but a confused *mêlée* broke out in which the two women and both dogs became entangled in the retractable lead while Bisto pursued his activities with renewed energy.

The abrupt parting came when a passing jogger broke up the canine bliss. Fortunately for Cleo, the other lady was so traumatised that the young jogger had to lead her away sobbing to recover herself on a park bench while signalling to Cleo that she should make a quick escape and take Bisto, who the jogger referred to as *Casanova*, with her.

Cleo was by now reaching the end of her own tether, but her ordeal was not yet quite complete. She turned back towards her flat, hauling Bisto behind her. The bereft lover kept trying to look back over his shoulder for a glimpse of his *amour*, but it was futile and he soon renewed his interest in the other scents that thrilled his nostrils.

An elderly lady bent over her stick was standing at the gatepost out of the park, a site that Bisto seemed to regard as one of almost religious significance.

'That's an unusual dog,' she said, squinting through her glasses at Bisto. 'What breed is it?'

Cleo had not the slightest clue about dog breeds and, taken aback, could only say what first came into her head. All she could think was that it might be a good idea to go for one of those artificial doodle breeds as there were so many of them and new ones were popping up all the time, so she was less likely to be caught out.

'It's a Doodlebug.'

'Really? I thought that was a German rocket. At least that's what we used to call them in the War when I was a girl[136].'

'Oh yes, sorry I meant a Doodlenoodle. It's a recent cross breed.'

'Well, fancy that. And what are the breeds it's crossed from?'

At this point Cleo should have shut up, but she ploughed on. Better make it sound rare.

'A Nova Scotian Doodle and a Bavarian Noodleholzhund.'

'Extraordinary. I thought a noodleholz was German for rolling pin, but I suppose they get up to all sorts these days.'

'Yes, well they're a kind of sausage dog, so the shape is a bit like a rolling pin. I imagine that's the reason.'

In her alarm, Cleo was losing her cool. Although there was a voice inside her head shouting at her to stop, her mouth just kept motoring on of its own accord as she struggled to find the off switch. It seemed to be inspired by dim memories of a German cookery course Cleo had attended and a knowledge of the Germanic love for linking words together like carriages until the train became too long for the platform.

'Their pedigree goes back to the rare Knoblauchkrautermitstrudelwursthund.'

The old lady was now looking astonished. 'Funny, doesn't that literally mean garlic and herb with strudel sausage dog? My little Chorizo[137] was a sausage dog. Sadly, he got caught on an electric fence and ended up like a charred chipolata only last week. I've been a judge at Crufts for a great many years but never heard of any of those breeds. Yours looks remarkably like a Corgi to me, but he can't be as he's black. I've never seen a black Corgi. They must be even rarer than black tulips. I suspect your dog must be even more of a mongrel than you think, dear.'

The old lady began reaching in her handbag for another pair of glasses so she could get a better look, but Cleo made polite excuses and hurried on as swiftly as Bisto's sedate pace would allow.

Dusk was falling. The last bright splinters of sunlight picked out the intricate skyline of the city. The roofs, towers, crenelations and spires of the palazzos were edged in gold. But the black canals and streets below only served to make the firefly lights within them burn brighter, as if a box of jewels had been opened in the dark. Cassie was almost invisible as she slipped out of the front door of the hotel where she was staying. She was dressed now in her catsuit and matching black mask, but it was Carnival in Venice. There was no need to slide out of the window and down a drainpipe. Anyone who had sharp enough eyes to see her would not have been alarmed or suspicious as they were all dressed in the most outlandish costumes, although most in the glittering colours of fireworks. This city of one hundred and eighteen islands, patched together with a tracery of stone and necklaces of water was at its most mysterious and playful.

At San Marco, Cassie had been intrigued by a couple of other fragments of information, even though they seemed more likely to be lost pieces from a completely different jigsaw. The guy with the blue rucksack, who had been in the Cathedral around the time of the crime, had been interrogated closely. Officially, he remained the chief suspect and his past showed that he probably should have been in jail for life many times over for other matters but had somehow, like Houdini, always slipped through the police net[138].

Cassie read the transcripts of his interviews but had to agree that they did not establish any clear link with the San Marco crimes other than the rough timing of the visit which he confirmed. The police were probably right to conclude that any answers lay elsewhere.

What he had mentioned in passing, however, was that he thought he saw a ghost emerging from the confessional box. The police dismissed this as the ravings of a man poised on the cliff edge of insanity, but Cassie filed it away in her mental "odds and ends" draw.

She also asked about Father Matteo. Everyone assumed this revered priest was an innocent victim of the gang who must have stolen St Mark. Wrong place, wrong time and all that. Otherwise he wouldn't have met such a gruesome end while quietly making himself available to others who needed to cleanse their souls. He clearly hadn't committed suicide. But one of the police team had let slip that the Tax Fraud Office had recently raided the restaurant in St Mark's square which Father Matteo frequented and whose owner had even written his obituary. His friend in the tax fraud team told him that a few weeks ago they had uncovered some surprising information about Father Matteo and his activities through a whistle-blower, but nothing more. Cassie was flying back to London tomorrow but had one last night and now also an idea of how she could put it to good use.

As she slid though the throng of revellers, keeping close to the frontages of the palazzos away from the canals, Cassie had the sense that she was being followed. She looked round a couple of times and once even slipped into a quieter side street and waited a couple of minutes to see who passed by, but there was nothing obvious she could put a finger on. Everybody was in high spirits and high on spirits, laughing, shouting and using swear words that even her excellent Italian shrank back from translating.

'Relax,' she told herself sternly. She soon turned into an alley that was almost deserted. No one was in a hurry to visit the offices of municipal bureaucrats and tax officials even in the daytime and certainly not in the small hours. Using the names the garrulous policeman had mentioned, and after some careful online research including a little hacking, she knew exactly where she needed to get to. Clicking open the small grappling hook on the rope she had taken from her small black rucksack, she threw it up over the roofline, pulling until it went taut and she was confident it would hold her weight.

Ten minutes was all it took, and her toes were touching down again on the flagstones. She had left the file she was interested in behind but had shots of all the paperwork on her phone. This might not be able to capture a grain of sand on Mars, like that American tourist's camera, but it did the job she needed. As she emerged again onto the sidewalk by the main canal she noticed a small figure on the opposite side, dressed as a jester save for the grinning mask of a horned devil. She couldn't place the memory, but she felt a jolt of current and connection. This was however displaced when she saw in the background behind him someone else she thought she recognised, a large, bearded gentleman with a mask adorned with sequins and peacock feathers. What caught her eye however was the flash of purple lining from his waistcoat.

Cavatappi was leaning forward with his head resting on his fist in the same dramatic pose as Rodin's Thinker. All around him steam was rising, and he was only wearing a towel round his waist. It was extremely hot, but nonetheless he reached out and poured a little more water onto the brazier from the wooden ladle that lay beside him, releasing a fresh cloud. He was in the sauna at his hotel back in Oxford and had arranged a couple of meetings here. It seemed as good a place as any for a quiet conversation.

Life was at present a bit of an *insalata mista* – a mixed salad – as his mother would have called it. On the one hand, he had temporarily extended his control over "pizza" supplies in New York. A text had also arrived with the good news that, "there is one more Angel in Heaven", so Angelo Capelli had been tracked down and rubbed out. On the other, Inspector Panettone was now in England as part of his investigation into the San Marco affair. Cavatappi was concerned that, if the Inspector had not already connected this to the relics scam, he would do so soon. His contacts had informed him of the current tax investigation. Although the tax fraud team often moved at a glacial pace and seldom thought outside the box, eventually they would surely get round to putting two and two together with the police investigation and uncover the truth about Father Matteo's unholy activities.

The phone call he had received from Fra Diavolo[139] in Venice only half an hour earlier had significantly raised the temperature, filling his brain with warm mist and giving him a headache. Diavolo reported that he had watched the History Mystery girl sent out from St Barbara's break into the tax fraud office directly after visiting San Marco and being briefed at the crime scene. It seemed likely this girl had picked up something while at the Basilica. How could she make that connection unless the police knew already? Things were moving faster than he had thought. At least Capelli couldn't do any more damage, although it wasn't clear what he had already divulged. Cavatappi could have kicked himself for suggesting that Cassie be sent out to investigate St Mark's disappearance. It seemed he had scored a spectacular own goal[140]. She was supposed simply to bring a different perspective to the search for the saint.

Finding and returning the saint's body would simultaneously have helped him restore the lost income skimmed from donations and, in all likelihood, provide enough to go on to identify the shadowy opponent who had murdered Father Matteo. Instead, it seemed she was opening up the very can of worms which Cavatappi had hoped to bury.

As he was still trying to work out his next step and how to stop Cassie from solving the rubik's cube, the Dean sidled into the sauna. He looked awkward, uncomfortable and already his face was lobster red. It wasn't often that Cavatappi lost his own composure, but his mouth dropped open now.

'Its like trekking in Costa Rica in here. My goggles have steamed up.'

'What the hell are you wearing?' Apart from the googles the Dean was clad in a full length wet-suit. 'It's a sauna, not a coral reef. Have you never been to a sauna before?'

'No, I haven't actually. But they're Nordic aren't

they? I thought you need to jump into an ice cold plunge bath…or does that come later?'

'I suggest you take that stuff off or you will boil alive.'

'But won't it also provide some protection against the thrashing? I have quite sensitive skin.

'What do you mean?'

'I read that it's a Scandinavian tradition to roll in snow while being beaten with birchtwigs after the bath? [141].

The Dean looked shocked as two Germans entered naked as peeled prawns. Since there was no chance now to talk confidentially, Cavatappi left in despair after signalling secretly to the Dean that he should wait a few minutes so as not to attract attention if they were seen together. Given the Dean's attire, that risk was clearly already much higher than it would otherwise have been.

The Germans swiftly felt they had to leave as well. Their efforts not to laugh fit to split their sides were coming close to causing them internal injury and sitting in that confined space next to some guy in a wetsuit also seemed from a teutonic perspective extremely unhygienic. As they went out one of them poured an entire bucket of water on the charcoal burner and the other turned the latch on the outside of the door so the Dean was sealed in. If they hadn't relented and told the Spa manager as they left that they thought someone was stuck in the sauna, it's unlikely that the Dean would ever have been able to peel himself out of the melting rubber.

CHAPTER 15 – A UNIVERSAL LANGUAGE

I've got nothing to say. Any questions? – A post-match interview by manager Ray Hudson.

For days now the team had been working hard at the projects they had prioritised. An air of studious concentration often pervaded the faculty for hours as they pored over maps and old texts or made calls to museums and experts all around the globe, trying to piece together as much evidence as possible.

As Tom had been researching Atlantis for some time already, he had a significant head start, but just one breakthrough could turn everything on its head. The variety of skills and knowledge within the team was already giving all of them new and valuable insights that they could never have achieved on their own. The total consumption of coffee was so great that their local supplier, *Full of Beans*, was having problems keeping up, especially as Tom was an afficionado. Sometimes he even insisted on *Kopi Iuwak*,[142] despite the expense. Still, Tom felt everything that could make a difference was worthwhile and the largesse from Cavatappi's investors seemed to be a bottomless pit – at least compared to the usual miserly sources of academic funding.

They needed it. The challenges they faced were unprecedented since the History Mystery Faculty was the pioneer in its field.

This morning, Tom had gathered the team together to take stock on the Atlantis project and to brainstorm next steps. The proposal was that they should do this with each priority project in turn. He was using a few PowerPoint slides to remind everyone of the key background.

- *Lost kingdom of Atlantis first mentioned in Plato's Repub lic, c. 380 BC.*
- *Waged a great war against Athens thousands of years before Plato.*
- *Large island of massive wealth.*
- *City had three great stone concentric walls surrounding a central mountain[143].*
- *Canals and docks within the walls with tunnels to allow ships to access sea.*
- *Ruled by a king, Atlas, after whom Atlantic Ocean named.*
- *Located beyond Pillars of Hercules (the Straits of Gibraltar).*
- *After defeat by Athens, "there occurred violent earthquakes and floods; and in a single day and night of misfortune all your warlike men in a body sank into the earth, and the island of Atlantis disappeared in the same manner in the depths of the sea. For which reason the sea in those parts is impassable and*

> *impenetrable, because there is a shoal of mud in the way; and this was caused by the subsidence of the island" (Plato's Timaeus).*

Tom's enthusiasm was apparent as he spoke to the team. 'Over centuries, many historians, cartographers and adventurers seeking Atlantis have argued for locations everywhere from America, Antarctica, Bolivia, Iceland and the Caribbean, to a range of sites in the Mediterranean[144]. The most popular theory has been that Atlantis was destroyed by the gigantic volcanic eruption of Thera, now known as Santorini. I've been there. It's a beautiful holiday island. You can sit at the top of the cliff on the crescent rim, which is all that remains of the original volcano, and drink cocktails looking over the tiny smoking cone of the new volcano that's growing out of the sea inside it's curve. But I don't think it can be Atlantis. That runs directly contrary to Plato's description which clearly places the city in the ocean named after it, the Atlantic.'

'So, what's your view, Tom? Couldn't it all just be an alluring myth?' asked Ming, flicking back his fringe so Tom wouldn't miss the hard question in his stare.

'Possibly, but I don't think so[145]. Plato's account is very detailed. This may seem far-fetched but I think it was probably located on the Dogger Bank in the North Sea.'

'That's on the list for the shipping forecast, isn't it? I thought it was where all the cod for fish and chips came from.' said Puk.

'And now the site of a huge wind farm,' Ming added 'So, lets hope Plato wasn't full of it.'

Tom didn't rise to the jibe, 'Yeah, both correct. But a few thousand years ago, Dogger Bank was land.

You could even walk over it from what's now Suffolk to Denmark without getting wet, at least if wearing wellies. But then there was a huge land slip called the Storegga Slide off the coast of Norway. It's thought it created a mega-tsunami that submerged Doggerland and turned it into a massive underwater bank. A great shoal of submerged mud, just as Plato says.'

'So, what other evidence have you found?' asked Finn running his hand through his ginger hair as if this would make it any tidier.

'It's obviously difficult, but there are some exciting archaeological bits and pieces coming to light. Usually they're dragged up by trawler nets, but often the fishermen don't tell anyone because they're not supposed to be dragging the seabed due to the environmental damage it causes. I've been plotting all the finds I can trace, and I've also been speaking quietly to fishermen, asking them to let me know of anything else they find.'

'So that's why you keep visiting Grimsby, Lowestoft and such like," Ming exclaimed, the thought striking him as unexpectedly as a finger of light piercing the heart of a long barrow at the winter solstice[146].

Tom projected a map onto the screen on the wall. They could all see a pattern was developing from the plotting of the finds. There was a buzz of excitement and ideas began to pour in as to how to narrow the search site down.

'It may not be Loch Ness,' teased Finn. 'But looks like you might still get a spot of diving in the freezing cold, Puk, without the risk of getting eaten by the monster. Shame Atlantis isn't near the Barrier Reef.'

'It's a bit like joining the dots in a dot-to-dot puzzle to build a picture.' Ming suggested (this turn in the conversation made me wonder if some of the group had also been receiving treatment from Dr Bacon).

Puk countered, 'Yes, but as they aren't numbered to help us, we could all end up with different pictures or pictures that just lead us astray. In a way, that's the story of the constellations. The Greeks joined some random stars together to try and find a story for the night sky by stitching them into imaginary patterns.'

'Okay, I get that, Puk. You're the astronomer. But what are we supposed to do? Give up on using our imagination? You may say zodiacs and horoscopes are all delusions but without drawing patterns, what would we do? How would we see and share our ideas or make any sense of anything at all? And anyway, constellations have helped sailors navigate for thousands of years.'

'I agree with you, Ming,' said Boudicca. 'It's like stringing pearls – pearls of wisdom – together to make a necklace. We create new meaning, new beauty by linking things and the patterns we draw from those connections.'

'That's all very romantic, Boudicca', Puk responded, 'I don't know if you have ever seen a *Fata Morgana*[147] – a shape on the horizon at sea? It's a sort of mirage caused by atmospheric conditions, but we often see them as castles in the air or ghost ships. Yes, they're beautiful, but we still need to understand that they're mirages not real structures or vessels. All I'm saying is that before we start drawing pictures from the finds Tom has plotted we need to check out that they really have a relationship to one another.'

Tom held up a hand. 'Look, guys, this is all fascinating, but let's save it for the pub. I just need some practical help with trying to make progress with these findings.'

As they crowded around the map and the conversation grew more heated, the door opened and the head porter came in. It was a long time since he and Tom had last clashed. The Dean had been forced to tell him to back off and leave Tom alone, but now Tom could see that he had the glint in his eye of a Rottweiler about to be let off the leash. He was carrying what looked like a large paperweight which he thumped down with obvious satisfaction on Tom's desk, together with a typed note. Turning on his heel, he left the room without bothering to shut the door behind himself.

Finbarr picked up the paperweight and turned it round in his hands.

'It's like a cube of crushed coke cans. Metal anyway, and very heavy. Looks like some bits were painted.'

Tom had meanwhile picked up the note, which he read with disbelief.

"The College Regulations, originally enacted in 1463, as amended, state that no vehicle, cart or steam engine, whether horse drawn or otherwise, shall remain stationary without written permission on any ground reserved by the college for other use, and particularly not in any space allotted for the use of the Dean. Transgression of this regulation shall be considered a trespass and felony which will result in the immediate confiscation and destruction of the aforesaid offending vehicle."

Tom groaned. It was the Dean's sick idea of a

momento from part of his beloved Mini[148]. He had bought it with his very first few months' salary as a lecturer and hadn't been able to bring himself to part with it. Even its many foibles and the many escapades they caused had become dear to him. The handbrake was so useless he could never risk parking it on hills. Many icy mornings had been wasted trying to coax the engine into life. The flattening of the garden shed at the bottom of the road and the boy next door's hamster had been costly and regrettable incidents, but in a way were also rites of passage that he and the little car had been through together. It was true, his rebellious streak had led him to park it that morning in the Dean's parking place. But only for a few minutes. He meant to move it as soon as another space came free, but had been distracted by his research.

It looked as if he had finally discovered, in a rather expensive way, the limits of the protection Cavatappi's support would give him against the Dean. He noticed a curious splinter of plastic in the cube. Then with bitterness he remembered the expensive new sunglasses he had just bought and had left in the glove compartment.

The police station in Oxford was pretty basic, or at least it was on this floor which contained a few cells and the spartan interview room in which he was sitting. Panettone wondered if it was the same as in Italy, where the ground floor would look very similar, but the offices of the top brass upstairs would be much plusher. Not gold leaf and designer wallpaper, exactly, but swanky. That was the thing he loved about his native land. So much more flair, thirst for beauty and disregard for legality. Britain seemed a bit dour and hidebound by comparison.

He took a sip of the tepid coffee in the chipped mug in front of him. It was instant and quite disgusting. Perhaps he had accidentally been given the stuff they forced suspects to drink to make them confess. He longed to stand at a proper Italian bar with an *espresso*. That would smoothly launch the morning like a ship sliding down the slipway after a christening of champagne.

He looked at his watch and wondered when the officers he had been told would be assigned to help him would show up. In the meantime, perhaps he could take a few minutes for his opening moves against ChesstWig. Whoever that guy was, he seemed to be a sore loser and had just sent a text asking for a rematch.

ChesstWig had just opened as white with the aggressive Ghengis Khan Gambit[149]. Panettone felt he had no option but to counter this with The Great Wall Defence, a rare sequence of moves last used in China against the Mongol hordes[150]. He had tried the Goliath Defence in the past but, although it looked impressive at first, he had been finally brought to checkmate by a pawn. The only other alternative seemed to be the recently invented Schettino Defence, but the Inspector was too honourable to ever contemplate that[151]. As he started to implement his strategy, the two policemen arrived, so he had to put the match on hold for now anyway.

The larger, and clearly senior, copper held out his hand, introducing himself tersely as DCI Boyle and his lanky young colleague as DC Peel. Panettone felt his fingers being crushed in Boyle's grip but tensed his own enormous hand just in time. He wondered why the English were either so embarrassed about greetings that they couldn't make contact at all or else turned them into a kind of arm wrestling contest. Why couldn't they just embrace and kiss on both cheeks like an Italian? But trying that with Boyle would be like colliding with an iceberg and he didn't want to share the fate of the Titanic[152].

If only the English were able to thaw a little and express themselves it would help build a bit more camaraderie. Small talk to get to know each other also seemed to be off the agenda. Boyle just sat down silently and propped up an eyebrow so that it hung there brooding like a vulture on a washing line. This appeared to indicate that he would like to know why he had been asked by those smart arses at Scotland Yard to interrupt his own investigations to make himself available to assist this foreign Inspector who had just waltzed in from Heathrow.

Panettone's English was reasonably fluent but he was keen to improve it and had been looking up a few idioms he hoped to practise while on this visit. It was easy to confuse them at times with their Italian equivalent. He understood that words should not just be sprayed around indiscriminately like deodorant. That could be overpowering and drive people away but he loved to try and make his speech graphic. As an Italian, he also liked to converse in gestures that would make most ballerinas look like statues, and found Boyle's eyebrow just a bit too cryptic.

Thinking relations might melt with a little lubrication the Inspector suggested they adjourn to the pub. Once seated at a table by the bar with their drinks, Panettone started talking about the weather. Everyone knew the English were obsessed with it. He could see that outside it was still raining, but only very lightly, and gestured languidly to the window.

'It's raining kittens and puppies out there.' Then realising from his colleagues faces that this wasn't registering with them, 'I mean it's raining a cat and a dog.'

They still looked blank so the Inspector adeptly changed tactics. He began to talk about football and beer, a global dialect with its own vocabulary, great and shocking moments, culture and songs. This was language Boyle and Peel revelled in. It turned out that in another life all three of them could have been football pundits, but why wait if you could just get on with it from the sidelines in this one? Soon, relations were warming up and the permafrost was vanishing.

After sharing trenchant views, and more recently recollections, of every World Cup since Uruguay won the first in 1930, the atmosphere warmed up significantly. Despite his passion for the game, Panettone exercised enormous restraint. Although he had to concede that England had invented football, he refrained from pointing out the World Cup tally which clearly proved that Italy was four times better at it. With this tactful preparation, the way was open for a helpful discussion of the Ashmolean raid. The Inspector leaned forward slightly as if to share a confidence. Given his height this always created a slight sense of anxiety that, like Pisa's tower[153], he might never straighten up again.

'Let the cat out of the sack and tell me without any hairs on your tongue how your investigation at the museum is going.'

'I think you mean spill the beans and say it like it is? DCI Boyle clearly felt that either he was getting the hang of this game or perhaps these idioms were contagious.

'Yes, but I'm confused, is it the cat or the beans that go in the bag? Anyway, go on please,' Panettone waved his hand in encouragement.

'To be honest, we don't have any active leads at present, although we can't show our cards to the public. We seem to be clutching at straws. '

'Ah yes, the straws, I know they suck. As we say at home, I am *climbing on mirrors* myself over the San Marco theft. If I pick up one more straw the camel's back will snap in half. It's *breaking my boxes* - I think you say climbing all over my nerves or something like that. One more dead end and I will be *at the fruit.* You, of course will be slapping your tough arses.

Boyle scratched his forehead, then hazarded a guess. 'Hitting rock bottom?' The Inspector gave a glum grimace of confirmation.

Peel took up the baton of conversation. 'After our initial interviews Scotland Yard barged in and took the lead in the investigation telling us to concentrate on local matters except when they needed support on the ground. We're pretty disheartened.'

'So they have poured frozen water on you with a dampener?'

'Exactly', said Boyle. 'Another round? Let's drown our sorrows.'

'That would be the knees of a bee', Panettone replied, giving a slow thumbs up.

Boyle was forced to laugh, 'Yeh what the hell is that one about?'

The Inspector shrugged, 'How would I know? It's your language. As for our mutual investigations, I think we need to *turn the omlette*, or I think you say the tables. If we could find some connection between both the Ashmolean and San Marco crimes we could have and eat your famous cake and in Italy we would not only *have full bottles of wine but a drunk wife as well.*'

Then, unfolding himself to his full height he added, 'Now about that drink, it's my turn and *I don't have short arms*...or, as you would say it, I'm not stingy.'

The bond now established between them led on to an even older foundation for building solidarity – grumbling. As Boyle said, crimes were often complex and took time. The public didn't seem to understand Murphy's Law[154] – that the more you investigate something, the more complex and time-consuming it would always become. On top of that, there would be more form-filling in triplicate and, put together, all of this would mean less time on the beat and more resources used up so, whatever the budget, it was always exhausted.

It was all a vicious circle, and the criminals didn't help. In many cases suspects seemed reluctant for some reason to just come into the local station to explain themselves. Rather than co-operate, a lot of the time they would lie low or even vanish altogether, like Lord Lucan, meaning that more public money needed to be spent going out to look for them. If you could find them and put them in an identity parade, the victim or witness usually couldn't identify anyone because they were drunk at the time or else they failed to pick the person the police had already pointed out as "the wrong un." If the police were just left to get on with their jobs without all this investigation malarky the real troublemakers would be locked up in no time.

On top of all this, the endless requests by the press for updates were deeply annoying. Fortunately, the police were now properly trained in how to say, 'No comment,' for legal reasons on all matters which were the subject of an ongoing police investigation, as the Ripper murders had been since 1888.

'Just earlier today we've been wasting time on a missing persons enquiry about a lady in Summertown' groaned Boyle. 'She's probably gone to visit a relative, but an elderly neighbour has been peeking through the net curtains and says the husband has been re-laying the patio at night.'

'I spent the afternoon watching it being dug up. The neighbour is probably just a local busy body, an amateur Hercules Poirot who overdoses on Hitchcock films and is convinced everyone in her street has something to hide,' added Peel.

'And we were robbed of our first sure-fire prosecution this month only a few days ago' Boyle continued glaring down at the dregs of the pint in front of him. 'The Dean of St Barbara's College stepped in to help a young lecturer get off scot-free even though he was banged to rights with clear evidence and a near confession. That was just the sort of conviction that would do wonders for the statistics without even leaving the office.'

Panettone expressed his sympathy, but in truth it was limited. In Italy the prosecutors, witnesses and defendants often all died before the case got to trial, either because the process was so slow or because they were shot by the mafia.

'In Italy we are eaten up by a monster with green eyes to see that British police can hang up their hats when they are still spring chickens and call it a day, although we are not sure which day that is. We hear that if suspended for making a hash you are never given a sack, a boot or any orders for marching or even told to pull your stockings up but can just climb a greasy pole to another rung of the ladder.'

Boyle got a little hot around the collar at this. 'That's fake news spread on the dark web by a secret network of conspiracy theorists, controlled by organised crime, the Joker and North Korea. It's only us boys in blue that stand between these shadowy forces and the collapse of civilisation[155].'

The Inspector listened, nodding sympathetically and keeping to himself the thought that at least they didn't have the mafia in their backyard. The important thing was not to wreck the bridges he had carefully built. Moving seamlessly back again to business, Panettone now quickly established that there was only one witness to the Ashmolean raid.

A couple of hours later, accompanied by Boyle and Peel, a further interview had been arranged and the Inspector found himself in a narrow, cobbled street.

The house was a small two up, two down in the centre of a long terrace, which was a good thing. It had seen much better days that no one currently alive was likely to remember. Had the house not been supported on the shoulders of the neighbouring terraces on either side, it would have collapsed long ago. The only distinguishing feature from the outside was that the door was painted a rather murky maroon and the window frames in a garish combination of blue and yellow. On the outside of the front door were two huge crossed yellow hammers of the kind used for heavy duty roadworks. With the astute intuition that only comes from years of detective work, Panettone realised that the house must have been marked out by the local council for imminent demolition.

As Joe led his guests through to the small living room, the Inspector had already started asking him where he was going to be re-housed, but then stopped abruptly. The whole room was festooned with team photos, scarves and other memorabilia. West Ham, the Hammers, of course. Panettone swiftly switched into football language yet again. He even remembered that Bobby Moore and Geoff Hurst had played for the Hammers and what the team was first called[156].

Joe was apparently quite happy to talk about West Ham until his final earthly breath and his greatest hope for heaven was that, when he got there, he would find the Hammers leading the celestial Premiership. Shifting the one-track conversation was as difficult as changing the course of an oil tanker while it was still navigating the Suez Canal. Panettone did at last manage this feat but only by accepting with apparent relish a deep-fried Mars Bar that Joe proudly pressed upon him.

Joe revealed he had discovered this culinary delight on a recent trip to Glasgow to enlarge his cultural horizons and was keen to share it. Maybe it was the skill of the questioning that followed, or maybe a little more time had cleared Joe's brain from the shock that night of the Hammers' win against Chelsea. Whatever the cause, some new and potentially interesting information emerged.

Joe now recalled a couple of snatches of

conversation between the gang members and, with the assistance of a short recording of one of Lenin's speeches on Panettone's phone, was able to identify that they had probably been speaking in Russian. What's more, Joe was sure he had heard them mentioning Chelsea, supporting his impression that they were Chelsea fans who were as interested in the match as he was. He said he believed the fact that the raid ended just in time to allow them to get away to watch the game was conclusive proof of this.

The police seemed less convinced by his reasoning, but everyone was aware of Chelsea's Russian links. Joe was adamant that only Chelsea fans would break into a museum and run off with as many treasures as they could carry, refusing to accept that this view might be a little tainted by ancient soccer rivalry. Panettone could not resist saying that if by treasure, Joe was talking about Chelsea taking home a lot more silverware than West Ham, then that was objectively undeniable.

Tom was feeling depressed. It was a few days now since Valentine's Day and he had no idea what Cassie was thinking. Probably not much. She was busy and would be having a whale of a time in Venice without sparing him a thought. He had to remind himself that this wasn't entirely fair. He had no reason to think she knew about his own feelings, although he was aware that female intuition was a remarkable thing that men were rarely able to hide from. His last girlfriend had cut off all his buttons and sewn up all the cuffs on his suit and shirts even before he had raised the courage to actually tell her he didn't think they were well-matched. There was something in his leg, digging into his trouser pocket. Taking it out now he realised it was his old car keys. Car keys looking for the right lock, a bit like him and Cassie, although he hadn't yet even been able to test his conviction that they belonged together.

He felt adrift and purposeless but told himself to perk up. More Dogger Bank finds had been coming in and he needed to be upbeat this morning for Finbarr's presentation to the team on their second project, Alexander's Tomb.

Apart from Tom, the team were all in good spirits. Finn was an engaging if idiosyncratic presenter, and they were excited to hear what he had to say. As Tom had done, he started with a few slides to cover the basics.

- *Alexander the Great died, aged 32, in Babylon 323 BC of fever or possibly poisoned*[157].
- *Not just the world's greatest general going beyond the edge of the known world to India, but established numerous cities, including the site of the first great public library open even to slaves, and initiated a diversity policy for multi-cultural integration that some say led to his assassination.*
- *Before dying, gave his signet ring to Perdiccas as Regent.*
- *When asked who should succeed him, Alexander said, 'To the strongest.'*
- *Alexander expressed the wish to be buried at temple of Zeus Ammon at Siwa in Egypt.*
- *Rival generals fought over his empire. Possession of the King's body key to power.*
- *Body en route via Syria to Macedonia when intercepted and taken by force by Ptolemy to Egypt.*
- *Initially buried in Memphis in gold coffin, then*

reburied in coffin of crystal in Alexandria.

- *Records show the mummified body was visited by Julius Caesar, Cleopatra and Augustus (who knocked off its nose) among others. Disappeared c. 400 AD.*
- *At least 140 search attempts to find the tomb so far. One of the greatest History Mysteries!*

Puk was wired-up with excitement. 'Wow, Finn. If we could find that it would be bigger news than Tutankhamen. There are still plenty of exciting things being found, so why not? We should remind ourselves that the terracotta warriors in China were uncovered by local farmers less than 40-odd years ago and there are eight thousand of them. It's easy to forget that Otzi the Iceman was discovered preserved in a glacier. Weren't you involved in the ongoing dig at Gobekli Tepe in Turkey quite recently, Ming? I think that's the oldest temple site ever found. Even in this country it's encouraging that the Staffordshire Hoard of thousands of pieces of Anglo-Saxon gold has fairly recently been uncovered and Richard III's grave found under the "R" of "PARK" in the second bay of the Social Services car park site in Leicester[158].

'That's true' said Ming, and I found it fascinating that he had a twisted spine, so all the hunch back stuff in Shakespeare we were told was Tudor propaganda turns out to be right after all. He clearly did need a bit of social service support so he was in the right place.'

'You need to be a little careful with Shakespeare, Ming. Have you read the bit where a Welshman claims that Alexander was Welsh[159]? And there's lots of other similar stuff one needs to treat with a little scepticism about Alexander's exploits, particularly in the later myths that grew up around him. For example, they include him yoking two birds together and flying up to explore Heaven, where he nearly froze to death.'

'Point taken, Finn. But the sources about his tomb you mention all sound reliable. Tom and Boudicca's find with the Ninth Legion confirms that it's still possible to uncover major treasures. From what you say, we know that the body was in Alexandria for at least 700 years after Alexander's death, don't we?'

Finn found his own reservations succumbing to infection from Puk's enthusiasm and Ming's reasoned argument. 'Yep, and some sources say much later,' he said. I've been cautious and gone for the last sighting we can be virtually certain of. A lot of historians still think the body is likely to be preserved somewhere, which is why there have been so many search expeditions. There were recent claims for possible finds at Siwa in Egypt and at Pella and Vergina in Macedonia where excavations of new royal tombs have turned up some incredible things, but none of these have been substantiated. Much of ancient Alexandria has yet to be excavated, so there's masses to go at yet. Too much! We're working hard on finding some clues in the ancient texts and reviewing the studies that others have carried out to check anything that's been missed before I ask Tom for the funds to go out to Egypt and have a look on the ground.'

After Panettone left the police station, Boyle and Peel grudgingly agreed that he had turned out to be quite good company. He certainly knew his football, even if his knowledge of real ale was distinctly dodgy. There was only one thing Boyle noticed that seemed out of place. After he followed the Inspector into the gents, he was surprised to see fumes rising from the locked cubicle. Hadn't the Inspector told them he didn't smoke?

Returning to his hotel Panettone passed an Italian café and gelateria, *Palline Congelate*. There was a guy outside at one of the tables with his back to him. Panettone could tell even from that angle that he was Italian from the cut of his suit. Over the guy's shoulder he could see he was studying an online chess board on his phone. He felt for a second that the bloke was vaguely familiar but put it down to a natural yearning for home when abroad. He needed to get back to his room and think through his own next moves, on the chess board and in his investigation.

CHAPTER 16 – TAKING THE BISCUIT AND PASSING THE GRAVY

There is no such passion in human nature as the passion for gravy … – Charles Dickens

Cavatappi was equally lost in concentration. He had never seen this defensive formation before. Somehow, he needed to prise it open and give ChessNut a good roasting.

In the meantime, he heard that Panettone had reinterviewed a witness who had been caretaker at the Ashmolean on the night of the raid. One of his henchmen, Fabrizio Boscaiola, was now tailing the Inspector and the two coppers assisting him to the guy's house. Cavatappi needed to find out what this witness knew quickly and get ahead of the Inspector so he could track down the Ashmolean raiders. It was clear that Panettone had reason to think that this and the San Marco incident were connected since otherwise he wouldn't be looking into a matter that was the responsibility of Scotland Yard.

An hour later, Joe heard a knock at the door and was surprised to find a very sharply dressed gentleman on the doorstep. Fabrizio had done his research and Pappa introduced himself as Secretary of the West Ham Supporters Club. He explained that Joe had won the raffle for Fan of the Month. The prize was a seat in the Directors' Box for the next home game, but the club wanted to include a short interview about Joe in the monthly supporters' magazine.

Once Joe had overcome his initial paralysis and his gaping mouth began to move, there was no stopping him. Cavatappi hadn't quite bargained for a full rendering, not only of Joe's life since he was delivered in the drum of his father's cement lorry on the way to hospital, but also his genealogy back to Spud, a peasant on Sir Francis Drake's estate who planted the first English potato crop after this wonderous new vegetable was brought back from America[160]. The drum of the cement mixer was fortunately empty. Joe explained that there wasn't enough legroom in the cab for his mother in the circumstances.

Pappa tried to extract all the information he was looking for as quickly as possible, but Joe gushed on like a burst water pipe. He only finally came to a halt when he tried to show Cavatappi the video he had taken of the West Ham v Chelsea win. The cassette became jammed in the slot of the machine because this was where Pannetone had previously posted the deep-fried Mars

Bar Joe had pressed upon him. Cavatappi made good his escape.

Unknown to Panettone, a race in which he was an unwitting participant was now underway. At his hotel, he took a shower and checked that the Great Wall was holding in his chess match. Then he focused on what he had learnt. After a few minutes he was clear on the next steps in his investigation.

He called his deputy in Venice, checked that Cassie was on her flight home from Venice and asked that a message be sent to her saying he would like to meet with her when she got back to Oxford to discuss whether she had uncovered any angles on St Mark's disappearance. He then called DCI Boyle and arranged to visit the Ashmolean the following morning. Finally, he spoke to Scotland Yard and suggested they run a check on all Chelsea season ticket holders who were Russian. It was just a hunch, but then Panettone believed that hunches were far more productive than losing the wood for the trees in endless detail that simply clogged up the brain.

It was only then that he started to feel really unwell. He tried taking a short power nap but found that not only could he not sleep but he seemed to be getting rather weepy and emotional. Eventually he felt there was no option but to call for some medical assistance.

Cleo had good cause to be worried. It was proving very difficult to keep Bisto hidden and, even though her attitude to him hadn't changed, for some reason, he seemed to be getting ridiculously attached to her. She felt that she had become the hostage. When she went out, he would start to howl and she was concerned the neighbours would hear. Her lease didn't allow pets. On the last landlord inspections, she heard that a baby alligator, an anaconda and several goldfish from other apartments in the block had been flushed down the toilets. The anaconda made it all the way to Ealing Broadway where it cornered an unfortunate workman sent down to clear a fatberg that had blocked the main Victorian sewer and squeezed him like plasticine.

The only way she could keep the hound quiet was to let it sit on her bed watching Scooby Doo while she fed it with steak almost continuously. She was sure that, unless he was put on a fast soon, his heart would give out. Things were made worse by the national hysteria whipped up by the press. If she had ever doubted that she lived in a country not simply of dog lovers but worshippers, she had none anymore.

Her Majesty had not helped matters by making a personal TV address asking anyone with any information to come forward and speak to Scotland Yard. Should the information lead to the return of Bisto the reward would be a life peerage and a romantic weekend for two at either Windsor Castle, Balmoral or Sandringham. The BBC presented a two-hour tribute biopic about Bisto on prime TV over the weekend. The viewing figures were so high that sequels were planned for all the Queen's current and dearly departed Corgis. As these numbered more than thirty, normal viewing was unlikely to return for months, although in the interests of accurate broadcasting the BBC made it clear that this number included the Dorgis.

The Dorgis are a hybrid branch of the royal Corgi line which began when one of the Queen's Corgis mated with Princess Margaret's Dachshund, Pipkin. Together the sisters encouraged this illegitimate line. Inbreeding has often been a problem in royal families, such as the Hapsburgs, so this adventure in canine crossbreeding was an interesting experiment, perhaps as a dummy run in plans to improve the royal gene pool by similar means. Over the years there have been more than ten Dorgis including Cider, Rum, Vulcan, Spock, and Berry[161]. Fortunately, the most engrained character trait of the Dorgi is loyalty to the throne so there is no suggestion that they have any pretensions to usurp the legitimate succession of the royal Corgis, even though they are affectionately known as the "little bastards."

The Royal family can also rely on centuries of experience in managing the pretensions of bastards and usurpers, although occasionally one got through the net. William the Conqueror is a prime example, but then he was French. Quite a few legitimate members of the royal family have however had an even better claim to the title, "Right Royal Bastard." Henry VIII and King John spring to mind[162].

Her Majesty had also summoned the Prime Minister very publicly to the Palace. He was televised leaving in a hurry, looking ashen after only ten minutes. A press leak from a royal footman confirmed that Her Majesty had given him a blasting that was as close to being dropped into the nuclear core of Chernobyl at the time of its meltdown as it is possible to imagine. She apparently said that, regardless of the strict protocol that the monarch should not interfere in constitutional or political matters, he was delusional if he thought she would re-appoint him after any future election, which against all the odds he might win, unless Bisto was already back at the Palace.

Sir Benedict was delighted that he was no longer Culture Minister when the anonymous ransom note arrived at Number 10. It made clear that unless the Elgin Marbles were in a shipping container on their way to Athens within five days, the consequences for Bisto would be unthinkable. The note threatened that the retribution would start with no doggie treats, then no daily walks and escalate from there[163].

The Greek Government swiftly disavowed all responsibility although no one believed them. It was thought that a group of artefact activists known as ROT were involved as a result of a tip-off M15 had received from a mole at a Greek restaurant called *O Live,* who called himself "Trojan Horse". The source admitted to having sympathies with the ROT cause but claimed not to have known about the planned kidnapping.

Ernest Pemberry was two minutes into his first TV interview as new Culture Minister after his abrupt transfer from Justice in the suprise reshuffle when the interviewer told him he had been sacked. He sadly reflected that he had not had the opportunity to write one single letter on the ministry's splendid, crested writing paper, not even a letter of resignation.

In view of Cleo's outspoken demands as cultural attaché in previous press coverage, it was probably only a question of time, but the treachery of Trojan Horse accelerated the inevitable. Cleo woke to hear a booming recording of the Queen calling the dog's name outside her windows. When Bisto began to bark, this was replaced with a policeman in a flak jacket standing in her front garden with a loud hailer through which he demanded that she come out peacefully with her hands up.

Peeking round the curtain she was momentarily distracted by a bulky passer-by sporting an unbuttoned, purple-lined waistcoat. Before she could remember the distant bell this was ringing, a couple of snipers scuttled like startled rabbits across the lawn and into the rhododendrons. There was a splash as one must have fallen into the pond. Others were positioned at strategic points on the surrounding roofs.

Through all this the hostage was laid out on Cleo's bed, blissfully asleep. Occasionally, as Bisto got closer to the rabbit he was chasing in his dream, his nose and legs trembled with the ecstasy of the chase. It was more running than he could ever manage in real life with his stubby legs and enormous belly.

A siege situation was swiftly developing. Cleo knew the game was up, but she had no intention of being rushed. She had watched lots of movies involving tense hostage situations so knew that a negotiator would seek to establish a dialogue with her and persuade her to come quietly. In the meantime, they would gradually send in things she requested to build the relationship. She therefore ran a hot bath and luxuriated in it while she waited. Sure enough, her mobile rang and she was able to have the conversation amidst a cloud of bubbles and steam.

As she skilfully alternated being obstructive and then appearing more pliable, the negotiator in stages agreed to more and more. She tried asking initially for a large bag of prawn cocktail crisps and gradually increased her demands. From the bath she could hear the footsteps on the creaky stairs of the landing as the deliveries were made one by one. When it got to a crate of Champagne, a bouquet of lilies and two dozen oysters she could tell that the negotiator was starting to crack under the strain. The Harrods hamper convinced him he was out of his depth and dealing with a psycho, but the final straw was the Wimbledon Final tickets. He broke down in tears and confessed that it was his first hostage situation so that Cleo was forced to comfort him.

It was at this point that a great hubbub broke out. Cleo could only hear weeping from her phone, but she had left the window open. The dustbin men had arrived, and the altercation floated through to her clearly.

'Get down! You're in the line of fire!'

'Look, mate, I don't care what line I'm in. We're here to collect the bins. Haven't you read the schedule?'

'This is a hostage situation.'

'Well, no one's taking me hostage. It's bin day[164]. You should have come another day. Make sure its's not one of our other collections days either. Today is plastics, tomorrow glass, then food, then it's garden, then electricals, then general household, so that only leaves Sunday, which is our day of rest. Best come then. Now move that vehicle there so we can get through.'

'It's an armoured van and its sited there so we can provide the maximum cover if needed when we go in.'

'Well then, since it's got those caterpillar tracks you won't have much problem driving it off the road for a few minutes while we get through, will you? Otherwise, could you just "go in" to wherever you're going, quickly now and we can all get on with our jobs. Looks like you've got a whole canteen set up there for your lot, so if you give us a cup of tea and one of those sandwiches, we don't mind waiting a couple of minutes. Is that pink stuff in them Spam? No, looks like smoked salmon. Pretty good rations you guys get. Maybe I'll swap jobs. Where can I apply?'

The situation was getting out of control and Cleo could hear that the commanding officer was also getting nervous. He must have seen the negotiator was still blubbing away and seized the phone from him because suddenly she heard his voice on her mobile. The abrupt switch caused her to drop her own mobile in the bath. At the other end the commander thought maybe it was the sound of the hostage being drowned or waterboarded and barked an order. Seconds later, the door to her apartment was smashed flat with a battering ram and an anti-terrorist team charged in.

Cleo's modesty was saved by the foam from her bath salts. After a female officer had searched the bath, presumably to check there were no hidden underwater mines, Cleo was given a towel behind which she was allowed to dress, although two guys with machine guns kept a watch to ensure there was no funny business.

She was then led away, to the astonishment of her neighbours, as Bisto trotted along behind. Cleo resented the Corgi's sense of entitlement. His captivity had been a gravy train so she wasn't surprised he was happy to follow her in the hope of staying on board. The dog obviously believed that sticking close held the promise of steak in abundance and that Cleo would be taking the biscuits with her. Cleo cursed Cassie under her breath for swanning off to Venice. If she had she looked after the brute instead as intended, the plot would never have been exposed so easily.

The Queen was delighted at the news and the flag

over Buckingham Palace, which had been at half-mast since Bisto's disappearance, was raised again. Her only disappointment was to hear that the kidnapper could not be immediately sent to the Tower. The Prime Minister advised her that he would have been delighted to arrange this, but as Cleo had diplomatic immunity there was no option but to release her.

It was lucky that she had held the hostage in her flat which was outside the Embassy building. That would have been very tricky as the special forces would not have been able to storm it. Twenty-four hours later Cleo was deported, and the Greek Government firmly advised that if they wanted any relations at all with Britain, they would keep her well away forever.

As she was about to board the plane, she found Sir Benedict waiting. Although no longer part of his responsibility, after the humiliation he had suffered at Cleo's hands he didn't want to miss this moment. Cleo knew what he wanted. He held out his hand and reluctantly she placed a small box in his palm. Opening it, he confirmed it was the ring from the Ashmolean.

ROT realised that the rot had truly set in and was untreatable for now. The group was temporarily disbanded. As a rebate on annual subscriptions, everyone was given a free meal voucher for *O Live*, a pop-up cardboard model of the Parthenon and was encouraged to go and see the Marbles as often as they could at the British Museum until a new campaign could be set up.

Dark suspicions of treachery circulated among the former ROT members when one of the waiters at *O Live* became Lord Odysseus of No Place in the New Year's Honours list. No Place was apparently a small village near Durham[165], and he picked it because his Homeric namesake had used the pseudonym, Nobody, to get out of various scrapes on his long voyage home. Odysseus, the waiter, couldn't resist the idea of being Lord Nobody of No Place.

In Accident and Emergency at Oxford Royal Infirmary, Dr Seuss was finding his work overwhelming. The case list seemed never ending but he was concerned that his exhaustion might be something more. Possibly salmonella from the rather greenish eggs and ham he had eaten for breakfast[166]. In reception, he could see more patients still coming in. A man who had broken his jaw while limbo dancing under a pole; an elderly gentleman wearing small, round glasses made of the silver rims of milk bottle tops and lollipop sticks for the arms who claimed he was John Lennon; a guy who had been run over while trying to walk in a straight line down the white markings dividing the outer lanes of the M1 to check if he was drunk before deciding whether to drive home; a mum with a small child who had sat on a dummy and got it stuck up it's bottom. The usual stuff, but a lot of it. Surely a chemist would have some cream that would sort out the last one, or as a last resort you could buy a plunger at any hardware store. He would get to these cases in due course, but first he needed to do his ward round.

The doctor was pleased to see Sister Hildegard. Her footsteps clicked as briskly as a typewriter in a shorthand dictation test. That said it all. She was very experienced and didn't take any messing. A little brusque with her bedside manner perhaps, but at least the ward round would be swift and orderly. Things would get done. One or two of the other nurses might be all heart, but they were also all chat. Like Dr Seuss, Sister Hildegard wanted to get on and didn't mind not being part of the crowd. As his maths teacher had told him, 'You've got to be odd to be number one.'

Together they whisked down the corridor and round the beds as if speed reading the alphabet from A to Z. Sister Hildegard ran her eye down the chart at the end of each bed, checked the patient's pulse and, if they were alive, swiftly moved on. Doctor Seuss asked a question only when necessary. If asked for a diagnosis he tried to give short, truthful but non-committal answers with no medical jargon as it reduced the risk of being sued. It helped, however, if the answer was sufficiently ambiguous that it took the patient a few seconds to work out, so he had time to move on to the next patient in the interim.

'Am I going to get through this doctor?'

'Of course, but if you're a betting man and you've already put the house on it, it may be best to give someone else your lottery ticket.'

Coming to the last bed on Ward 3B, Doctor Seuss was surprised to see two new patients. One was so tall his feet were projecting into the corridor in breach of regulations. Sister Hildegard gave him the option of tucking them in immediately or having them amputated. Dr Seuss tried to take the briefest details for a check-up and diagnosis but found this surprisingly difficult.

'Occupation?'

'Italian police Detective.'

'And I'm the Pope.

'I regret to tell you that you must be delusional. I met him very recently and you don't look remotely like him.'

'Look, I'm the one making the medical diagnoses round here.'

'But you said you are the Pope.'

'That was just a way of saying that I think you are the one who is clinically delusional, before you tried to reverse roles and pretend to be the doctor.'

'I'm not pretending to be a doctor. I only just told you I'm a Detective.'

'Ok. Let's just run with that for a moment. So, in that case what are you investigating?'

'I'm looking for a missing Saint.'

'Well, you've come to the right place, or at least lots of my colleagues think they're Saints.'

'The one I'm looking for is headless.'

'That certainly narrows the field. We don't have any of those. Just lots of headless chickens.'

'Chickens?'

'Look, I haven't got time for this. I have checked you over and there's absolutely nothing wrong with you other than that you're insane.'

'I have all my marbles and quite a few more than most. I am Detective Inspector Panettone. I can say even with humility that in Italy everyone has heard of me.

'Panettone ! So, you admit that you are insane.'

'How do you reach that conclusion?'

'Well. I don't know much Italian and I've never heard of you, but I do know panettone is a sort of fruit cake.'

'I insist I am fine. Not mad as a hat person, no vampires in the bell tower and all screws are firm, as you say here.'

'Then why are you hugging that vase.'

'It's my mother.'

'Really? Well, there you are then. Completely insane. I'm discharging you as a bed blocker and by the way you should stop smoking.'

'How do you know I used to be a smoker.'

'Used to be? Well, there's the glow-in-the-dark yellowish eyeballs, the tremor, the stains on your teeth, the furtive glances searching for an ashtray, the hand gestures and the Malboro voucher in your top pocket for starters.'

'I don't think you're the Pope or a Doctor. You must be a Detective.'

The other new patient was stretched out on top of the bed rather than under the sheets and every inch of him was bandaged from head to foot. It wasn't even possible to see his eyes in the dark slit left open above his nose; well, the place where his nose should have been as he seemed to have lost that. He can't have lost his sight because in his hand he was holding an article roughly torn out of a newspaper in a foreign language the doctor vaguely recognised but couldn't read. It had a photo on it of what seemed to be of a ring. Sister Hildegard looked cross. The checklist on the clipboard at the end of the bed was blank. When asked, another nurse passing through the ward didn't seem to know much either.

'Seems he was picked up and brought here by ambulance from the airport, but we don't know anything more. He's not very talkative. In fact, he hasn't said a word. Obviously been in some terrible accident so probably traumatised.'

Dr Seuss looked at his watch. The guy needed closer attention but taking all those bandages off to find what was wrong with him was going to take some time. Best to come back in half an hour when they had finished with Ward 4 as well.

Sister Hildegard agreed and told the nurse to have a full history and the patient's medical records available when they returned to avoid wasting time. She had taken an immediate dislike to the guy and as she was a great believer in preventative medicine adopted her normal practice in such cases of ticking the box on the checklist to put him on the list for a vasectomy, although it looked as if he might have had one already which had gone very badly wrong in which case another would do no harm. Either that, she decided, or he must have had a life and death struggle with a lawnmower.

When, they eventually returned, the bed was empty. It seemed the guy had discharged himself without even telling anyone. Perhaps he had read his checklist. That often had the desired effect. In any event he had taken the dressing gown of the elderly gentleman in the next bed off its peg, along with the beanie the old man had been wearing when he was brought in, and left.

The nurse who had been asked to check up on the patient's history was puzzled. It seemed the guy had arrived at Heathrow on a flight from Thessalonika with a note saying he should be urgently transferred to Oxford, so he had been brought by ambulance. She assumed it was for some specialised treatment, but the notes didn't specify what. The despatch notes from Thessalonika, presumably from a consultant, were unsurprisingly in Greek and signed by someone called Iskandar, although there didn't seem to be a consultant listed under that name at Thessalonika General Hospital.

After some discussion, it was decided that a missing person's report should be filed with the police who would also be asked to speak to the local paper so that the local community were alerted.

As Dr Seuss's bleep went off calling him to yet another crisis, he noticed that the missing patient had dropped his newspaper article. He picked it up in case it might give the police any clues in trying to track him down before he came to serious harm.

When Cassie breezed back into the faculty office at St Barbara's, the atmosphere was as taut and skittish as a kite in a gale. She could tell immediately that something was up, and it wasn't just that Tom had a strange new metal paperweight on his desk. Everyone grabbed a chair and joined the circle. Cassie had brought everyone a coffee and Finn raised a laugh by reminding them all to, 'Beware the Greeks bringing gifts.' They were keen to hear what Cassie had to tell them about St Mark and what she had discovered in Venice, but, overripe with the seeds of their own discoveries, they were bursting to share them.

Finn had been trying for some time to decipher an ancient script called Linear A using the Phaistos disk, a clay-fired circular tablet found at the Palace of Phaistos in Crete. For breaking down languages, as for algorithms, his maths skills came in very useful. Tom was convinced that Linear A might help throw light on Atlantis, particularly by proving or disproving the commonly held theory that Atlantis was Santorini and was destroyed by the Thera eruption. If that was the case, then Tom and everyone looking for Atlantis in the Atlantic had been wasting their time. But at least the mystery of the submerged city would finally be solved, and they would have solved it. The disk was one of hundreds of other surviving tablets preserving Linear A, which was the writing of the Minoans, the great civilisation centred at Knossos on Crete that had traded all over the Mediterranean and beyond. A young architect, Michael Ventris, had long ago successfully decoded Linear B, the script of the Mycenaeans, who succeeded the Minoans, but Linear A remained impenetrable[167].

Now, it seemed, Finn had cracked it and although there were many more tablets to read, the disk already revealed some tantalising hints. It mentioned trade in amber, tin and gold with a great city forty days sail beyond the Pillars of Hercules, which was about right for Dogger Bank. There was also information on the constellations that could be seen overhead, and Puk was studying these to work out whether they provided further geographical clues.

Boudicca had re-examined some of the fisherman's finds from Dogger and these fragments suggested that whoever crafted them had done so with exquisite skill. Ming's anthropological input was helping to identify some of the functional uses of these artefacts within the ancient society that had created them and suggested that this had been highly organised.

Cassie reported on her own findings, which met with a certain amount of confusion and scepticism.

'So, what you're saying is that the fibres found in San Marco predate St Mark? Maybe some much older cloth was used to bandage his body or as coverings on which the mummy was laid when it was brought to Venice,' suggested Boudicca.

'Yes, that's possible,' Ming's voice was muffled behind his black hair curtain. 'But what seems even stranger is your impression, Cassie, that it was a break-out rather than a break-in. That can't be correct, unless someone tunnelled into the chamber and I'm sure you or the police would have seen if that had happened.'

Cassie shrugged. 'It's all Greek to me, too. But even being one, I can't make sense of this.'

The Inspector turned over in bed and virtually dislocated his arm. He had been relieved that the hospital had discharged him so swiftly the previous afternoon but had resolved on getting a good night's sleep. He could diagnose himself and that was what he most needed to calm the emotional sensations he was feeling. His mother might possibly have left him a fortune, but she had also left him a broken heart.

Unfortunately Panettone had forgotten that he had handcuffed himself to the bedframe so that he wouldn't be tempted to get up in the middle of the night and buy some fags, particularly after Dr Seuss's ominous warning. He hadn't been able to avoid noticing that there was a small newsagent round the corner that seemed to be open all hours. Now he scrambled for the key in his pyjama pocket, unlocked himself, dressed, had breakfast in the dining room downstairs, then returned to the hotel room. It wasn't quite what his mother was used to, but it was comfortable enough and the fireplace was quite impressive.

She seemed to be content sitting on the mantelpiece next to a large arrangement of flowers, even though these were artificial and had faded a little.

Initially, the Inspector was going to leave her there for a nap, but then he remembered what had happened the previous day and thought better of it. He had fortunately returned to his room while the cleaner was still there. She had given him a wink and asked if he wanted her to clean out all the cigarette ash, clearly angling for a tip. He had pointed out that it was a no smoking room and, anyway, he didn't smoke.

She had responded with a knowing smile and, waving her hand at the ice bucket, said, 'What's in there then? All that must be a week's rations at a hundred a day.'

It was obvious she found his explanations wholly unconvincing, so Panettone had now stuck a large label on the ice bucket saying, 'Hands off. This is my mother.' Perhaps he should play it safe and take her with him. The Ashmolean was only a few minutes' walk away and a bit of fresh air would do her good. She might also quite like to see some of the museum's many treasures, at least the ones that hadn't been taken in the raid.

Having made this decision, he picked her up under one arm and headed for the lift and the lobby.

As he entered the Ashmolean through the imposing portico, the Inspector had forgotten that Joe might be on duty. He was forced to introduce him to his mother as Joe seemed to think her urn was some form of football trophy. They had a short but lively discussion about Vic Watson, the club's leading goal scorer, who had compiled his prolific record in the 1920's.

Joe was, of course, also bursting with joy at the gift he had received from his other visitor. He was full of thanks, assuming that Panettone had somehow pulled some strings with the club, since the Secretary of the

Supporters Club appeared on his doorstep only hours after the Inspector and had asked a lot of the same questions.

Rather than disillusion him, Panettone simply smiled and shrugged while casting around in his mind as to what to make of this unexpected information. Joe was annoyingly vague in his description of the other visitor. Although clearly foreign, it didn't sound as if he was Russian.

Boyle arrived and gave the Inspector a detailed account of what the police had found following the raid, with photos of DJ's sarcophagus and everything else that had been stolen. Panettone then inspected the room from which the ring had been taken. It was a long way from the galleries in which all the other items had been on display. The replica that had been left in its place was still there and didn't seem especially prominent among the other small items of jewellery that surrounded it in the case. It was hard to imagine why someone would pick it out or why they would leave a replica.

As he leaned forwards, Panettone noticed something else. A small dark crescent, lying close to the replica ring on the velvet that lined the case. He could see that the glass of the case had been opened with great skill leaving only a couple of barely detectable scratches. There was no sign of the brute force evident in the removal of the other stolen items. Opening the case with the key he had been given, he picked up the tiny arch with his tweezers and using a small magnifying glass examined it more closely. As he thought, it was an eyelash thickened with mascara. Joe had been clear that the raiders he had seen were all huge men and they didn't sound like the types to be batting their eyelids. Everything now pointed to the ring somehow being stolen by someone else, either a woman or a man with a love of make-up, and stolen for some other reason.

Working backwards from all the later publicity the ring had received, the motive was now clear. The ring was Greek and had been used to embarrass the Government over the Elgin Marbles. Whoever took it was concerned that the theft shouldn't be discovered straightaway so that they could raise the pressure later, hence the small size, relative obscurity of the item and use of a replica to postpone any discovery of the theft until the most opportune moment to reveal it.

But that still left a lot of questions unanswered. Cleo Popillopolis, who must be the prime suspect, had been deported so Panettone wasn't sure those questions would ever be fully put to bed. In any case, his task was to investigate the San Marco crime and it now seemed unlikely that the ring had anything do with that. He needed to find out what had happened to the other stolen items to see if that gave him the connection he was looking for.

Panettone's phone pinged. ChesstWig had just made his move and the Inspector could see it had the potential to be a fiendish one, threatening to prise open the Great Wall with a knight fork on his king and queen unless he could repel it.

CHAPTER 17 – LOVE AND LYCRA

My wife is really sentimental. On Valentine's Day I gave her a ring and to this day she has never forgotten those three little words engraved inside – Made in Taiwan – Leopold Fechner

The artists who originally protested against the building of the Eiffel Tower had a point[168]. It really was just a grotesque and overgrown electricity pylon, thought Cassie. There were thousands of those in England and, so far as she was aware, no one called them national treasures. But then, the French often had a different view. Even in Greece, no one thought snails were delicacies. But according to the French putting a pylon on steroids and installing it in Paris did not just transform an ugly bug into a butterfly but into a temple of culture. It was however a sunny day and the shadow of the tower stretching down the Champs de Mars was impressive. The monstrosity itself was growing closer as Cassie zipped along on her skates.

She was early and had some time to kill before she met her unknown Valentine at sunset, so she had come prepared. At the base of one of the massive legs of the structure there was a toilet, which enabled her to remove the summer dress she had on over her catsuit, and a cloak room where she could leave her rucksack with the dress and her skates safely inside. Although her new attire attracted a fair amount of attention, Paris was a city of fashion and gave free licence allowing people to wear anything at all, provided of course that it was something the French considered chic.

Looking around, Cassie could see that meeting her date at the appointed time might be a challenge. There were already about fifteen men and some women with red roses gathered around the base of the tower[169]. Perhaps a little more imagination with the secret symbol would have been helpful. Still, that was a problem for later.

Cassie had intended to take the lift as far as visitors could go to the restaurant at the second level and start from there, but she hadn't had much exercise with all her recent travelling to Venice. On the spur of the moment, she felt like taking on a bigger challenge.

As she began to climb, she found it relatively easy to make progress up the lower flex of the giant steel girder that capped the outer corner of the leg she had chosen. Soon, however, the angle of the curve steepened. By then, people on the ground were gathering as swiftly as pigeons to birdseed. Many were shading their eyes as they craned their necks to gaze upwards. Some were pointing and shouting.

Her lithe movements were carrying her up so swiftly that already their calls seemed thin and muffled. The booming pre-recorded police announcement was much clearer.

'Retournez immédiatement à la terre' – Return to earth immediately.

She wondered if this was the same announcement they used for astronauts whose rockets had developed a fault after launch.

'L'escalade est interdite'- Climbing is forbidden.

Then more interestingly, harking back perhaps to the French Revolution.

'Vous serez envoyé à la Bastille' – You will be sent to the Bastille.

By now, she was climbing past the windows of the first level restaurant. An elegant lady, seeing her view blocked, initially obviously thought Cassie was a window cleaner, then choked on her *Poire Belle Hélène*. The steelwork was now approaching the vertical and Cassie had no time to waste but she gave the diners a wave as she disappeared upwards out of view.

She soon reached the second stage restaurant, where some of the staff had by now been warned. A chef in full regalia, with a hat that seemed to have risen like puff pastry, unlocked a window and was calling out. Cassie asked, in her politest French, if he had anything she could eat as she was feeling faint and might fall off at any moment. The chef's eyes widened in alarm. He rushed back into the kitchen, returning a moment later with a bag. Cassie thanked him but, rather than take his outstretched arm, gripped the bag in her teeth and kept on going.

Finally, she reached the top of the third stage of the tower, crammed with various antennae and forbidden for anyone except service engineers. She got herself comfortable, looking out at the incredible view as Paris unrolled like a map below her in every direction. The pastry selection in the bag was utterly mouth-watering. She just hoped it would leave room for dinner later with her date, assuming that's what he or she had in mind. She hadn't got a particular gender preference, nor did she have any idea who the mystery person could be.

After a short fling with Cleo, things had become a bit tense. Although both were still dedicated to the ROT cause, they had agreed to give it a break. So Cassie had no ties at present and was happy to see what was out there, as she was doing now from the highest point in Paris. The nights had been clear for several days now and Cassie was tempted to stay up to wait for the stars to overcome their shyness and gradually emerge, but that would make her late for her secret admirer. She could hardly leave someone waiting who had gone to so much trouble to bring her here in the first place and, although she had some suspicions, she was intrigued to discover who it was.

Leaving the Ashmolean, Panettone decided to take his mother for an ice cream and *Palline Congelate* was the obvious place. He chose a table in the far corner where he would have some peace and quiet. Fortunately, these days his mother was happy to let him get on with his work without the constant interruptions of the past. He ordered two scoops, one for her and one for him. It was a good arrangement. He had to choose a flavour for her that she would have liked but he got to eat both scoops without feeling guilty.

It was just as the spoon reached his mouth that the call came in on his mobile from Scotland Yard. They had sorted through the Chelsea season ticket holders. There were over four hundred Russians but searching for a grouping of three they had identified three students who seemed to be linked together. Two were on nuclear physics courses, learning how to enrich plutonium and the other was an aging athlete now doing a pharmaceutical PhD in anabolic steroids[170]. The season ticket photos however showed that the first two were thin and beany and the third, although larger, looked out of shape and certainly incapable of lifting a sarcophagus.

After eating his ice cream, Panettone was about to get up from his table to pay the bill at the counter. As he did so, he came to a halt as sudden as a sentence hitting a full stop. A few yards away a very snappily-dressed Italian man had entered – someone he knew very well from police records and many past investigations. The mutual recognition was instant. Even though they had never met face to face, both knew so much about the other that felt they had almost grown up together. Cavatappi was aware that Panettone was coming to Oxford but not that he had already arrived. The Inspector would, of course, take great pleasure in putting him behind bars if he could, as he had so many other mafiosi.

Panettone thought Cavatappi was in Italy or else New York. Although the Inspector knew Pappa was the puppeteer who pulled the strings of a major international criminal cartel, he was also all too aware that the file of evidence on him was too thin for an arrest. The question buzzing around him like a mosquito was, why Cavatappi would be in Oxford, of all places? The irritation would only stop when he knew the answer but, from past experience of the mafia, by then he would know that somewhere he had already been bitten.

Without knowing it, both men were sharing the thought: that it was like a meeting between James Bond and Goldfinger. They eyed each other for a moment then with elaborate courtesy Pappa removed his hat. Each gave a slight bow of respect like two wary fencers before a bout begins, neither lowering their guard for a moment.

'It's good to meet a lucky man. Maybe some of it will rub off,' said Cavatappi.

They both knew that Panettone had already survived at least three recent mafia attempts to assassinate him, and there were probably others he didn't know about. One involved a small explosive device hidden in his electric razor. Fortunately, that was the only morning in his life that the Inspector had overslept. It had wrecked his bathroom. A close shave, indeed.

A few weeks later, a crane had dropped a grand piano from several storeys above the front door of Panettone's home in central Rome just as he opened it. But he had just turned on his heel, realising he had forgotten his wallet. Black and white keys were scattered all over the street as if a zebra crossing had been blown to smithereens.

On the last occasion, a sniper's bullet ricocheted off Panettone's hearing aid, went straight through the plate glass window of a Turkish takeaway and buried itself in a doner kebab. The hearing aid made a strange whistling noise after that until the Inspector was able to replace it and the Turkish takeaway's next customer broke his dentures, but otherwise there was no harm done.

Tom arrived at the Eiffel Tower in a mucky sweat. His plane had been delayed and the setting sun was already skimming the horizon. After a final intense blush, the oranges, reds and pinks infusing the waters of the Seine were fading into dusk. Perhaps he had missed Cassie altogether. He couldn't be certain she had made the trip to Paris at all. After her return from Italy, she had casually mentioned that she was going abroad for a couple of days but perhaps she meant somewhere else or maybe she had changed her mind about responding to an anonymous Valentine invitation.

Staring around frantically, he couldn't see any sign of her and his desperation rose as swiftly as mercury in a thermometer dropped in scalding water. Then a commotion at the base of one of the vast steel legs of the tower caught his eye. A young woman in black, yes surely Cassie, was being manhandled down the last few feet to the ground by several French paratroopers. As Tom tried to make sense of it all she was bundled into the back of a police car by a couple of gendarmes.

Another British tourist eagerly gave him a garbled version of what had happened, triggering a brief spasm of doubt in Tom's mind for the first time. Perhaps Cassie was just too much of a handful for him?

He wavered for a second amid mental images of butterflies catching fire as they fluttered too close to the flames of candles and of Icarus spiralling down towards the sea in a tangle of feathers and molten wax. Tom was momentarily tempted to take this last chance to slip quietly away, but then a mist descended again and obscured everything else.

It was love, although it could have been the effect

of that all that sweat. This was the moment when he must show what he was made of by committing himself to the charge like the Light Brigade. The verses of the stirring poem drummed into him at school echoed in his head. "Into the valley ... rode the six hundred ..." A few words forgotten, but the message seemed clear[171]. Cassie was Tom's mission, and he needed to blot out any thought of retreat.

Running to the roadside, Tom flagged down a cab and persuaded the surly driver to set off in hot pursuit of the police car with the promise of a tip that would enable him to indulge himself with frogs' legs, nettles, snails, horse, truffles, sea urchins and other culinary delicacies for several weeks.

Cavatappi had committed many terrible crimes so had no difficulty in swiftly suffocating any trace of emotion. Showing only a perfect set of flashing white teeth he gave Pannetone a charming smile, graciously gesturing them both back to the table the Inspector had just been vacating as if this was a prearranged meeting. He then asked Pannetone if he might join him.

The Inspector was thinking about the small boy he had rescued in Rome. Although Cavatappi was a monster perhaps he had also started life as a vagabond child on the streets of Rome or Naples. Perhaps ice cream was the only taste of something sweet they could experience in their lives. Pannetone recognised he had been fortunate. He could only hope that the young boy didn't follow in Cavatappi's footsteps.

'You look as if you have something on your mind?' Cavatappi enquired.

'Yes, excuse me I was miles away for a moment. It's just that you reminded me of someone.'

Cavatappi knew that the Inspector had a reputation for behaving strangely at times, so simply raised a quizzical eyebrow. Remembering that Panettone smoked he offered him a cigarette. The Inspector took it out of politeness but put it in his pocket.

'I'm trying to give up.'

'Don't bother. Even for the lucky, life is too short and all the best bits are bad for your health.'

'My Doctor tells me that the choice is to give up the fags or give up the ghost. I would prefer not to kick the bucket.'

Cavatappi thought the Inspector was referring to the strange object he had been carrying under one arm and had now placed on the table. 'Well, if you really want to stop then you need to find another addiction. What's the celebration? Do you always carry an ice bucket.'

'Oh, excuse me. I should have introduced you. This is my mother, well really my grandmother. But tell me, why are you in Oxford?'

'Just to indulge a hobby really, my interest in ancient history.'

'In that case you must surely have visited the Ashmolean Museum?'

'There didn't seem to be much point as I heard that a lot of the treasures had been stolen.'

'Yes, including a dead body. In fact dead bodies seem to be vanishing all over the place.'

'Ah. You are referring to St Mark. The ways of the saints are a mystery to us all.'

They were both old hands and knew that this verbal fencing wouldn't reveal anything. When Panettone left,

Cavatappi ordered a coffee. He was still puzzled by the ice bucket and all this confusion over grandmothers. Genius and insanity were different sides of the same coin, so perhaps in grief the Inspector had flipped over from one to the other.

At the police station in the Rue de Vaugirard, Cassie found the gendarmes were easily persuaded that her antics were simply an impetuous escapade and not a sinister terrorist plot. The prejudices of a lifetime had taught them that such offences were never committed by attractive women.

When Tom arrived, she was initially relieved to have some additional support, but matters took a turn for the worse when the gendarmes assumed that he was her boyfriend. Not only did this put an abrupt end to their own flirtatious daydreams, but he was clearly a *rosbif*. Once he had been ejected to wait outside, Cassie was able to convince her captors with difficulty that she was Greek, and this certainly helped.

But the key to her release was joining the poker game they and their colleagues were playing for serious money. Cassie didn't have any on her, but they accepted her stake based on how many nights she would be spending in the cells.

Within a few rounds, Cassie was not only free but had a large pile of cash in front of her, which she graciously handed back to the losers. She then proceeded to beguile her new comrades with her skills at every card game they could think of. It was impossible to understand how the aces flocked to her hands like bees to pollen. Suspicions were aroused when Cassie repeatedly declared a full house of trumps whoever was dealing, but no one could fathom how she did it. Her father's old magic tricks came in useful sometimes.

Although the card games consumed some of the evening, it was fortunately still not too late for Cassie to swiftly slip her dress back on in the Police Station toilets and for Tom to take her for a wonderful meal at *Le Petit Zinc*. They then returned to the hotel where she discovered he had booked two adjoining rooms, the perfect balance between desire and decorum or invitation and disappointment.

Puk was taking advantage of a spell of darkness unblemished by cloud, a rare event in Oxford, and was still trying to work through what she had found. Her desk in the University observatory was surrounded by a litter of empty coffee cups and half-eaten biscuits that had somehow kept her awake over the last twenty-four hours.

The script Finn had deciphered was tantalising. It described the stars and constellations visible at a number of stages on a voyage from Crete through the Pillars of Hercules to Atlantis. Puk believed she could identify most of them, but only by observation could she try and confirm the match. The telescope she chose had quite a low magnification, just sufficient to compensate for light pollution, as she assumed that all the stars mentioned in the script must at that time have been detected with the naked eye. Anything more powerful would potentially lead her astray by bringing into consideration thousands of other stars invisible at that time.

She felt a deep anger that the sky was becoming so congested now with satellites and other modern trash. Without the aid of space telescopes, it seemed that astronomers observing the night sky from earth would increasingly become like the elderly, struggling with cataracts and floaters until they became partially blind. The clutter just added to the many factors that could lead stargazers astray.

A couple of years earlier she briefly thought a comet shower was coming down in Oxford until she realised they were glowing Chinese lanterns released from a college ball. Her professor caused himself greater embarrassment by pointing out one of Jupiter's moons, only for a member of his class to quietly interrupt to show him it was a fleck of toothpaste on his glasses.

Puk's spirits were in free fall as she plotted the results of her observations against the star charts in front of her. Everything seemed to point to a location for Atlantis somewhere near the Canary Islands and there was no other evidence consistent with that. She stood up, about to pack it in and get some sleep, when a sudden thought slapped her in the face.

Of course, half asleep, she had adjusted for the position of the stars for the date at which Plato first wrote about Atlantis rather than the much earlier date when the Minoans would have been writing the Linear A script that Finn had decoded[172]. Plato had, after all, made it clear that he was writing about a time already long past. Shaking off her fatigue, she set to work with renewed purpose.

Tom was mesmerised as he gazed into Cassie's eyes from a couple of dreamy inches away. He could see the flecks of burnt hazelnut and swirl of chocolate now as the hidden intimacies and dark warmth drew him in. This moment was even more blissful than he had imagined. They were sitting on an indigo sofa with the silver fragments of stars frozen in the night beyond the open curtains. The crazy patterns you could draw between them were like the cracks stamped into an icy puddle.

After the frustrations of their disrupted rendezvous the gates of paradise were now slowly opening. In Tom's mind they were encrusted with pearl and the iridescent sheen from the secret inner chambers of oyster shells. The alcohol and the conversation had both been shared in easy abundance so, once they reached Tom's room, everything else came together in a natural flow. Cassie's lips were a caress of blossom; buds that sense the restraints of winter are receding and gently relax as the urgency of spring overtakes them. No need for more words; impossible anyway now they were tongue tied.

Pale but excited, Puk was passing on her news to Finn. Her new calculations pointed to a location somewhere roughly midway between what was now London and Copenhagen – in other words, in the middle of the North Sea and a perfect fit for the Dogger Bank. It was frustrating that they needed to wait for Tom's return. As their boss he should be contactable and concentrating on the job as they all were, but his phone just rang out unanswered. No one seemed to know where he was, or Cassie for that matter. When Finn said that there was little point in staying up any longer, she was reluctantly forced to agree. They had no alternative but to wait and see if the truants would reappear in the morning.

Tom ignored the stale croissant offered to him. Staring out of the port hole he wondered what it would really be like if you could walk to the end of the grey wing that tapered out towards the horizon and then dive off it. The endless duvet of pure white cloud below was so fluffy you would surely just be left bouncing around behind the aircraft. It was hard to believe that you could just plunge through it. Where had everything gone wrong? He found it hard to work out, although when he really trawled through the evening and tried to be honest perhaps he could think of a few possible reasons.

The red poppy field dress slipped off like a dream but then he had been faced with the catsuit. He hadn't bargained on that. Apparently Cassie didn't have time to change fully after her climb and just pulled her dress on over it. All the buttons, zips and fastenings confounded him. She probably felt she was a parcel he was tearing open as he struggled with the squid-like suction of the Lycra. Still, probably not a great idea to joke about two rubber bands trying to make love.

Maybe Cassie had also caught a glimpse of the small silver foil bullet he had bought, just in case, from the dispenser in the gents on departure for Paris and had accidentally left on the coffee table. What was a sign of gentlemanly forethought to one could seem presumption to another, or worse still a casual readiness for any opportunity that might present itself. He just hoped she hadn't seen the branding on the outside which was certainly crass enough to make anyone cringe – "Poppets…just pop it on, pop it off, but don't pop it."

Then of course there had been a few interruptions. He rolled on a drawing pin someone had carelessly left on the sofa. The plaster falling like chunks of packed snow was due to the guests in the room above allowing their bath to overflow. The knock at the door turned out to be a Chinese takeaway with the wrong room number which left a pervasive stale aroma of fish, ginger and garlic as if the chef had built up a sweat in the gym. Then Cassie suddenly became rigid as if struck by rigor mortis. Only seconds earlier there had been no warning that she was on the verge of dying of excitement. Tom was about to call for an ambulance before it turned out it was just acute cramp after her climbing exertions. At least it gave him an excuse to spend a few minutes giving her a massage.

Tom silently admitted to himself that maybe he had also been pretty tense for different reasons. Cassie's exploits in scaling the Eiffel Tower increased his nervousness that she might just be hotter than he could handle. She certainly seemed to like going to extremes. He wasn't sure how he would cope if she started shredding the wallpaper, wailing like an air raid siren or giving him a spanking. Perhaps as a result he had been a little hesitant. Keeping his socks on was always a symptom of stress.

He had tried to remember the only advice his father ever gave him about what he had called "the birds and the bees", an odd concept to Tom's mind as surely these two species never mated with each other. Inevitably the guidance had been heavily veiled in ambiguity rooted in his father's deep embarrassment, "Relax, son. It's like golf. All in the mind, so just keep your focus on the fairway and you will be fine." Tom had no idea what his father meant, but whatever it was he still always ended up in the bunkers.

As quickly as Tom burst one bubble of doubt

another floated up. As if he was a souffle exposed when the oven door is accidentally left open, he felt his confidence deflating. Irrational concerns he would normally have dismissed as ludicrous loomed larger and took menacing shape. The absurd legalism of St Barbara's college regulations had provoked only laughter in the past but now silently resurfaced like an enemy submarine.

"In these regulations '*intercourse*' is strictly defined as academic dialogue involving the exchange of ideas. By contrast '*intercoarse*' is a biological process for exchanging bodily fluids driven by instinct with minimal intellectual content. It disrupts academic study and the harmony of college life. '*Intercause*' is intercoarse that results in unintended consequences. Staff who mix intercourse with intercoarse may end up with intercause. If confused about this staff must make an urgent appointment with the college matron. Also be aware that there is no accomodation on site for children, who under these regulations are classified as illegal subtenants liable to eviction. A member of staff who still plans to indulge in intercoarse should ensure that a consent form signed by all parties concerned is lodged with the college office at least forty eight hours in advance for approval by the Dean."

It was a little late at this point. Cassie was also a member of staff so she could equally have mentioned it? The paperwork could surely wait? That these thoughts were even vague shadows in Tom's mind was evidence of its febrile state.

Completing his virtual replay of the night before, Tom concluded that what finally killed it was when he had been wavering between wanting to say something about love while aware Cassie would think it much too soon. Three little words with only three syllables and eight letters between them. They could work like magic, but only if used at just the right time and in the right way. Tripped up by indecision whether to go the whole hog or say nothing at all, Tom had fallen into the crevasse in between. With hindsight he realised his compromise was far worse than either. At first Cassie could hardly hear the soulful whisper that came out at as more of a mumble.

'What are you trying to say?'

'That my mother would love you.'

To Cassie at first it had all been quite unreal. Tom seemed caught in a tide of passion as he was swept out to sea, but she was still only knee deep, the sand dragging out through her toes. The swell kept slipping past without holding her firm in it's embrace. She was tired from her climb, tipsy from the champagne and a bit confused about a date with her boss. These confusions were struggling with her desire to let go and see where the current carried her. Tom was amusing and she found him attractive but wasn't yet sure if this alchemy was a beguiling spell. Would it forge fool's gold or could it mysteriously become the real thing?

In any case did she want the real thing? And if not, then why not? She did not herself fully understand the knotted contradictions between her deep homesickness and fierce determination to force it's suffocating boundaries back to establish her independence. Again she felt torn, as she did whenever she thought about getting a dog. There were the upsides of affection, silky ears, companionship and another living being always sensitive to your mood, always pleased to see you. On the other hand, there was cleaning up after them, the tiresome regime of feeding and walking schedules and the big doleful eyes when leaving them in kennels. Cassie had no intention of being pinned down by a pooch just yet.

Perhaps the comparison was unfair. Men were seldom as trustworthy as dogs. Tom seemed the long term loyal sort perhaps but that was the underlying problem. That and her increasing awareness that while he might look like a fully grown hound, inside he was still just a puppy.

Quite soon the answer to her immediate dilemma became clearer. She found herself reliving the excruciating embarrassment she had only felt this sharply once before, although for very different reasons. Her first date at school in Mytilene. A rite of passage summed up in her memory by the brief exchange afterwards.

'*Alithino i pseftiko?* - Real or fake?'

What did the boy mean? Life? Who knew? No, she must be misunderstanding him. He had a cute face but his grades suggested that he was like moussaka; the topping looked creamy there was only mushed vegetable underneath. In any case it seemed an odd moment to ask an existential question.

'*Ti* - What?'

'*O organismos.*'

Clearly the oik had been truanting not only from Biology but from Greek as well. A few years later, she would have told him that if a plankton like him wanted to grow up into a real 'organism' this would involve a bit more than clumsy fondling, but back then she was too shy. There were sometimes earth tremors in Lesbos but the ground wasn't moving as far as she was concerned. And her ordeal was not over. Even the darkness of the cleaner's cupboard could not protect her from further shame.

During the next history lesson when the teacher was telling the class about Columbus, all eyes turned towards her. Whispers of breathless wonder were spreading from one desk to another as swiftly as bubonic plague. When the cleaner had hauled him out of their hiding place by the ear, the plankton still had one foot stuck in her bucket, but shame did not deter him now from seizing the moment to claim a much more significant discovery than Columbus' - *I thili!* If only she had not been so overcome by humiliation, Cassie could have told them all that explorers often convince themselves that they have found what they were hoping to discover. Columbus[173] hoped and thought he had found India or China. The plankton had made an even more fundamental error, mistaking the quilted button on the front pocket of her blouse for something else. In any case his discovery certainly wasn't a new one. Every single human being has a couple and a few are even lucky enough to have a third as a spare.

For Cassie the very final nail in the coffin of her date with Tom was none of the many mishaps of the night that he was now so painfully reliving, or even his obvious nervousness. That was something she had enough empathy not only to understand and forgive, but to see as a sign of an engaging vulnerability that stirred some deep instinct within her. What killed it was when he went through every single tool on his Swiss army knife to find the right implement to cut the Lycra free, making her feel like a rotisserie chicken about to be ritually sacrificed.

The Queen's veterinary surgeon examined Bisto carefully. The dog had been almost unrecognisable when he returned to the Palace. Even the footmen, Doggie One and Doggie Two, were shocked at the change that had come over their protégé. It wasn't the black coat. The dye was indelible, but he had been given the same short back and sides by the royal barber that the royal children received when they were sent off for a spell in the army. New fur was already growing, so now he was just left with a strange black fringe with patches of toffee and cream showing through.

It wasn't that he was half starved, as is often the case with hostages, and he certainly hadn't gone off his food, quite the opposite. In fact, he resembled a barrel while refusing to eat anything except steak or to drink until his water bowl was filled with champagne. No, the problem was that he seemed to have suffered a profound personality change and this couldn't all be blamed on the strict diet the vet had prescribed. The dog no longer seemed to have the same affection for the footmen or even the Queen.

Her Majesty was not simply displeased but upset, particularly because Bisto was apparently pining for Cleo. On several occasions, when he had seen Cleo's picture in the papers he had started whining and trotted over to lick her face. The royal vet was desperately searching for something diplomatic to say to explain the dog's strange new attachment when a sudden brain wave flashed into his head.

'I think this may be the first canine case of Stockholm Syndrome, Your Majesty[174]. You may have heard of those unusual instances where hostages become emotionally attached to their captors, even when this appears completely irrational. Some have even joined in their captors' crimes. It's a sort of brainwashing. I suggest referring Bisto to a psychiatrist. I'm not quite sure how it works with a dog in terms of communicating his inner feelings, but I understand there are dog whisperers just like horse whisperers. Bisto will love lying on the couch.'

Cassie elbowed Tom so hard in the ribs that he doubled up and cracked his forehead on the seat in front. It was unfortunate that they were booked back on the same flight. Tom had just assumed it would all work out so differently and even now she could see he hadn't entirely given up. Seeing how crestfallen he was Cassie felt sorry for him, but not sorry enough to give him false encouragement. If a kamikaze pilot crashes their plane but survives you shouldn't let them get straight into another one.

'Tom, I enjoy your company, but we can be mates without mating. I'm sorry, but the connection isn't right.'

'I thought we were a natural pair like ... well for example Adam and Eve.'

'That's not very flattering.'

'Why not? Weren't they made for each other?'

' Think about it Tom. Leaving aside the fact that she was a temptress, Eve was also the only option Adam had. I wouldn't go quite as far as oil and water, but you're goat's milk and I'm ouzo. Fiery alcohol just makes the milk curdle.'

'Goat's milk?'

'Well that's what we had at home. Goats are

inquisitive, like you, and they're not timid like sheep so no need to be offended. My father used to keep a small herd. They were so difficult to catch and bring down from the mountain pasture that he used to joke he would fix up a zip wire and hang them on it by the horns. But they don't drink ouzo.'

'That sounds definite. So, my life has turned to sour milk.'

'Tom, don't be so melodramatic. You would look less miserable in a selfie from your own funeral. It was my catsuit that was destroyed. Even if I could forgive you for that, we just weren't meant for one another. There's a buzz between Barbie and Ken[175] but not between Cruella de Vil and Shrek. That may sound harsh but remember Shrek was the soft-hearted one who found love in the end.'

Tom looked as if he had been tasered. Cassie realised her efforts to be honest but lighten his mood with humour weren't working.

Reining back a bit, she cantered on at a gentler pace. 'I believe in love at first sight too, Tom. But just because it's at first sight doesn't mean it can work with everyone first time. Otherwise, you would have shacked up with the girl from the local chip shop at seventeen and I would be back on Lesbos mending some fisherman's nets while he strummed his *bouzouki*. Mind you, if first sight did always work, it would save a lot of grief and put thousands of dating agencies out of business. This love stuff is as hard to catch as a waterfall in cupped hands and even more unfathomable than the ancient mysteries we are trying to solve. You need to keep the faith and carry on looking.'

Tom had read that one of the key psychological

elements of love at first sight was a mutual memory of a wonderful initial bonding experience. He had to accept that his and Cassie's memories would be an elasticated bad dream, not so much bonding as involuntary bondage.

He tried to persuade her that, sometimes, things that seemed ill-matched, and even apparent opposites could work perfectly together – like breakfast for lunch or laughing so hard you cry. But Cassie told him that he was trying to push Niagara Falls uphill. If it was just all a question of wishful thinking, she would already be in a relationship with Percy Blakeney the Scarlet Pimpernel[176], D'Artagnan and the other three musketeers all at once[177] or else Cathy in *Wuthering Heights*.

Tom was stubborn as well as still smitten, suggesting that Cassie might come round, more like Elizabeth and Darcy in *Pride and Prejudice*. She was however adamant and pointed out that anyway if that was the story they were following it certainly couldn't be love at first sight. Facing up to the inevitable, Tom felt he had no option but to make a confession.

When he admitted that he had sent her the other two Valentines as well, she laughed so her dimple danced on her cheek, but pointed out that if you try to cover every angle it shows you don't understand what it is you are really trying to find. Then she made a suggestion about the Valentines that might be an adventure for both of them. Tom wasn't looking for another adventure, nor was he ready for one, but he was too bruised to respond.

After they landed at Heathrow, Cassie parted from Tom in Baggage Reclaim. It seemed deeply symbolic. He imagined that no one would ever come for him, and he would be left going round and round on the carousel like some rucksack abandoned from an unknown flight to a forgotten destination.

Cassie headed back to her flat. On arrival, her first act was to fill out an insurance claim for her catsuit, which she stated had been shredded by someone who had suffered an epileptic fit while mugging her. It was only then that she noticed she had received a missed call. It was from Venice, saying that the Inspector who had authorised her access to the San Marco crime scene would like to meet with her.

She was intrigued to meet Inspector Panettone anyway, as she had heard he was both a very cultured man and a very famous detective in Italy, albeit also known for his modesty. She suggested the British Museum as it wasn't far from her student apartment, and she was interested to see if any changes had been made to security arrangements since her break-in. Cleo had got in touch as soon as she had reached Athens following her deportation, advising Cassie to lie low for the time being, like the rest of ROT.

When Panettone approached her table in the museum café, Cassie's attention was glued to a small article about a seriously injured patient from Thessalonika who had gone missing from Oxford Royal Infirmary. The whole affair seemed very odd. She could see why no proper description could be given because the photo showed that the bloke was bandaged up like a mummy from one of those horror movies.

When Panettone coughed gently, she quickly rose and shook his hand before offering him a cappuccino. As the coffee arrived she noticed that he had a little difficulty sipping it when the level dropped because his huge, ridged nose reared up from so close above his moustache and top lip. The gunmetal hair and grey eyes were very distinguished, yet there was a tenderness in them and she found it very touching when he explained the ice bucket which she had already noticed was engraved with a name in her native tongue. Panettone said that his mother had always wanted to see the Elgin Marbles.

Without even realising it, Cassie found herself drawn into a conversation about her own love for the Marbles, her mother and father and her childhood in Lesbos. The Inspector was a wonderful listener. Cassie almost had the feeling that they were in a mutual counselling session as he also shared memories of his mother and her extravagant embrace of life.

Panettone thought Cassie was delightful, but he had not forgotten that he also had a job to do. There was something about her he couldn't quite put his finger on until the mention of the Elgin Marbles set off a small avalanche of various facts, stored like knick-knacks in odd corners of his mind. As he almost subconsciously began to assemble them, he listened to her report on her visit to San Marco and then saw a moment of indecision in her eyes.

Cassie was wondering whether it was wise to tell Panettone how she had broken into the Tax Fraud Office, but unless she did how could she explain what she had found out about Father Matteo or give him the photos she had taken of the file on the priest and the restaurant. She was still hesitating, her slim hands clasped together in her lap, when Panettone said gently:

'Sitting on a fence can be uncomfortable.'

'What do you mean?'

'Well, I can see there's something you think you may be able to help me with, but perhaps you will find it easier to tell me if I dangle a carrot you can't refuse?'

Cassie had noticed the Inspector's rather eccentric use of idioms, and like Peel and Boyle was finding it contagious, responding nervously with a few Greek ones before she could stop herself, *'I am doing the duck. You are eating my ears. Grab an egg and shave it.'* – I'm staying quiet, you are being too pushy and asking me something impossible. But Panettone was not to be put off and although his tone did not change its measure slowed a little and he sighed as if pushed to the verge of being impolite.

'Perhaps I can be more persuasive. You see, we were just talking about the Elgin Marbles, and I know you are both an expert in ancient history and that you are Greek. It's also just occurred to me where I've seen you before. On the news on Sunday evening there was quite a stir about a young lady who was arrested after climbing the Eiffel Tower right to the top. I think that's only the second time anyone has managed it and I saw footage of the arrest afterwards. It's obvious that the cultural attaché, Cleo Pillpopper or something like that ... the lady who was deported....she can't have climbed into the British Museum through a tiny skylight. No disrespect, but there's a reason you can catch tadpoles in jam jars but not whales. Perhaps you might like to come clean...get a load off your mind?'

When Cassie remained silent, Panettone smiled without smiling and ordered another cappuccino for them both, then continued. 'So, we have the Elgin

Marbles connection and then there's the ring taken from the Ashmolean, also used as part of the same campaign. I think it was ROT; sorry I don't intend to be rude, I mean the name of the group involved who were trying to get the marbles repatriated? I know the ring wasn't taken by the same person as the other items stolen from the Ashmolean.'

'How do you reach that conclusion', Cassie asked as innocently as she could.

'It's partly that the other stolen artefacts are still missing and no replica was left of those. Also even the museum didn't regard the ring as a great treasure and was still investigating its provenance. But the killer is that I found an unusually long ladies' eyelash in the display case that held the ring and the caretaker only saw three huge men. I hope you don't mind me saying, you have lovely long eyelashes, Cassie. And, of course, you're not only Greek but an amazing climber.'

'Coincidences don't prove anything.' Cassie said with more than a dose of defiance.

'So you may say, but if I felt compelled to do my duty and report my suspicions to Scotland Yard, no doubt you would be happy to take a DNA test as a match against the eyelash to prove that my theory is insane? That would give a definitive answer. But I'm not really interested in the Elgin Marbles, just in St Mark. So if you promise to help me in any way you can, I'm happy to accept your word, and I can certainly help you stay out of jail. At my age, it's shocking how easy it is to forget things.'

Cassie saw there was no escape. In any event, she wanted to help with the recovery of the Ashmolean treasures and solve the mystery of St Mark's disappearance as well. Also, she liked Panettone and his dry wit. As she told him about her night-time escapade in Venice, he steepled his fingers and listened with both keen interest and amusement.

The scans of the tax investigation files Cassie showed to the Inspector revealed that the tip-off had come from an informer, Angelo Capelli, who seemed to have been keeping the books for various mafia operations including the relics scam. Capelli was now stated to be under the protection of Interpol and Panettone made a mental note to find out where he was and arrange an interview as soon as possible. Father Matteo had been co-ordinating the process of creaming off around ten percent of all the donations received from all relics in Italy and, in particular, those given for blessings from St Mark.

All these funds had been funnelled through the restaurant's secret set of duplicate financial records and paid on to an offshore bank account in the name of a Panamanian entity which went under the innocuous name of the Promotion of Educational Studies Trust. The records also contained regular monthly payments from PEST to Father Matteo's personal account which he drew on for his expensive tastes in food and wine. The different tentacles of Italian bureaucracy rarely thought to speak to one another. They just stuck to their own lanes like cars in a motorway traffic jam. It hadn't occurred yet to the Tax Fraud Office to tell the police about Father Matteo, even though the police were investigating his murder.

Panettone couldn't yet see the Oxford connection to all of this, but he was beginning to think there must be one somewhere. This scam and the obvious mafia link had the hallmarks of Cavatappi's handiwork stamped all over it, and Cavatappi wasn't in Oxford for sightseeing or study.

Then Cassie provided the Inspector with an unexpected bonus. She explained that she had known about the Ashmolean raid in advance because she had managed to secretly hack into the raiders' communications. Not only did this confirm that they were the Bolshie Bears, who had been causing so much clandestine chaos around the world, but Cassie told him that the leader of the raiders was Dmitry Collossovitch, a member of Russian special forces.

Panettone immediately put in a call to Scotland Yard. When they searched the Chelsea database again, sure enough, not only did Collossovitch come up with a photo but also his two colleagues. A quick cross check with Border Force showed that their visas had been issued on entry to the UK two days before the raid. They had put down the reason for their trip as visiting historical sites, including the Ashmolean Museum and particularly Salisbury Cathedral[178].

Panettone felt he could finally see some progress; even more so when Cassie suggested that she might be able to use her hacking skills again and maybe find some clues to the gang's current whereabouts. He was however getting increasingly fidgety, which was so obviously out of character that Cassie asked him if he was okay.

What she didn't know was that he had covered his body with nicotine patches and must have overdosed on them[179]. Alarming surges of adrenalin were coursing through him with growing frequency. Panettone apologised to Cassie for 'giving her the bum's rush' by leaving in such a hurry. Leaping up he asked her over his shoulder to let him know as soon as she had any news, then began running in strange jerky movements towards the exit.

CHAPTER 18 – CARPE DIEM

[180]

Dating is when you pretend you're someone you're not to impress someone you don't know – Melanie White

The wall of the office at St Barbara's looked like a collage. There were thousands of pieces of paper stuck, apparently randomly, over a large board. Finn thought that, if he had been named Hockney or Pollock, he could probably have sold it for a fortune. Standing back, however it gave him an overview of all the fragments of evidence he had found to date. There were several balls of coloured string on the table in front of him and every now and then, as a link occurred to him, he would cut a length off and use it to make connections.

The progress with the Atlantis project was exciting but the thing that was really occupying his attention at present was the ring from the Ashmolean. He had even been along and inspected the replica, as the original hadn't yet been replaced, and was also able to compare this with the original through enlarged photos. The head in silhouette was Alexander the Great. The rams' horns around his ears confirmed this as they were a long-established symbol of his claim to be the son of the Egyptian god, Ammon Rah, whose temple Alexander visited at Siwa. Alexander appeared like this on hundreds of the coins minted during his reign.

What was so special about the ring was the inscription. It seemed as if no one had picked this up before but, as Finn had mentioned in his team presentation, "To the strongest," were the words that Alexander used on his deathbed when giving his signet ring to Perdiccas to act as his Regent. Finn was beginning to wonder if anyone had considered whether this could be that very signet ring. Its survival might seem improbable at one level, but, at another, that would explain why the ring had passed through so many hands yet been preserved.

If so, it was an extraordinary treasure and a symbol of Alexander's power expressed in its most personal form; the ring that gave authority for rule over an empire that had stretched from Greece to India.

Tom had returned the previous evening, morose and dejected. Finn knew him too well not to put two and two together, given Cassie had also been away. They had obviously met up somehow and it seemed clear Tom's hopes had been shot down without even the consolation of a blaze of glory.

The developments on the Atlantis project, at least, acted as a partial tonic. Puk was bubbling over to tell them both about her revised calculations based on the Linear A script. These suggested that the star constellations mentioned in the script were consistent with a voyage that placed its destination, Atlantis, exactly where Tom had suspected. The possible significance was still sinking in when Tom received a call and left again in a mad rush with Boudicca.

He grabbed his car keys before he was reminded that a small cube of metal wouldn't take them very far, so Boudicca was driving. She owned an ancient Citroen which some rudely called a tin snail or upside-down pram. The model was referred to in France as a *deux chevaux*, although this was an exaggeration[181]. The engine was really only equivalent to an aged donkey, not two horses. But when it proved stubborn and refused to start, there was always the crank handle. Despite the Gallic quirks, with Boudicca at the wheel it was transformed into the closest vehicle you could get to a chariot of the Iceni tribe who, under the leadership of her ancient namesake, terrorised the Romans. She'd told Finn that's why she bought it. That, and the fact you could peel and roll the canvas roof right back like a sardine can, so it became a windswept convertible as it bucketed along.

The call had come from Captain McKracken, skipper of a small trawler called, Gone Fishing, in Grimsby. When he first bought it, the boat had been called, Wet Dream, but his wife insisted he changed it. The seaman was a taciturn man. He therefore renamed the boat to say where he was and what he was doing without the need for him to say anything at all. The call to Tom had been very short. 'Found something,' he'd said and then the line went dead, but Tom didn't need any more encouragement.

As they reached the quay and Boudicca screeched up, just missing a couple of huge bollards. Gone Fishing was already casting off. They leapt out and jumped across the widening gap just in time. Soon, the little boat was plunging up and down like a dolphin on a pogo stick. Holding on as if their lives depended on it, which they very probably did, Tom and Boudicca grappled their way along the rail and collapsed on the small bench in the cabin. McCraken stayed at the wheel and said nothing but pointed at a strange object on the floor.

Tom picked it up and they examined it carefully. It was covered in barnacles and badly cracked, but there was little doubt about it. In their hands they had part of an ancient amphora and, stuck to it by the sea debris it had accumulated, was a piece of amber. Tom worked the amber loose and Boudicca carefully washed the surface to reveal engravings of a ship entering a port with mighty walls. The design of the ship was not one they had ever seen before, but it fitted Plato's descriptions.

A couple of hours later, Gone Fishing cast its nets over Dogger Bank and the Captain silently gestured to some diving equipment in the corner. One of the crew helped them get kitted out.

'It's not too deep here but its murky. Don't stay down long.' Then he added apologetically, 'The skipper's almost forgotten how to speak. He used to have at least two words to rub together but he forgot what they were due to his wife's constant jawing and took up fishing as the next best way of getting some peace.'

At the hospital Cassie was told that they had given all the details of the missing patient to the police, so she went on to the police station. Luckily, DC Peel was on duty. When he saw Cassie he was only too keen to assist, 'a member of the public,' as he insisted on calling her as if the public were a neighbouring tribe with whom the police were trying to establish friendly relations after years of internecine conflict.

What Cassie read on the despatch notes from Thessalonika Hospital left her feeling light-headed and when she saw the scrap of newspaper the missing man had been carrying as well, she really did have to lie down while Peel grabbed the first aid kit and tried to tend to her.

'Bit rusty with this, miss. Last time I used it was at a student riot when one of them hit DCI Boyle with a hockey stick. Serious incident. Went down for a long time.'

'Poor guy. How long?' asked Cassie, thinking that a lengthy prison sentence seemed more than a little disproportionate and would have put an end to the student's entire career.

'Ten minutes, at least. Good job the DCI had his helmet on,' he told her. Then he asked, hopefully, 'Any chance you would feel better for a bit of mouth-to-mouth resuscitation?'

As she left the police station, Cassie could sense she needed a break to clear her mind. The ease with which she had opened up to Panettone reminded her again that, deep down, she was homesick. Her restless thirst for adventure was still at war with the draw of family and lifelong affection.

Fortunately, she had just received a message that gave her an opportunity for a some fun and time out that might possibly also be an antidote. She would do some hacking to assist Panettone as soon as she could, but it was important to get your priorities right in life. The Bolshie Bears had been causing mayhem for some time now and another twenty-four hours of robbery and murder wasn't going to change a world which was full of it already.

When Panettone arrived back at his hotel, his heart sank. He quickly put on his reading glasses and lowered his gaze in the vain hope of passing by unnoticed. The lugubrious receptionist with the walrus moustache was at the welcome desk. Every day he had something depressing to say, often about the news. Everyone expected most of the news to be full of doom, but there was no need to search out the very gloomiest item. Panettone was convinced the guy spent most of his life reading the obituaries but concentrating only on how people died rather than what they had done in their lives. It was like an encounter with winter in the middle of spring.

'Afternoon, Inspector. Did you see there's been a pile-up on the M1? Canada has declared war on Denmark[182] and Elvis has died again. In fact, one thousand five hundred people have died in the UK today already.'

'But that's just the national daily average', Panettone replied, 'and as for Elvis I'm sure he will pop up again somewhere.'[183]

The Inspector rushed past before the receptionist could say anything else, so when he reached his room, he didn't know a couple of guests were waiting. Because they were so obviously distinguished, the hotel had been happy to give them a key. Panettone was therefore taken by surprise to find Cardinal Cantucci and Sister Felicity perched on the edge of his bed as the chairs were laden with clothes he hadn't properly unpacked and books by various chess grandmasters.

Panettone's normal calm was already ruffled, if not to say flustered, by the nicotine patches, so his behaviour had become a little erratic. He made a pot of tea but, as well as the tea bags, accidentally put in a couple of the pills his doctor had given him. He had forgotten to take these when he first got up and it was in his mind to do as soon as he got back to his room, but the combination of excess nicotine and his unexpected visitors had confused him. The pills were for his low thyroid and helped adjust his sense of balance.

The Cardinal explained that the Pope had sent them to obtain an update in person. He was becoming increasingly concerned that the Inspector's failure to report back suggested he was getting nowhere. Until Panettone's meeting an hour ago with Cassie that was true, but now he had something he could tell them. Cantucci listened attentively, only distracted for a little when Panettone, thinking it was a sugar bowl, poured some sugar into the red velvet skull cap the Cardinal had left upside down on the table.

Satisfied at last, the Cardinal left but said the Pope had insisted on putting Sister Felicity at the Inspector's disposal. The Popemobile was in the hotel car park ready and waiting should he need it. This took one weight off Panettone's mind. With Cassie's help, he might soon be able to catch some criminals, but everyone knew that this would be impossible without a terrifying car chase first. DC Peel had driven him to Joe's house and Panettone didn't think the young policeman would be able to keep up with a child on a bike who hadn't yet learned how to ride without stabilisers. Sister Felicity could teach him a thing or two.

While Sister Felicity retired to her own hotel room, Panettone went down to the lobby with the Cardinal to say farewell. In fact, he had to ask the gloomy receptionist to help him get the Cardinal to his taxi as the poor man seemed to have some problem with his balance and was wobbling around all over the place. As he left and they walked back inside Panettone was able to cheer up the receptionist with the good news that he had just seen Elvis going into Marks and Spencer's.

Dan's mobile rang again. It was the third time from the same number within a couple of hours. The first at breakfast went dead when he tried to answer. The second only a few minutes ago did the same again, but before it cut off he caught a handful of words from a muffled conversation. It sounded something like, 'I just can't do this, Fi' before the line abruptly died. He would have assumed it was a scam but the words seemed intriguingly at odds with that. Now with the call coming in again he hesitated a couple of seconds, then answered suspiciously.

'Who's that?'

'My name's Finn.'

Ah, Finn not Fiona so it had been a bloke with a different voice talking, not to a woman as he had thought, but to this guy Finn who for some reason was now calling instead but using the same phone. The voice continued in a soft Irish lilt.

'You don't know me, and it's a bit difficult to explain this.' Dan waited in silence sensing some embarrassment at the other end of the line.

'I'm calling about a girl...' So that explained the embarrassment.

'Look I don't need a girl or if you're asking me to arrange one for you you've definitely got the wrong number.'

'No, no, I'm sorry. But you gave it to this lady and she's passed it on to my friend and he's asked me to contact you.'

'What the hell are you on about? Gave what? If this is some joke about paternity or contact tracing for something contagious then I'm hanging up.'

'Your mobile number. You gave it to her. Remember the girl you met at the British Museum? Short dark hair. You gave her your number. Remember now?'

Then slightly belligerently, 'Perhaps you think you are such a prize you just hand your number out like a raffle ticket to every girl you meet. But even if you do you wouldn't forget this one unless you have a guide dog. She's Greek and her looks would make even her own mirror feel insecure.'

Dan felt a sudden quickening of his pulse which he instinctively struggled to suppress. 'She was brunette when I met her, if you mean the archaeologist?'

'Yes, that's the one. Thing is, I've got a Valentine gift you could give her if you are interested.'

'But Valentine's Day was a week ago. I suppose a turkey might celebrate if you gave it a Christmas present at New Year but otherwise wouldn't that just be a bit insulting.'

'Well, it was her suggestion.'

'Does she know what the gift is?'

'No, just where to meet you if you turn up with it, but she's sure to love it.'

'So, what happened and how do you fit into this?'

'I'm best mates with the guy who sent her the Valentine card telling her where and when to meet. She asked him to call you and suggest you give it to her instead.'

'This is possibly the most confusing conversation I have ever had. So why isn't he calling?'

'He tried a couple of times, but he's still heart broken and just couldn't bring himself to do it.'

'So he asked you?'

'Yep. Like I said we are best mates.'

'You two sound like teenage schoolgirls if you ask me.'

'I wasn't asking you and I if I put this phone down what will you do about it? Seems you haven't got her contact details. But given your attitude I'll tell her it's a "no" anyway and make my mate happy as well.'

Now Dan unexpectedly found himself on the back foot. 'No, wait...' , but the phone had gone dead again. He put his head in hands, shocked at how a spark of excitement could just die in an instant, even before it had time to take hold. What should he do? It stuck in his throat to call the idiot back but there seemed no option. After a lot of ring tones he heard the same Irish voice again but this time dead flat with no lilt.

'Your call is important to us. You are held in a queue and will be answered shortly... what do you want?'

'You cut me off.'

'Went through a tunnel. Ok, I'm lying. I knew you would call back. Changed your mind?'

'No. I was just about to say I'd like to meet her when you hung up. Where?'

'Newcastle station.'

'What? That's a long way north. A couple of hundred miles at least.'

'Ah. There is a whole alien world north of London you know and even far distant lands beyond Newcastle. Never heard of Scotland or ventured beyond the safety of Watford Gap? It's an industrial wasteland up there full of ravening beasts and old mine shafts. I wouldn't risk it if I was you.'

'Hey, Finn you said your name was. Give me a break. I'll come. Just satisfy my curiosity and tell me why it didn't work out with your mate?'

'Wrong chemistry she said. Like goat's milk and ouzo apparently.'

'And which of those was she? Just need to make sure I can get it right.'

Fabrizio had done an excellent job. Normally it would have been extremely difficult to tail Panettone without him noticing, but he had left his mother at his hotel table over breakfast to go to the gents. Fabrizio had seen the chance to bribe the receptionist to carefully remove the lid of the ice bucket and bury a small transmitter in the ash.

The only problem had been the guy's negativity. He seemed convinced that the large wad of cash must be counterfeit. It was, of course, but Fabrizio still found it annoying that the receptionist's belief was clearly based on a glass-half-full view of life rather than any insight or even instinct. Despite this, the plan had worked a treat. Not only had it been possible to track Panettone remotely to the British Museum, but Cavatappi had overheard the Inspector's entire conversation with Cassie.

He now knew it was the Bolshie Bears he was looking for. Either he would get to them first through his own enquiries or else, as a fall back, if the ice bucket was close enough, he would hear what Cassie had to tell Panettone when she reported the results of her hacking. All he had to do was relax and wait. That gave him time for an ice cream at *Palline Congelate* and another attempt to break down The Great Wall in his chess game.

Children, parents and tourists were streaming through Regent's Park. Although it was building up to be hot and humid, Tom was downcast and miserable. Why had he come? Although he hardly cared, things were made more complicated as he had no idea who was going to turn up today. The deal he had made on the plane with Cassie was that he would call Dan and line her up for the date he had booked with the second Valentine's card he had sent her. In return she had someone in mind to join him for the third, the special outing to London Zoo. She had assured him it was nothing serious and on his return Finn had said in that case he might as well go. Anything to take his mind off his misery.

Now however he was getting a little nervous. Perhaps he should just run away. But then a woman he knew came round the corner and it wasn't as bad as he had feared. Someone he felt comfortable with and might even be able to open up to.

Tom had been in denial but Finn's insight about him had a lot of truth to it. He had often been secretly attracted to older women. He found the idea of being taken in hand by someone who knew what they were doing reassuring and Boudicca certainly knew exactly what she was doing.

The zoo tour which earlier had seemed a ludicrous and cruel frivolity gradually lifted his spirits. Coming hot on the heels of their dive together on the Dogger Bank, Tom felt increasingly at ease with Boudicca. He had to admit that swimming with the zoo seals was fun. By feeding time he was even acting the fool, copying them by catching a fish thrown by the keeper in his mouth and swallowing it whole, although he was then violently sick.

It was just the sort of idiotic and juvenile behaviour that Boudicca found irresistible. She also enjoyed running her hands through the chest hair of Kong the gorilla, which was a very close match for her own tawny locks. Her slight twinge of disappointment when Tom admitted his own chest was as smooth as a bar of soap was swiftly banished. She consoled herself with the thought that gorilla hair would block the shower. Kong's keeper said he was very tame, but Tom turned down the chance to give the gorilla a hug in case Kong hugged him back[184]. Apart from fracturing his skull, he had also broken a couple of ribs when he had walked into the lamppost while ogling that blonde woman at the bus stop on the night of the Ashmolean raid and he didn't want to risk a recurrence.

The only moment that briefly threatened to disturb a perfect afternoon was when Tom received an unwelcome call but fortunately he had the presence of mind to deal with it. The Dean was trying to contact him for an update on the faculty projects to pass on to Cavatappi. When his video call was accepted, instead of Tom's face as expected the Dean found himself staring at a bright pink expanse with a deep crevice through the centre, encircled with purple, blue and yellow. He had no idea what he was looking at but it was clearly a wrong number. He rang off just as the baboon dropped its tail and Boudicca's stifled laughter got the better of her.

Towering meringue clouds had been piling up to impossible heights above them, shaping new fantasies from thin air. They drifted slowly as their own creations became increasingly unstable and their darkening bellies snagged on the skyline. Sure enough the first scattered drops of a warning salvo spotted the ground as if from a dam that had sprung a leak.

Tom and Boudicca reached the striped awning of a bandstand just as a ferocious belt of rain raked the paving stones, ricocheting off them like machine gun fire. As the initial fury abated Tom sprinted to a small shop on the corner opposite and returned, soaked but self-satisfied, clutching a golfing umbrella emblazoned with the slogan "Drop in or drop out." There hadn't been much of a selection to choose from.

As they made a break for it towards the nearest tube station, this small fabric circle drew them into it's orbit, forcing them to synchronise their steps and cadence in a mutual concern not only to avoid getting drenched themselves but to ensure that the other also stayed dry. Dr Bacon would no doubt have described it in astronomical terms as a kind of emotional gravity.

The candlelit dinner that evening had all been part of the same Valentine package Tom had booked for Cassie. After far too much wine, he was already running miles ahead of a heart that wasn't quite ready for it, telling Boudicca that she was unique. Just like everyone else, of course, but she seemed to understand that his earnest attempt to compliment her came from his nervousness not to make a mess of things, which, of course, he then immediately did by suggesting that if they were the only two people left on earth the human race would have a flourishing future.

In this state, he was as subtle as Moby Dick trying to dance Swan Lake. Yet, it was Tom's youthful awkwardness and eagerness to please that Boudicca found somehow charming. It filled her with a tender feeling that she needed to protect him. She wasn't entirely sure if it was just some maternal hormones getting a bit confused, but frankly she didn't give a damn.

Discussing their Dogger dive, they were in no doubt that they had discovered Atlantis. In the beams of their headtorches, and through the waving forests of seaweed, they had been able to trace the outlines of extensive walls, temples and the footings of huge towers – the skeleton of a drowned city stretched out on the seabed.

But somehow, they both felt that to reveal a mystery that had lasted for thousands of years would be wrong. It might illuminate history but only at the cost of impoverishing the imagination. And it was also intensely romantic to be the only two people sharing such an incredible secret.

In fact, had Tom been giving it any thought he might have realised that this was just the sort of foundational memory he had read was so psychologically important for a lasting relationship. Instead he did tell Boudicca what Cassie had said about ouzo and goat's milk and she reassured him that, unless provoked, she was more like richly mature dark chocolate than ouzo herself. It seemed likely therefore that hot chocolate made with goats milk would be just fine.

When Boudicca asked him if he would like to

have one at her place rather than the restaurant, Tom hesitated for a moment conscious that as a matter of common sense everything was yet again moving far too quickly. But this only lasted a moment as Tom didn't have common sense in abundance, and it wasn't much fun anyway. If things went beyond hot chocolate he just hoped Boudicca wasn't wearing a catsuit under her little black number.

As Cassie's train came into Newcastle station, she felt a surge of excitement. After her evening with Tom, she felt surer of what she wanted at the moment from any relationship. That was some fun with no strings attached and Dan had seemed the type. Although he clearly had some complicated baggage in his past and a small boy to look after that might well mean he was looking for a light interlude as well.

The long platform stretched away to infinity and, at first, she couldn't see any sign of him. A glimpse of purple distracted her as it had momentarily in Venice. Then she picked Dan out on the edge of a clump of people all jostling for position as they tried to outguess each other as to where exactly the train would come to a halt.

The game was to be in a good position to board first but without too obviously barging others out of the way. This little snapshot of the tension between self-interest and a veneer of civilisation struck her as a microcosm of life generally. Dan was wearing a leather jacket and looking quite well-groomed in a casual way. She thought he had visited the barbers since she had met him at the museum and wondered where his son was. With grandparents probably.

'Hi. I hope you don't mind, but I'm standing in for

Tom.'

Cassie laughed and was pleased that he accompanied the greeting with a kiss on the cheek. He had hired an open-topped sports car which he drove very fast. The afternoon and chat seemed to be disappearing behind them just as quickly. Cassie was, however, itching to have a turn at the wheel and Dan was soon in no doubt as to which of them was the natural rally driver.

As the needle of the speedometer threatened to spin off its dial altogether, Dan asked whether she had any points on her licence and whether she was at all concerned about speed cameras. Cassie laughed and replied that if you went fast enough the photos of your number plate would be too blurred to read. This seemed to amuse Dan, but not entirely reassure him. As Cassie gunned the engine out of a chicane, overtook a silver Range Rover and sped along the next straight, Dan instinctively clutched his head. But it was too late.

The elderly driver of the Range Rover was already shaken by the tailwind Cassie had created when there was a loud thwack as a squirrel hit the windscreen. At least, he thought it was a squirrel, but his wife was shrieking that it was a rat. Her screams were pitched high enough to shatter glass, but luckily the windscreen was laminated. The sound was off the spectrum for his hearing aid which just distorted the whistle to a level that he thought might melt his brain.

'Get rid of the horrid thing!' she shrieked.

In desperation he switched the windscreen wipers to their highest setting. They whipped the squirrel backwards and forwards like a mop but still didn't dislodge it. How had the creature jumped so high in the first place or had it just fallen from a branch? These thoughts flashed through his mind as his hearing aid exploded and he hit a signpost before crashing into the ditch. All he remembered as the car came to a halt were the words on the road sign: "Beware of the wildlife."

Back in the sports car, Cassie was oblivious to the fate of the Range Rover but had almost driven off the road herself. Dan's appearance had completely changed. He hadn't turned into a werewolf, but he was totally bald[185]. She had just seen what must have been his toupee disappearing in the rear-view mirror at the speed of light as he clutched at his head. She thought at the station that his hair was shorter, but it was just a different wig.

Clearly embarrassed, he tried to pass it off. 'Just too much testosterone.'

Cassie didn't mind. 'Well you certainly are a smooth operator. It looks as if I'll never be running my hands through your hair, but you may still need a bit of polishing.'

Dan laughed. 'At least you can be confident that I'm not one for partings and I've nothing to hide. You can see immediately I've no head lice, and if I did, they wouldn't stay around as they'd be homeless.'

Everything literally whizzed by. In what seemed like no time at all, they were luxuriating in their hot tub. Other couples were dotted around at a discrete distance in hot tubs of their own. Those who were more serious about their astronomy, and perhaps had more inhibitions, restricted themselves to viewing the stars through the giant Kielder telescope. Cassie sipped her champagne while Dan insisted on beer. Overhead the misty scarf of the Milky Way, spangled with brighter diamonds, unfurled across the dark and the moonlight reflected from the twin domes - Dan's and the Observatory's.

Cassie's mind was still half occupied with the theories she was developing about St Mark. The fact that she was able to share them with Dan at all when they were so obviously incredible showed how relaxed she was in his company. He told her he found her barmy ideas mildly erotic. She was a very intelligent woman and if that meant she had episodes bordering on insanity, it seemed that Dan didn't mind.

'So, what do you think? You're the first person I've told about this.'

'Crazy. Totally crazy. If you tell anyone else, then you will be sectioned and our dates will be limited to the visiting hours at the mental asylum.'

CHAPTER 19 – STRANGER THAN FICTION

If you tell the truth, you don't have to remember anything – Mark Twain

When the call came, Panettone was rummaging through the bin in his room. He had thrown the ash tray in there to avoid temptation, but temptation had overwhelmed him all the same. In fact, his cravings seemed to have become stronger since he had overdosed with the nicotine patches. The grey tip accumulated on the end of the cigarette he had begged from the cleaner was already fragile and close to the point of crumbling. Unable to find the tray quickly enough, he tapped the tip on the side of the bin instead and answered the call.

Cassie gave him swift and precise details of the Bolshie Bear's present location, including a numberplate and a brief description of the blue Transit van the gang were now using. It was parked outside the Pitt Rivers Museum, so perhaps they were casing the joint and planning another raid.

The disappointing news from the Inspector's point of view was that Cassie's detailed search of their communications, including with the Kremlin, contained no mention at all of San Marco. It seemed that their aim might simply be to cause the maximum chaos they could in the UK. Further investigation was needed but there was no time for that now. The immediate priority was to apprehend them.

Flinging on his coat, grabbing his mother and stuffing his revolver into a pocket, Panettone strode to the door. The gun was clear evidence that while airport security might be hot on detecting ice buckets, it didn't always find the items about which questions really should be asked. Equally Panettone hadn't thought to declare it as in Italy it was as much part of his daily attire as his socks.

By some sixth sense, Sister Felicity was already dashing down the stairs much to the surprise of other guests who had never seen a nun on the run. When Panettone stepped out onto the pavement outside the hotel, he was almost flattened by the Popemobile as it screeched to a halt.

It was only then that he noticed an old man wrapped in blankets and dirty plastic sheeting propped up by the side of the hotel entrance. Panettone paused, then despite Sister Felicity's strident honking of the horn, turned back. Finding he had no coins in his pocket, he handed the old guy a creased twenty-pound note from his wallet. When he saw the tears welling up in those pale rheumy eyes the Inspector found that his own cheeks were wet as well. Sister Felicity was on the verge of having a seizure with frustration, but the ancient gentleman was struggling to say something.

'Don't suppose you've got a fag as well?'

Panettone buckled his mother into the back seat, making sure her seat belt was secure. The car was already moving off as he jumped into the passenger seat next. Within seconds Sister Felicity was accelerating straight through a red light and speeding towards the Martyr's Memorial. This was originally erected for the protestant bishops who Queen Mary had burnt there for heresy. Panettone wasn't aware of any heresy he had committed, but he felt that, at the speed they were travelling, he might well be martyred in the same spot nonetheless.

'*Mamma Mia*,' a severe female voice squealed, clearly sharing his sentiments. Panettone was momentarily at a loss as there was no one else in the car, until he saw that being in unfamiliar territory, Sister Felicity had switched the Sat Nav on. He urgently punched in the destination Cassie had given him. As they hurtled onwards the disembodied electronic voice continued a commentary of exclamations. Some, including, 'Holy Mother of God,' and, 'Saints preserve us!' were, perhaps, to be expected. But, sprinkled among these shrieks were others that were more unusual, such as, 'By St Geronimo and all his cherubs.'

Somehow, they survived and arrived only just in time. As Sister Felicity turned abruptly into Museum Road, the blue Transit was already pulling away from the kerb in front of the museum itself. She would have tried to follow them inconspicuously at a distance, but it was hard to be inconspicuous in the Popemobile. Pedestrians and other cars recognising the distinctive vehicle, and assuming that His Holiness was on a poorly publicised visit, honked their horns and waved with wild enthusiasm. Sister Felicity had no choice but to accelerate to avoid getting snarled up. Hearing all the din, the Bolshie Bears must have looked in the mirror, as the van suddenly took off. Of course, their van was no match for the Popemobile's supercharged aircraft engine, so Sister Felicity was easily able to keep pace and when they reached a stretch of quieter road outside Oxford she was even able to pull alongside. Panettone didn't need to get onto the front seat to stand with his head almost pressing the top of the bulletproof glass turret that the Pope used to wave to the crowds. From this vantage point he was able to exchange shots with the Bolshie Bears through a small side window left for ventilation. But it quickly became apparent that they were much more heavily armed as one of them lent out of the car and riddled the Popemobile with machine gun fire, blowing out the front wheels on the passenger's side so that it swerved through the hedge and into a field.

Cursing in a wide variety of languages, including Latin and Hebrew which she had supposedly learnt for Bible translation, Sister Felicity got out the jack and spare tyre. The Sat Nav only made matters worse by quoting the Book of Proverbs, Chapter 15 v 18, 'Hot tempers cause arguments, but patience brings peace.'

Meanwhile, Panettone tried to divert the angry bull in the field by waving his sweater at the beast. He couldn't quite remember if it was red or green that calmed them down but red certainly wasn't working[186]. The Inspector hadn't loped along so fast since a Rottweiler bit him on the backside as a child. He managed two complete circuits of the field, but by then he was exhausted. He only saved himself from being gored with three improvised *pase de pecho* – chest high passes, and a *rebolera* – a final pass, that would have made any matador proud and brought the crowd in the Plaza de Toros de la Ventas, Madrid's most famous bullring, to their feet. All this gave Sister Felicity just enough time to change the tyre and bolt the wheel back on.

Then, they were away again, leaving the bull still rolling its eyes like bloodshot billiard balls with Panettone's torn sweater dangling from one of its horns.

The Bolshie Bears were long gone, but Cassie had fortunately told Panettone that a lot of the gang's internet traffic seemed to be coming from a large country house called Bling Hall and a little more research showed it was owned by an Oligarch with close links to the President. Checking the map, the Inspector could see that they were only a couple of miles away, so it was highly likely that this was the gang's destination. In the stress of the journey, the Sat Nav seemed to have forgotten its real vocation altogether and was of very little assistance with directions. Only occasionally it threw in, 'Do a U turn as soon as possible,' and once, when faced with a choice between a dual carriageway and a small lane, it recited the Book of Matthew, Chapter 7 v 13-14. 'Take the narrow road, for broad is the road that leads to destruction.'

When they arrived at the edge of the estate, Sister Felicity drove through the imposing entrance. Panettone noticed that the ironwork, both on the gates and the railings either side of them, was contorted into strange bulges and bends. Sister Felicity parked on the side of the gravel drive as soon as the Hall itself came into sight through the trees. Sure enough, the blue van was drawn up outside the vast gothic pile.

Circling round one wing, Panettone eventually found a side door. When he tried the handle, it opened easily enough. Before entering, he put in a call to DCI Boyle and explained that they might need some support. The house was eerily silent as they crept through a maze of corridors into a large hall at the base of a gigantic stone staircase overhung with old portraits. Sister Felicity was just whispering that one, a haughty-looking lady in a pink ball gown the size of a punctured hot air balloon, looked remarkably like her Aunty Lil when they heard a cough behind them.

Finn was reviewing some articles about previous searches for Alexander the Great's tomb when Cassie came in. She propped her skates up against the wall and made them both a coffee. Having failed to find Tom, Finn was as jumpy as a vat of fermenting cider. Connections and ideas kept bubbling up inside him, but most of them popped immediately on exposure to the air as they were obviously preposterous.

Still, he badly needed to talk to someone to get his own head in order. He wasn't to know that Cassie felt exactly the same. Her date in Northumberland had been exciting, but her increasingly crazy thoughts were also keeping her buzzing and she had not been able to sleep at all. The glitter sparkling in her peroxide ponytail reflected her febrile mood.

Finn told her about the ring. Cassie had examined it far more closely than Finn knew, so she could immediately picture what he was describing, although of course she couldn't reveal how or why. She had read the inscription, "To the strongest," but hadn't realised its significance. If she had understood it might be Alexander's own signet ring, she would have persuaded Cleo not to hand it back at any cost. It was a major national Greek treasure in itself.

Finn's latest information was also sending her own thoughts racing into orbit. She told Finn about the white figure that had escaped from Oxford Royal Infirmary. The newspaper cutting the patient had been carrying was about the Ashmolean raid and particularly the disappearance of the gold Greek ring. Then there was the referral note from Thessalonika Hospital. None of the Oxford medical staff were able to read it but at the police station, Cassie had recognised immediately that it was written in ancient, not modern, Greek. There was no consultant called Iskander in Thessalonika, but as she and Finn both knew, "Iskander" was the name by which Alexander the Great was known in much of the eastern part of his empire.

Their brains were fizzing as they tried to add all these fragments to Finn's wall chart and connect them, but this was more like making crop circles or drawing ley lines between the Great Pyramids of Egypt[187] and the Aztec pyramids of South America than building with the logic of Lego.

Another thought suddenly rooted Finn to the spot and he began searching back online through old magazines and newspapers. Cassie helped him at first, but finally gave up through exhaustion while Finn continued to the early hours. When he finished he was dizzy and shaking.

In the ballroom, Dmitry Collossovitch was standing in

front of the huge fireplace, keeping his muscles in prime condition by bending a thick steel bar backwards and forwards until, eventually, the fatigued metal snapped. He looked at the broken pieces with disgust. Steel wasn't made like it used to be. He had already been round the entire perimeter of the estate bending the railings so there wasn't much left to go at. On the dining table the vodka shots waited in a long queue. Without waiting for the others, he started knocking them back one at a time, hurling each empty glass into the grate. It was a typical and extravagant Russian toast but rather expensive on crystal. Fortunately, the house was well equipped for huge parties, so there seemed to be an ample supply.

When Vassily and Igor returned, they were frogmarching a couple of reluctant visitors in front of them at gunpoint. They tied Panettone and Sister Felicity to chairs. Igor, had clearly not forgotten the skills learnt in gaining his rope-master badge in the Boy Scouts[188]. He made no attempt to hide the joy he felt in making the knots as complex and tight as possible.

Dmitry asked his captives a few questions, but when they refused to answer he swiftly concluded that a little persuasion was in order. Usually, he would not have hesitated to use the thumb screws and other similar implements. These might seem a little medieval and outdated to some but, in his view, they worked remarkably well. Less a question of, if it ain't broke don't fix it, and rather more a case of if it breaks something, then he would get some answers.

The problem was that even he had scruples about using such techniques on a nun. Fortunately, there were other subtler methods available. He started by lowering silver helmets with wires attached over the heads of his captives. The domes looked like old-fashioned hairdryers. That's because that's exactly what they were, except that they had been adapted to pipe recordings into the ears of the victim – a form of brainwashing the Bolshie Bears had found highly effective. Ten minutes of Swiss yodelling usually made even the toughest man break down in tears and beg to tell all, if only the torture was switched off.

As luck would have it, however, Panettone was a great lover of yodelling. He had his own *lederhosen* and often went on yodelling tours of the Alps with other friends and afficionados. Sister Felicity, on the other hand, completely blanked out the terrible din by intoning the hypnotic and monotonous chants of the whirling dervishes that she had memorised while travelling in Turkey.

Dmitry rapidly lost patience with them both, particularly Panettone's obvious pleasure in the experience. It was time to try another approach. Removing their shoes and socks, the giant feather duster was applied to the pair's bare feet, but with no more success. Panettone gave an occasional rasping chuckle when the tickling became too intense but did not surrender and tell all, as expected. Sister Felicity had been on so many pilgrimages with no footwear that her calloused feet couldn't feel a thing.

There was nothing for it. They would have to use the truth drug. Syringes were swiftly brought in by Vassily. He preferred to administer injections in the victim's bottom but the task of untying and re-tying Panettone and Sister Felicity, then getting them to bend over, would have taken too long. Rolling up their sleeves, Igor reluctantly injected the two captives in the upper arm instead. Had Dmitry been watching more closely he would have seen Panettone show just a flicker of fear at this point. The Inspector hated injections as he associated them with his dentist, the Marquis de Sade. If the gang had exposed him to the shrieking pitch of a dental drill poised for a filling, he would have capitulated straight away. As it was, after a struggle, the Inspector managed to get his nerves back under control and keep up the appearance of *sang froid*.

The truth drug took much longer to work than usual. Panettone had been trained to resist interrogation by putting himself into a catatonic state in which he convinced himself he was someone else[189]. In this case he chose Sherlock Holmes. Dmitry's questioning at first only succeeded in establishing that the Inspector's address was 221B Baker Street, his associate was called Dr Watson, he had a pet called the Hound of the Baskervilles, was a heavy drug user and kept tobacco for his pipe in the end of a Persian slipper[190]. He also kept calling Dmitry, "Moriarty."

Eventually, however, the prisoners' defiance was overcome, and they were both babbling like babies in a bath full of bubbles. Dmitry now discovered everything he wanted to know and quite a few other things as well, such as that Sister Felicity had once been a lap dancer, thought celibacy was over-rated and had become a nun because she liked the idea of the uniform – at least until it became a habit. An even less expected outcome was that both of the prisoners then told Dmitry, rather more truthfully that he had bargained for, exactly what they thought of him as well.

While Panettone used robust but gentlemanly

terms, describing Dmitry, for example as a cad and a rotter, Sister Felicity let loose a torrent of gutter swear words so foul they made the Bolshie Bears shudder and turn pale with shock. Even during stints in the gulag in Siberia for political re-education they had never heard anything quite like it. Had Vassily not put a large piece of sticky tape over Sister Felicity's mouth, it was quite possible that they would have been the ones broken by the interrogation.

When Boyle received Panettone's call, he and Peel were having a morning coffee break while playing a game of Scrabble. Boyle was on a run with words like rythumb, seperate and greatful,[191] although, just as he was about to clinch the win, Peel came in with "supercalifragilistic," and used up all his letters in one go before running out of tiles to pip his boss at the post. This led to a bitter argument about the number of tiles that could be used in one go, the spelling, whether the word had any meaning, was incomplete without the "expialidocious" and if it was in the Scrabble dictionary. The argument only ended when Boyle threatened the young whippersnapper with demotion, although as Peel was only a constable, there really was nothing he could be demoted to.

Eventually, they set off. Boyle thought about using the blue light, but he generally reserved this for the evenings when he needed to get home for dinner. Panettone had asked for help urgently but using dinner as a comparator, it couldn't be as urgent as all that.

En route to Bling Hall, they were diverted several times by other pressing police business. A cat had to be rescued from a telegraph pole and Boyle pulled over to give a caution to a cyclist with no lights even though it was broad daylight[192]. Peel also received a call to say that a woman's body had been found under the patio at the property he had visited, so the gossipy neighbour had been vindicated. There was, however, no need for Peel and Boyle to turn back. Scotland Yard were taking over the investigation as, having checked past crime records, a further fifteen similar cases had now been uncovered which Oxford police had failed to connect.

The current theory, for what the press were christening the Patio Murders, was either that a serial killer was on the loose or that the idea of claiming life insurance by this means had gone viral on social media. All over Oxford, people who had recently laid crazy paving were being viewed with suspicion. Those with longer memories wondered if there could even be a link to the gruesome BBQ Murders that had rocked Oxford a decade earlier and had led a dramatic slump in the popularity of ribs, sausages and finger buffets.

Now that Dmitry knew Panettone was the Italian detective who was famous for never giving up on a case and always solving it eventually, he could see there was no option but to feed him to the fishes. Conveniently, there was a large lake in the grounds of the hall that the Russian owners continually re-stocked with piranhas for just this sort of eventuality. The fish had been so well fed they had reached a significant size. Dmitry thought of getting the Inspector to walk down to the lake and then dive in, but it seemed easier to shoot him first and then carry the body.

He took out his pistol and screwed on the silencer. There were owls nesting in the roof, and he didn't see any need to disturb them. In any case, proper assassins always used silencers.

The truth drug didn't last long and was now swiftly wearing off, so Panettone and Sister Felicity were coming round just in time to realise the fate that was awaiting them. Dmitry was about to raise his gun. Panettone couldn't understand why a squad of police cars hadn't arrived long before as back-up, but it was now clear that he and Sister Felicity might well be in another world before Boyle could help them in this one. The Inspector could only try and buy some time.

'Please could you turn my mother to face the wall? She wouldn't want to watch.'

This wasted a few minutes as Panettone then explained about the ice bucket which Igor had taken from the Inspector when tying him up and had placed on the mantelpiece above the fireplace. Dmitry grudgingly obliged by turning the bucket round so the small plaque on the front was now staring at the garish gold wallpaper which Panettone thought his mother would rather approve of. He had nothing to lose by playing for a bit more time.

'Its usual to offer the victim a last wish or moment of prayer.'

'Da. Okay. Which you want?'

'Well, Sister Felicity can say a prayer for me and, as she has received absolution for the lap dancing, it's more likely she will be listened to. So, how about as a last wish we all enjoy a staple of Russian culture together.

'Borscht or vodka?'

'Well, I had in mind reciting a chunk of your great literary heritage. "What about Tolstoy's "War and Peace"? Have you read it?'

'Part.'

'Oh, which part?'

'War part.'

'So I suppose something similar may be true for Dostoevsky? I expect you've read the crime part but not the punishment? Perhaps now is a chance to fill in some gaps.'

'No reading! These books too many words!'

'In that case just the usual request, a last packet of cigarettes. In all the films I've seen, that's a wish that's always granted by anyone with even an ounce of sensitivity.'

Dmitry was a total thug with no sensitivity at all. If he had been asked to save the planet by reducing his carbon footprint, he would have said he didn't have one because he always drove everywhere. He was also a little wary. He remembered what had happened to the police officer who offered a former member of another gang a last wish. The guy's wish was for the officer to hold his hand when flicking the switch on the electric chair. The officer had fallen for it, and they went up together in a flash and some acrid smoke. On the other hand, Dmitry liked to delude himself that he was a cut above the normal hoodlum and blended ruthlessness with a sense of style.

'Only one cigarette in film I see,' he said, holding up a single crooked finger that seemed lost without a trigger.

He beckoned to Igor, who made no bones about his unhappiness at wasting a fag on the Inspector. Eventually, and only grudgingly, his boss convinced him to put one between Panettone's lips. Even then, the Inspector still had to ask for a light as well. This clearly snuffed out Igor's hopes that Dmitry would just get on and shoot the Inspector since, strictly speaking, his wish was to have a cigarette and he hadn't said anything about smoking it.

The Inspector was filled with a sense of contentment. This last cigarette was definitely better than all of the last cigarettes he had enjoyed before put together. He inhaled and savoured the bittersweet fumes, while stretching out the conversation for as long as he could. After all, you never knew what might come up and while there was life there was hope. He could see Dmitry was becoming impatient and might just pull the cigarette out of his mouth and stamp on the butt so he could get on with the shooting unless he was distracted.

'I see your pistol's Italian, a Beretta. Six chambers, so perfect for Russian roulette, although I'm sure you guys have never really dared to play.'

Dmitry looked annoyed. 'Of course, play all time. Before eight man in gang. Why you think now only three?'

'So, you're one of the lucky ones.'

'Make own luck. I play six bullets. Let five others make first shot. They all unlucky. Now just me, Igor and Vassily.'

A sudden crash from the top of the staircase outside the Ballroom made all the Bolshie Bears swing round. Vassily grabbed his machine gun and, urged on by a nod from Dmitry, ran to investigate. There was no sign of anyone on the landing, but the fire extinguisher had been knocked off its wall bracket and lay on the floor. The door to the gallery opposite was also ajar. Vassily was sure he had left it locked after all the treasures taken in the Ashmolean raid had been carried up and stacked inside. On tiptoes now, he gently pushed it open. As the door swung back, he saw a white figure in a beanie bending over DJ's sarcophagus. The lid had been removed and the figure was searching inside. The covers left over the other treasures had been pulled back, so it was clear the intruder had been rummaging through them all.

As Vassily moved forwards, the fire extinguisher suddenly exploded spraying white foam everywhere. The impact when it hit the floor must have caused a delayed build-up of pressure that now acted as a trigger.

Through the cascade, Vassily saw the figure look up sharply, then start towards him. A staccato arc of bullets from his machine gun blasted chunks out of the panelling and left a string of holes across several paintings and through the chest of the figure. It paused only for a moment, shivered and shook itself vigorously like a maraca, then kept coming.

Seconds later, more steps came drumming up the stairs. On the landing by the gallery door, the newcomers found the body of a muscular giant dressed in army fatigues lying stretched on the floorboards. He was motionless which perhaps wasn't surprising. It would be difficult to describe his position. Either you could say he was face up but with his actual face facing down or that he was face down but with his body facing up. Either way it was as if Vassily had been caught in a corkscrew and truly uncorked.

Boyle and Peel had meanwhile just driven past a strange-looking white vehicle a bit like an ice-cream van as they came down the drive. As they drew up outside the Hall, there were two other vehicles already parked there, a blue van and a black Mercedes with tinted windows. They were just getting out as they heard the burst of gunfire.

Boyle looked at Peel, Peel looked at Boyle and they both looked down at their batons. These suddenly seemed about as adequate for the job as two flabby sausage rolls. Discretion was clearly the better part of valour. DCI Boyle called his Chief Inspector as they swiftly jumped into their police car and drove back to the gates to wait for reinforcements.

In the brief conversation, Boyle mentioned that Panettone seemed to believe that the perpetrators of the Ashmolean raid were a Russian gang with direct links to the Kremlin. The Chief Inspector expressed alarm. He had apparently been briefed, along with all senior police, that anything relating to the Ashmolean raid should be immediately reported to the Home Office. This Russian connection simply underlined the gravity of the situation.

The Home Secretary received the call like a hot potato best passed on before it burnt his fingers. He tried to call the Minister of Defence and eventually tracked him down on the golf course, where the call was answered with a stream of expletives. The Home Secretary was not to know that this was because the Minister's ball had just landed in a bunker nicknamed by locals, Death Valley, which stood very close to the flag for the notoriously tricky eighteenth green, otherwise known as the A-Hole[193]. The Minister was therefore desperate to finish the round and drown his sorrows in gin and tonic in the club house, but what the Home Secretary had to tell him brought him up even shorter than the detour he had just taken from the fairway.

To be fair, the original message had now become distorted out of all proportion by the bureaucratic Chinese whispers it had undergone. In the face of what now seemed to be near Armageddon, the Minister had already concluded that this needed a response beyond what the police could provide. Checking the map he saw Bling Hall was only a few miles from the SAS base at Much Wallop. He called the commander.

'We're relying on you, Jack. Heavily-armed Russian special forces have been parachuted into a country house in Oxfordshire. Who knows what the Ruskies are up to?'

Putting down the phone, the Major felt a surge of adrenalin and his thoughts went into overdrive. It could be a prelude to invasion. Unless the threat was nipped in the bud, matters could quickly escalate to a nuclear confrontation, or, worse still, Oxfordshire might become a distant suburb of Moscow.

He, Major Potts, might be remembered as his country's saviour and he was already ecstatic with anticipation. This was the moment he and his finely-honed battalion had been training for. All those exercises where they had yomped up mountains and climbed waterfalls, carrying packs weighing half a ton with one leg tied behind their backs, were about to be put to the test. He would need to think of a suitably glorious code name for the operation[194].

CHAPTER 20 – THE GAME IS UP

Football is a simple game. Twenty-two men chase a ball for ninety minutes and at the end, the Germans always win – Gary Lineker

In the ballroom, Dmitry grew tired of his chat with Panettone. From the burst of gunfire outside, it seemed Vassily might need a hand. He was raising the Beretta when Sister Felicity sprang out of her chair. She made a grab for the mantelpiece. Before Dmitry could overcome his surprise and react, she had seized Panettone's mother. Then a super nova exploded in Dmitry's head as the ice bucket, which Sister Felicity was wielding by one handle, caught him just above the ear.

Dmitry went down like a boulder falling off the Empire State building and hit the floor so hard that Panettone found himself looking for the crater. The Inspector was in no doubt that his mother would have enjoyed delivering the knockout punch, even more than Rocky Marciano. Certainly, she hadn't been involved in anything quite so exciting since her funeral.

Panettone's wonderment at Sister Felicity's timely escape was explained as she swiftly cut his own ropes with a razor blade.

'I always keep one to shave my legs. Otherwise they look like moon boots. Mother Superior doesn't approve so, to avoid the tedium of all those extra Hail Marys, I keep it hidden in my cuff.' She removed the butt of the cigarette that Panettone was still trying to savour down to its dregs, chucked it on the floor and stamped on it. 'A filthy habit. At least mine's clean.'

The Inspector felt as if he had been caught behind the bike sheds, kept behind after school and told to write five hundred lines saying, "Smoking is bad for your health." On the other hand, he found Sister Felicity's feistiness quite magnetic and was convinced he could just detect a whiff of Chanel No 5 from her. From close quarters, he also couldn't help noticing that, if it wasn't for that sacking she was wearing, and with a lick of paint, she could look quite attractive. Perhaps it was just that the concept of a sexy nun was alluring.

He realised this was a train of thought he needed to firmly put a stop to before it missed the signals and crashed off the track altogether. This was just the sort of temptation to eat forbidden fruit that had derailed the whole of human history right at the beginning.

Everything had been moving faster than a cheetah in full stride and both the Inspector and Sister Felicity had forgotten Igor. It was clear that he was as bright as a broken light bulb. Many amoebas had more brain cells. But, unlike them, Igor had a machine gun. Initially diverted by the shooting outside, he was heading towards the ballroom door just as Panettone's mother delivered her *coup de grâce*, sending Dmitry's consciousness into orbit.

Looking round as he heard the noise, Igor's mind had been momentarily paralysed, jammed by the need to change direction. At last, the gears clunked into action and now he was ponderously turning back, finger on the trigger. Panettone saw him coming and pointed urgently to the ceiling.

Someone had told Igor about this old trick, but the dim memory was taking far too long to retrieve from the archives. It was like searching for one book in a huge library of endless rooms and echoing corridors that contained only empty shelves and one hidden copy of the Beano. Just too hard. Igor gave up and looked up all at the same time.

As he did so, Sister Felicity and the Inspector both dived. Igor was perplexed to be hit hard in the midriff by a flying nun who had obviously played a lot of rugby but, however good the tackle, a fly can't knock over an elephant. He swayed a little on his feet before steadying himself.

Sister Felicity craned to see what was keeping Panettone. As she expected, he had plunged across the floor for Dmitry's pistol, but she was incensed to see that he had paused on the way to pick up his crushed cigarette. This was on life support already but sadly the final spark had already been stamped out by the sole of Sister Felicity's shoe. She found it inexplicable that this diversion could hold up the Inspector at a moment of such acute peril, but he was still quicker with the Beretta than Igor was with his machine gun[195].

Panettone would have got his shot in first but, before he could, three other armed men burst through the door. Igor and Panettone both dropped their weapons as instructed.

Cavatappi stepped forward and bowed slightly to the Inspector. The situation was a little ironic. He had out manoeuvred his rival and now had Panettone at his mercy, but it seemed that the Inspector may have inadvertently led them both up the garden path as it was looking increasingly doubtful that the Ashmolean raid had any connection with San Marco or the murder of Father Matteo. Cavatappi had already heard the results of Cassie's hacking research through the bug in the ice bucket, which had also enabled him to track the Inspector to the Hall.

Fabrizio now subjected Igor to detailed and painfully slow questioning in which Igor finally confirmed that the gang were the Bolshie Bears. They were working for Moscow to cause disruption and embarrassment in the UK, and he knew nothing about San Marco. It was apparent that Igor must be telling the truth because an amoeba is quite incapable of double-crossing anyone.

A swift hunt also located all the stolen treasures from the Ashmolean stacked in the gallery opposite the ballroom, although it looked like someone had been searching through them. Fabrizio and Luigi didn't think to look behind the curtains draped from the vast windows overlooking the balcony at the front of Bling Hall.

Panettone and Sister Felicity swiftly found themselves tied up yet again, this time accompanied by Igor. It was all getting a little repetitive, but the Inspector wasn't going to lose the opportunity to repeat his final request.

Cavatappi could, of course, not refuse him as he was unaware how many final, last or ultimate cigarettes Panettone had already enjoyed or that he was about to grant an encore to the rigamarole that had taken place in this same room only moments before. He did see the ropes Sister Felicity had previously cut on the floor and she reluctantly gave up the razor to her latest captor. Cavatappi also took the precaution of banishing Panettone's mother in case she caused any more trouble. Her ice bucket was removed to the gallery with the Ashmolean treasures.

Almost immediately, as Fabrizio closed the gallery door, a white figure emerged from behind the curtains, grabbed the ice bucket, opened the window, slipped out onto the balcony and shimmied down the drainpipe with remarkable agility.

DCI Boyle was sitting on a bench by the grand gates to the Hall with DC Peel. Their back up was due any moment, so they were listening to the Ashes cricket commentary on the radio. There had been a lot of excitement as England scored a historic thirty-seven off their last over and then took a hat trick of wickets off the first two balls as Australia opened their innings. It was all going fantastically well until someone pointed out that the Barmy Army had been tampering with the scoreboard.

Boyle looked up as the Popemobile sped past in the opposite direction. He just had time to glimpse a white figure at the wheel and what looked like some sort of bucket in the passenger seat. The vehicle was clearly going too fast and, had it not been on private property, Boyle would have given chase. As it was, just at present, he had other priorities. Nonetheless, he told Peel to make a note of the number plate before the strange-looking car vanished over the rise. VATICAR1[196].

'White robes and some fake personalised numberplate. Who does he think he is? The Pope or something?'

However much he tried to prolong the experience, the Inspector was finally coming to the end of his cigarette when they all heard a booming announcement.

'Come out with your hands up. If you fail to comply you should note that the scenes that follow may cause you considerable distress and may be much more painful than flash photography. Please be aware that guns are not toys and that we will not be firing any warning shots as this is a waste of public money. We are required now by law to advise you of our diversity and equal opportunities policies. We take these issues very seriously and seek to shoot everyone impartially regardless of race, gender and existing physical or mental capacity or impairment, although mistakes do frequently happen. We aspire to avoid bias of any kind, including in relation to any wrongdoing or criminal behaviour committed, whether past or present.'

While the announcement dragged on, Cavatappi had ample time to leap to the window and, crouching down, scanned the drive below. He could see the policeman, DCI Boyle, on the edge of the lawn with his megaphone. Behind him, with their guns trained on the Hall, were dozens of tanks in a circular formation that seemed to surround the entire building. Gun emplacements with trenches and sandbags had been prepared with lightning speed and soldiers in green camouflage were packed into these like clumps of asparagus. Every line of fire bristled with machine guns, bazookas and self-propelled grenades.

Behind this formidable force, the sight of a large gardener with a purple waistcoat putting stripes into the lawn on a large sit on mower was a little disconcerting. Fabrizio had been checking the windows on the other side of the ballroom and confirmed that there was no hope of a getaway there. Little mushrooms were floating down from the sky and he realised that the paratroopers were about to land on the roof.

Cavatappi knew that the game was up. He took out his phone. In the previous couple of moves in his chess match he had finally managed to breach the Great Wall and was closing in on a win. Now with a flourish he resigned in what he saw as a symbolic gesture. There would be no visits to *Palline Congelate* for quite a while and, even if he was able to play online chess in prison, they were sure to confiscate or wipe his phone first. It was unfair to his opponent to leave him hanging there indefinitely for a finale that would never come.

Over the other side of the ballroom, Panettone heard a ping from his own phone which had been confiscated and placed on the mantelpiece, but he was still tied up so couldn't check it. Only later, to his amazement, he found his nemesis ChesstWig had conceded when on the verge of victory. Quite why his anonymous enemy would do this would always remain a mystery to him. Perhaps he or she had a death wish, or maybe they were just too soft-hearted.

The Dean was already feeling rather unwell from a

surfeit of venison and sherry trifle at the college dinner he had hosted the previous evening to announce the college's expansion plans. Architects had prepared drawings of the new quad. This was to be called Templeton Quad in his own honour and was designed to preserve his name forever in the college annals.

It seemed to him a fitting reward for his unprecedented contribution as Dean which had seen the college rescued from near destitution and elevated to the richest in the university. The Dean's own rather undistinguished academic career had been in the study of propaganda, and he had become very familiar with the various ways in which history could be shaped like putty in the hands of an arch manipulator. The work of Tom and his team therefore received no mention whatsoever and, of course, Cavatappi had conveniently requested total confidentiality in relation to the torrent of money that his investment fund was supplying. That left the field free for the Dean to take all the credit and exaggerate his own role with no real constraints.

Now, however, as he clutched his stomach and reached for the indigestion tablets, he was unaware that the bottom was about to fall out of his world, although all too conscious that the reverse was becoming inevitable.

A few days later, Panettone was having dinner with Sister Felicity at his hotel. He felt as if his life had been shaken up like a newly-invented cocktail. He wasn't yet sure if he liked the taste of it or not. In fact, it was a bit of a sweet and sour mix. On the positive side, after years of cat and mouse, he had finally arrested Cavatappi and some of the leading members of his outfit, but there were still a lot of missing pieces in relation to

Cavatappi's operations and the relics scam. He would need to find these to be sure of securing convictions. Perhaps the pending interview Interpol had now arranged for him with the grass, Capelli, would help. It was convenient that this could take place in London since this was where Interpol had moved Capelli to try and keep him alive at least long enough to debrief him.

The Inspector knew even this would only cause a temporary disruption to the drug underworld. Already other gangs would be fighting to step into the shoes that Cavatappi's gang had so suddenly vacated. Nonetheless it was a setback for the mafia and should also at least put a stop to the scam involving relic donations. Although the Vatican found Father Matteo's activities embarrassing, the Pope had sent the Inspector a personal message of thanks. His Holiness had however predictably ended this by asking what on earth was happening with the investigation into St Mark?

The Pope suggested, rather discourteously, that rather than stick to his brief, the Inspector seemed to be wandering around like a stray cat sniffing at any old sardine can that came near him. Panettone felt this was harsh, but he didn't yet have a satisfactory response. His instinct still told him that there was some other connection between the Ashmolean raid and the events at San Marco, but he couldn't yet explain what had happened to the Saint. The Bolshie Bears and Cavatappi were as silent as the grave on nearly everything, but all denied knowing anything about St Mark's body, which was disconcerting to say the least.

Panettone's private life was also topsy turvy. Sister Felicity had accepted his invitation to dinner. He had always understood that old habits die hard, but she seemed to have forgotten her time as a nun all too easily and slipped back to an outfit more reminiscent of her dancing days. It was a distraction he could neither ignore nor afford. Unless he solved the mystery of St Mark, he would never be able to claim his mother's inheritance and, to his greater distress, she had now gone missing. He had searched Bling Hall from top to bottom with no success and, when interrogated, Cavatappi's men were adamant that they had just left her in the gallery.

The hotel receptionist wasn't helping. He had just pushed the cork from the very expensive bottle of wine the Inspector had ordered into the bottle rather than out of it and was now fishing about with a skewer borrowed from a kebab that had been served to the neighbouring table. Sister Felicity, at least, took that problem into her own hands by saying he should pour the bottle down the drain and bring them both a vodka. She added that she needed it because she had her own problems with the Pope, who was asking for the urgent return of the Popemobile. It was difficult to ignore the repeated warnings that both the Ducati and hitching were high risk.

Shortly after that, but while he was still sober, the Inspector received a call from Cassie, who said she had a theory she thought was crazy but which she wanted to discuss with him and the History Mystery team. It seemed to the Inspector that crazy things were colliding with each other all the time and the world was making less and less sense to him.

He had been shocked to find that he really did seem to have smoked his very final cigarette. The craving had vanished. Nothing could ever again come close to the transcendental experience of his two last cigarettes, both enjoyed in the belief that they were leading to the imminent and absolute butt end of his worldly life. He had always feared that Heaven would be a no smoking zone, while harbouring the secret hope that it would just be unfiltered delight. If he was destined for Hell, then it would be hard to enjoy a cigarette if he was on fire himself.

CHAPTER 21 – COMPLETELY DOTTY

A line is a dot that went for a walk – Paul Klee

Perhaps I am at last gaining something from Dr Bacon's treatment. The dots seem to be connecting in a rough picture and the marbles have become less of a distraction. I can sense my imagination navigating its own course with greater confidence through an infinite number of different perceptions.

As you join the dots of my account of events you will probably come up with a completely different picture. I hope however that as my version crystallises it will hopefully be one you can at least recognise in outline, like stargazers looking for the Plough, the Big Dipper or now the Kite, in the night sky, although of course with many variations of your own.

But now I need to tell you about my own interview with Inspector Panettone.

'We have buried you here right here next to Karl.

Interpol thought you would prefer politics to science or sculpture as otherwise they would have tried to squeeze you in alongside Michael Faraday or Henry Moore.'

I found I was looking at my own grave. The inscription "Angelo Capelli – Fallen Angel" left me feeling strangely empty inside. I wasn't keen on the glassy emerald gravel the colour of a rabid dog's vomit which filled the stone surrounds marking out the area six feet above where I was supposed to be. Like the gold on black headstone it looked both a bit garish and cheap. But then I wasn't exactly in a position to ask for my own mausoleum. No doubt Interpol had a budget to stick to and I didn't want to seem ungrateful so I didn't comment and simply observed that Highgate Cemetary seemed an odd place to meet.

'Interpol suggested it,' said the Inspector. 'I imagine they thought they could kill two birds with one stone, or catch two pigeons with one bean as we would say. One bird or bean is that the mafia think you are dead so Interpol need to put up a headstone for you somewhere. The other is that I asked for a meeting somewhere quiet.'

'So why are we two Italians talking in English?'

'For three good reasons. We are less likely to attract attention if anyone overhears us, your Sicilian accent is not always easy for me to understand anyway and the practise is good for both of us.'

We were standing next to the huge bearded effigy of Marx since the only places to sit were on people who were dead. Panettone had brought along a large thermos of black coffee which was very welcome but I couldn't help feeling sorry for myself.

'Next to Karl would be fine. I doubt many people

would have turned up for my funeral even if I'd had one.'

'Well only eleven came to Karl's so I wouldn't worry about it. He died broke and at one stage in his life his wife pawned his pants for food so he couldn't even go out on the town or anywhere. Perhaps you should look on the sunny side up. After all not many people can expect to be alive after their own funeral.'

'I'm not sure how long I can expect that to last.'

'Well, it's true that everywhere the mafia have their ears in the ground and will hear through the vines of the grapes, so soon they will work it out. Although Cavatappi will be in prison you will always be in danger until his living daylights are beaten out of him, but we will do our best to ensure you stay officially dead as a duck.'

'Duck? Isn't it doornail or maybe dodo?'

'I think any of those. Anyway the point is we want you to remain stone dead as one of those for as long as possible as far as the mafia are concerned. So now I need to know everything you can tell me.'

It was far too late to turn back. As the Inspector said, I had already burnt all my bridges so I might as well add fuel to the fire. I confirmed everything Cassie had told him and he had already gleaned from the tax investigation files. Cavatappi had fingers in many pies, most of them other people's. The relics scam was a big money spinner. Father Matteo had been perfectly placed to set this up and oversee it based on the national survey of relics he had conveniently been asked to undertake by the Church.

As a sideline to this, Cavatappi's network acquired a great deal of knowledge about ancient artefacts and spread their tentacles into the illegal trade in antiquites.

These were stolen from numerous archeological sites in Italy and across the world.

'Ah that's very interesting,' said the Inspector. 'I know these treasures are smuggled out of their homelands and sold like hot cakes and grannies to private collectors or even unsuspecting museums, but I didn't know any mafia were knee deep in it.'

'They weren't knee deep They were up to their necks. It's a real problem that goes back to the tomb robbers even in ancient Egyptian times. I think it was this line of business that gave Cavatappi the idea of using academic institutions as a front for his operations. But remember when I turned informer he was still only at the planning stage for the Oxford venture.'

I was able to confirm to Panettone that PEST was the vehicle through which all of the gangs illicit profits were routed, particularly those from "pizza" or drugs, which was the mainstream profit earner. In order to launder these funds they needed to be "washed" through a legitimate organisation by mixing them with entirely legal income streams. Otherwise all those ill-gotten gains were pointless as they would be tracked down eventually and confiscated. As Cavatappi realised, nothing could act as a better money laundrette than the faculty of an Oxford University college endorsed and supported by "clean" funds from many global academic institutions. The more prominent it was in the public eye the less questions would be asked.

Then there was the added attraction of using the faculty in the future to give a veneer of credibility to sales of stolen artefacts verified by acknowledged world experts as genuine. It seemed that as the faculty was still in it's early stages, matters had not yet got that far. But, as I told the Inspector, given time Cavatappi would have looked for a way to blackmail or threaten members of Tom's team and other academic experts in the University to confirm not only the authenticity of such treasures, even if fake, but also that they came from real archeological sites and via legitimate sources..

The Inspector had already combed through the faculty accounts and the Dean's own bank account, tracing the entries relating to PEST and the transfer of monies paid out from the faculty's account to Swiss accounts in the names of mysterious third parties. It was clear that the Dean would already have known enough to realise that the faculty was living largely off the proceeds of crime and that the benefits he was receiving personally were in effect bribes. Although it was a near run thing,[197] Panettone seemed to think Tom should be given the benefit of the doubt. There was no concrete evidence that he knew anything.

We turned to leave, the Inspector leading the way but following a different path to the one I had come by. He paused abruptly and a question that had been lurking in the back of my mind came flashing back to me.

'The lady who was shot in my place?'

Panettone nodded towards another fresh grave that had just caught my eye.

The sharp edged inscription engraved on the granite stone read, "Catrina Tuner, affectionately known as Tina to her friends ...'.

'We've put her next to Mary Anne Evans.'

'Who? Never heard of her. And why? Was she very beautiful?'

"No, she wrote under the name George Eliot and according to her fellow novelist Henry James was "magnificently ugly, deliciously hideous." Perhaps that was why on her honeymoon in Venice her new husband jumped off a balcony into the Grand Canal, although you would think he might have taken a sneak peek under the veil beforehand.

As I've said, my heart may still be beating but it's also had a beating over the years and toughened as a result. Yet standing there I really did feel choked up, only just managing to mumble words thickened with emotion, 'Tina Tuna. Cod shave her shoal.

Panettone could see that I was really floundering. 'You mean her sole?' He put a long arm round my shoulders while momentarily forgetting his own warning that we should speak in English, '*Si, povera donna* - poor woman. For the sniper it was like shooting fish in a barrel. She just went down hook, line and sinker.'

Through my sobs I tried again to say something profound. 'She's had her chips'. Then we both lapsed into silence.

CHAPTER 22 – WHERE WILL IT ALL END?

When you reach the end of your rope, tie a knot in it and hang on – Franklin D Roosevelt

The team were all gathered round the office table eating arancini, the sticky little Italian rice balls that Panettone had brought with him to lighten their spirits. They were dismayed that their projects and their jobs now faced the axe. The news that they had inadvertently been funded by the mob, who were covertly using the faculty as a front for money laundering, was a real shock. With the arrest of Cavatappi and the Dean, this flood of income had abruptly dried up and the faculty's account had already been frozen as the proceeds of crime.

The question was whether anything could be salvaged from the wreckage? This seemed unlikely, given that their projects would all require a great deal of further speculative research, assuming they had any prospects of success at all. Tom was sorely tempted to brighten everyone up with the news of Atlantis. That incredible find would reignite the team's reputation and possibly encourage some other sponsors to come forward.

But he was now hitched to Boudicca's chariot, and she had a firm hold of the reins. She was adamant that, having sworn to keep the secret, nothing had changed, and Tom was too smitten to demur. So, all that remained was to listen to some theories on Alexander's tomb that Cassie had already told them all were crazy ideas.

'Okay, Cassie and Finn,' he said. 'You've got some things to share with us and you think it will be helpful to have the Inspector's views. Go ahead.'

Cassie and Finn looked at each other a little nervously, then, as Tom requested, she briefly reminded everyone of what had already come to light so they could concentrate on the new fragments they had uncovered.

'So, since my visit to San Marco, I've been thinking about the white figure. You will remember that the first sighting reported was by the guy with the blue rucksack who was initially regarded by the Italian police as the prime suspect. He said he had seen a white figure in the Cathedral, but everyone dismissed this as him trying to distract the investigation; just a red herring or the imaginings of an unstable person[198]. But Finn and I have pieced together a lot of other similar sightings since then. These have taken place all over Turkey and Asia as far as Afghanistan, India and Egypt. We've put together a timeline for these which Finn will say a bit more about. Then there were the reports in Oxford of the missing patient, completely bandaged in white, and apparently interested in the missing Ashmolean ring. I've been back to the police station yet again since the events at Bling Hall to have another look at the newspaper cutting and the referral note the patient left behind at the hospital. Both DCI Boyle and DC Peel mentioned that they saw a white figure leaving the hall in the Popemobile just before the SAS arrived. And they saw a silver bucket of some kind on the front seat.' Cassie paused and looked inquiringly at Panettone who clearly wanted to interject.

'That must be my mother. One of Pappa's gang put her in the gallery, but then she just flew the coop.'

Finn winked at Cassie to show he was ready to step in. 'As Cassie says, we traced all the sightings of the white figure we could find. This may sound far-fetched, but they are all from places Alexander the Great visited and, apart from the temple at Siwa, which is where he wanted to be buried, are all sites of cities he established. That pattern explains them all and I can't think of anything else that would – although, of course, these reports are mostly from newspapers and we don't know if they are complete or how accurate they are. Cassie, you forgot to mention the thread.'

'Oh, yes. DCI Boyle told me that in the gallery with the Ashmolean treasures the police also found a few strands of white thread. I suggested that these should not just be forensically examined but carbon dated and, like the threads found in San Marco, they were made roughly around 300-350 BC. Alexander died in 323 BC.'

Tom was getting impatient. He could not hide the shedload of sarcasm in his voice but, detecting it himself, wondered if any of it was the pique of recent rejection. 'So, what are you suggesting, Cassie? That St

Mark was Alexander the Great and came back from the dead?'

Instead of the swift denial he expected, her reply knocked him off balance and she, in turn, was a bit sharper than she had intended because she was feeling defensive.

'I know it seems mad but that's the only explanation I can think of. I accept that quite how he got to all these places is to say the least unclear and for the time being we will just have to add it to our list of mysteries for further investigation. But taking it a step at a time, the mix-up between St Mark's body and Alexander's really is plausible. You should listen to Finn before you shut your mind. We're supposed to be open to any possibility in our work and I'm sure the Inspector would say the same in his.'

Finn came to her aid again before matters got out of hand. 'One of the recent pieces of academic research on Alexander's tomb does put forward some detailed evidence that there was a mix up between their bodies[199]. There's no mention of St Mark's body until around 400 AD when, out of the blue, ancient sources suddenly refer to it being in Alexandria where we know Alexander's embalmed body was still on display. In 832 AD, St Mark's body was allegedly taken by two Venetian merchants from Alexandria to Venice. All except the Saint's head of course, as that remained with the Orthodox Church in Alexandria. The merchants smuggled the body out in a cart of pork to save it from possible desecration by the Muslims who had conquered Egypt.

In Venice, the Cathedral of San Marco was then built to house the body and to venerate the saint. Over a thousand years later in 1811, the body was moved due to flooding into the High Altar. This exhumation provided indications that the body was mummified, like Alexander's, but that was contrary to the traditions of the early Christians who would have originally buried St Mark. It also revealed a large corner segment of an Egyptian sarcophagus which has Macedonian carvings on it and is very probably the one in which Alexander's body was first buried. Cassie noticed this stone segment as well and took a photo of it when she was in San Marco at the crime scene. When Ptolemy originally kidnapped Alexander's body and took it to Egypt, this sarcophagus conveniently happened to be available. The previous Pharaoh, Nectanbo II, for whom it had been made, never used it and died elsewhere, so Ptolemy popped Alexander in it for safekeeping. So, there you have it. The body at San Marco is probably Alexander's.'

There was a stunned silence. Everyone in the team was trying to join the dots to draw a different picture that still made sense and they were all drawing a blank. Then Panettone had a sudden thought.

'Did any of the sightings of the white figure suggest it had no head?'

Cassie shook her head. 'No, and you're right. If it had been headless, they surely would have commented on that. At the Oxford Infirmary, the staff commented on his piercing eyes and the fact he seemed to have no nose, but of course that just confirms there was a head.

'No nose?' Finn said. 'Well that is another pointer. You remember from my presentation that the historical sources mention that the Emperor Augustus knocked off Alexander's nose when he visited the tomb in

Alexandria?'

'So,' Cassie followed up. 'Let me tell you a story, and then you can all tear it apart. The mummified body buried in the High Altar of San Marco is Alexander the Great, not St Mark. St Mark's head is in Alexandria so the body in San Marco can't be the Saint's since it has a head. On the Day of the Dead when, according to Italian tradition, the dead come back to the world of the living, Alexander breaks out of the tomb, kills Father Matteo, the only person he sees, and escapes from the Cathedral. He then spends the following few weeks trying to find the cities he founded, which are either now in ruins or unrecognisable. Virtually all trace of his empire and the world he knew has gone. But then he picks up news of the ring which has just been stolen from the Ashmolean. There was global press coverage but particular interest in the theft in Greece since it was a Greek artefact and ROT was stirring up publicity as part of its campaign for return of the Marbles. Alexander recognises the photo in a Greek newspaper and kept the cutting which he had with him at Oxford Infirmary. He sees it is his own signet ring, the symbol of his kingship and authority. He is determined to hunt it down and recover it. Even if he has a little difficulty with modern Greek he can read enough to tell him where to look; in Oxford where the theft took place. Once here he probably follows the Inspector, who he has read is heading an investigation and trying to find whoever stole the Ashmolean treasures as well as solve the crimes at San Marco.'

Everyone looked at each other as if they were all participating in a séance and had just seen the glass spell something out. Cassie seemed completely bonkers, but no one could think of another narrative that made sense of everything or of any objection to her theory, apart from the glaringly obvious.

Panettone leant back in his chair and said calmly, 'Well, we can test all this. The ring is back in the museum and I'm sure that has already been reported in the Greek press as well. Alexander – if we call the white figure that for the time being, has proved to be cunning and tenacious so he's sure to track this down soon enough if he hasn't already. All we need to do is get all dressed up for somewhere to go and be ready to roll there. Hopefully, he'll also bring my mother back with him when he comes, although I can't quite understand why he took her in the first place.'

'Well maybe it could work', Tom said doubtfully.

'What other option is there', Panettone asked shrugging his shoulders. 'It's the weasel's last fart....sorry, that's Japanese...I think you would say it's the last resort.'

CHAPTER 23 – WHAT GOES AROUND …

Don't worry about the world coming to an end today. It's already tomorrow in Australia – Charles M. Schulz

Joe was on late night duty again. It was a few months since the raid and the museum's treasures had all been restored to their rightful place. West Ham were playing the return leg of the season against Chelsea. Joe had a funny feeling in the pit of his stomach. He would have described it as *déjà vu*, but couldn't because it wasn't one he'd ever come across before.

He cleared the last visitors out of the galleries. As usual, there was the Professor with the purple waistcoat. He had come to see the enamelled astrological bowl now it had been returned to its cabinet. Joe shooed him out. He was leaning forward to press the red security button to set the systems for the night when the side exit door burst open.

This time, however, the intruder wasn't one of the Bolshie Bears and, if he was either another West

Ham supporter or a Chelsea supporter, he had already been seriously beaten up by the other side. The bandaged figure was wearing a beanie and a dressing gown, and was clutching an ice bucket under one arm. The piercing eyes fixed on Joe were like those of a basilisk and Joe felt the pre-match pasty he had just been eating turn to stone inside him. In a moment, he was trussed up on the floor like a haggis.

Cassie, Panettone, Finn and Tom were all watching on the security cameras with DCI Boyle, who now gave the signal for the police firearms squad to move in and surround the museum. This time round, the SAS had been confined to barracks to reduce the risk of any escalation in hostilities.

The figure knew exactly where to find the ring, broke the glass in the display with his fist and slipped it on his bandaged finger. The museum would no doubt like to recover it for a second time but Cassie thought that perhaps now they would need to be satisfied with the replica. After all they hadn't realised before that it was a copy. In any case, she thought this was one small way in which a Greek treasure could be returned to its rightful owner.

The question was, what would Alexander do now? In 323 BC, on his deathbed, he was still making extravagant plans to build a huge fleet, conquer the Arabian peninsula, Italy and Sicily, and to build a road all the way to the Straits of Gibraltar. Now he had seen that his empire had disappeared and the world had changed irrevocably, what would he do?

What happened next surprised them all. The figure went to the case in which the Alfred Jewel had been restored and splendidly mounted. For a moment

Cassie thought he was about to seize that as well, but after gazing on it intently he turned away.

'That's interesting', Finn was whispering although there was really no need in the back office in the museum from where they were watching. 'Some think the figure carved on the jewel is Christ, but other scholars believe it's of Alexander the Great.'

The mummified figure seemed tired, as if he suddenly felt nearly two thousand four hundred years old. He yawned, or at least his jaws opened and his head seemed to droop. Could it be that the world's greatest conqueror was finally experiencing career burn out? He appeared to be looking around for somewhere to take, at the very least, a long nap. Returning to the main gallery he levered open the lid of DJ's sarcophagus. Then scooping out the priest's body he chucked it on the floor. On impact the head rolled away down the gallery clunking down a short flight of steps before coming to rest against a display about some of the most extraordinary artefacts ever found including the London Hammer, the Baghdad Battery and the Antikythera Mechanism[200]. Alexander wasn't interested in these distractions. He just tenderly placed the ice bucket inside the sarcophagus, climbed inside himself in DJ's place and pulled the lid back shut so that he and Panettone's mother were sealed in together.

Panettone was speechless. They were all bemused. DCI Boyle asked if Alexander the Great liked champagne or just the idea of lying next to an ice bucket. Finn pointed out that, although he was certainly recorded as often drinking rather too much wine and Macedonian beer, champagne hadn't been dreamed up back then.

Somewhere in the recesses of Cassie's mind a dim light flickered and she turned abruptly to Panettone. 'The inscription on the ice bucket!' she cried. 'It's in Greek!'

'It's just my mother's Christian name, Roxanne,' said the Inspector.

Cassie's eyes rounded wide from dark almonds into hazelnuts. 'Ah, that explains it then. Roxanne was the name of Alexander's queen. She was a princess from Uzbekistan who outlived him by thirteen years before being murdered in the strife that followed his death. And what's more I've just realised that DJ's own curse has also been fulfilled. His mummy was taken by Collosovitch, who is now in solitary confinement in Belmarsh prison, and then removed by Alexander who is indeed now entombed just as DJ was. In fact in DJ's own tomb!'

Panettone's initial reaction was that he would need to rescue his mother but after giving it a little more thought, he changed his mind. The old lady would have loved the idea that her last resting place was in the arms of Alexander the Great. It was a more flamboyant and dramatic end than anything even she could have dreamed of.

As for DJ, he provided the perfect solution all round. Had Alexander's body been returned to San Marco many would have doubted whether it could really be St Mark. It had a head after all although without a nose. Instead, DJ's now headless body was successfully restored to the Venetian Cathedral amidst great pageantry and rejoicing with no questions asked. The Pope himself presided over the ceremony on a day which was declared a national holiday in Italy.

CHAPTER 24 – SEARCHING FOR THE SINGULARITY

Reality is merely an illusion, albeit a very persistent one – Albert Einstein

Reality leaves a lot to the imagination – John Lennon

Some of you will by now be yearning for an end that joins all the dots neatly and completes the picture. Although Dr Bacon's therapy has taught me this is just fantasy, I have connected below some stray dots that you may feel need to be tidied up.

Tom quietly disposed of DJ's inconvenient head. Uncle Albert had seemed increasingly lonely, but now that DJ was next to him on his archive shelf in the Pitt Rivers, they both looked a great deal happier. When Tom's father returned from the outback, he said it was clearly a case of two heads being better than one. He then had a riotous weekend in Rome with Tom's mother.

Nursing hangovers the following afternoon when they finally crawled out of bed after partying into the early hours, she explained that she could never return to a country where rather than cakes and espresso, breakfast consisted of tea and porridge. Tom's father finally capitulated, promising to hang up his boots after one last trip, this time to the Arctic to catalogue the four thousand different words the Innuit use to describe ice in all its many forms.

The restoration of St Mark to San Marco had the added advantage that Panettone now inherited his mother's fortune. Sister Felicity gave up holy orders and the Inspector was delighted to discover that the most powerful aphrodisiac of all is years of pent-up celibacy. They married with almost indecent haste and the Pope allowed them to borrow the Popemobile for their honeymoon. Having expected to complete his days as a confirmed bachelor, Panettone found that, in a remarkably short time, he had fifteen children who filled every room of his mother's huge mansion with screaming. The speed of these developments was helped by Felicity's propensity for triplets which enabled them to have five waves of children, a batch at a time.

The Inspector did not, however, forget his mother's cat, Felicette, and adopted her before Uncle Ugo could find a method of getting rid of her in a more terminal way. While the cat continued to viciously attack Panettone and Felicity's guests, it gambolled with the children like a kitten, indulgently allowing them to pull out it's fur until it became a sphinx.

Cavatappi was given permission to play online chess

from the solitary confinement wing in Pentonville, so intense battles between ChesstWig and ChessNut soon resumed without either of them ever knowing the identity of their opponent. When he was eventually released, Cavatappi called in a few favours from old mafia mates and bought out Palline Congelate. He refined his ice-cream making skills and devised several new flavours. It was however only a few months later that his body was found packed deep and perfectly preserved in a freezer full of traditional Sicilian lemon with a vengeful twist, always the best seller[201]. The murder weapon could not be found until forensics took a closer look at the raspberry gelati in a large, discarded ice cream scoop. If you have me down as the prime suspect, then for the record I honestly had nothing to do with it. Cavatappi had such a queue of enemies that whoever it was just who happened to be the first to get there.

Dan's baldness meant it was even easier for him to change his hairstyle regularly than for Cassie, and over the years he had already acquired one of the world's largest collections of toupees. Keeping up with Cassie's hair-raising activities would have resulted in total hair loss at some stage, anyway, so it might be said that Dan had just gained a head start. But sadly, like Tom, he soon found her too hot to handle.

After they split up, Cassie returned to Lesbos to visit her family and found her mother had set up an art history group in the small, whitewashed church in the village. While there, she met Adonis, a local fisherman, who took her skinny-dipping with dolphins. Over the next couple of years, she alternated between the pull of home and rediscovering, then excavating, several lost

Alexandrias in remote regions of Turkey and Pakistan in between climbing a crop of Himalayan peaks.

Finally, she asked Adonis if he would promise to mend his own nets and he accepted her proposal. Cassie's father said nothing but showed his deep pleasure by teaching Adonis all the magic tricks he knew. This was also a great help when two grandchildren came along. Alexander and Roxanne had an unconventional upbringing in a house full of lavender and rabbits where they took turns to saw each other in half.

Every winter when it was too rough to fish, Adonis would look after the children for a few weeks, while Cassie packed her catsuit and disappeared. Every spring, her mother's art history group found new pictures on display for a short period in the small whitewashed Church. The aged priest and local women who came along never realised that the painting of the guy with one ear was a genuine Van Gogh or that the molten watches on a beach were original masterpieces by Salvador Dali[202].

The priest was particularly scandalised by the chubby lady without even a bikini posing in a ridiculously large clam shell. It was worse than the foreign tourists who flocked to the island's beaches in the summer and wanted to cast off any semblance of decency. At least the woman in the painting was hiding her modesty with her long blonde hair. His mood was not improved by overhearing a snatch of conversation between two aged widows from the village.

'The notice says this one's a famous painting by Botticelli[203] although it must be a copy.'

'I've used that jelly myself. It's very soothing for

my haemorrhoids.'

Cassie felt she was quite entitled to borrow these treasures from other countries, just as the British Museum had. The only difference was that her loan was a short term one. She took them all back after a few weeks, leaving the owners of the private collections they had usually come from at a loss as to what had happened and red-faced. How could they now explain the reported theft? They needn't have worried. The police just assumed the owners had hidden the pictures themselves before submitting a fraudulent insurance claim but then got cold feet about it.

Tom didn't quite confirm his theory of love at first sight with Boudicca, but he did statistically prove that, if you do this often enough the probabilities of your wish being fulfilled eventually tend to improve.

With the Dean gone, life at St Barbara's became much more enjoyable. Tom and Boudicca took students on many exciting field trips and archaeological digs, still hoping to uncover other historical mysteries. When the Dean was released, he reappeared in Oxford as a parking warden and tried to take his revenge by giving Tom tickets for the tiniest infringements in a game of cat and mouse that lasted for years. This only ended when the Dean tried to hide behind a double decker bus to catch Tom out, only for the unsuspecting driver to reverse over him.

Puk renovated her ancestor Tycho's observatory on the island of Hven, which was generally regarded as heaven with just a couple of bits missing. Many astronomers came to gaze into the dark sky over the island through its state of the art telescopes. Puk herself became a leading expert in the study of space rocks from meteors, meteoroids and meteorites to comets and asteroids. She allowed a herd of elks to roam free on the island but did not permit them any alcohol[204].

You may be wondering about the Professor with the purple waistcoat. It's hard to know whether all those sightings were real or imaginary and, if real, what the explanation is, if any. Possibly he was an MI5 agent with some unknown mission or was planning to steal the bowl he coveted from the Ashmolean himself before the Bolshie Bears made off with it. It all depends on how you would like to join the dots. But, then again, maybe his appearances are just a series of coincidences that have no relationship with each other, except for the ones we invent in the fevered hot-houses of our minds.

I'm sure there's something else important I've forgotten but I seem to have lost it. Something Dr Bacon warned me about. Of course...the marbles!

A couple of months after St Mark was joyously reinterred at San Marco, a large container ship wallowed slowly out to sea from the jetty at Felixstowe. The deck was piled so high with multi coloured boxes that the boat seemed to be sinking under the foundations of an unfinished Lego skyscraper. It was a calm day but even so the vessel's wake cut a broad arrow through the swell. Two figures hung over the deck rail at the stern watching the widening white scars peel away towards the shore. In their greasy overalls and woollen beanies they were indistinguishable from the rest of the crew, except that both were on the short side and one seemed far too slight to manhandle a winch.

'Well, I must admit I never thought we would

actually get away with it', Cassie said as the wind whipped and cuffed her face.

'We haven't yet. We may soon find Admiral Nelson, Sir Francis Drake and the whole Royal Navy in pursuit. Hopefully that Greek ship, the Argo, will act as a decoy and keep them guessing as long as possible. The captain, Jason, struck me as a real toughie along with his crew. He called them the Agronuts and came out with some of the longest swear words I've ever heard when I mentioned the name Elgin[205]. He's someone who would go to the ends of the earth for the Greek cause, although given half a chance I'm sure he also would happily fleece you.' Despite these words of caution, Cleo could hardly hold back her own delight but no one would have detected it under her false walrus moustache.

'It was a good tip off from that informer Angel to use a British vessel ourselves and make a customs declaration for a consignment of construction materials. He's obviously learnt a trick or two from mafia drug smuggling.'

Cleo was laughing now. 'Yes. I was shaking at first when Customs insisted on checking our container, but then when the guy said he couldn't understand why anyone would want to go the trouble of exporting chunks of broken rubble I almost had an embarrassing accident.'

'Shame we could only take ten blocks but they are the best preserved ones.'

'Look on the bright side Cassie. We were lucky to have this chance at all. We never thought when you redecorated the marbles that the museum's restoration team would shift them all to a warehouse for cleaning and checking over or that their security systems would be so hopeless. It was so much easier to nick them from there than the British Museum. Once you had hacked into their system they didn't think to ask any questions at all when you booked in our hire truck to collect them on the basis that the best marbles needed to be returned pronto. I suppose it made sense that the government would be applying pressure to get the marbles back on display quickly to put a stop to all the negative publicity. But even then we wouldn't have managed if you hadn't persuaded Tom and the History Mystery team to give the ROT network a hand to get them loaded up.'

'I feel almost sorry for the British government.'

'I wouldn't spare them a thought. In the negotiations over the future of the marbles with our own Minister of Culture the best British offer was to give us a set of plaster casts for the Parthenon in return for a free bowl of olives and shot of ouzo for every Brit tourist visiting Greece. They had it coming to them.'

So now here you are at an end, or the beginning of a possible end[206]. My lapse in forgetting to join up the marbles was a salutary lesson that we are never really at the end but always somewhere in the middle. Some marbles are kept, some are lost and some are found or even re-found. It all depends how you look at the dots and connect them.

At least I've joined up some dots and written a small part of my story linking it with some other stories. There's a lot more that's missing, just as constellations miss out most stars. It's a work in progress, I suppose. With Dr Bacon's help over time I will write more of it but, as you can imagine, a lot of my past is dark matter

I would rather not explore or disturb at all. There are black holes lurking there that could easily suck me in and tear me apart, extinguishing the light altogether. Places where no stars can survive and no constellations can be created.

When I last went back to see Dr Bacon he was still talking in the same mysterious pseudo-scientific terms. Although I've become accustomed to using them myself, I'm still not sure that I understand a lot of it. The impending singularity he mentioned in my first session still appears to be a long way away and until then apparently our stories will continuously be rewritten. He says this next singularity will be like a return to the previous one. That was the moment before the Big Bang when allegedly all the dots of matter in existence in the universe were not simply connected but crushed together into just a single dot smaller than the full stop at the end of this sentence. Against that measure almost any fantasy or fairy story seems entirely credible.

Apparently at that moment no imagination was or will be necessary. The density of gravitational forces is so intense that time and space have no meaning and there is no 'when' or 'where'. No forces or laws of physics exist to explain the relationships between things because everything is one. A singularity. There is just what is with no room for argument. Just fact with all the fiction squeezed out, although I'm still not sure if that explains the ultimate coincidence of how the singular dot itself first came about or what will happen when we reach the next one. Maybe to understand that we would need to read the Book of Life in which it is said that the final version of all our stories are recorded.

Postscript

If at this point you wish you had never read this book please at least recycle the materials by using the pages for bathroom wallpaper or to make a *papier maché* model of the Taj Mahal. I can only hope that the fact you have persisted this far may be an encouraging sign that you have gained something from doing so.

For my own part I have found the therapy of joining the dots to be helpful and would like to give my heartfelt thanks to Dr Bacon. He tells me that the next stage of my treatment is to reconnect the dots I have selected already in this story with the Unjoined Dots in the endnotes that follow to make a new pattern. All unjoined dots will eventually find themselves in someone's story at some stage. Those in the endnotes are only a draft list to which I am adding all the time and of course you will have unjoined dots of your own.

Find out more at angelcapelli.com.

As you will have picked up from my story life has been hard, but underneath the scar tissue I'm a sensitive soul just trying to turn away from past crimes and live up to my name. So if you could find it in your heart to give me an honest and kind or even constructively critical review that would help me to do better with my next book, that would be very much appreciated. Direct link - amzn.to/3qRKDzN

CULINARY ENCRYPTION

Codenames and Pasta Sauces

Alfredo – Invented in 1908 in Rome by a guy called Alfredo to tempt his wife, who had lost her appetite after giving birth. The rich sauce of butter, young parmesan and sweet spices combined with *fettuccine* became famous and Alfredo was feted as a celebrity. In 1950, he set up a new restaurant with other family members and gold cutlery donated by the silent movie stars Mary Pickford and Douglas Fairbanks in honour of Alfredo's hospitality. He was known as the Emperor of *Fettuccine*. Part of the appeal of the dish was the performance of preparation at the table, described as a spectacle reminiscent of a grand opera.

Boscaiola – Means woodcutter or woodsman and this rich sauce is based on the most popular ingredients foraged in woods, porcini mushrooms.

Capelli d'angelo – These long strands of very thin pasta dating back to the 14th century are often sold in a nest like shape. The name means angels' hair and because it is light this pasta goes well with soup and seafood.

Cavatappi – This means corkscrew and the pasta is *macaroni* in a spiral shape. It is a hollow tube not to be confused with fusilli and other flat pastas which also have a helical shape. It was invented by accident at Barilla's factory in Parma in the 1970's when a set of pasta moulds for *cellentani* were made in a spiral shape by error.

Fra Diavolo – A hot spicy tomato sauce with crushed red pepper, garlic, onions and herbs named after the freedom fighting guerrilla, or bandit to some, Michele Pezza (see footnote 140), although some attribute it to the opera of the same name by Daniel Auber.

Genovese – a slow-cooked meat and onion sauce that, despite its name, comes from Naples not Genoa. It should be served

with a cylindrical pasta that can hold the sauce, either *paccheri* or *rigatoni, ziti* or *candele.*

Linguine – This pasta really is from Genoa and the Ligurian region and originated in the 1700s. The name means little tongues and National Linguine Day is celebrated in the United States on 15th September every year.

Norma – A Sicilian sauce from Catania made from aubergines, tomato, basil, garlic and *ricotta salata.* See Chapter 5.

Orzo – Derived from the word for barley and also known as *risoni*, it is a very small pasta shaped like a large rice grain.

Pappardelle – A very wide flat pasta whose name is based on the Tuscan *pappare*, meaning to eat with childlike pleasure (showing Cavatappi's charming and generous side).

Penne – A pasta with an undisputed birthday. On 11th March 1865 pasta-maker Giovanni Battista Capurro from San Martino d'Albano applied for a patent to cut pasta diagonally. Its name comes from the shape of a pen quill.

Puttanesca – A vibrant tasty sauce which includes tomatoes, capers, black olives and oregano. It can be cooked easily and quickly, and the name means, "In the style of a lady of the night." It's origins are unclear, but it is suggested it was something that such ladies could easily cook between shifts with clients.

Vermicelli – Similar to *spaghetti* but thicker in Italy and thinner elsewhere, the name means "Little worms," which doesn't immediately sound appetising.

Ziti – A small extruded pasta from Campania traditionally served at weddings. Zita and zito mean bride and groom.

(You are probably already aware that *Calzone* is a form of folded over pizza, a bit like a large pasty, originating from Naples, *Panettone* is a sweet bread from Milan studded with candied fruit and raisins and *Cantucci* are crunchy almond biscuits that are good for dunking.

UNJOINED DOTS

Dots that have some connection with this story, however tenuous, but didn't make the cut - as Dr Bacon says (Prologue), they may come in useful sometime.

---

[1] Winston Churchill giving the British people a rather confusing progress report in the middle of WW2 in 1942 after the very first allied victory at Alamein. Perhaps he was under the influence of alcohol at the time, as he frequently drank a full bottle of champagne for both lunch and dinner together with a great deal of scotch and brandy. When Bessie Bradock told him in 1946 that he was disgustingly drunk he famously responded that she was disgustingly ugly but he would be sober in the morning, although perhaps less so later in the day

[2] People often talk about the 'year dot' but no one seems to know when it was. The origins of the phrase are unclear but it seems to have emerged from the idea of something so distant it couldn't be clearly identified. Strangely in our Gregorian Calendar there is no year zero and history goes straight from 1 BC to 1 AD without missing a beat. The Year Zero was however a concept invoked by the murderous dictator Pol Pot to signify the irrelevance of past Cambodian history and culture so that his revolution could start again from scratch.

[3] Book 2, Ch 173. Herodotus (484-425 BC) invented history, or at least the term, and the concept of trying to explain what happened in the past, but some of his findings were bizarre. For example, he gives an account of super sized ants in Persia that ate adult camels and dug up gold while making their burrows.

[4] It seems Joe had not inherited the athletic prowess of his great great grandfather, who ran in the 1904 Olympic marathon at St Louis. It was a remarkable event with the lowest number of finishers in Olympic history, not assisted by the decision to have only one water stop to see how well the runners could cope with dehydration in temperatures of over 40C. One contestant was chased over a mile off the course by a pack of wild dogs. Another hitched a ride and was even crowned the victor before he was rumbled and initially banned for life. A Cuban ran in leather boots and took a nap in an orchard to recover after eating an unripe apple but still managed to come in fourth. As stimulants were allowed, when the eventual winner began to struggle seven miles before the finish his team gave him a mixture of rat poison and egg whites which he washed down with a brandy chaser. This enabled him

to stagger over the line where he promptly passed out for over an hour.

[5] Rasputin was a mystic who became a close confidant of the Imperial Russian family (allegedly, one factor leading up to the Russian Revolution of 1917). He proved extremely difficult to murder. Tea and cakes laced with poison had no effect on him. Nor did poisoned Madeira wine. He was then shot in the chest but sometime later jumped up again and had to be shot in the forehead but still needed to be finally finished off by being thrown into a frozen river.

[6] This forms part of a set decorated with astrological symbols from the Safavid dynasty (1501-1722) of Iran. Ismail I, the founder of the dynasty, used the skull of the Uzbek warlord Shaybani Khan as a bejeweled goblet.

[7] Joe's attitude to technology had some similarities to Napoleon's. When told of a new design for a steamship, Napoleon said: 'What, sir, would you make a ship sail against the wind and currents by lighting a bonfire under her deck? I pray you, excuse me, I have not the time to listen to such nonsense.'

[8] A masterpiece of goldwork and rock crystal with the inscription, "Alfred ordered me to be made," making it a priceless royal relic. It was discovered in 1693 near Athelney Abbey in Somerset from which Alfred launched his successful attack on the Great Army of the Vikings who he defeated in 693 AD. So it seems he was a successful soldier even if he is mainly famous for poor baking skills and burning cakes.

[9] Dating from around 2500 BC, it was found in 1669 in Ireland by some men who were looking for a place described in an old Irish song as a burial site containing gold for "A man of gigantick stature".

[10] Donated by Prince Chichibu of Japan. The Samurai often tested how sharp their swords were by chopping up random civilians.It wasn't a great idea to be married to one as wives were expected to commit ritual suicide when their husbands died.

[11] Carried by Guy Fawkes when arrested underneath the House of Parliament on the night of 4-5th November. He managed to light his lantern but not the fuses for the kegs of gunpowder he had hidden there. Such was the national rejoicing at the uncovering of the plot that until 1959 was it was illegal <u>not</u> to celebrate Bonfire Night.

[12] Probably from Urbino and bearing a Latin inscription showing

remarkable self awareness, "*Every man looks at me as if I were a head of dicks.*"

[13] He was a priest from Thebes in Egypt around 770 BC and his name means 'The God Thoth says, May he live.'

[14] The three Laws of the Jungle which, according to Rudyard Kipling's Jungle Book, must always be remembered are: wash daily from nose to tail tip; drink deeply but never too deep; remember the night is for hunting and forget not the day is for sleep.

[15] A major fire was caused by beef stroganoff in the kitchen in 2015. When the hotel reopened the General Manager, Michael Grange, said safety measures had been reviewed and tightened up by taking beef stroganoff off the menu.

[16] The nickname of the Eagle and Child pub on St Giles in Oxford where Tolkien and C.S. Lewis used to meet in the Rabbit Room.

[17] The most famous West Ham song dating back to the 1920s is often adapted to the tune of Chitty Chitty Bang Bang.

[18] Particularly if you're in Korea. Kim Jong il is alleged to have scored eleven in his first ever round of golf.

[19] Hoyle as astronomer, pointing out that what's remote is mainly in the mind as Space is only 62 vertical miles away.

[20] The need for anger management is an ancient one and anger often has complex causes. The Iliad is about the anger of Achilles, first because his girlfriend is stolen from him, then because his boyfriend is killed. But underlying this is his anger that he can't be a god. Therefore, he must make the choice either to live a long life and be forgotten or a short one as a warrior and be remembered forever. In the Dean's case, there was no complexity at all. He was just a nasty piece of work.

[21] Archimedes (287-211 BC) invented a water screw for pumping water to a higher level through a pipe. He is also famous for jumping out of his bath and running down the streets of Syracuse stark naked shouting, 'Eureka.' This may have been because (a) the water was too hot, (b) he had just found the plug, (c) it was the name of his girlfriend or d) he had discovered why ships float and coins sink.

[22] In Genesis, the attempt to build a tower up to Heaven is said to have resulted in the confusion of languages. Hence our word Babel.

[23] It could have been much worse. For example, it could have been the mummy of Amenenope, slayer of Wahibre Ibiau, a pharaoh of the 21st Dynasty and son of Psusennes 1st and Queen Mutjedmnet,

or else Aahotepre, slayer of Djedkohnsuefrankh, a minor pharaoh of the 14th Dynasty. But Egyptian pharaohs generally were a strange lot. Pepi II kept the flies away by ordering slaves to strip naked, cover themselves with honey and follow him around so the flies would prefer them to him. Actisanes dealt with criminals by cutting off their noses and sending them all to a town called Rhinocolura populated entirely by other noseless criminals. The Romans regarded him as a softie.

[24] Mummy curses are rare but certainly send chills down the spine. An example is the inscription in the tomb of the 10th dynasty pharaoh, Khentika Ikhekhi: "As for all men who enter this my tomb ... there shall be judgment ... an end shall be made for him ... I shall seize his neck like a bird ... I shall cast the fear of myself into him." Yikes! Lenin was embalmed after his death in 1924 and visitors still flock to see him in his mausoleum in Moscow's Red Square. In Victorian times there was a craze for all things Egyptian and 'Mummy Unrollings' were spectacular events where large audiences sometimes paid to see mummies being unwrapped.

[25] This was because his cat Cleopatra had recently died and, as expert in the field, he had read in Herodotus that if a cat died a natural death in an Egyptian household all its members would shave off their eyebrows.

[26] Ovid was exiled by the Emperor Augustus, probably because of his racy verse about seduction which Augustus thought encouraged loose morals.

[27] The Aztecs thought chocolate was a gift from the Gods and who would argue with that? They even used cacao beans as currency and valued them more than gold. Montezuma II drank gallons of chocolate each day and regarded it as an aphrodisiac. Probably the greatest ever human inventions along with the wheel are however the chocolate bar, first invented in 1847 by Fry & Son in Bristol, and milk chocolate, invented by the Swiss chocolatier Daniel Peter in 1876.

[28] Tom's father also told him how the Aztecs played a game Ullamaliztli with a rubber ball that they had to hit through stone hoops without it touching the ground, a bit like Quidditch. There were real incentives to try hard to win as the captain of the losing team was usually sacrificed by decapitation.

[29] Being hit by bird poop is very widely believed to be associated with good luck in many countries including particularly Russia and Turkey, where people may apparently buy you a lottery ticket if you

mention that you have been pooped on in the hope that you will share the winnings with them.

[30] There was good reason to be frightened of Boudicca. After the rape of her daughters in AD 60-61 she sacked three cities including London and killed an estimated 70-80,000 Romans. Unlike Asterix the Gaul she didn't even have the benefit of a magic potion.

[31] A great English victory in 1346. At school we all learn that in the last 1000 years, since Hastings (when we take care to refer to our conquerors as Normans not French), we have won virtually all our endless battles against France – Sluys, Agincourt, Poitiers, Blenheim, Trafalgar, Waterloo to name a few – and then of course that we had to rescue the French in both World Wars. We are given the impression that they are hopeless soldiers and even their greatest general, Napoleon, was, in the end, a loser. It's not surprising therefore that Parisian waiters sometimes seem a bit resentful. In French schools however, we can be sure they they are taught that, in the end, even if they never won a battle, they won the Hundred Years War and that England has in any event been a French colony since 1066.

[32] The first instance of spontaneous combustion was documented by a Danish doctor who claimed that an Italian knight called Polonus Vorstius was enjoying a few glasses of wine with his parents at home in Milan when he burped fire and died. The most recent incident was of a Mr Flaherty in Ireland in 2010 and was officially recorded as death by spontaneous combustion by the coroner. There are many other cases including a woman who "roared like a dragon" as flames burst out of her stomach. It's a little suspicious that most cases have involved an excess of alcohol. Dickens was a believer and in Bleak House his character Krook, the brother of Mrs Smallweed, dies by spontaneous combustion.

[33] Contenders for an early date suggest the Giant is Cenric, son of Cuthred, King of Wessex who died in battle in 748 AD and those proposing the seventeenth century have suggested Oliver Cromwell. Another local tradition suggests it is a caricature of the last Abbot of Cerne Abbas Abbey, Thomas Corton, who was accused of fathering illegitimate children. The sixth Marquess of Bath claimed to have visited the giant when having trouble conceiving a child. He later said, 'We were very much in the dark as to what he [the giant] could do. I explained the problem and sat on him.' The couple had a daughter ten months later.

[34] As Tacitus said, 'In stature she was very tall, in appearance most

terrifying, and her voice was harsh; a great mass of the tawniest hair fell to her hips.' And, of course, she told the foreman that if he so much as turned the ignition key on one of his bull dozers she would ensure that his company never got a contract from the Department of Transport again.

[35] Chance or random? This is a question that underlies all of life but particularly strange meetings. Often there is an explanation, but the connection isn't obvious. Take, for example Einstein and Charlie Chaplin, who it turns out were friends. When they met, Einstein said, 'You don't say a word, but the world understands you,' and Chaplin responded, 'True. But your glory is even greater! The whole world admires you even though they don't understand a word of what you say.' Missiles brought together "Little Rocket Man" and "Dotard," as Kim Jong-Un and Trump endearingly called one another. Alice Cooper, the extreme rocker, and Col Sanders of Kentucky Fried Chicken fame met up because they were both notorious chicken killers.

[36] Just checking if you are still awake. Thucydides in fact only wrote eight books, or at least eight that survive. This quote was in fact invented by a prankster from the US Naval College in 1960 and has since taken on a life of its own, showing just how difficult it can be to sift fact from fiction.

[37] Being a gondoliere should be one of the world's most sought-after jobs. Not only do you get to float around in a setting of incredible beauty, but they are extremely highly paid. There are now only around 430 compared to 10,000 in the 1500's and their number is limited by a permit system. There is currently only one female gondoliera. As Steven Wright quipped, 'I think it's wrong that only one company makes the game Monopoly.'

[38] The head of St John the Baptist can still be found in four places – the Basilica of St Silvester the First in Rome, the Residenz Museum in Munich, the Ummayad Mosque in Damascus and the Cathedral of Amiens in France. If two heads are better than one, then four is presumably better still. As for other relics, St Claire's fingernails and hair clippings are in Assisi as she was very beautiful so cut them off to avoid provoking temptation. The tongue of St Anthony is in Padua but was taken on a full tour of New York in 2013. At least eighteen churches have claimed at various times to hold the Holy Foreskin, removed during Jesus's circumcision. The last sighting was at Calcata in Italy, but it mysteriously disappeared from the church there in 1983 and has yet to be found.

[39] The romantic legend says that this small bridge was named because of the sighs of lovers who met there after dark. It's good to look on the bright side but, in fact, the sighs were those of prisoners viewing their last glimpse of Venice before execution as they were sent across the bridge from the palace to the prison on the other side of the canal. The notorious lover Casanova was one of the few who made the crossing and lived to tell the tale.

[40] Built originally in 800 AD, it is prone to collapse – several times due to lightning, so approach with care! The most recent collapse was in 1902 and reconstruction was completed in 1912.

[41] St Mark's body was allegedly rescued by two Venetian merchants from Alexandria where the Muslim conquerors were about to destroy it in 842 AD. The merchants allegedly smuggled it out in a cartload of pork to discourage the Muslim guards from searching their wagon and installed it in San Marco (although Cassie comes to doubt this account).

[42] A famous piece of bragging by Julius Caesar – 'I came, I saw, I conquered.'

[43] Tom's article was titled *Fallen Eagle – The Fate of the Ninth*. The dig provisionally suggested that the massacre took place around 110 AD. The last mention of the legion is in an inscription over a gate in York built by soldiers of the Ninth dated 108 AD so this fitted perfectly and also explained the reason for the building of Hadrian's wall (to hold the Picts back) which began in 122 AD. Hadrian's family came from Spain where the Ninth Legion had previously earned great honours (it was called the Ninth Legion Hispana), so he would have been particularly distraught at its destruction. This explanation also fits well with the fictional account in the popular book, *Eagle of the Ninth*, except that the author, Rosemary Sutcliffe, envisaged that the legion had marched much further north and was annihilated in Scotland.

[44] For example, the time when the Dean seemed convinced that Tom's seminar implied comparisons between himself and the Emperor Caligula who was known for his sadism and insane extremes (including ordering his army to flog the sea to show he had conquered it, having a section of the audience in the Coliseum thrown down among the wild animals for sport and proposing to make his horse Incitatus a senator).

[45] This isn't quite true. He did take a little cannabis very occasionally which he called simply recreational. He justified this

to himself on the grounds that Coleridge had gone much further as a regular opium user, which had only seemed to help his poetry, as had Sherlock Holmes to solve his cases. Coleridge describes his poem Xanadu about the palace of Kubla Khan as a "fragment of a vision or dream," very probably inspired by opium.

[46] Although now a robot called RePAIR has been invented that may solve this problem by scanning millions of fragments and using mechanical arms to put them in the right position relative to one another. The first literary reference to robots is in the *Iliad (18.418-422).* Homer says that the god Hephaestos made serving girls out of gold who spoke, used their limbs and had intelligence like humans.

[47] Berlusconi has become notorious for sexism and has been prosecuted for abetting illegal activity involving Ruby 'the heartstealer' Rubacuore. It would not have been suprising if his reported comments about Angela Merkel to a news editor in 2011 had caused Germany to break off diplomatic relations and invade Italy, but they were so rude you will have to look them up for yourself.

[48] The Shard had only been completed very recently at 72 storeys and already the Blot had proved it's point by going one better. The numbering of the top floor was however the same for both buildings as the Blot didn't have an unlucky 13th floor whereas the Shard does, perhaps because it was built by an Italian. In Italy 13 is lucky and it's 17 that's unlucky, probably because one anagram of XVII in Roman numerals is VIXI or "I have lived" implying I am now dead.

[49] *Palline Congelate* means 'little frozen balls'.

[50] There are over 350 different pasta shapes and a great number of sauce flavours (see Appendix for those relating to Cavatappi and his henchmen). Furthermore, many types of pasta have four or more names in different dialects so the potential to build a complex code of identities is almost endless.

[51] All victims of assassination. Others at the party that Tom didn't spot included Benazir Bhutto, Abraham Lincoln, Caligula and a lot of other Roman Emperors, Indira Gandhi, Gianni Versace, Pancho Villa, Archduke Franz Ferdinand, Emile Zola, Mussolini, Rosa Luxemburg, Archbishop Thomas Becket, Philip II of Macedon and Alexander the Great (who was let in, even though it's not clear if he really was assassinated), Alexander Litvinenko, Georgi Markov and Edward II. The last three were killed in ways too gruesome to

describe in a book that is intended to entertain.

[52] Examples of these epitaphs include: "I like gardening but I never planned to become compost." "My friends can now stop complaining that they can never get the last word." "Just thought I might lie here for a bit and watch the clouds." "I've always believed in pudding and that God saves the best till last."

[53] Choosing who to benefit in a will can be tricky. A childless Portuguese aristocrat dealt with this by picking his randomly from a Lisbon telephone directory. Shakespeare, rather callously, left his wife Anne Hathaway in his Will his "second best bed". There is no record of who he gave his best bed to.

[54] The Vatican tends to be tardy when it comes to change. The Roman Catholic Church only formally recognised in 1992 that the earth does in fact go round the sun and that Galilleo, who it convicted of heresy in 1633 for saying just that, was right all along.

[55] Apparent correlations need careful analysis. For example, there are very close statistical correlations between the level of ice-cream sales and the number of murders, a shortage of pirates and global warming, Mexican lemon imports to the US and the prevention of highway deaths, the per capita consumption of cheese and the number of people who were strangled by their own bed sheets. Correlation is not necessarily a result of causation!

[56] Rabbits were first introduced to Austalia in 1859. They bred so fast that they soon became a major ecological hazard. In the 1950's the Australian government introduced the myxoma virus, which is specific to rabbits, from South America. It killed over 90% of the rabbit population through myxomatosis, but the remainder developed immunity and will soon overtake humans as the dominant species on the planet.

[57] Parchment fragments discovered by Bedouin shepherds in caves near the Dead Sea in 1947 containing nearly a thousand ancient manuscripts including the oldest surviving copies of some biblical texts. Among them was also the mysterious Copper Scroll, a sort of ancient treasure map listing 64 underground hiding places around Israel where gold and silver possibly from the Temple in Jerusalem was allegedly stashed for safekeeping. None of these stashes have yet been found. The Copper Scroll is written in a strange vocabulary and spelling that is as yet unexplained.

[58] When Biagio da Cesena, the Papal Master of Ceremonies, complained that Michelangelo's painting of the Last Judgment

contained too much nudity, the great artist took his revenge by depicting Biagio naked in hell on the wall of the Sistine Chapel with a snake wrapped round his waist and biting his genitals.

[59] *I regard golf as an expensive way of playing marbles* – Gilbert K Chesterton. Ducks, Mibs, Taws and Immies, End of Days and Bumboozers are all different marbles ranging in size, pattern and what they are made of. The most expensive marbles are Lutz marbles.

[60] Michelangelo put it more eloquently: "I saw an angel in the marble and carved until I set him free".

[61] The first yo-yo was invented in Ancient Greece. There are plates showing pictures of children playing with them dating from 500 BC. They became popular in 18th Century Europe when they were called by a range of names including Whirligig, Bandalore, Quiz, Incroyable and Coblentz.

[62] A Yorkshire farmer, George Bamber, invented double yellow lines in the nineteenth century, using them as boundary lines around his land.

[63] Julius Caesar originally crossed the river Rubicon on the border between Cisalpine Gaul and Italy in 49 BC. It was a symbolic step he took in deciding to march on Rome as once he crossed the river he knew there was no turning back.

[64] Famous Freemasons include Charles Darwin, Robbie Burns, all the US presidents who came from Tennessee and Buzz Aldrin, who went to the moon with a special dispensation from his Grandmaster to claim it as the territory of the Grand Lodge of Texas. Napoleon declared himself a protector of Freemasonry and many of his family were Freemasons including his wife, Josephine, but it's not certain if he was one himself. Two common phrases based on the Masonic symbol of the square and compasses and the Masonic concept of honesty are "square deal" and "on the level".

[65] Ivan the Terrible liked to eat swans with gold plated beaks and served roasted in vinegar and the food preferences of many dictators are a little bizarre. It seems particularly surprising that Hitler was vegetarian, but this was not borne out of kindness to animals but rather the belief that it helped to reduce the flatulence to which he was prone. He was paranoid about poisoning and had a team of fifteen food tasters. Only if none of them had dropped dead after forty-five minutes would he touch the food prepared for him. Idi Amin took the five a day principle to new heights eating

around forty oranges each day as he thought they were a form of aphrodisiac, although he was also partial to KFC. Pol Pot loved cobra stew and Kim Jong Il had all the grains of rice served to him compared so that they were perfectly matched in size and colour to accompany his favourite dog-meat soup.

[66] Who were the victims of these two operations and why might a later one be called Project Cathedral.

[67] Not to be confused with the military intelligence group *The Fancy Bears,* responsible for a series of cyber hacking attacks by using malware code-named *Sourface* and *Chopstick.*

[68] The longest recorded champagne cork flight is just over 177 feet. There are roughly 49 million bubbles in a standard bottle of Champagne.

[69] In 1531 Richard Roose was convicted of treason and (perhaps appropriately) boiled alive for making porridge that killed two beggars and made other guests of the Bishop of Rochester seriously ill.

[70] The shooter is the marble used for knocking the opponents marbles out of the ring, which is the field of play.

[71] He had perhaps forgotten that in 1671 a Colonel Blood posing as a vicar almost managed to steal the Crown Jewels from the Tower of London after getting friendly with the family of the Keeper and distracting him by arranging a meeting between his wealthy nephew and the Keeper's daughter. Blood used a mallet to knock the Keeper unconscious and flatten the crown to make it easier to carry, then stuffed the orb down his breeches and tried to saw the sceptre in half before being apprehended. Alternatively perhaps Sir Benedict was thinking of the Irish Crown Jewels successfully stolen in 1907. This mystery has never been solved or the jewels ever recovered.

[72] The Benin bronzes were looted by Britain from Benin, now part of Nigeria, in 1897 when the kingdom was ransacked. They include more than 3,000 items (many of which are not made of bronze) dispersed around the world and held by at least 45 museums, but the largest collection is in the British Museum. The looting took place when a British explorer and 200 porters were welcomed by Benin's King Oba Ovonramwen, but then massacred when they interrupted a series of rituals. The British sent troops to avenge this incident and they came away with the bronzes.

[73] But not as wildly as victims of St Vitus's dance, a frenzy

of compulsive dancing affecting hundreds of people who danced to exhaustion or even death, first recorded in Aachen in 1374. Subsequent outbreaks took place up to 1518 in Germany and other areas. The cause is unknown but is now believed to be a mass neurological condition called Sydenham Chorea. At the time it was thought to be a symptom of demonic possession or the result of spider bites but then perhaps that's what future generations may think about modern pop concerts. St Vitas is the patron saint of dance, epilepsy and boilermakers. The Emperor Diocletian boiled him in a cauldron of liquid tar and lead without effect and when he was thrown to the lions they just licked his feet, but he was successfully martyred eventually.

[74] The odds between the opposing forces in each of these battles were: Rorkes Drift - 150 British (11 VC's awarded, the most in any one engagement) vs 4,000 Zulus; the Alamo – 200 Texans vs 1,500 Mexicans; Thermopylae – 7,000 Greeks (including 300 Spartans who all died) vs 70,000 – 300,000 Persians.

[75] Saint Gummarus is the patron saint of difficult marriages after his own to the shrewish Guinmarie failed. Perhaps he could be considered a forefather of marriage guidance counsellors.

[76] In 1959 he entered the Bleriot Race which involved getting from Marble Arch in London to the Arc de Triomphe in Paris as fast as possible by any means of transport. Boaks took part on roller skates but didn't win.

[77] Perhaps almost as fragile as that of Charles VI of France who, in common with others in 15th- 17th century Europe, suffered from a delusion that he was made of glass. As a result the king would not let anyone touch him and had iron rods put in his clothing, among other protective steps to prevent himself from being dropped or broken. Strangely there are earlier records of 'Earthenware Men' who believed they were made of pottery so there are modern theories that these neuroses were somehow influenced by a fear of new technologies.

[78] Songlines sometimes include Petrosomatoglyphs which are natural marks or depressions in rock that are regarded as images of human or animal body parts.

[79] Tycho himself died of a burst bladder at a banquet where he apparently over-indulged.

[80] The Sect of the Phoenix is a book by Jorge Luis Borges about an ancient and mystical eastern cult whose membership consists

simply in the performance of a secret ritual. The nature of the ritual, being secret, is of course not revealed in the book but is thought by many experts to be sexual intercourse, a theory that certainly has the merit of explaining how the sect has managed to survive so long.

[81] Bellagamba, Pelaratti and Mezzasalma are all genuine Italian surnames meaning literally, beautiful leg, to skin rats and half-cadaver.

[82] The largest surviving Bohemian crystal chandelier was given by Queen Victoria to the Dolmabahace Palace in Turkey and weighs 4.5 tons. Reflective Flow in Qatar, the world's largest modern chandelier, has 165,000 LED lamps.

[83] Wills can often both express and be a cause of bitterness. German poet, Heinriche Heine, left his estate to his wife on condition that she remarried, "so that there would be at least one man alive to regret my death." Felicette was not the first feline beneficiary. There is a case of a wealthy millionairess leaving her mansion to her cat for its lifetime, but sadly the cat did not enjoy its fortune for long. It was sunning itself on the drive when it was run over by the hearse taking the old lady's body to her funeral.

[84] Shakespeare provided his own explanation of love at first sight: "Love is blind."

[85] He also blocked his mind to the joke lines a friend had recently suggested to him. 'I love you with all my butt. I would say my heart, but my butt is bigger.'

[86] In Victorian times, "showing a bit of leg" even extended to ankles and revealing them was considered immodest. Even table legs were covered as they were considered too suggestive. Other weird Victorian fashions included excessively tight corsets and phrenology.

[87] Dan Quayle when visiting an elementary school in 1992.

[88] Mafia boss Sonny Corleone is murdered by the Barzini family in the famous toll booth scene in *The Godfather.*

[89] This well-known phrase was used to lobby the Government in 2010 by a campaign to allow gap year students to defer their University places for 2011 without incurring the higher tuition fees introduced in September 2012.

[90] Lucky Luciano was born Salvatore Lucania in 1897 in Sicily and became the leading gangster boss in New York. Lucania seems to have become Luciano simply through mispronunciation. Lucky

was ironic because he allegedly survived a beating and throat slashing by three men for refusing to join another gang.

[91] Although as the philosopher Bertrand Russell said, 'I would never die for my beliefs because I might be wrong.'

[92] Perhaps the most famous predictions of the future are those of Nostradamus, a French astrologer (1503-66) who has been claimed to have foreseen many world events from the French Revolution and the Great Fire of London to the World Wars, Hiroshima and Nagasaki. Popular authors claim that he predicted whatever major event has occurred just before publication of their book and also when the world will end although Nostradamus' prophecies don't mention the end of the world. The Nazis dropped pamphlets of Nostradamus's prophecies on France because they thought these predicted their victory. Paco Rabanne, the French designer, cancelled all his shows for 1999 based on Nostradamus' prophecies, believing that the world was predicted to end in July and leaving Paris because he thought that the Russian Mir space station was going to crash there during an eclipse.

[93] Although it has happened. Six mummy parts concealed inside two loudspeakers were recently confiscated at Cairo airport. Another repatriated mummy hand was assumed to be a sci fi prop. The mummy of Rameses I was eventually sent home from Canada.

[94] Admittedly he was a man and supposedly men smile on average 8 times a day and women 56.

[95] It only became common practice to brush one's teeth daily after WW2 when many soldiers acquired the habit while in the army.

[96] Plato's cave is a philosophical allegory about reality and our interpretation of it. If you want more detail you will have to read Plato while remembering that philosophers are still arguing about it 2,500 years later.

[97] Captain Nemo is a strange character who hates surface civilisation and avoids dry land, preferring to voyage around in his submarine, the Nautilus, sinking the ships of imperial powers who he regards as oppressors, particularly Britain. He rediscovers Atlantis and claims to be the descendant of an Indian prince who developed rocket technology. Submarines have a long history. William Bourne designed one in 1578 that was enclosed in waterproof leather but there are suggestions that submarines were used at the siege of Syracuse 415 BC. Alexander the Great is said in the medieval Alexander Romance to have been to the bottom of the

sea in one.

[98] This is according to the philosopher, Hobbes, in his book Leviathan, although he himself lived until the age of ninety-one. Hobbes was born prematurely in 1588 because his mother was frightened about the impending Spanish invasion as the Armada approached.

[99] Mermaids, and sometimes mermen, appear in accounts from all over the world. They may be influenced by the sirens encountered by Odysseus in his travels and are often associated with shipwrecks. Among seafarers who claimed to see them are Christopher Columbus and the pirate Blackbeard's logbook records sightings. Our modern perspective is very different as it has been radically re-shaped by Hans Christian Anderson's tale, *The Little Mermaid.*

[100] One of Macbeth's most striking comments on time in Shakespeare's play. Time is after all hard to pin down. Einstein's theory of relativity tells us that the closer you are to the centre of the Earth the slower it goes and a difference of 15 microseconds has been measured between the summit of Everest and sea level.

[101] Laurence Sterne encourages his readers to take up his own pen and draw Helen themselves: "as like your mistress as you can – unlike your wife as your conscience will let you."

[102] Two separate quotes here brought together.

[103] You may wish to try drawing your own picture of Humbaba.

[104] Marilyn Monroe had an arranged marriage to the boy next door a few days after she turned sixteen. Otherwise she would have been sent to an orphanage. Once, after she had become a star, Joe DiMaggio and Frank Sinatra assembled a crowd and forcibly broke into a house where they thought Marilyn was having an affair. It turned out to be the wrong house and the owner sued them for trauma.

[105] *No One Sleeps.* The record for staying awake is 264 hours set by Randy Gardner in 1965. He was of course a teenager at the time.

[106] Popularly known as *Tomba the Bomba* because of his explosive style and tremendous speed. In later life Tomba has said he is now passionate about sleeping (but presumably not for as long as Randy) and automatic car washes, where he likes to go late at night when there is no queue.

[107] Fellini's famous film from which the term *paparazzi* first originates. The male star, Marcello Mastroianni, had to wear a wet

suit and drink a bottle of vodka to keep himself warm during the shooting of the scene in the Trevi Fountain with Anita Ekberg who, being Swedish, didn't seem to notice the cold at all. In the final scene the emptiness of life is summarised by images of a dead fish washed up on the beach.

[108] Rather than a crowd, a group of penguins is technically called a 'raft' if in the water or a 'waddle' if on land.

[109] The only one of these that Leonardo did not design is a frying pan.

[110] To be fair it was encrusted with diamonds which seems an easy way to make anything valuable, although Henry Kissinger pointed out that a diamond is just a lump of coal that has done well under pressure.

[111] This is what Clemenza in *The Godfather* says to his new protégé who has just shot someone. The gun apparently represents the unpleasant past to be left behind and the cannoli the sweet future that lies ahead. Cannoli are a traditional Sicilian street food of sweet pastry tubes filled with ricotta.

[112] Galante was a New York crime boss who was gunned down by rival gangsters in Brooklyn with a cigar still in his mouth. He was shot on Knickerbocker Street which was named after short trousers worn by New Yorkers rather than glorious gelati.

[113] That's me. As I still keep a low profile if you want to get in contact just leave your message in a brown envelope marked *Pasta Pronto* under the third pot plant on the left just inside the main entrance of the Temperate House at Kew Gardens. Take care to follow these instructions precisely as this is the greatest glasshouse in the world containing over 10,000 plants.

[114] Sun Tzu was a military strategist and philosopher thought to have lived around 500 BC. The King of Wu put his generalship to the test by getting him to organise his harem of 180 concubines. Sun Tzu put two in charge but executed them when the others giggled while following their commands after which the rest were perfectly obedient. His advice in *Art of War* has inspired many including Gordon Gecko in Wall Street.

[115] Invented in 1867 in New Orleans to honour the purchase of Alaska by the USA for $7.2m from the Russians after the British turned down a prior offer. A reverse variant is the Frozen Florida, which is a frozen shell of meringue filled with hot liqueur. This was made possible by the microwave and invented in 1969.

[116] In 1972 the finding by a team of zoologists of a 1.5 ton body in the loch described as having a bear's head and a brown scaly body with claw like fins also gave rise to much excitement. It turned out to be the disfigured body of a bull elephant seal with it's whiskers shaven that had died a week earlier in York's Flamingo Park Zoo and had been dumped in Loch Ness by another zoologist to fool his colleagues.
[117] A polygon with 10,000 sides and a lot more corners. A polygon with 999 sides is called an enneahectaenneacontakaienneagon.
[118] In the sixteenth century the geographer Zeigler of Strabourg and the natural historian Ole Worm believed that lemmings were created in the sky and dropped to earth during stormy weather. Perhaps they were under a cliff in a Norwegian fjord at the wrong time. In 1958, the award-winning Disney documentary, *White Wilderness* included scenes of lemmings committing mass suicide over a cliff in Hudson Bay. However a subsequent documentary, *Cruel Camera*, revealed that the makers of *White Wilderness* had transported the lemmings from Hudson Bay to Calgary for the filming where they were dumped over a cliff by the camera crew filming the creatures allegedly, 'Casting themselves bodily into space.' Because they didn't have very many lemmings, they used a tight camera angle and a spinning turntable covered in snow to create the impression that there were hordes of them.
[119] The first was performed in 1899 on a 19-year-old inmate in an Indiana prison by Dr Sharp, which must have been some consolation for the patient. In the 1920's, the operation became popular with wealthy individuals, including Sigmund Freud and W.B.Yeats, who believed it would restore general vigour and sexual potency.
[120] Agamemnon was murdered in the bath on his return home from Troy and other bathroom deaths include Elvis Presley and Jim Morrison, lead singer of the Doors. Around 14,000 people died in the bath in Japan in 2011, over three times the number of road traffic fatalities.
[121] Lycra is also known as Spandex and was originally nylon 66 polyamide. Two early names considered by the manufacturer Dupont were Klis and Duparooh. Klis is silk spelt backwards and Duparooh is an anagram for 'Dupont pulled a rabbit out of a hat'. It's perhaps not difficult to see why even Lycra could beat this competition.

[122] The Duke was not well liked despite his victories. The future King George IV even admitted he liked Napoleon better. Wellington was a good violinist but burnt his instrument in a fit of anger when his marriage proposal was rejected.

[123] Eton Mess was invented during a school cricket match at Eton in the 1920's. A strawberry pavlova was waiting in a picnic basket for the boys as an after-match treat, but an over excited Labrador sat on it.

[124] Among many acts of upper-class vandalism in both 1894 and 1927 members smashed all the lights and all 468 windows in Christchurch College's Peckwater Quad.

[125] Nelson joined the Royal Navy at the age of twelve and early in his career used the butt of his rifle to fight off a polar bear. He suffered from sea sickness and frequently disobeyed orders. On one famous occasion he put the telescope to his blind eye claiming he could not see the signal to withdraw. After he was killed at Trafalgar his body was preserved in a brandy cask on the voyage home.

[126] It was a Russian Orthodox tradition to exchange eggs at Easter and there was great demand for those produced by Fabergé at the Russian Imperial Court. In 1885 the Tsar Alexander III ordered the Hen Egg for his Tsarina. It was made of white enamel with a belt of gold round the middle and inside a yolk of gold containing a golden hen with a diamond miniature of the imperial crown within that and, finally, a tiny ruby pendant. But, of course, everyone has their own preferences when it comes to eggs, and some might prefer theirs to be free range, chocolate or sunny side up.

[127] There have been many "Broken Arrows" or near accidents involving nuclear weapons. Since Kennedy every US President has had a nuclear "Biscuit" and a "Nuclear Football". The biscuit is a card containing the nuclear codes. Jimmy Carter allegedly lost his when he sent his suit to the dry cleaners. Under Bill Clinton, the code may have been missing for months. An aide asked Clinton for it the day after the Monica Lewinsky sex scandal broke but Clinton had apparently been a bit distracted and couldn't find it. The case containing the means for the President to communicate with the Pentagon command centre is called the Nuclear Football because it was part of an early nuclear war plan code named, Operation Drop-Kick. Nuclear warfare seems to provoke dark humour. India's first nuclear weapon test was called Operation Smiling Buddha.

[128] Site of the first penal colony after Captain Cook's visit in 1770. Between 1788 and 1868 over 160,000 convicts were transported to Australia mainly for petty crimes and it is estimated that around 20% of the modern population can trace ancestry back to them. Botany Bay is now home to Sydney Airport and the world's largest population of Weedy Sea Dragons.

[129] The highly successful video game, Assassin's Creed is based on a fictionalised version of the medieval Order of Assassins. Their first grand master was Hassan- I -Sabbah, described by Marco Polo as the Old Man of the Mountains. The ruins of his castle, Alamut or Eagle's Nest, lie near Tehran in modern Iran. Between 1090 and 1275 AD from here and a network of other mountain fortresses in Persia and Syria the Order arranged covert murders of hundreds of Christians and Muslim leaders considered enemies of their Ismaeli sect. They used daggers, nerve poison or arrows, but they were not always successful. Edward I of England escaped one attempt and Saladin two. Assassinations in fact quite often go wrong, particularly where they involve US Presidents. Roosevelt was saved by a steel glasses case and 50 page speech in his breast pocket, then beat his attacker with his cane. Andrew Jackson was saved when both of his assailant's guns misfired one after the other. Ronald Regan's attacker failed to hit him with any of the six shots he fired although the President was wounded by a ricochet. JFK sadly didn't enjoy the same luck although debate still rages as to who actually shot him.

[130] Yes these really were names of two royal corgis.

[131] OXO seems to be Ox turned into an ambigram so that it conveniently be read either way.

[132] Surprisingly few famous people were killed by arrows in history, but they include three English kings. Harold Godwinson at Hastings. William II (or Rufus) while hunting. Richard the Lionheart while besieging a French castle.

[133] St Sebastian joined the Roman army to convert soldiers to Christianity but the Emperor Diocletian ordered him to be killed by being used for target practice and shot full of arrows. However he was revived by a widow and went to see Diocletian to complain, so the Emperor had him beaten up and properly killed this time.

[134] There can be worse punishments for illegal parking. In 2013 in Russia, a man was so irate that his drive had been blocked by illegal parking that he called a cement lorry and had the car filled with wet

cement (after he had first moved it down the road).

[135] Originally a royal hunting ground, Hyde Park was opened to the public by Charles I. It has a secret pet cemetery with over 300 pet graves and it's Rotton Row was the first road in the country to have street lighting.

[136] Over 8000 V2 rockets were launched at Britain during WW2 killing over 23,000 people. Other nick names were Pill Bug, Roly Poly and Buzz bomb. Doodlebugs are also the larvae of insects known as Ant Lions.

[137] Already popular with the Spanish by the time of the conquest of the Aztecs. Cortes bred pigs so he could make it in South America.

[138] Harry Houdini's most famous tricks were escaping from giant milk churns full of water and straitjackets but he eventually died from a burst appendix at Halloween.

[139] Fra Diavolo was the popular name for Michele Pezza an inspirational guerrilla leader who led resistance against the French occupation of Naples in the late 18th century. His fiery temper, as hot as the Devil's, is still remembered through the pasta sauce of the same name, the Italian equivalent of a vindaloo curry.

[140] Sunderland scored three own goals in 7 minutes in 2002/3 in the Premier League.

[141] Both quite common pursuits in Finland where people seem almost to live in saunas. There are over 3 million of them, an average of one per household. The birch twigs are supposed to improve circulation and help relieve frequent mosquito bites, which can drive people almost as mad as Scottish midges. Before modern hospitals existed, Finnish mothers always gave birth in saunas and, in pre-Christian times, they were a place for casting spells. More recently, beer is often poured on the stove in saunas to give them a beery smell.

[142] This is a rare bean from Indonesia. A wildcat-like animal called the Iuwak eats the ripe coffee cherries of the bush but can't digest the stone, which farm workers collect in the wild once it has passed though the animal.

[143] In the middle of the mountain was a love nest that Poseidon made for his lover, Cleito, who bore him five sets of male twins, which must be some form of record.

[144] Another Atlantic island recorded in ancient times whose whereabouts are disputed is Thule, first by mentioned Pytheas in voyages around 320 BC when he was probably trading amber

and tin. He describes the midnight sun and says that the island was made of a sort of mixture of earth, sea and air, giving it the consistency of a jellyfish so it was hard to walk on. He was probably describing a Scottish peat bog.

[145] There have been hundreds of invented islands. Examples are Treasure Island; Alca, an island where penguins were transformed into humans; Fernandos, the destination for couples sent out as part of a TV dating series; Crab Key from a spy movie; Gulliver's Lilliput; Avalon from the Arthurian legends; Rugged and Craggy Island from a TV sitcom; Sodor within the area managed Thomas the Tank Engine's Fat Controller; Utopia invented by Sir Thomas More; Numenor and the moving island San Serriffe. It's worth noting that there have also been many mistaken maps including ones showing the world as square, California as an island or hoax islands such as Crockerland, alleged to be located on the North Pole. The Mountains of Kong appeared on many maps of Africa in the 19th Century until they were shown not to exist. When Christopher Columbus first reached America he thought he had arrived on the far side of India (i.e. its eastern coast) by sailing round the world, since no one knew the Americas were in the way.

[146] At Newgrange in Ireland, for example, for three days at the Winter Solstice light penetrates the stone hole above the entrance and illuminates the passage and chamber at the centre of the barrow. A lottery is held to decide who can access the inner chamber for this special experience.

[147] *Fata Morgana* are mirages caused by the refraction of light due to temperature differentials between the sea and the land. A thermal inversion results from a layer of cold air beneath warmer air. Usually the mirage is of something real that is below the horizon. *The Flying Dutchman*, the ghost sailing ship often sighted by sailors which legend had it was doomed to voyage the seas forever, is now thought to have been a *Fata Morgana*. A similar mirage is suggested as a possible cause of the failure of the *Titanic* to detect the iceberg that sank it as the cold Labrador currents would have created perfect conditions. *Fata Morgana* are named after Morgan Le Fay, an enchantress of Arthurian legend, sometimes seen as Arthur's sibling and often as his evil nemesis.

[148] The Mini was revolutionary because it had a transverse engine and front wheel drive designed by Issigonis (known to his friends as the Greek God). This created much more space in a small car and it became iconic. When Michael Caine filmed the Italian Job

using Minis, he couldn't drive and didn't have a driving licence. Stirling Moss was famously banned for driving for a year in 1961 for speeding in a Mini and 27 is the record for the most number of people crammed into a Mini (2014).

[149] Ghengis Khan invented the first international postal service. Although he was tolerant of all religions, he can hardly be called a peacemaker as he probably massacred in the region of 40m people. He believed that someone's legacy should be measured by the number of their children. By this yardstick he was very successful indeed. It has been suggested that he was the most prolific biological father of all time and today has descendants assessed to number around 16m, so almost half of the number he is estimated to have killed (and still counting).

[150] The Great Wall of China is 75 times longer than Hadrian's Wall (5,476 vs 73 miles).

[151] Effectively a resignation, named after the approach adopted by the Captain of the Costa Concordia, Francesco Schettino in 2012. He took his huge cruise liner too close to shore (allegedly showing off to his girlfriend) and capsized it with disastrous and tragic results, then abandoned ship himself leaving many passengers still on board.

[152] Unintended consequences occur all the time in history. The Titanic (whose Captain went down with his ship) only had lifeboats for 1178 people but was licensed to carry 3500. This was to avoid obscuring the view from the promenade deck. After it sank in 1912 with the loss of 1514 lives it was made a legal requirement to have enough lifeboats for all on board. However 3 years later in 1915 the Eastland sank under the weight of it's additional lifeboats with a loss of 850 lives.

[153] Pisa's leaning tower, completed in around 1350, took nearly 200 years to build. During construction there were a number of attempts to stop it leaning but on each occasion this just caused it to lean in a different direction. Mussolini thought the tower was a national disgrace to the reputation of Italian engineering and tried to rectify the problem but without success. To be fair to him Superman also failed in the 1983 film Superman III. Pisa's famous tower is in any event not alone as Italy has at least 9 other leaning towers, including two more in Pisa and three in Venice.

[154] Murphy's Law says that everything that can possibly go wrong, will go wrong at least eventually. Really this is just entropy or, if you prefer, a tendency towards chaos. If you dump a box of puzzle

pieces on the floor, theoretically they could all just fall out perfectly in place, but in practice the odds are overwhelmingly against this as there are so many other possible permutations. Captain Edward Murphy was working on U.S Airforce experiments in 1949, measuring the effects of forces of deceleration. His assistant made an error with the wiring and Murphy reportedly said, 'If that guy has any way of making a mistake, he will.' This was subsequently picked up in a press conference.

[155] Recent conspiracies include QAnon, that the moon landings never happened and strange explanations for the death of famous people such as JFK and Princess Diana, but such rumours have always been around. The Popish Plot was a ficticious conspiracy invented by Titus Oates that there was a Catholic plot to assassinate Charles II. It led to mass hysteria and executions between 1678 and 1681.

[156] Thames Ironworks, as it was drawn from the workers of the last shipbuilding company on the Thames.

[157] The following all died under 32 – Otis Redding, Rupert Brooke, Jimi Hendrix, John Keats and Tutankhamen. Bruce Lee died at 32. Che Guevara, Lord Byron, Mozart, Ayrton Senna, Cleopatra, Emily Bronte,

Caravaggio and Princess Diana all died under 40.

[158] In a rare act of mercy, Leicester City Council waived the parking penalty they could have charged Richard for occupying a parking bay for over 500 years since 1485, but they did confiscate his body which many maintained should have been returned to his home city of York.

[159] Henry V (VI.vii.18-32). The Welsh Captain, Fluellen, compares Alexander to Henry, initially calling him Alexander the Big, which he pronounces Pig because of his accent. He ridiculously bases the comparison on the argument that there is a river in Monmouth where Henry was born and a river in the town where Alexander was born.

[160] Drake was the first Englishman to circumnavigate the world (1577-80). He started with five ships and ended with just the Pelican, renamed The Golden Hind. When he set out, his men thought he was only sailing to Egypt. The Spaniards believed he had supernatural powers because he was such a successful commander, and the King of Spain placed an enormous bounty on his head. He died of dysentery off the coast of Panama and his body, clad in full armour and placed in a lead coffin, was dropped

overboard in Portobello Bay. There have been several attempts to find it, so far unsuccessful.

[161] All true except there was no Spock.

[162] Both King Henry VIII and King John treated their wives badly. If you think calculating the survival rate of Henry VIII's wives refers to how many he killed, then 33% as he beheaded two out of six. If how many survived him, then 16.7% or one out of six. If, however, you take the most literal approach then 0% as they all died eventually. Whereas Henry divorced two of the wives he didn't murder, King John divorced one – Isabella, then married a 12-year-old, Isabelle, and made her live with his first discarded wife, which must have been awkward. But perhaps we shouldn't think too badly of our worst monarchs. Ivan the Terrible outdid Henry with eight wives of whom he killed 3 and to put the contest beyond doubt by also beating his own son to death. But then he had started torturing cats at the age of twelve.

[163] It is alleged that there is a connection between the shape of the port at Gioia Tauro in Calabria, Italy, and a famous kidnapping. In 1973, John Paul Getty III, grandson of the American oil tycoon and at one time the richest man in the world, was kidnapped by the 'Ndrangheta, a mafia organisation based in Calabria. His ear was cut off and sent to a newspaper, after which a ransom was agreed. Some have suggested that the port in Gioia Toro in Calabria was built using the ransom money and note it is shaped like an ear. In 2006, it was estimated by the Italian authorities that the 'Ndrangheta were supplying 80% of the cocaine market in Europe through shipments from Columbia coming via this port.

[164] The first law introduced in England making it illegal for people to dump rubbish outside their homes was passed in 1297, but around 500 BC, Athens opened one of the first known municipal landfill sites.

[165] It is near Beamish. The local Council wanted to change it to Cooperative Villas in 1983 but some residents objected so, in a classic fudge the signs now say both No Place and Cooperative Villas.

[166] A Tweetle Beetle is a character in *The Fox in Socks* by Dr Seuss, one of his many books designed to help children to read. They love fighting and for those who like nonsense, the description is highly recommended.

[167] If you want a new hobby, why not try translating one of the

many ancient writing systems still not deciphered? These include Ronga Ronga (Rapa Nui), Olmec (the oldest Mesoamerican scripts), Quipu (an Inca script), Pictish and the Ikom monoliths (Nigeria). Meroitic is the language of the ancient Nubian civilisation of Kush (2450 – 1450 BC) in what is now Sudan. The script was deciphered in 1911 but so far has proved impossible to translate. Perhaps one for a rainy afternoon?

[168] The tower was originally only intended to be temporary and was projected to be dismantled after twenty years. Hitler ordered that it be destroyed, although only after he had his picture taken in front of it, but the order was never carried out.

[169] The Eiffel Tower is an extremely popular place for a rendezvous between lovers and particularly for proposals. In 2007 an American lady called Erika LaBrie took matters a stage further by marrying the tower itself after falling in love with it three years earlier and changed her name to Erika Eiffel. The Tower was also once successfully "sold" by an Austrian conman, Victor Lustig, in 1925.

[170] Doping in athletics has many negative side effects, including for men, shrunken testicles and enlarged breasts, and for women, baldness. It just shows how driven athletes must be. Russia's reputation for doping that is systematic and state-sponsored reached a height at the Sochi winter games. Every night, urine samples taken from Russian athletes were exchanged for clean samples, prepared in advance of the games, through a specially-constructed hole in the wall of the lab where they were stored.

[171] In the Crimean War in 1854, the Light Brigade (a cavalry unit) attacked the wrong guns due to a miscommunication. The disaster was immortalised in the poem Tennyson wrote six days later in which he described the charge into, 'the Valley of Death.' Casualties totalled 278 dead and wounded out of 600 before they withdrew. Not quite as bad as the retreat from Afghanistan in 1842 when, out of a column of 16,000, only one British military surgeon and a few Indian sepoys reached Jalalabad.

[172] Apparently minor mistakes in calculation can be very expensive in astronomy and in space exploration. The Mars Orbiter cost NASA $125m and was specifically designed for its Mars mission, but as it commenced its orbit of the red planet, the craft burnt up in the atmosphere. Unfortunately, one engineer in the team had carried out his calculations in imperial units of measurement and another in metric.

[173] Columbus even compelled his crew to sign a deposition that Cuba was part of China in which they agreed that if they later denied this they could have their tongues cut out. When he discovered Venezuela he claimed this was the outer region of the Garden of Eden. He also thought the earth was pear shaped and miscalculated it's circumference by 25% possibly to convince his backers that the voyage to Japan, his intended staging post en route to China, was much shorter than others thought.
[174] This syndrome was first identified in 1973, when four bank employees were held hostage in a vault for six days and developed a bond with their captors. The most famous example is, however, the heiress Patricia Hurst who helped her captors, the Symbionese Liberation army, to rob a bank in California in 1984.
[175] Mattel, who manufacture Barbie, announced in 2004 that Barbie and Ken had broken up. But don't worry, a further announcement in 2006 said that they had got back together after Ken had a make-over.
[176] The charming, understated English hero who rescues fellow aristocrats from the guillotine during the French revolution. His dual identity and rather bumbling cover character started a trope for others such as Clark Kent and Batman. The author was Baroness Emma Magdolna Rozália Mária Jozefa Borbála Orczy de Orczi. Sir Percy escapes from his evil pursuer, Chauvelin, at the Chat Gris in Calais by offering Chauvelin a pinch of snuff that turns out to be pepper.
[177] The motto of the Three Musketeers 'All for One and One for All' is also that of Switzerland.
[178] A clever alibi successfully used already by some of their comrades to cover up the Skripal poisonings.
[179] "Nicotine patches are great. Stick one over each eye and you can't find your fags." Bill Hicks
[180] Carpe Diem does not mean "Fish of the Day".
[181] Originally designed in the 1940's for farmers the briefing concept was for an "Umbrella with four wheels" robust enough to carry 50kg of potatoes and eggs off road without breaking them. The high roof was designed to be tall enough to allow front seat passengers to go to church on Sundays wearing their hats.
[182] The Whisky War was a border dispute between Canada and Denmark from 1978 to 2022 over the tiny, barren and uninhabited Hans Island near Greenland. The conflict earned its name after

Canadian troops planted a flag there and left a bottle of Canadian Whisky, after which both sides made repeated landings to plant flags and leave bottles of alcohol in order to claim the island as their territory, turning the place into perhaps the world's best venue for picking up liquor that is not just duty free but completely free. Matters were only resolved by an ingenious solution – a new treaty divided the island down the middle. This is a relief, as wars can be started all too easily. The Pig War was started in 1859 between Great Britain and the USA over a slaughtered swine. The Nika Riot in Constantinople in 532 AD over a chariot race resulted in 30,000 casualties. The War of the Stray Dog in 1925 between Greece and Bulgaria was triggered when a Greek soldier was shot when he inadvertently crossed the border while chasing his runaway dog. In 1618, the Defenestration of Prague, in which various Catholic officials were thrown out of a window, led to the Thirty Years War, causing an estimated 4.5 to 8 million deaths across Europe. What is particularly strange is that there had been two previous defenestrations of Prague in the fifteenth century, although how this custom developed is as unclear as a lot of other human behaviour.

[183] Some believe Elvis got involved with the mafia, faked his own death to escape them and attended his own 82nd Birthday Party.

[184] When producer Merian C. Cooper told Fay Wray that her co-star would be, 'The tallest, darkest, leading man in Hollywood,' she thought he meant Cary Grant. In fact he was refering to King Kong in the famous 1933 movie, which was so successful it was the first movie ever to be re-released.

[185] There's no rhyme or reason for baldness. It happens to good guys like Mahatma Gandhi and bad guys like Voldemort. Baldness can save you a lot of money over a lifetime on haircuts and help your finances – it seems to have worked wonders for Jeff Bezos.

[186] It's not really the colour red that angers bulls as they are colour-blind. It's the movement of the matador's cape that annoys them.

[187] They align exactly with the three stars in Orion's belt, Delta Orionis, Epsilon and Zeta (showing how we join dots in the stars).

[188] The following have all at one time been genuine scout badges: Nut Culture, Bookbinding, Stalking, Atomic Energy, Pigeon Raising. Stalking which existed between 1915-52 was about tracking animals by stealth, not humans.

[189] As S.E. Hinton said, 'I lie to myself all the time, but I don't believe me.'

[190] He kept his cigars in the coal scuttle.

[191] Peel's spelling of supercalifragilisticexpialidocious is correct as far as it goes, but Peel should himself have challenged Boyle's spelling of rhythm, separate and grateful.

[192] It's an act of treason to put a British stamp on upside down, but just illegal to sound your car horn in anger, to jump the queue at a tube station, to linger after the end of a funeral, handle a salmon suspiciously or to knock on someone's front door and run away.

[193] The Hopi tribe consider the Grand Canyon to be the gateway to the afterlife and on average two or three people every year fall into it. It is around 6,000 feet or 1,829 metres at its deepest point so it can take a long time to hit the bottom.

[194] The military are great at code names. The following were all WWII operations: Toenails was an operation to capture New Georgia (part of the Solomon Islands); Slapstick was a British airborne landing at Taranto in Italy; Dracula was a plan for an attack on Rangoon, Burma. The later Project Fat Fucker was an unkindly titled CIA undercover programme to put pressure on King Farouk of Egypt.

[195] Beretta is the oldest active manufacturer of firearms in the world and made gun barrels for the Venetian fleet at the Battle of Lepanto 1571.

[196] The Popemobile's registration is really SVC1, which stands for *Status Civitatis Vaticanae*, or Vatican City in Latin.

[197] As Wellington said of the battle of Waterloo.

[198] There is no such fish as a red herring. The consensus is that a red herring is a kipper that is cured for so long that its flesh turns reddish and the smell is particularly pungent. It seems to have been used to distract hounds from the path of a fox in hunting (although some suggest it was used to guide them, but this was misunderstood).

[199] The Quest for the Tomb of Alexander the Great by Andrew Michael Chugg, Third Extended Edition, January 2020.

[200] The London Hammer is a hammer of iron and wood found in London, Texas which some allege must date back 400m years because of the age of the rock encasing it. The Baghdad Battery is a set of artefacts consisting of a ceramic pot, tube of copper and rod of iron which is is suggested in combination may have been used

as a galvanic cell. The Antikythera Mechanism has been described as the oldest analogue computer and could predict astronomical positions and eclipses of great complexity.

[201] It was, after all, lemons that first gave rise to the Mafia. The origins of the Mafia emerge just after the liberation and unification of Italy in the 1860's. Law and order in Sicily was weak and huge profits were being made from lemons because of the recent discovery that citrus juices were needed to avoid scurvy when at sea for long periods without fresh vegetables. Sicilian landowners used the Mafia to protect their valuable lemon groves, or, if they didn't, risked retribution (as in the Galati incident in 1872, the first Mafia violence on record).

[202] Dali got the inspiration for his "soft watches" from a piece of runny Camembert melting in the sun. Fortunately, his paintings didn't convey the smell.

[203] You have to admit that the idea of Venus being born in a clam shell is a bit odd. We only have one possible self portrait of the artist but that's not the reason why there are grounds to think he was probably short and stout. That is based on Alessandro di Mariano Filipepi's nickname, Botticelli, which means "little barrel."

[204] For reasons you will remember from Chapter 7 her ancestor Tycho's elk had a fatal accident when drunk.

[205] But not as long as the longest word ever to appear in literature. This is ancient Greek and has 171 letters and 78 syllables. It is the name of a fictional food dish mentioned in the Assembly Women, a comedy play by Aristophanes dated 391 BC. I won't include it here as it would need another appendix of its own.

[206] Ends have, after all, often been wrongly predicted. The Prophet Hen of Leeds predicted the end of the world in 1806 through messages on eggs that turned out to be fake. Haley's comet triggered similar fears in 1910 and only shortly after that the Mayan Calendar predicted Doomsday on 21 December 2012. The Millennium Bug was expected to wreak havoc by causing all computer systems to crash on 1 January 2000. Gordon Brown predicted the end of boom and bust in the economic cycle but look what has happened since then.

ABOUT THE AUTHOR

Angel Capelli

The author is still in hiding, for reasons apparent from this story, venturing out only in disguise. This passport photo is the only known picture of Angel and was kindly provided by Interpol.

A written description of his appearance by Inspector Panettone can be found in the "about" section of Angel's website at angelcapelli.com. There you can also read Angel's blog and even contribute your own suggestions for the Unjoined Dots which appear as endnotes in this book.

Alleged sightings of Angel in obscure parts of Italy are regarded as unreliable since he surely wouldn't take that risk. Rumour has it that he enjoys running around in mountainous areas (so as to keep himself fit enough to escape when needed) as well as studying history, cosmology and of course all things Italian, but then again rumours are often wrong.

Printed in Great Britain
by Amazon

33679137R00249